THE WORST KIND OF KILLING

Kate Harrod was police chief of San Madera now, after sacrificing her marriage for her career. That meant she had cops under her to do a lot of the dirty work in the dirty business of hunting a monstrous murderer.

In addition, she had a couple of tough cops from Stockton, who came to town following a trail that began with the corpse of a gorgeous nude woman, to offer their aid and advice.

Kate was more than willing to push all the buttons at her command as hard as she could to send her investigation into overdrive. But no matter how many helping hands she had, she wanted to get her own hands on this baby killer. . . .

A LYING SILENCE

OCT 97

TERROR ... TO THE LAST DROP

A LYING SILENCE

Laura Coburn

AN ONYX BOOK

ONYX
Published by the Penguin Group
Penguin Books USA Inc., 375 Hudson Street,
New York, New York 10014, U.S.A.
Penguin Books Ltd, 27 Wrights Lane,
London W8 5TZ, England
Penguin Books Australia Ltd, Ringwood,
Victoria, Australia
Penguin Books Canada Ltd, 10 Alcorn Avenue,
Toronto, Ontario, Canada M4V 3B2
Penguin Books (N.Z.) Ltd, 182–190 Wairau Road,
Auckland 10, New Zealand

Penguin Books Ltd, Registered Offices:
Harmondsworth, Middlesex, England

First published by Onyx, an imprint of Dutton Signet,
a division of Penguin Books USA Inc.

First Printing, August, 1997
10 9 8 7 6 5 4 3 2 1

PUBLISHER'S NOTE
This is a work of fiction. Names, characters, places, and incidents either
are the product of the author's imagination or are used fictitiously,
and any resemblance to actual persons, living or dead, events, or locales
is entirely coincidental.

*Dedicated to Katherine, my daughter,
whose triumphs overwhelm me. Your
mountains will always be there for you.
As will their Maker.*

*With love,
Your Mom*

CHAPTER ONE

I saw the tape across the mouth and retched. I pulled myself together, crouched down, and looked at her. I saw pale skin, fine hair, a dimple in one cheek. She was only two feet long and less than five months old.

The baby lay there like a piece of tossed-out trash. Forlorn, unwanted, a bit of useless baggage slung aside like so much swill.

I had to move on past it, so I could do what I must do, but it wasn't easy. God help me, I prayed. God help me now, please give me strength.

I knelt beside her, my face tight, my body feeling hollow. My eyes observed the dove-soft skin, the tiny fingernails like petals off a rosebud, the deep dark bruises shading arms and thighs.

"So tell me," I said, and you'd have thought I was asking for a game score, "what do we know here?"

I stayed hunkered down, wanting not to leave her—wanting to protect her, to stand guard—and so I craned my neck to look up at Davey Johnson.

The sergeant's eyes were wet with tears but his voice was steady.

"Cook was putting out the garbage"—he jerked his head toward a greasy spoon behind us—"and saw something in the bin he knew wasn't his. He spread out the shirt and found the baby." Now his voice began to break. "And then he called us."

I glanced across the parking lot and saw a little man with dirty smears across a dingy full-length apron leaning back against a wall. His feet crossed loosely at the ankles and his shoulders hunched far forward as he stared steadily at the ground in front of him, as if standing in a trance.

"That's him?" I asked as I let my hand lay close against the little body. "Have you questioned him at all?"

"Nope, Kate, leaving that for you. We've notified the coroner, though."

Johnson bent his head and locked his eyes with mine.

"Who the hell, Katharine"—he ran a hand roughly through his hair—"who the hell would do a thing like this? To kill a baby's bad enough but to tape its lips together so it couldn't easily breathe is too monstrous to take in." His eyes mirrored his agony.

Reluctantly I rose to face him, glancing down at the tiny bundle lying there beside me.

"Nothing should surprise us, Davey, not after all this time. We've learned all too well that cruelty knows no limits. And there's this. The taping may not be what caused her death. She may have died by means other than smothering."

My eyes lingered on the blue-black arms and thighs, and Johnson's glance followed.

"Like booting her to hell and back," he spat out angrily, "or squeezing her and shaking her till her brains snapped loose."

I nodded grimly and began to walk away.

"Take care of her, Davey. Penross should be coming soon, then he'll take over."

Though it was nearly midnight, a jostling crowd had gathered behind the yellow tape. Pressing forward, pushing hard against one another, they craned their necks and tried to see the little girl lying on the green plaid shirt. Two uniformed patrolmen stood before the tape, trying to keep order.

And what would you do if you could break on through and rush right up to her? I thought disgustedly. Gawk and stare and maybe poke a bit just so you could say you'd been there? Then puff up around your friends and make yourself important?

I looked around the parking lot. It ran in a long rectangle behind a set of eight or nine small shops, all joined together. There were apartments on the second floor. I saw people in their nightclothes leaning out across the windowsills upstairs, but on the lower level all the stores were dark and silent save for the kitchen of the restaurant straight in front of me.

The lot was paved with asphalt and pockmarked with random holes that held water from a recent rain. Little chunks of pavement lay broken here and there, and weeds pushed their way through a myriad of narrow cracks.

Opposite the shops, along the other long side of the lot, a row of trash bins stood end to end to hold debris that the businesses produced. Each was large and square, made of heavy metal with fitted tops, the kind that get hoisted high above garbage trucks and emptied once or twice a week. The baby's body lay on its back on the asphalt, five feet in front of the third bin from the end.

I sniffed the air and drew in a cloying greasy scent coming from the door in front of me. The whole scene—the run-down lot, the little shops with broken screens and peeling paint, the restaurant with its heavy odor—spoke of long neglect and cheap unsavory merchandise.

The cook looked up and saw me coming. He straightened hard against the wall and stood there waiting, wary eyes scanning up and down my face.

"Arturo Gomez?" He nodded quickly. "I'm Detective Katharine Harrod, San Madera Police Department. Are you the one who found the little baby?"

"*Sí.*"

He shifted uneasily from foot to foot and now kept his eyes focused on the ground.

"Can you tell me about it?" I watched him closely as I spoke.

The man pulled nervously at his thick mustache but didn't speak. An inner sense based on long experience told me what his trouble was.

"Arturo, we're not Immigration. We don't report to them or have any dealing with them. Relax. I don't even care to know if you're illegal or not, I just want you to tell me about finding the baby."

The little dark-skinned man looked visibly relieved and I saw his whole body loosen as the tenseness fled.

"*Sí*, señora. Okay. What do you wanna know?"

I stuck a piece of gum in my mouth and offered one to him. He readily accepted it and began to peel the wrapper.

"How did you know there was a body in the trash bin?"

"I took the last load of trash out when I'd finished up my work. I pushed up the lid and was just about to dump it in when I saw this shirt. You see, the pickup comes tomorrow so the bin was almost full and so this shirt was sitting up real high and I saw it right away."

Now that Lopez felt at ease, his words rushed easily from his mouth.

"What made you notice it?"

"Ah, I think maybe it's good and I can use it and so I go to reach for it, but then I see it is, how you say, *pesado* . . . heavy, and I wonder what's inside."

He paused suddenly and looked down at the

ground again. When he glanced back up at me, I saw a sadness had consumed his face and an anguished pleading stare filled his eyes.

"I know it's hard, Mr. Gomez, but please go on." I pushed my hair behind one ear and leaned my hand against the wall.

"I picked it up and put it on the ground"—he began to gulp and choke—"and then I start to unfold . . . and I see the little baby. I can't believe it. I don't know what to do."

"What *did* you do?"

"I covered it back up and ran inside and told my boss. He called police."

I turned around and looked behind me at the baby girl, lying all alone in a glare of light from a covered bulb high above the parking lot. I longed to go to her, to be with her, but I could do more good for her by staying where I was.

"Arturo, listen to me and please tell me the truth. Did you take anything from the baby or the shirt? Did you change anything at all, make it different from the way you found it?"

Shock filled his face and his eyes sprang open wide.

"Oh, señora, no. I would never. I only looked and went inside."

I believed him and I gave two quick pats on his upper arm.

"Mr. Lopez, when did you last empty the trash before you found the shirt?"

"Not since last night. You see, my helper does it while he is here. Then he goes and I am last man out so I throw away the final load."

"Did you hear or see anyone near that bin tonight, or any unusual occurrence in the parking lot?"

"No, señora, *nada*. I just cook and cook, the oil, how you say, seezles, and I hear nothing. I stay right by the stove."

He looked at me expectantly, waiting for my next question.

"Is your boss still here?" I glanced toward the restaurant.

"Sure, inside. Señor Waters."

I hit the back screen door with the heel of my palm, bouncing it back to me. I felt the need for harsh contact. My flesh stung but the pain didn't matter. It helped relieve the misery I felt. I saw a man standing by the counter, his back turned to me, his hand resting on his hip.

"Mr. Waters?"

He spun around to face me and I saw a pale-faced man in his early forties with thin blond hair that lay in fine straight lines across his scalp.

"Yeah, that's me."

"I'm Detective Katharine Harrod, San Madera Homicide. Were you at the restaurant tonight when the body was discovered?"

"I'd been out," he told me, none too friendly, "depositing the receipts in the bank. I'd been back no more than five minutes when Arturo came running in yelling about a body."

"Where did you park? In the lot?"

"Yeah. Right behind the building."

"Did you see any other cars moving in or out at that time, or earlier when you left? Any persons near the Dumpster?"

"Cars, sure, two or three at least, but they didn't look suspicious, if that's what you want to know. They could've belonged to any of the apartments up-stairs. All the tenants park back there, one space per unit. As far as anyone near the trash, only old Henry poking his way along."

"Who's Henry?"

"The street person who's been hanging out in that park down the block for the past year or so. He makes his nightly rounds and then again in the morning."

"What's he look like?" I asked, making a mental note about the park.

"Old, dirty, gray hair to his shoulders with skin that street-baked brown shade. Limps a little sometimes."

Waters gave an unsympathetic sneer and began to walk around, picking up, then laying down, various utensils.

"What a bitch!" I heard him murmur to himself.

"What's wrong, Mr. Waters?"

"Well, some beaner's gone and dumped her unwanted baggage right behind my store. What d'ya think that's going to do for business? Not a hell of a whole lot. Which matters, since it hasn't been that good anyway lately."

I stared at him in disbelief.

"A little baby has just died," I said, "and there's no doubt in my mind it's homicide, so show a little respect, please, sir. And for your information, the child appears to be Caucasian, not of Mexican origin. Didn't you go to look?"

He jerked his head back in surprise.

"No, no, I didn't. I didn't want to see it, didn't think I had to. It just seemed like something one of them would do. Them or blacks. Just pop it out and toss it. A white kid, huh? I didn't know."

I yearned to get away from this callous bigot but I needed him just a little longer.

"I'm going to have to ask the staff to stay awhile. Are any patrons left in the dining room?"

He shook his head.

"Kitchen closes at ten-thirty, last one usually leaves around eleven. We don't serve the kind of food it takes too long to eat."

"Yo, Kate, the coroner's here. So's Mungers."

Johnson's deep voice bellowed through the screen and hastily I turned to go.

"I'll be back, keep everybody here," I told the owner curtly, glad to leave the greasy smell and the meanness of his soul.

I pushed the screen and saw the square black van pulling slowly to a stop. A hand touched my shoulder and I started. It was Carl, my second in command and my friend and confidant whom I trust without reservation. His bulky frame loomed tall beside me.

"Have you seen her?"

He nodded grimly, his round, fair-skinned face grim and set.

"Haven't had a baby in a long, long time, Kate. Hoped I'd never have another." He ran his hand quickly through his unruly straw-stick hair.

Howard Penross, the county coroner who could've retired several years ago but could not give up the work he loved, climbed down from the van. A perfectionist who would not lay down a case till he knew he had his answers, he locked his jaws mentally on his corpses and kept them tight till he was satisfied. Like a dog worrying over a bone.

The three of us converged on the tiny bundle lying in the spot of light. So small, so still, she could've just been sleeping. Or so you would've thought, until you saw the cruelty of that length of silver tape.

"Howard." I acknowledged him with a nod. "It's pretty bad."

He pursed his lips and stared down at the victim as the uniformed officers drew back in quiet solemnity. I saw his eyes blink quickly behind the steel-rimmed glasses but his face showed no expression.

"Have you touched her, Kate? To find ID?"

"No, we left her as she was," I answered. No need to add how much I'd longed to take her in my arms. "But she was moved from that Dumpster to the ground by the man who found her."

Carl and I crouched close behind her as Penross began to examine her. I suddenly felt the cold, a typical January night near the foothills, where our breath came out in whitish puffs of vapor.

She lay there naked, the cool strong wind of winter blowing across the smooth pink flesh. I wanted to draw the shirt around her, to protect her from its harshness, but even more I wanted to find some clues so I could catch her killer.

Penross gently raised her, first one side and then the other, and felt beneath her, shaking his head slowly to himself. He lowered her and probed the pockets of the shirt, which lay spread out on either side of her, then he looked at us.

"There's no ID on this child," he said. "So this far into this investigation she's a Baby Jane Doe. Let's hope we can put a Christian name to her before we have to bury her."

My head swung around as a sudden commotion broke out behind the yellow tape. A pushing, shoving woman held a camera high above her head and was attempting to force her way through the gawking crowd. Those she was jostling aside pushed back and her camera fell heavily to the ground. I heard her yell "Shit!" in loud disgust.

I rose and strode quickly toward the tape.

"One more word from any of you and this area will be cleared," I yelled angrily. "Just one more word will do it."

I turned to the young officer closest to the crowd.

"I want this circus stopped," I told him. "Understood?"

"Yes, ma'am," he answered as he reddened. "I'll try my best."

"Just do it."

I knelt again beside Carl and watched Penross do the liver probe, to determine present body temperature that, in turn, would help determine time of death. He used the same long chrome thermometer used on adult victims, and it looked grotesquely oversized as it entered the tiny abdomen through the hole made by a small three-bladed knife. I winced and looked away and I felt Carl put an arm around my shoulder.

When the coroner had finished his examination, we stepped back and let the crime lab take their pictures, then the baby's body, wrapped once again in the green plaid shirt and with the silver tape still sticking to its mouth, was carried to the waiting van and strapped upon a gurney. Penross walked back to me.

"I'll let you know just as soon as I have something, Kate. I'm going to work nonstop on this one." He slowly stroked his neat gray mustache. "I can give you this right now, though. The child's been dead no more than a few hours. Two, maybe three outside."

Slowly the van pulled away and left the pock-marked parking lot, driving past the silent gaping crowd, heading for the county morgue. I stared at the cold hard spot beside the Dumpster, now empty of the little human body it had held. In my mind, I saw the lashes laid against the cheeks and the tiny nails like petals off a rosebud.

"Let's get to work," I said to Carl, and brusquely I spun around and headed for the units on the second floor while he went to quiz the workers at the greasy spoon.

CHAPTER TWO

A foot stuck out below a pile of brush. The Labrador began to sniff its sole, then zeroed in on the delicious smell of death and rapidly caressed the skin with grateful loving strokes.

Its master missed all of the enthusiasm. When he jerked back the lead and spied the object of his pet's affection, his eyes popped open wide with nonbelieving, nonaccepting stares. He pushed the brush aside, thinking maybe she was only sleeping, but when he saw the purpled face and the swelling of the tongue, he knew she wasn't just taking a nap.

He scampered backward, stumbling all behind himself, till the lead abruptly tightened and the dog fell backward on his lap. He dropped the leash, freeing the dog to return to serious licking of the smooth still flesh, and ran as fast as his chubby little legs would carry him.

Detective Robert Michael Harris, an ex-Los Angeles police investigator working Stockton PD for the past eighteen months, took the call and grabbed his pencil.

In LA, this would've been an everyday occurrence. In Stockton, it was every bit as serious an event, just one that didn't happen quite so often.

"Did you determine she was dead?" he asked, his body taut with tension.

"Yeah, I looked at her"—the voice huffed and puffed from lack of breath—"and she was purple. She's a goner."

"Did you take the pulse? Did you put your fingers to her throat?"

"Hell, no. I told you, she was purple, almost black. What else do you guys need?"

Harris took the caller's name and the location of the woman, told the man to stay in place, then phoned communications.

"Get a unit out to Thurston Road, forty-seven hundred block south side, sixty feet back in a vacant lot between two stands of pine. She's probably dead, but I'm not sure, so send an ambulance as well."

It was just by chance that he had been there, sitting in an empty squad room at eight a.m. on Sunday morning. A trim athletic man with hard-packed muscles, he'd gone for an early-morning run, all the while chewing over details of a case that had been bothering him.

As he pounded down the pavement, the logic of his thoughts began to jell and he headed for the station, running suit and all, and bounded up the stairs to pull the file and check on several details. He'd just sat down, sweat pouring from his brow, when the phone began to ring.

Ordinarily the call would've gone straight through to patrol, but somehow it'd found its way to him. He didn't even think to wonder if he should go home and change. Instead, he dialed the number of his partner, rousing him from a cozy weekend sleep, then bolted out the door, down the stairs to the nondescript gray Chevy parked against the wall, then pointed it toward the south end of town.

The lot lay on a little-traveled two-lane road in a rural part of the city, where houses sat on several acres, separated by stands of trees and ground not yet built on.

Harris pulled up behind the black-and-white that had only just arrived and he and the officers walked together toward the porky little man standing near the middle of the field. His eyes were open wide and beads of perspiration rode his brow while he panted oddly, as if hyperventilating. Beside him, a black dog whined plaintively and tugged steadily at its leash, straining toward the woods.

"She's there"—he pointed a shaky finger toward the center of a line of scraggly brush and overgrown stumps—"beside that big green bush to the right. See all that dead stuff in a pile? Well, under that."

Harris looked questioningly at the chubby man,

who seemed to read his mind and shook his head wildly.

"No, I'm not going back there. I don't want to look at that again. I've told you where to find her. You go do it, that's your job."

The three officers walked straight ahead, their eyes scanning the ground around them with every step they took. The grass in the front part of the lot was closely clipped, so short that in several spots the dirt showed through. If any clue lay here, it should be easy to pick up, but nothing caught their eyes so they continued moving forward, toward the thick green bush standing on their right.

Harris saw it first—the long, thin, high-arched foot that lay sole up, toes pointed toward them. He motioned to the others, gestured toward it, then carefully stepped forward. His face was grim, his normally laughing eyes dead-serious.

He used his hands to part the pile of dry, decaying brush, much as the owner of the dog had done, and saw the graceful fair-skinned body of a woman lying on her stomach.

There was nothing graceful about her neck and head, however. Angry blackish marks, mottled here and there with duller red ones, ringed her throat and the flesh beneath her long dark hair. Her face showed a bulging open eye, thickened tongue protruding between swollen lips, and the same dark uneven discoloration.

She lay naked, her arms stretched out in front of her and angling outward from her torso. Not a stitch of clothing, not a bit of jewelry, was visible on any part of her unmoving body. Her legs lay straight, from hip to toe, touching at the thighs and calves. Had she fallen that way, so neat and linear, he wondered, or had she been arranged?

As he bent forward, his nostrils widened as they suddenly filled with the thick, sure scent of death. He wasn't the medical examiner but Harris had attended enough murder scenes to be able to give the time of death a ballpark figure by the visible signs of putrefaction he observed.

From the evidence of the growth of bacteria within this particular body—the presence of the odor, the slight degree of swelling, the greenish-red discoloration of the groin and abdomen, apparent when he tried to peer beneath the torso—he concluded the victim had probably been dead between twenty-four and forty-eight hours.

A car door slammed and he turned to see his partner, Charlie Rhoads, emerge from a shiny dark blue van. Simultaneously, ambulance shrieks tore the air and the city rescue squad, lights blazing, jerked to a stop behind the van. Paramedics raced across the close-clipped grass.

Harris held his hand up as he walked to meet them.

"No need," he said. "You should've been here yesterday or maybe even earlier."

They slowed their pace but decided to take a look anyway. One glance and they turned and left, without even taking a pulse check.

He looked at Rhoads, a tall, rugged man in his mid-forties dressed in tan slacks and a cotton windbreaker. They'd been friends longer than either could remember but only recently had begun to work together.

"She's back there, Charlie, lying stark-naked underneath some brush. Been there awhile, I'd say. Unless the M.E. finds a bullet hole or stab wound when he turns her over, I'd pick strangulation as the cause of death. Go on and take a look. I'm going to hurry them up with that tape."

Harris moved toward two members of patrol, who were dawdling along and chatting as they unwound the yellow tape used to secure all crime scenes.

"Get hustling," he told them, "the looky-loos are coming." He waved toward several people gathering across the street and pointing at the lot.

As he threw up the trunk of the gray Chevy and began to pull the homicide kit out, another van, this one black and longer than Rhoads's, drew in behind him. The county coroner, a large, burly man with florid cheeks, eased himself out with a grunt and nodded to Harris.

"Too damn early in the day for this thing, buddy," he threw out in way of greeting. "And on a Sunday at that."

The two men walked back toward the woods, each with a kit swinging from his hand.

The coroner gave another grunt and went to work while the two detectives stood close by. The morning sun was moving on toward nine and cast a shaft of brightness on the scene beneath the brush, but the air stayed crisp and cool, as it does in January in these parts.

Harris glanced around. They'd get the lab boys to check for footprints but he doubted that they'd find any. The ground was winter hard.

"Ummmm," the coroner murmured, more to himself than to anybody listening. Then, "See this here?" He pointed to purplish discolorations on the hips and back. "Lividity suggests she laid primarily faceup for at least several hours shortly after death."

He began to turn her over and the long dark hair fell slowly to one side. The woman now lay fully on her back and the three men stared down at her. They saw a white female, maybe twenty-eight, maybe thirty years of age, with a face of frozen agony that when filled with life must've been vivacious and attractive.

The features—those that were untouched by the trauma of the violence—were regular and appealing, the figure full-breasted and slim-hipped. Her pubic hair, like the hair upon her head, was dark and thick, her legs shapely and smooth. Harris observed the fingernails, gracing the ends of long, thin fingers.

They were beautifully manicured and painted in an appealing off-rose shade. This woman, whoever she might be, had obviously taken good care of herself, right up until the end.

He shook his head. He never would get used to it, the wasting of a human life. Any human life but especially one that was in its prime. He glanced at Rhoads and saw him staring at the corpse, his eyes resting on the distortions of her face. His expression, too, was somber and filled with sorrow for the figure lying there in front of him.

"Someone's sister, someone's wife, who knows?" he mused. "And she had to end like this."

The coroner wheezed a little, then pointed to the stomach.

"No lividity present here," he said, "or on the sides, so I stick with what I said before. She either fell or was placed on her back at some point shortly after death and stayed that way for maybe five to six hours. It was only after that that she was placed here, on her stomach. So you know this much already. She probably wasn't killed at this location but somewhere else, then transported here and dumped."

"What about the cause?" Harris asked, leaning forward, one hand on his hip. "I'd say strangulation, wouldn't you?"

"Maybe, maybe not." The coroner sounded surly, as if he didn't like being second-guessed. "Right up front, it looks like that, sure. No obvious stab wounds, no signs of blunt force trauma, but I've got to get her back to the lab and do my work. And if it *is* death by strangulation, I've got to determine whether it was manual or ligature. All this takes time. You wouldn't want a half-assed job now, would you, Bobby?" The coroner squinted up at the two detectives.

They didn't answer but instead started to slowly part the bushes and move away the brush surrounding the body while the coroner began to do the liver probe.

"Maybe he threw her purse away or something fell off of her," Rhoads said without much hope, "so we can get some sort of ID."

"Sure, maybe he dropped a little address book with both his name and hers inside," Harris shot back, "but I wouldn't count on it. It looks like he's stripped her clean of every single identifying factor that she carried. I'll bet he brought nothing to this lot except her naked body."

The two men worked for several hours, stopping briefly to watch the bundling of the corpse into the long dark body bag and its transport to the coroner's van. Their search yielded nothing except an empty soup can, long since rusted and deteriorated, and an equally empty dirt-encrusted whiskey bottle from some long-ago party. No fresh cigarette butt, no fallen earring or signature pin, no scrap of paper holding out a promise.

The lab men didn't help them either. No footprints could be found on the short-clipped, hard-packed earth, no tire tracks showed by the roadside save for those of the official vehicles. Now that the corpse itself had been removed, the empty lot offered nothing—not a whisper, not a trace—connected with the violent death it had sheltered and concealed.

Harris and his partner looked at each other and shook their heads in puzzlement and disappointment. It was as if their victim had dropped cleanly into those woods from the skies above, untouched by human hands.

CHAPTER THREE

I climbed the weary stairs to the second floor, above the restaurant. The banister beneath my hand felt rickety and I didn't trust it with any of my weight.

The apartments' tenants, all lined up along the common walkway that ran before the fronts of the shabby units, turned to stare at me, mute and solemn as they gazed. They'd thrown on some clothes, left the safety of their windowsills, and moved outside as the action down below them had intensified.

I stopped outside the first apartment door and looked down the row of silent people.

"A little baby has been killed," I said, "and found lying in a Dumpster in the lot. I'm going to need to talk with all of you, unit by unit, so please don't leave the building till I'm through. Right up front, though, can any one of you tell me anything to help me?"

Collectively they shook their heads.

"I was all tucked in watching television," one finally volunteered. "Maybe we all were."

"All right," I answered. "Please go inside now and wait till I can talk with you more privately. In the meantime something may come back to you that will help us."

Reluctantly they dispersed and went behind each of their respective doors.

The occupants of the first unit, a young couple in their twenties, led me into a tiny living room furnished with odds and ends that looked as if they'd come from the Salvation Army or some in-law's attic.

The woman looked to be at least eight months pregnant, and she moved ponderously toward the faded sofa and sat down heavily, clasping her hands protectively on her stomach and waiting for my questions. Her husband, a wan, thin youth with pimples mixed among some freckles, sat down beside her and laid his own hand on her thigh.

"Did you go outside this evening," I asked, "or glance out the back window? And if you did, did you see anyone near that trash bin?"

They shook their heads in unison.

"We came in together shortly after six," the girl replied, "and we've been in ever since, eating and watching TV. I pulled the shade and never looked outside again till we heard all the commotion a little while ago." I saw tears begin to gather in her eyes.

"A baby," her husband murmured, staring straight ahead, "a little baby just like ours. Just a little while ago it was inside, too, and safe, and now it's dead. I cannot take it in. So cruel." He stroked his wife's full belly while she began to cry.

"What was wrong with its mouth?" he asked, staring at me through his horn-rimmed glasses. "From up here it looked like something was wrong with its mouth."

"You'd rather not know," I told him and rose to go, leaving with the certainty that their unborn child had become even more precious than ever to them within the hour just past.

I began to work my way down the row, hearing the same story from each occupant I talked to. They'd come home, pulled the shades or drapes, and settled in for a comfy evening without outside interference. Does no one ever come or go here? I wondered to myself.

I was sitting in the sixth apartment down, talking to a portly cigar-puffing gentleman and his hard-of-hearing wife, Velda. I'd just raised my voice for the fourth or fifth time, asking if she'd had an eye out on the parking lot, when movement on the walkway caught my eye. I saw the shadow before I saw the man, but he quickly followed, moving rapidly toward the stairs.

I sprang to my feet, leaving the woman and her husband with their mouths gaping wide, and ran to the door, wrenching it open. He was already two steps down, heading for the parking lot—a tall, slim, blond-haired fellow in his mid- to late twenties.

"Hold on a minute," I called out harshly, rushing toward the stairhead. "I thought I asked you to stay put till I could talk with you."

He spun around, nearly losing his balance in the process, and I saw frightened eyes above a full-lipped mouth. A neatly trimmed blond mustache bristled above the upper lip.

"Look, I can't do you any good so just let me leave, please." His tone was pleading, not belligerent.

"I'll be the judge of that," I said. "What unit do you live in?"

The man hesitated, shifting from one foot to the other on the step.

"Why don't you come back up here on the walkway," I asked him. "We're going to have to talk and I don't want you falling down the stairs."

Unwillingly he climbed slowly up and stood there facing me.

"What unit?"

"Aw, fuck it!"

"Excuse me?"

"I don't live in any unit. I was visiting in number eight, second from the end."

"Well, let's go down there, then," I said, waving him ahead of me.

He brushed past me, a defeated look upon his face, and pushed the door to number eight roughly inward when he reached it. I followed close behind.

"It won't work," I heard him say to someone in the interior. "I've got to stay."

I saw a red-haired woman close to thirty standing in the doorway to the kitchen. Attractive in a tarty sort of way, she was tugging on the belt of a long flowing housecoat, tightening it around her waist. The guilty looks on both their faces made me wonder what they'd been up to, though I was pretty sure I knew.

"Would you please tell me why you tried to run?" I asked. "This is a murder investigation I'm conducting here."

They looked at each other, grimacing.

"Because I'm not supposed to be here," the man said finally. "Ah, fuck it! Will this have to get out?"

"It depends on what you have to tell me, but I'll try to be discreet. What do you mean, you're not supposed to be here?"

"Because I'm a married man and Caroline's a married woman. Her husband's out of town and I came over."

"Jesus, Curt, you've got to run your mouth, don't you!" The redhead slapped her hand angrily against the wall.

"Let's all sit down," I said, pointing to the sofa and two chairs, "and get this things sorted out. Did either of you see anybody near that Dumpster down below at any time this evening?"

The woman shook her head but the man stayed silent.

"Curt?"

He looked down at the floor, then up at me. Despair filled his face.

"Caroline was in the other room, changing. I was standing by the window, just passing time, when I saw someone walk away from the Dumpster toward that alley on the other side of it. Then I heard a car start up and saw the taillights moving down in that direction." He waved his hand to the left.

"What time was this?" I asked, no longer angry at his obvious reluctance to get involved.

"Maybe nine-thirty, maybe ten. I wasn't checking." He gave an exaggerated sigh.

"Was the figure male or female? And what about the car? Make, model, color?"

"I couldn't tell a thing. The person was already behind the Dumpster when I saw him. Or her. Moving into the shadows. And the car was in the darkness, too. Like I said, I only saw the taillights as it drove away."

"You're absolutely sure that's all you saw?"

A child was lying dead but he was minding his own sweet hide to cover up a wrongful assignation with Mrs. Wonderful.

"That's all, I swear," he whined, squirming in his chair.

"Give me your full name and address, then," I told him. "I'll be in touch only if I have to be."

I glanced around the apartment while he wrote out the information. All the while, the redhead watched distastefully, propped against the doorjamb.

A photo of a husky pink-faced male, presumably the absent husband, smiled broadly from a table. Beside it sat a framed enlargement of a little girl with a mouthful of tiny baby teeth. As I looked at her, I heard a little whimper from the rear of the apartment. The sound a child often makes involuntarily in its sleep.

Screw around but do it on your own time, I thought scornfully to myself. Don't drag in the children.

And then I scolded myself for my moralistic view. Perhaps the husband was a right bastard, perhaps this was true love standing here in front of me, perhaps I had no right to judge other people's lives.

The last apartment on the row yielded nothing and I walked down the stairs to Carl. I told him about the shadowy figure and the car, for all the good it did us.

"At least we know there was a car," he pointed out. "She wasn't walked up." A toothpick, one in the endless daily chain he chewed, bobbed in the corner of his mouth.

"There's that, yes," I conceded. "How'd you make out with the restaurant staff?"

"Nothing. No one saw or heard anything. Seems they only go out in that parking lot to empty the trash or get their cars to go home. And there's no window looking out on it, only that door that leads into the kitchen."

He shifted from one foot to the other and I noticed his stomach, never trim, spilled more than ever over his belt line.

"What about the patrons? Did Waters think any of them parked out back earlier this evening?"

"He says no, that they all use the larger lot across the street, come and go by the front door. Bigoted bastard, ain't he?"

I nodded, tucking my hair tight inside my collar to keep my neck warm. It was the early hours of morning now and the air felt as cold as the color of the deep black sky above.

"Let's check out that alley where the car's supposed to have stopped," I said, "before we tackle the Dumpsters. After that, we've got to see a guy named Henry who hangs out in the park."

Carl plodded forward, his big hands jammed deep into his pockets, his large head with its unruly fair hair bent down to gain some warmth.

Little girl, I wondered sadly as I followed him, where are you now? Are you on the cutting table yet, are you in the holding crypt, are you still strapped upon that gurney, waiting in some lonely hall? And does the cruelty of that silver tape still bind against your mouth?

CHAPTER FOUR

"So who is she?" Harris looked across the desk at Rhoads. "Where did she come from and how did she get inside those woods?"

His partner shoved a stick of gum inside his mouth and began chewing rapidly.

"Can't say. I've never seen that face in town, that's for sure. Have you checked missing persons yet?"

"Just now." Harris motioned toward his phone. "Nothing's on file that'd fit. Nothing that would even come close. Damn"—he bit his lower lip, thinking back to the vacant lot—"I've never seen a cleaner crime scene."

Rhoads called downstairs to the watch commander in patrol.

"Jerry, pull the roster for all three watches for the past two days and nights and then get back to me. I need to know who was working 8A27." He looked at Harris. "Maybe the beat cop saw something that'd help us. Someone stopping at the lot or coming from the woods." He ran his fingers through his thick dark hair.

The two men were unlike, both physically and in temperament. Harris was smaller, more compact, with light brown hair and eyes that smiled easily while Rhoads was big, with a football player's build and carried an intensity about him that his partner seemed to lack.

Extremely self-assured, he tended to wear this assurance like a badge upon his chest. Except for the occasional times when he fell moody, internalizing things a bit too much instead of letting them all hang out.

Harris, on the other hand, though every bit as much in possession of himself, stayed quiet and self-contained. Comfortable with what he was, without too many ruffles and flourishes. He was more even, less flamboyant, while Charlie was the loud and noisy one.

But they were friends, as tight as if they were blood brothers. Their differences of personality didn't seem to matter in the way they got along. And then there was the other thing, the other bond between them. The debt Harris felt he never could repay.

"Okay, baby." Rhoads slapped the desk. "Let's get our artist to make a sketch of the victim as she'd look if she were living and we'll circulate it to the papers and TV, then get on out and talk to the folks on Thurston Road."

He'd just hung up with the artist when his phone began to ring. It was the watch commander on the line.

"Stillwell's been working days on 8A27," he told Rhoads. "He's in the jail now, booking a burglary suspect. Wanna catch him up?"

"Sure thing," Charlie said, rising. "Robert and I will be right down. What about the other watches?"

"Brown and Carrow on P.M.s, Jason and Telforth on A.M.s. They're all coming on later on today, but I pulled their field activities reports. Neither car reported seeing anything suspicious at your location during the past two nights and early morning. I'm assuming you want to talk to them because of that body out on Thurston Road, right?"

"Right, Jerry, and thanks. We're on our way."

The two men clattered down the stairs and swung the jail door open. They found Stillwell, a beefy, grizzled old-timer, fingerprinting a scared weasel of a man who'd been caught with his hand in someone else's cookie jar.

"Warren, you know that lot on Thurston Road where we found the female victim this morning?"

"Damn right I do," he growled. "I'd have been there code three myself but I was chasing down this scumbag."

"You notice any unusual activity there the past two days when you been driving past?" Rhoads did the talking while his partner listened.

"None at all. Quiet and peaceful. Pleasant spot, I always thought. You think she was dumped there in the past forty-eight hours, do you?"

"Give or take a little, yes we do."

"Well, sorry, boys, I can't help you. Sometimes I'll see a repair man sitting there in his truck eating lunch or going behind a bush to take a leak, but not this weekend."

Rhoads and Harris left the jail and started out to Thurston Road. They'd already asked the porky little man with the questing hound if he'd walked that way the previous night or day. No, he'd told them, he'd taken a different route, so his pet hadn't had a chance to make an earlier discovery, even if the corpse had been lying there before this morning.

"Used to think a dog wouldn't touch a dead person, Bobby, that it'd shy off. Then I found out different."

"Maybe we just don't like to think that sweet old Fido doesn't show respect," Harris answered, "but here we have the proof. I recall an animal behaviorist once telling me a dog will lick, chew, and eat human remains with relish. And then lie down and roll in them with pure delight."

The day was clear and bright, with the chill of early morning replaced by winter warmth—a slight rising of the temperature that pleases but never holds the promise of full-blown heat. They drove toward Thurston Road and gradually, as they left the center of the city, the houses became sparse and open fields and woods appeared.

Stockton was a pleasant little city, neither too big nor too small. It lay ninety miles inland from the ocean, northeast of San Francisco and south of Sacramento in the sprawling acreage of the San Joaquin Valley. Harris thought how it suited him just fine, away from the hurly-burly of Los Angeles, and how glad he was he'd returned to his hometown. Though he regretted why he'd had to leave L.A.

Long past, he thought, looking out the window, all long past now. He glanced at Charlie, concentrating on the road ahead. He's made the difference for me, Harris thought, just like he's always done.

The house closest to the lot came into view and Rhoads pulled the Chevy to a stop.

"Come on, kiddo, let's get cracking," he told Harris. "Maybe these fine folk saw the Whole Thing and are dying to tell us all about it."

He arched his eyebrows and gave a little whistle, mocking his own words. And then a look of darkness fell upon his face as he stepped out of the car.

CHAPTER FIVE

It was Saturday morning, the brightness of a new day just beginning, and we weren't any closer than we'd been eight hours ago to finding out who our baby was, let alone who killed her.

Carl and I, joined by Steve Darrow, the third man on my team, had donned long rubber gloves and sifted through the top layers of the trash in every Dumpster. At times the stench had overwhelmed us—thick, rotten, clinging—and the decomposing mater itself had stuck firmly to our hands and arms.

It would all have been worth it, of course, if our efforts had produced a clue. But there was nothing. Nothing we could tie definitely to the baby or the person who had brought her there. Sodden food was mainly what we found and it didn't help us.

"An outside chance," Darrow had muttered, loud enough to be heard by me.

A seasoned investigator, he'd only recently returned to my unit, after department disciplinary action for conduct unbecoming. He was handsome, he was brash, and despite his talent as a homicide detective, he and I didn't always get along. He tended to go his own way too often and held a cavalier attitude toward women that I didn't like: using them up, then tossing them out like worn Kleenex.

"I think the baby was the only thing he had to dump, so that's all we had to find. No weapon used, as far as you could tell, no bloody gloves or clothes to throw away."

"Probably right," I conceded, "but we had to search."

The asphalt driveway likewise told no tales. Too hard to hold a print, we could find no other evidence to indicate a car had parked there for the few moments it would take to toss a baby in the trash.

Old Henry was our third disappointment. We'd found him sleeping underneath an oak tree in a little city park frequented by the homeless and other down-and-outs, but we might as well have let him rest.

We'd had to rouse several graying long-haired men before we'd found our quarry, but once we located him he was immediately awake.

"What Dumpster? Nah, I haven't been there." His breath rode strong and fetid through the air.

"We know you were there, Henry," I told him, "the owner of the restaurant spotted you. And there's no problem with that. Just tell us, please, what time it was and if you saw anything unusual in the trash bin, then we'll go away."

He pulled his blanket tight around him and gave in.

"Okay, it was close to eight o'clock. I know that because I always do my rounds on a set schedule and I always get to that parking lot around that time. Anything unusual? Nah! Even less good stuff than there usually is."

"What about the third Dumpster from the end?" I asked. "The one directly behind the restaurant. Concentrate on it."

"Old Nellie?" He looked surprised and sat thinking as he picked his teeth. "I name my Dumpsters, you know. A silly thing, I guess, but it's just a little game with me. Harmless, after all. Well, Nellie's my favorite in that lot 'cause she's right behind the food joint, so sure, I remember her. And she was disappointing. Just some scrappy leavings a dog wouldn't touch and wads of tossed-out paper napkins."

I'd seen the napkins. They'd lain underneath the flannel shirt, beneath the baby's body, so if Henry had seen them, too, but had not seen the little girl, that meant that the infant had been placed in its resting place sometime after eight o'clock but before ten forty-five p.m. Which tied right in with the sighting at nine-thirty or so by Curt, the lothario in unit number eight. With nothing more to offer, we thanked the gray-haired man and told him to go back to sleep.

"Carl," I called, rising from my desk to get a cup of coffee, "has the print info come in yet?" I'd not slept since Thursday night, having just been ready to crawl between the sheets last evening when my phone rang to tell me a baby's body had been found. I'd thrown on some clothes, kissed my sleeping son good-bye, and raced on out the door. Now I needed a good strong jolt to keep me going.

"Just did," he answered, and showed me flyers of the infant's hand and footprints, as well as a morgue photo of a little face that looked as if it slept. The silver tape was no longer in evidence.

"Get the prints out to all hospitals and clinics in the area," I told him, "just on the off chance they keep a copy of the set they give the parents. Send the photos to the papers and TV as well as to all local doctors, especially pediatricians. No baby's been reported missing so we've got to start stirring things up somewhere."

My phone rang shrilly, startling in the quiet around me, and I quickly picked it up.

"Katharine, it's me. How're you doing?"

I stiffened.

"How did you know I was here?"

"Where else would you be if you weren't at home?" he asked sarcastically. I ignored the tone and asked him what he wanted.

"That father-son Cub Scout dinner. When is it, Kate?" My estranged husband spoke normally now.

"I'm not certain, Jon. Next Friday night, I think. I thought you had the date."

"Just double-checking. Forgot to write it down." And, without the nicety of a good-bye, he hung up.

Putting down the receiver, I caught a glimpse of my reflection in a nearby mirror. My brown hair was disheveled and my hazel eyes—sometimes gray, sometimes green, depending on my mood and the colors that surrounded them—were dulled with weariness and a slight anxiety. I may've been only in my late thirties but suddenly I felt much older.

My phone rang once again and I gave a little jump, slopping the coffee over the edge of its container.

"Harrod here."

"Katharine, it's Penross. I've got a cause of death for you and it's pretty much as we suspected. The infant died from deprivation of oxygen to the lungs or, in your words, smothering, brought about by the binding of the tape across its mouth and nose."

"Her nose?" I asked, frowning. "I saw no tape across her nose."

"Yes, Katharine. There's evidence that a strip of the same tape or similar had been placed across the child's nostrils at some point, then removed."

I started to gag but controlled myself.

"What about the bruising, Howard?"

"Inflicted before death. Injurious, yes, but not fatal. Made with some powerful object to cause such severe trauma, possibly a fist or booted foot."

"God," I heard myself murmur, as much to myself as to the coroner, "a perverted monster."

"Yes, Katharine, a monster," he agreed. "Controlled and calculating enough to cut that tape and lay it on, wild and raging enough to smash a baby violently."

I wiped a tear away and asked about the tape and the flannel shirt.

"Negative on those. The lab boys tell me the tape's just ordinary duct tape, available in any hardware or convenience store. It came up clean of fingerprints. The shirt's an adult's, old and worn with the label missing and the pockets empty. It could've lain in the back of someone's closet for many years."

I hung up and watched Carl and Steve leaving with the flyers. I sipped my coffee slowly, listening to the silence of the squad room and reflecting on my case. We'd done everything we could for now, unturned every stone that lay within our sight. We'd come up empty and now we could do little more than watch and wait. And wonder who she was and what she'd done to deserve her awful death.

CHAPTER SIX

The house, a restored Victorian two-story painted deep green with black and white trim, sat well back from the street. A faded brick sidewalk led to its three front steps, breaking off near the porch to form a second path to the structure's rear.

Harris looked to his left, toward the woods and vacant lot. A split rail fence separated the house from the lot, and against the fence a low row of trees was planted, low enough that the view beyond them would not be obscured to the Victorian's occupants.

He rang the doorbell while Rhoads stood to one side, glancing at his watch.

"Hope they skipped church today, Bobby. It'll save us coming back."

As he spoke, the glass-topped front door opened and a patrician-looking woman, possibly forty-five or fifty, gazed at them with questioning eyes.

"Detective Robert Harris, Stockton Police Department, and my partner Detective Charles Rhoads. We'd like to talk with you a moment if we may."

She relaxed and smoothed her ash-blond hair with a soft and delicate hand. Rhoads spotted the diamond rings on her fingers and mentally gave another whistle.

The woman, who introduced herself as Mrs. Burke, led them to a den just off the hallway, waved them to a sofa seat, and settled comfortably into a wing-backed chair.

"I heard all the commotion, of course, so I dressed and went outside. I know what happened. That poor, poor woman . . . how can I help you?"

"Mrs. Burke, we have reason to believe the victim may have been placed in the woods well before the time she was discovered—maybe as early as Friday night or Saturday morning." Harris spoke earnestly, leaning forward just a little. He'd changed from his running clothes and was now wearing a gray suit with dark blue tie. "Have you noticed anyone on that lot or parked in front of it at any time since then?"

The woman stared at him as if frozen.

"My God," she cried, "I just assumed she'd died there early this morning. I had no idea . . . you mean it's possible she's been lying dead right next to me for nearly two days?"

"It's possible, yes," Harris told her.

She shuddered. "How creepy! You see, my husband's away on a business trip and I've been here all alone since Thursday." She looked perplexed and on the verge of tears. "Suppose the murderer had come here and killed me, too?"

"If it's any consolation, we don't think the victim was killed here," Rhoads told her, "and we don't think her killer lingered long in this area. Just took enough time to hide the body and then he split."

"Did you notice anything connected with the lot?" Harris swung back to his earlier question.

"No. Only . . . wait, there was something, something small and maybe meaningless. I'm a nervous sleeper when my husband's not home, so I got up around midnight Friday to get a drink of water. Just then Jessie began to bark." She motioned toward a golden retriever sleeping in a large pen by the side of the house. "I keep her outside while Bill's away so she can stand guard.

"Anyway, she began to raise a ruckus—a cat or raccoon, I thought—and I looked out the upstairs hall window but there wasn't any moon that night so it was hard to see. Then she quieted down a bit and I went on into the bathroom." The woman paused, her hand going to her throat.

"I came out a few minutes later and went back to bed, but Jessie started up again. I got back up and saw the taillights of a car moving slowly down the road, but I thought—and I still really don't know any different—that it was a car that had passed this house and was proceeding on its way. Do you mean, do you think, it was parked first at the lot to unload that woman's body?" Her eyes were open wide.

"We don't know that, Mrs. Burke, but it's certainly possible. How precise can you be about the time?"

"Within ten minutes or so. I know the bedside clock said midnight either before or just after I got the drink of water."

"Did you notice anything but the taillights?" Rhoads queried. "The height or width of the vehicle, how far apart the lights were placed on the car's body?"

"No," Mrs. Burke replied, "only the red lights themselves, moving slowly away."

She told the two men she'd lain awake for five or ten minutes, to see if Jessie started barking again, but the dog stayed quiet and the woman had fallen asleep and slept till dawn.

None of the occupants of the other homes within a quarter of a mile of the lot reported anything unusual occurring within the past forty-eight hours, but Mrs. Burke had been reward enough.

"Friday night," Harris said as the two drove back to town. "I'll bet her body was dumped Friday night at midnight. He was probably back at the woods, car parked at the road with lights out, when that woman first heard Jessie barking. The second time the dog barked, he was returning to the vehicle to drive away."

Rhoads nodded absentmindedly, his thoughts temporarily elsewhere. Then, "We'll get those sketches out and send her prints to Sacramento, to see if they've got a match on file."

"Right. I'll call the coroner as soon as we get back,

to find out when they'll be ready. And to see what else he has to say. Hey, Charlie"—Harris moved quickly to another thought—"there's a real possibility she's not from Stockton at all, you know. She could've been driven in from anywhere. Maybe the artist's sketch will stir things up, especially if we get good circulation."

"I'll bet she's local," Rhoads countered. "Feeling in my bones says she's local, even though I haven't seen her around."

They parked the car, grabbed some takeout from a lunch stand beside the station, and walked inside. Crime was light on Sundays in this town and the halls were clear of cops and citizens alike. The desk officer in the lobby sat behind the long rectangular counter wrapped in utter boredom, thumbing through a hunting magazine and waiting for a phone that didn't ring.

Harris sat down at his desk, took a bite of his chicken-on-rye, and dialed the coroner's number.

"Whaddya think I am?" the coroner grumbled. "A bloody miracle man? I haven't been back here that long myself."

"Can you give us anything?" Harris pleaded.

"Official no, unofficial yes, and then stop bothering me."

"I'll take the unofficial."

"Cause of death was strangulation, no doubt in my mind about it. Manual strangulation, not ligature, with the killer facing her. Big hands. They damn near went all the way around her neck. Big and powerful. No other signs of trauma on the body. Liver probe says she's been dead well over twenty-four hours. I'd guess thirty-six or so. I'll get back to you when all the tests are done."

Harris looked at Rhoads and squeezed his open palm around his own neck while he listened, indicating to his partner the cause of death.

"What about the prints for Sacramento? Okay, good, we'll send them off. And the dental charts? Tomorrow early? Right."

The two men checked the missing persons reports again, just to make sure no new ones had come in. They distributed the artist's sketch of the dead woman—a remarkable rendering of how the attractive brunette must've looked before death took her over—and later in the afternoon they fired the prints off to the state capital for possible matchup.

And then they went on home and waited. Because there was nothing else that they could do.

CHAPTER SEVEN

I slipped on my socks and stepped into a pair of low-heeled shoes. I liked this combination—dark socks and heels topped by slacks and jacket. If a murder happened and I had to rush out to the scene, I could quickly pull on the old pair of Reeboks resting in my desk without the chafing feel of nylon stockings rubbing on my heels.

Monday morning. Would it all start to come together today? I wondered as I hurried down the stairs. There'd been time for the prints and photos to reach their destinations. Would some hospital or doctor phone? Or some man or woman who, right now, was scanning the morning paper and stopping short with widened eyes as they saw the picture of a familiar little face?

Tommy, my nine-year-old, was walking into the kitchen just in front of me, dressed in jeans and T-shirt and ready for another day of school. He hadn't seen me coming down the stairs and I snuck up behind him and gave him a soft and playful smack as I said, "Good morning, kiddo," and bent to kiss his cheek.

He took the kiss but tucked his bottom in, pulling away from the smack, and I saw a slight frown edge his face as he did so. Just another reminder, I thought, that he was growing up, becoming more mature, and that the welcomed touch of yesterday was not so appealing to him today.

"Cub Scouts after school?" I asked as Mrs. Miller set bowls of steaming oatmeal down in front of us.

"Uh-huh." He shook his blond head vigorously up and down as he swirled his spoon around the porridge, mixing in liberal helpings of milk and coarse brown sugar.

"And then straight home, right?"

"Sure, Mom, like always." He drew out the words, exaggerating them, as he rolled his eyes toward the housekeeper. I knew he grew tired of my constant admonition but I couldn't help myself . . . especially after that little boy last spring and now the murdered baby. He poked my arm, his mouth filled with oatmeal.

"There's a field trip coming up real soon, Mom," he managed to push out, as if talking through a twist of socks and marbles, "and they're looking for parents to volunteer as chaperons. Do you think maybe you could go?"

"Find out the date," I told him, "and I'll certainly try my best."

He quickly finished eating and took his dishes to the sink. My eyes followed him and I noticed he seemed to have grown another inch or so since the last time I'd looked, just the other day.

"He's doing okay, don't you think?" I asked Mrs. Miller as Tommy left for school and she settled opposite me with her cup of morning tea.

"Seems to be," she answered, patting the white bun behind her head. "Cheerful, cooperative. But he's growing up, I notice that. Getting more serious, interests changing. Becoming a little man and starting to put away childish things, so to speak. Which is just as it should be, of course." She paused, then, "Hardly ever mentions his dad."

"I know," I told her, "but I *don't* know if that's good or bad."

I leaned back as she began to clear the table, sipping at my strong black coffee, letting my mind drift backward through my life.

I'd been born and raised in this beloved valley nestled near the foothills of the Mariposa mountains, and I'd been a cop here for nearly all my adult life. And I'd had a good marriage here, or so I'd thought, and been happy, despite the loss of my own baby girl eleven years ago.

Happy till the case of that missing little boy had come along last spring and flamed Jon's smoldering anger at my work as head of homicide till it built to a crescendo and overflowed into our lives—a tumultuous entry that carried us to a bitter separation and a pending divorce that would leave no bridges we could ever hope to cross to meet again.

But I was coping. As a single parent, as a soul without a mate, as a person who, naive romantic that I was, had felt a pain I'd never thought I'd have to feel. Coping, yes, and finally starting to be comfortable with the life that now was mine.

I drained the cup, set it in the sink, and called good-bye to Mrs. Miller. A smile found my lips as I bent to pat the sleeping pile of fur named Molly, stretched out all doglike on the rug, and I suddenly realized how much easier it was for me to smile than it'd been just several months ago. To smile and to be happy.

Except for times like now, I thought, as I straightened up and felt my face grow grim. Except for times like now, when a baby girl lies dead without a name or a single soul to claim her and the killer of that baby girl runs free.

I saw her just ahead of me, hurrying toward the station—half walking, half trotting, her shoulders hunched, her blond hair streaming out behind her. Slight of build and delicate, her waiflike features gave off an air of youthful vulnerability.

"What brings you here," I wondered, "in such an urgent manner? A stolen car, a break-in? What's your great concern to drive you here so hurriedly?"

She threw a backward glance, as if she read my thoughts, and I saw a strained and worried face, mouth grimly set, that looked no more than twenty-three or -four, if that.

I followed her into the station and saw her moving toward the counter in the lobby and the uniformed desk officer standing there behind it. I turned right and headed down the hallway toward the stairs, my thoughts leaving her behind and turning to the work ahead.

I'd just swung the stairs door open when I heard my name called out from somewhere far behind me and I spun around to see the desk man waving at me, motioning to me to come back.

Wondering, I retraced my steps, my eyes now focused on the blond-haired childlike woman standing by the counter. What do I have to do with you? I puzzled as I approached the two of them.

"Detective Harrod, I think you ought to hear this right along with me," the officer told me, concern filling his face and eyes. Then, turning to the woman, "Tell us both together, ma'am."

"My baby's gone, she's disappeared. She's not where I left her Friday night." Her eyes were frantic, filled with fear, and tears ran over from their corners.

My soul chilled and I knew. I knew before she said another word whose mother was standing here in front of me. I felt my stomach sicken and my heart fall low at the thought of the ugly task now facing me. To lead her slowly down a sad, sore path and take her to the blinding killing pain waiting at its end.

"Come upstairs with me," I told her gently and I took her by the arm. "We can talk much better there."

I nodded to the officer. "I'll take over now," I told him grimly and I saw him slowly nod. He knew, as did all patrol and most detectives, about the finding of that battered little body Friday night.

I felt her tremble as her pale blue eyes fixed on me and we started walking down the hall. Not a word was spoken as we passed through the door and climbed the concrete stairs to the squad room. In the silence of the moment, I became vividly aware of the stairwell's musty worn scent.

"I'll get some coffee for us both," I told her when we reached my desk. "How do you take yours? With cream and sugar?"

Wordlessly she shook her head.

"Just black, then," I said softly. "Please sit here." I pulled a chair close beside my own. "I'll be just a minute." I glanced around as I was speaking. Carl and Steve were nowhere to be seen.

Miserably the woman grabbed my arm.

"No coffee, no," she cried out frantically. "I just want to talk to you, so you can find my baby."

"All right, I understand," I said, starting to sit down. "Please tell me why you think your infant's missing."

I couldn't come right out and say I had to take her to the morgue. In the slim off chance this fragile being wasn't who I thought she was, I must go slowly, step by step, as if I didn't hold the dreadful knowledge that I held. I could not unnecessarily subject some other mother, whose child was really on a day trip with an aunt, to the vision of that soft-skinned black-bruised body lying on a slab.

She gulped and choked, then fumbled in a tannish vinyl purse, taking out a pale green hankie that she held against her mouth.

"I live in Vegas but I came to San Madera late Friday afternoon to leave Lucy with a friend of mine. I needed to see my parents in Bodega Bay this week-end but I had to go alone. I dropped my baby off a little after seven, then drove on up north. I just got back in town this morning and they're not there, either one of them, and there's no note, nothing."

"Who's your friend?" I asked, reaching for a pad, "and where does she live?"

"Meryl Masters. She's got a town house at 4608 Rimerton Place."

"And you are?"

"Wanda Brighton. Please, ma'am, please go look-ing for them."

She leaned forward anxiously and bit her lip in clear distress.

"Does your friend work?" I asked, letting her plea go unanswered. "It's Monday morning. Perhaps she didn't expect you quite so soon and she took your child along with her to the office."

"No, no!" she protested loudly. "I called. I used her phone and called. She's with social services downtown and they said she hadn't come in. And the papers are on the doorstep."

"What papers?"

"Saturday's and Sunday's and today's. Not touched, not taken in. And Lucy's formula was still in the paper bag on the kitchen counter. It's not been used, not even one can." The woman buried her face in her hands and started sobbing. "She seemed so happy when I left her. Meryl was holding her and bouncing her and she seemed so happy and content I didn't worry at all about leaving her."

"How did you gain entry to the town house, Mrs. Brighton? Was the door unlocked?"

"No . . . I don't know . . . but I had a key and I just let myself in when no one answered the doorbell. Please help me, please."

There was no turning back, no taking of a different, brighter path. It was time to move ahead to the cruel crescendo of this whole pathetic interview. This woman's missing child wasn't on some happy outing with her sitter. The papers, maybe, would've lain uncollected if they'd gone off on such a lark, but the formula would never have been left behind.

"Do you have a picture of your Lucy?" I asked reluctantly, covering the woman's hand with mine.

"Yes, yes I do. It was taken just two weeks ago, on her four-month birthday, so it's very recent. She looks just like this."

She reached hurriedly into her purse—full of hope, certain now we'd start to make some headway—and drew out a worn wallet overstuffed with photos. She flipped to the topmost plastic holder, withdrew a colored two-by-three, and laid it down in front of me.

My eyes rested on it and I felt my heart contract. A smiling baby girl looked up at me, her dark brown eyes a startling contrast to the fairness of her skin and the lightness of the hair that fringed her round soft face. She wore a little sleeper suit with flowers and strings of hearts embroidered on a yellow collar.

I stared long moments at the picture. I saw little lips curving up in happiness at some unseen delight; I saw the sweetness of a dimple in the fatness of one cheek; I saw the battered little being who'd been thrown in a Dumpster on a cold clear winter night.

"I'm going to have to ask you to come with me." I heard my voice and it sounded as if it came from far away. Someone else, not myself, speaking for me. "A child very much resembling Lucy was found late last Friday evening. She was not alive. I'm very sorry but I need you to look at her for identification."

The woman stared at me as I reached out to put my arms around her. To console her, to offer her some sort of strength. She gasped, half rising from her seat, and then she fainted as her body swayed and fell across my desk.

*   *   *

I'd taken her to the morgue myself, rushing Carl
and Steve to 4608 Rimerton, to seal off and protect
the possible crime scene. They'd been out doing
fieldwork with the hospitals and pediatricians, but
their beepers soon brought them to the station.

She didn't speak as we rode down the sunbathed
city streets, just sat limply beside me, staring straight
ahead. Her pained face looked even paler and more
girlish, more vulnerable and helpless, than when I'd
seen her first, and her hair swung in uncombed
strands above the slightness of her shoulders.

I led her through the swinging doors and down
the silent corridor to the deep cold chamber where
her baby lay. It only took a moment. A moment that
forever changed her life. The sheet was drawn back
and the little face of Lucy Brighton, now devoid of
binding tape, rested there in front of her. Mercifully,
the same white sheet hid the ugly bruises on the
infant's arms and thighs.

Wanda Brighton took one look and wailed her anguish. A wrenching high-pitched utterance born deep
down in her gut. I held her close and rocked her back
and forth as she reached out and fought to touch her
baby.

"Is it Lucy?" I whispered, for I had to hear her
say it. "Is it your baby, Lucy?"

Miserably she nodded, her face contorting violently, tears flowing freely down her cheeks and
dropping on her blouse.

"Yes," she screamed, *"yes, yes, yes, yes, yes."* She continued to chant the words hypnotically, as if her voice had snagged and stuck, until I nodded to the coroner's assistant, then put my arm around her and led her from the room.

"Do you have any other friends in town?" I asked when we were settled in the car. "Any relatives that you can stay with?"

She shook her head, then bit the knuckle of her thumb so hard I saw it start to bleed.

"How did my baby die?" she asked, looking at me through a haze of tears. "What happened to her?"

"She died from lack of breath," I told her gently, determined not to mention the cruel silver tape. "Her breathing process was restricted and she was deprived of necessary oxygen."

"But how?" she persisted. "Was she smothered? Did someone mean to do this to her?" Her eyes sprang open wide in shock as the dreadful truth began to find its way into her mind.

"We'll talk more about that later on," I told her, starting the ignition. "Right now we need to talk about your husband. Where can we find him, to notify him? In Las Vegas?"

"Not my husband." Wanda Brighton hung her head. "I'm not married to my baby's father. Maybe someday . . . I want to but . . ." She drew herself together for a moment, straightening in the seat. "We live together back in Vegas. His name is Sonny

Mitchell. Can you call him? Can you tell him for me?"

"Of course I can," I assured her, "but right now I want to leave you at the station, where a friend of mine will take care of you. She'll take you to the doctor, who'll give you something to sedate you, and then she'll find a place where you can get some rest and sleep. I'll need to talk more to you later but now I want to relieve you just a little from this awful strain."

Wanda Brighton suddenly tried opening the car door, attempting to climb out.

"I can't leave her," she sobbed uncontrollably. "I need to go to her again. I want to hold my poor, poor little baby."

I pulled her slowly back inside the car.

"Not now," I told her softly, imagining the depth of pain consuming her. "Later but not now. You're with friends. Let me take you where they'll care for you."

She collapsed beside me and I drove her to the station, passing children bouncing balls on nearby sidewalks, mothers pushing carriages around a city park. Once she glanced up and saw a woman sitting on a bench, cooing to a baby much like Lucy. She began to sob again and doubled over in her seat.

I'd radioed ahead and Patti Burke, my old partner from patrol, met us in the lot and helped Wanda Brighton from the car.

"Look after her," I said. "I'll be in touch."

I watched them walk into the station, the slight blond figure leaning heavily for support against the uniformed figure of the other woman, and then I left the lot and raced the car to Meryl Masters's town house.

The two-story buildings were set in clusters around a common courtyard, their front doors facing one another, their rear doors opening on an alley or on the street behind them.

I walked slowly up the four brick steps flanked by wrought-iron rails, glancing at the dark green shutters flung back against a wall of deep red brick. The whole complex reminded me of pictures I had seen of town houses in the Fan District of Richmond in Virginia, or in Boston's Logan Square.

I saw the papers lying near the doormat, probably right where they'd been tossed by the paperboy, and the whiteness of an envelope showing through some slits in the mailbox to the side. Carefully I opened up the lid. Saturday's mail not yet collected.

My hand touched the bright brass handle and I pushed the front door inward. A Christmas wreath, thick with cones and rich red berries, still hung above the heavy knocker, though the holiday had ended several weeks ago.

"Find anything?" I called as I stepped into a small square entrance hall covered by a Persian rug.

"Nothing, Kate." Darrow clattered down the stairs from the second floor.

His dark hair was combed neatly back, his brown eyes large and shining. A crescent scar, newly healed from an altercation with a suspect last month, grooved his cheek beside one ear. Probably another thing the girls will find attractive, I thought. Another thing to suck them in and fall victims to his charm.

"It's as if no one even lived here, it's all so neat. Everything in place, no sign of any struggle, no evidence we can find to indicate a crime was committed here." His brash good looks were clouded in perplexity.

"How did you gain entry?" I asked, moving to the living room. "Was the door unlocked?"

"The front one was," he answered. "Did you ask the mother if she secured it when she left or not?"

"No, I didn't. I'll check on that next time I see her, though I doubt she'll even know. I imagine from the state she was in when she reached the station that she flew out of here without regard to too many particulars."

"All the windows are latched tight," Carl told me, coming from the kitchen. "The back door's locked, too, but not by the dead bolt, just by the handle lock that automatically works when you pull or push it shut. No sign of forced entry."

His round face wore its usual flush above the V-necked sweater pulling slightly awry across his chest and sporting little nubs of wool that attested to its wear. The inevitable toothpick hung loosely from his mouth.

Darrow, on the other hand, was bandbox-fresh and neat, carrying an air of cool imperturbability. Where Mungers was the plain white bread on my team, Steve was the showy high-yeast loaf with a glaze and flash that wouldn't stop. And sometimes it wore me down and made my patience thin.

I looked around me and saw a small and elegant living room fitted with fine, expensive furnishings. Someone obviously had taste along with money to indulge it. A framed photograph of an attractive dark-haired woman, maybe twenty-eight to thirty years of age, caught my eye from a narrow end table. I bent to look at it, then straightened up and strolled through to the kitchen.

A paper grocery bag stood beside a diaper kit on the long tiled center counter. I peered inside and saw the cans of formula stacked one atop the other. The diaper bag was zipped and bulging, probably unmoved since Wanda Brighton set it down there Friday night.

A thorough search of the rest of the downstairs and the two-bedroom upstairs yielded nothing helpful. As Steve had pointed out, everything was in its place or put away, except for the formula and the baby's diaper bag. If anything untoward had happened in this house, it had either been a swift clean

act or someone had straightened up very well behind him.

"Where's her purse?" I asked. "I haven't seen a
purse anywhere except those empty ones hanging in
the closet. Where's the one she used on Friday?"

We searched the town house all over again but
could not find a handbag crammed with wallet,
credit cards, and keys. Not pushed inside a drawer,
not slung across a chair. Had she taken it with her
when she left? Had someone else made it disappear?

I checked inside the closets till I found the one
where Meryl Masters stored her luggage. A set of
expensive leather bags sat neatly in a corner. The set
looked complete as it now stood but it was also possible one piece could be missing.

I turned from the closet to the message light blink-
ing on the answering machine beside the phone. I
went to it and started to rewind the tape, hoping it
would offer us a clue. The three of us gathered
around as it began to spin but its words didn't help
the situation. Just several everyday reminders about
lunch dates the coming week or a girlfriend saying
hi and that they'd get together later. All innocuous,
all far too ordinary to be useful.

Except for one small fact. The caller on the first
message named the time as ten p.m. on Friday night.
Why hadn't Meryl taken that call? Had she chosen
to ignore it or had she already left the town house,
either by force or by her own free will? Had she been

taken with the baby or had she gone separately, at some other time? Was she herself the victim of foul play or was she, perhaps, the perpetrator?

"Where is Meryl Masters?" I asked out loud, swinging around to Carl and Steve. "We've got to find her, to start to learn what happened to the baby."

I walked over to the little table and picked up the photograph.

"Let's go door-to-door to see if we can get an ID on this face," I told them. "Also find out when Masters was last seen or heard from by her neighbors."

We had our answers in less than thirty minutes. Two neighbors named Meryl Masters as the woman in the photo and an elderly gentleman in the town house on the right told us he'd seen the Masters woman come home somewhere close to six last Friday evening but hadn't seen her since. No one else we spoke with had noticed any movement at all or had heard any sounds, usual or unusual, connected with number 4608 during the past three days.

"Do you know what kind of car she drives?" I asked the oldster, figuring he probably spent some time watching from his windows and might know a thing like that.

"Mazda RX7, dark green. Real sporty little thing. It's parked around the back. Been there all weekend."

"That the only car she drives?"

"Yes, far as I know. Only one I've seen."

We walked through to the lot behind the unit's rear door and saw the car sitting right where he said it'd be. I peered inside—no purse, no keys, just Friday's morning paper lying on the seat. Stepping back, I took its license number, then phoned downtown.

"Run a make on California plate 3WGD321 and tell me who it's registered to."

I tapped my foot impatiently while I waited for Sandy, one of the records clerks and a close friend of Carl's, to do her work.

"It comes back to a Meryl Masters, 4608 Rimerton Place," she told me.

"Okay, now run 'vehicles registered to' and tell me if she owns any others."

Again a wait, then, "Negative. Only the Mazda."

Her car was here, her purse was gone. Two clues in apparent conflict with each other. Had she *walked* out? Had someone grabbed both her and her pocketbook and abducted her in some other vehicle? Or, and it had to get back to this, was 4608 Rimerton really even the scene of either the disappearance of Meryl Masters or the murder of the baby?

I turned to Carl and Steve.

"Seal it off and get the lab boys here," I told them. "Check for prints and have them search for anything unusual. Stains, fibers, mud, anything. We don't know what we're looking for but let's start looking nonetheless."

"You think Lucy was killed here, don't you, boss?" Carl queried. "She could've been taken somewhere else, you know, and smothered there or even been abducted from another place entirely."

"Right," I answered, "I'm well aware of all of that, but this is all we've got right now. This is the last *known* location of both Lucy Brighton *and* Meryl Masters so we've got to assume they disappeared from here till something tells us different."

I tossed the photo of the missing woman on the car seat and hurried to the station. I'd check the airlines and the bus and train depots to see if she'd left town by those means, but first I wanted to circulate this picture for everyone to see. Within hours, copies of it were in the hands of police throughout the state as well as with the TV and the papers. The search for Meryl Masters had begun with full, far-flung exposure.

CHAPTER EIGHT

He lit a cigarette and threw the match into the gutter, then bought an evening paper from the newsstand on the corner. He'd thought of stopping smoking but never very seriously. Got to die from something, he told himself. Besides, he enjoyed it far too much to quit.

Opening up the paper, he scanned the front page while he walked, then stopped dead in his tracks and riveted his eyes on a picture in the lower left-hand corner. He stared at it a long, long time, then headed for a nearby phone and dialed a number he knew by heart.

"Get the hell to the station, Bobby." Rhoads's voice was terse and low. "Our Jane Doe's on the front of this evening's paper. She's a missing female from down in San Madera, last seen there sometime Friday night."

He hung up the phone, took another long look at the photo, then headed back to homicide division.

*   *   *

They arrived together and rushed up to the squad room. Harris took the paper from his partner and spread it on the desk to study the photo for himself. Simultaneously, a records clerk laid down a fax of the same picture that had come in that afternoon.

"It's her, no doubt about it," Harris said, reaching for the phone. "I'll notify San Madera PD."

"Give me homicide," he stated curtly when the call was answered. He waited several seconds, then heard a woman's voice on the other end.

"Robert Harris here. I'm with Stockton PD homicide and just received your fax of the missing female. I'm sorry to have to tell you she's no longer missing. We found her body yesterday morning in some woods near the edge of town."

He listened carefully for a moment, then began answering questions.

"Manual strangulation and lying stark-naked. She's been dead for several days at least and lividity suggests she was killed somewhere else, maybe down in your town, then transported here and dumped. Where did she disappear from, her house?"

He sat still, eyes narrowed, while the San Madera homicide detective filled him in.

"Christ, no!" Harris suddenly groaned, causing Rhoads to swing his head around to stare at him. "Not that, too. Okay, gimme that name and number. As soon as we get a positive ID, we'll get down there to join you and try to sort this thing out."

He hung up the phone and turned to Rhoads.

"The killer took out a little baby along with our victim—threw its body in a restaurant Dumpster. It was found Friday night and San Madera's been carrying it as Jane Doe, too, till this morning when the mom showed up looking for it."

He held a piece of paper up to Rhoads.

"Meryl Masters is from the Bay Area originally. Got a pretty wealthy family still living there. We'll have to contact them and get them up here to identify."

Rhoads rested his large frame on the corner of the desk.

"What's this about going to San Madera? Are we going to give up control, hand it over to them?"

"Well, it makes sense to work with them, doesn't it?" Harris answered. "We're not sure yet who has jurisdiction on the adult victim's murder so we might as well lend a hand and maybe do ourselves some good at the same time."

He paused and pursed his lips.

"Head of homicide down there's a woman, name of Katharine Harrod. That was her I was talking to just now. Sounded like one very sharp detective."

CHAPTER NINE

I hung up the phone and looked across at Carl.
"Meryl Masters didn't walk away and she didn't kill the baby. Her body's been lying cold in Stockton woods for the past three days."

I pushed my hair back with one hand, knowing it needed a good brushing out but not really having time to do anything about it. Of course I'd never seriously believed Meryl had murdered Lucy, then disappeared of her own volition, but it was a possibility that had to be set out and examined. Now it was null and void and could be left alone.

"Talked to a fellow up in Stockton named Harris," I told Carl. "He's in charge of the Masters case on their end. He's doing the notification to the next of kin, then he'll come on down here so we can put our heads together."

"How'd he sound?" Carl asked cautiously. "Like one of those hotshot Willies who turn out to be a pain in the ass?"

He picked up a baseball cap and began to twirl it. It bore the logo of his beloved Atlanta Braves and I knew he longed for winter to end and spring training to begin.

"Nope, sounded okay. Pretty sharp and level-headed. Not a lot of bluff and bluster like you-know-who."

Darrow's hearty-Charlie personality didn't bother Carl like it bothered me, but then he wasn't a woman and I think that had a lot to do with it. I saw a little grin begin to curve his lips. I knew my annoyance amused him even if he didn't fully understand it.

I pushed back from the desk, thinking maybe a trip down the hall to freshen up might be a good idea after all. Not only would I look less battle-scarred but some cool water on my face and a smoothing out of my tangled hair might refresh me psychologically as well as physically. Anything to keep me going. This, coming on top of the whole frenzied weekend, had been one tough day.

I walked down the hall, reflecting on where we were with the two cases—now dual homicides, both probably having been committed in our jurisdiction. I'd get out to Rimerton after I'd freshened up but I didn't expect anything from the lab boys. When I'd left there earlier, they'd been scouring for several hours without reward.

"Clean as a whistle, Detective," one told me. "If this is a crime scene it sure disguises itself well.

We're lifting prints now. Maybe they'll give you something to go on but that's going to be about it unless I'm badly mistaken."

I'd had the Mazda impounded, just in case the killer had used it to transport Lucy, and possibly Meryl, from the town house, then returned it to its proper spot and picked up his own car. Granted, it was a two-seater but I never forgot anything is possible.

Now, however, I knew the impound was probably futile. I'd glanced at the odometer and saw it read "thirty." But now I'd learned the Masters woman had been dumped in Stockton, a city more than a hundred miles to the north. I seriously doubted any killer would've gassed up the car, then returned the odometer to the "zero" position in order to check the Mazda's fuel consumption.

I'd left Rimerton and gone back to try to talk with Wanda Brighton, to find out about her friend, but she'd been under sedation and was of little help to me. Patti sat beside her while she rested on a small bed in the cot room, a room usually reserved for officers taking a break on a long shift or needing a nap while killing time before a court date.

Earlier, she'd given me her home phone number, but attempts to reach the boyfriend had been unsuccessful. If he didn't answer soon, I'd contact Vegas PD and ask them to drive around and personally notify him of the death of his baby daughter.

Unable to gain much information from Wanda, I'd gone down to Meryl's work at county social services, a dingy ragged-out building on a crumbling corner of the city, and they'd informed me she was originally from San Francisco and given me the data I'd passed on to Stockton.

What was a woman with the tastes of Meryl Masters doing working in county services? I thought. It just doesn't seem to fit.

Come to think of it, she and Wanda seemed unlikely friends, too. I'd never met the dead woman but judging from her photo and her furnishings, I'd guess she was a sophisticated lady who usually moved in different circles than those traveled by the childlike unstyled Wanda.

Something to sort out when the baby's mother felt more like talking, something that maybe could have some bearing on the case. Relationships, I mused as I'd done so many times before, the answer's usually found in relationships. Work those out and study them and a pattern usually emerges that begins to point the finger.

I hurried through the station door and drove back to Rimerton. The slap of water had refreshed me and the brushing of the hair had perked me up, too. No need looking like a slob just because I worked hard.

The early darkness of a winter evening had come down and settled on the city. Lights flicked on in houses and apartments as I passed, and when I reached the buildings clustered round the common square, I thought how cheerful and homey they appeared with the warm glow coming from their windows, an inviting refuge from the January night.

Then I realized they must've looked that way on Friday, too. The glow of number 4608 would've promised warmth and comfort just as it did now. But that promise would've been deceptive, for though the lights had beckoned with their signal of safe succor, a killer had nonetheless crept in and done his work.

The last of the lab men was coming down the brick front steps and I saw Darrow close behind him. He'd stayed when Carl and I had left, to search and search again for any clues the unyielding town house might finally offer up.

"She's a homicide now," I told him when I reached him. "Masters was discovered up in Stockton yesterday morning, strangled, lying naked in the woods. Did you find anything, anything at all?" The urgency for solid leads was twofold now, with the discovery of the second murder.

He raised his brows and gave a long low whistle at the news.

"Hate to disappoint you, Katie baby, but I didn't find a thing. And neither did they"—he nodded toward the departing car—"except those prints, which they'll advise us on tomorrow. And you know something? There weren't too many of them either— nowhere near as many as you might expect."

"Wrap it up for the night, then," I told him, ignoring the jocular familiarity. "Go on home. We'll hit it again bright and early in the morning when the baby's mom can talk to me and Stockton's got a positive ID on our adult victim."

"*You* go on home, lady," Steve told me with a wink. "I've got something blond and soft waiting for my call."

I'd missed dinner but I was in time for the dessert, and I scooped ice cream on top of cherry pie and gave a plate to Tommy.

"Let's sit around the fire and eat it, kiddo," I said to him. "It's cozy and we can relax."

"What'd you do today, Mom?" he asked after we'd plopped down and crossed our legs on the rug before the fireplace.

"Two murders, Tommy," I told him. "I investigated two murders, of a little baby and the woman who was minding her." I never glossed over or lied about my work. If he asked, I answered, and anything that bothered him we talked out.

"A baby, Mom?" His eyes popped open wide as he licked the back of his spoon. "Someone would kill a little baby?"

"Yes, Tommy, someone would. For some perverted, twisted, upside-down reason. That's why it's important that I work really hard to catch that person. To punish him and to make sure he can't stay free to do it again."

"It was a man who did it?"

"I don't know. I just *say* 'him.' It could've been a woman."

"What did the baby look like?" he asked. "Was it very hurt?"

"She looked as if she were sleeping. Her eyes were closed," I said. I didn't see any need to mention the bruises or the tape.

"But that was so mean. How can people be mean like that?" He seemed honestly bewildered and I reached over, put my arms around him, and hugged him to me. He didn't pull away.

"Some people come that way," I told him, "and others get that way as they go along. But remember this. Most people in this world are good and kind and decent. I truly believe that, despite the things I see."

Molly, her frowsy hair standing up above one eye as if she'd just awakened, ambled into the room and dropped down on the rug beside us. Her nostrils flared as she scented the remaining pie crumbs and I picked up several from the bottom of my plate, placed them on the tip of my index finger, and let her lick them off.

"Okay, kiddo, time for homework," I told Tommy, "and I've got to hit the sack. I'm bushed."

"Alllll right." He drawled his voice in halfhearted protest, then gave a little jump as if he'd had a sudden thought.

"Mom, can I take drum lessons? Cubby does and it's so cool. Bang, bang, bang, rat-a-tat-tat!" He simulated sticking, moving his hands up and down.

"Funny you should say that," I responded, surprised at my own words. "I've always loved drums myself. Maybe we can take some lessons together."

Happy with the thought, he scampered off and I sat a moment, looking fondly after him. Could he really grow up okay without a father figure in his life? I wondered. So far, it seemed to be working out all right but for the long haul? I worried about it sometimes, but really, what could I do? Not much, not much at all. For now, it was him and me, taking it one day at a time and doing the best we could.

Don't ask for perfect, I told myself whenever these thoughts surfaced. Don't ask for perfect and don't ask for guarantees. Just go with what you've got and make it work for you.

Lucy filled my dreams that night. Not as I had found her—naked with binding tape sticking to her lips—but as she must've looked that morning, as her final day on earth had started to unfold.

I saw the image of a chubby little child waking in a crib and stretching tiny arms upward as her mother bent to pick her up. I heard the gurgle of contentment and delight and saw the happiness shining from her eyes.

She'd probably been bathed and fed, then bundled

up in warmer clothes and fastened in a car seat. She'd not known where she was going to, of course, but the hazy fragments of my dream imagined she'd been happy. Drowsing as the rhythmic motions of the auto lulled her, waking and watching trees and fields and cows spin past in rushing color.

There'd been no need to fear for there was nothing there to frighten her. Just the familiar feeling of the inside of her car and the reassuring presence of her loving mother. And then the car had stopped and she'd been lifted gently out and carried into Meryl Masters's town house.

Perhaps she'd wondered at the strange surroundings and the dark-haired woman reaching out to take her, but soon she'd grown used to her and didn't even whimper when her mother turned to go. To Lucy, who'd never known cruelty, this was just one more new adventure in a baby's life, one more sunny day filled with sweet surprise.

But suddenly, from somewhere, I saw a shadow loom and a crashing ugliness change those soft and powdered moments into brutal pounding ones as that little baby's gentle world reversed and ended in the violent downturn of that sun dance night.

I moaned and shuddered as the images grew stronger in my mind, tearing at me, striking at me with their horror, and I jerked myself awake and sat up on the bed, my face covered by my hands as tears streamed down my cheeks. The pain and terror she had felt engulfed me as I replayed that gruesome scene through a mind no longer drugged by sleep.

I would do my damndest to find the murderer of Meryl Masters, but it was the violation and destruction of that little girl that would eat at me, never leave my mind nor let me rest, until I caught her killer.

I hurried through the tiny lobby, my hands thrust deep into my pockets. It'd been another chilly night, extraordinarily so even for this foothill land so near the mountains, and I couldn't seem to start warming up.

Unable to locate her boyfriend, we'd rented a room for Wanda Brighton in a small hotel near the station. She might've been all right on her own, but Patti Burke stayed with her through kindness and concern. When the shot had worn off, she'd still been distraught, seeming sometimes on the verge of fresh collapse.

I hoped the pills the doctor had prescribed had afforded her some sort of good night's rest for I badly needed to talk with her, to begin to paint a background to my case.

I didn't know if they'd eaten yet or not, but on impulse I stopped in the coffee shop set off to one side of the lobby and ordered heated Danish and several cups of strong hot brew to go. Chances were Patti had already taken care of this but it couldn't hurt to have some more to eat and drink.

Balancing the container box with one hand, I pressed the elevator button with the other and soon ascended to the second floor.

I knew as soon as I reached number 203 that something had gone very wrong. The door stood partially open but I heard no sound, and as far as I could see from where I stood, no one was in the room.

Cautiously I set the containers on the carpet and pushed the door slowly inward. The twin beds had both been slept in but both now stood mussed and empty. Patti's overnight bag sat open on the luggage rack and several clothing items lay in disarray on a corner chair. I looked all around the room. Except for the clothes and unmade beds, it was neat and clean, showing no signs of a struggle.

I moved into the bathroom. No one at the basin, no one in the shower. Several toiletry items rested on a glass shelf above the sink, apparently where they'd been placed the night before, but nothing else indicated occupancy.

Returning to the bedroom I peered into the closet and beneath the beds. I saw no shoes anywhere nor did I see Burke's holster or service revolver. Wherever the two women had disappeared to, they'd put on their walking shoes first and Patti, or someone else, had taken the gun along, too.

I wouldn't have been unduly concerned except for the open door. If I'd just found the room empty, I'd have thought they'd gone out for a bite to eat or maybe back to the station, though I'd have found it odd that Patti hadn't phoned me first. No, it was the door ajar that rang the warning bells. Burke would never have gone off without securing it. Except, perhaps, in a moment of severe distress.

I started walking down the hall, puzzling over what I'd found and what I was going to do with it. Vaguely, I heard sirens screaming in the distance but in my absorption I paid them little heed. Then I felt a vibration in my pocket as my beeper suddenly sounded.

I checked the number—homicide—and raced to a lobby phone.

Carl's voice graveled out at me.

"Get over to Fourth and Alvarado. Wanda Brighton's unconscious on the ground there, waiting transport by an ambulance. Burke's with her. Apparently stuffed herself full of sedatives, then decided to take a walk."

Stunned, I slammed the phone back on its hook and sprinted out the door. Fourth and Alvarado was only several blocks away and as I darted toward it I remembered the sirens I'd heard earlier.

I turned the corner and saw a silent crowd of onlookers watching while two uniformed attendants strapped a pale limp body on a stretcher and moved it toward the open doors of a red-and-white emergency vehicle.

I could see no sign of life in Wanda Brighton. No

breathing movement in the chest, no flutter of the eyelids, only the stillness of her body and the gray-white pallor of her face.

A dark-haired figure also moved beside the stretcher, stroking, bending, talking to the girlish form that lay there.

"Patti," I called, "Patti, I'm over here."

She broke away and came to me, her face filled with awful anguish.

"I was so stupid," she cried, taking me by the arm, "but I had no reason to think she'd try anything like this. We went to sleep and I guess I slept a little bit too soundly. When I woke up this morning, I saw Wanda gone and the pill bottle empty on the floor. I looked out the window and she was walking down the street. She must've left just before I woke."

She gulped and stopped for air.

"I threw my clothes on and tore out of that hotel and ran to her, but just as I caught up with her she began to stagger, then collapsed."

"It's all right, Patti," I told her. "Don't berate yourself. No one could've known she was pushed to this point. Did she say anything before losing consciousness?"

"I asked her why. She murmured she had nothing else to live for. She could not go on without her baby."

"What's the prognosis? Do they offer any hope?" I nodded toward the departing ambulance.

"Too early to tell, but they said her vital signs are good."

"Where're they taking her, to Mariposa?" I asked, naming the hospital closest to us.

"That's right. Are you going down there?"

"Not right now. In an hour or so. But I'll monitor her by phone. I've got some other catching up to do."

Patti nodded slowly, still looking distracted and distressed. Then she looked up at me.

"What if she'd found my gun? What if that had happened?"

"Well, she didn't, so put it to rest. We all feel bad this thing happened—we feel bad the woman took it to the limits—but you could not have known what was coming. You did the best you could."

I walked back with her and picked my car up from the hotel parking lot.

Three victims, I thought as I drove away. Three victims—two dead, one still alive. And the living one will feel the suffering long after they've pumped out the pills.

"You know who you're dealing with here, don't you?" The Las Vegas sergeant's voice barked at me across the wires. I'd phoned him when I'd reached the station, to ask him to drive on over to Wanda's home address and make the notification to the father.

"Sonny Mitchell?" I asked, surprised. "Only that he's the baby's father."

The sergeant chuckled.

"So you haven't run him yet. Well, why don't you get over to your computer and see what you pull up."

"Why don't you just tell me and save some time," I retorted. I wasn't in the mood for playing games.

Silence followed. Las Vegas didn't like that. Then, "Well, if it's the Sonny Mitchell I'm thinking of, he's done time—in California, too—for armed robbery, grand theft, assault, and a whole bunch of petty nickel-and-dimers. Got a sheet you could wrap a gift box with and still have some left over. He's on parole right now but we keep a close eye on him. He's trouble through and through."

I sat still and listened, taking it all in, no longer in the mood for sharp retorts.

"Thanks, Sergeant," I told him when he'd finished. "I'll go do my own homework now. Get back to me when you've notified him."

"Righto, Detective. You'll hear soonest."

Why was I surprised? Because Wanda Brighton didn't seem the type to get mixed up with a convicted felon? I knew better—far, far better. How many sweet-faced weak-willed girls had I seen on the arms of cons and ex-cons? Far too many.

Usually of a trusting nature and possessing low self-esteem, they were easy prey for the rough domineering type of criminal, a type who nearly always failed to treat them right. They were pummeled physically, punched emotionally, and left without a will to make things change.

Yes, I knew better but the surprise had still come anyway. I'd pictured Lucy living in a loving, stable home with a caring set of parents, married or unmarried, who lived a normal life and were law-abiding citizens. Because I'd wanted it to be that way, I'd wanted that for her. Not to have a violent ex-con for a father.

I pulled up Mitchell's rap sheet and gave a little whistle. The sergeant hadn't been exaggerating about the gift box covering. Sonny's record dated back ten years and would've gone back even further, I was sure, if it'd shown juvenile offenses.

He'd done time twice for armed robbery, several times for felony assault, once for grand theft auto, and on and on down the line. He'd spent Christmases in some of California's roughest prisons and July Fourths in those he'd missed before.

I perused his physical description so I could conjure up some sort of mental image of this man in Wanda's life. Male white, twenty-eight years of age, six feet one, two hundred pounds. Blond hair, brown eyes. Just like Lucy.

Where is he now? I wondered, and will he care when he finds out? Will he truly care his little girl is dead and gone, violently removed from this world forever, or will he shrug it off without a tender thought to kiss the memory of her face good-bye?

Come on, I told myself, jerking my mind sharply, you can't prejudge this person's feelings, you can't assign a callousness toward Lucy to him just because of who he is. Perhaps she meant the world to him, inspiring feelings of a sort he hadn't known he possessed till she came into his life. Perhaps the hardness of his criminal heart had flooded full with deep true love at the sight and sound of her.

I swung away from the computer and walked back to my desk, Mitchell's rap sheet dangling from my hand.

"Take a look at this," I said, thrusting it at Carl. "Seems like Vegas knew what they were talking about."

He scanned it quickly, arching his eyebrows.

"Any chance they're talking about a different guy?"

"Very little, I should think. Unless two Sonny Mitchells are living at the address Wanda gave me. As soon as I read it out to them, they tied it in with this guy."

"The father to that little kid . . ." His voice trailed far away and his pale blue eyes stared off into the distance. I guessed he was thinking of his own child. His own beloved Betsy who'd been hospitalized almost since birth with severe mental retardation. He was thinking how every baby born should be cherished without reservation and was wondering, as I had, if Lucy had been as well loved as she deserved.

I saw him glance at Betsy's photo—the picture of

a bright-faced smiling child—and knew that I'd been right. Thank God, I thought, that Lila had brought her back to town, thank God that Carl had found Sandy, to take his mind off the long-time string of troubles foisted on him by his ex-wife's flighty fancies.

Darrow wandered in and sat atop the corner of my desk, his dark eyes grazing teasingly across my face. Thoughtfully he stroked the tiny scar.

"Saw a mutual friend of ours downstairs, checking out the daily occurrence sheets. She looked a little peaked, a little harried and frustrated. Maybe I should ring her up and offer consolation."

He swung his loafered foot casually back and forth in front of me while watching to see if he'd gotten underneath my skin a lot or just a little bit. He always had the needle out, ready to jab it in if the flesh were soft. Especially so since the time he'd tried it on with me and found it wouldn't play.

It'd happened several years ago, when my husband Jon had undergone a nervous breakdown and Steve believed his charm and sexual prowess could help me through tough times. He wasn't easily scorned and I knew full well he still recoiled from the bite of my rejection.

"Karen's doing fine without you," I bluffed, offering a bright cool smile. "I don't think she needs the call or cares especially if it comes."

"Oh, she cares," he commented cockily. "Ol' Steve makes a pretty deep impression."

Karen Windall, a local crime reporter, had fallen under Darrow's spell back in summertime, when days were sultry hot and evenings long and languid. A self-possessed and stylish lady who'd bragged to me she knew the score and called the shots, she'd nonetheless been heedless of the clanging warnings and readily bought the chatter Steve had handed to her, much to her regret. One day he'd been there, the next day he'd moved on and taken her heart with him.

We were friends—close in some ways, far apart in others—and she'd come to me, crying towel in hand, when the downfall came and several times thereafter. I'd lied now when I'd told him she was doing fine. Steve was right. If he'd bothered to ask, she'd have jumped right back into disappointment.

"Stockton should be calling shortly," I told the two of them. "I'm heading over to Mariposa to check on Wanda, to see if she can talk yet. In the meantime, phone down to the lab, see what they've got on the Rimerton prints and the Mazda impound. If I need to know sooner rather than later, beep me at the hospital. Otherwise, I'll be back by twelve."

I stood up, tucking my blouse inside the waistband of my slacks, then slipped on my dark blue jacket. I'd just slung my bag across my shoulder when the phone rang.

"Homicide, Detective Harrod."

"Harrod, it's Robert Harris, Stockton PD." The

voice, crisp and clear and friendly, came across the wire. "We've got a positive ID on our Jane Doe. She's your Meryl Masters, just as we suspected. Parents came up from San Fran earlier this morning and just finished viewing her. We're wrapping up some odds and ends here now. How about my partner and I come down there, oh, say, middle of the afternoon?"

"Sure thing, we'll be glad to see you," I responded. "Maybe between the lot of us we can get going on this thing."

"By the way, you know the baby maybe wasn't hers? The family was ambiguous on the subject. Said as far as they knew Meryl had no kids, though they didn't lock it up real tight, just sort of let it hang there. I gather there was some estrangement going on between them."

"I know the baby wasn't hers," I told him. "She was minding it over the weekend for its mother, who, for some unknown reason, had to go out of town without it. Fact is, this wasn't even her town to go out of. She came here Friday from Las Vegas, purposely to leave the child. She returned yesterday and that's how we ID'd the baby and learned Masters was missing. The woman tried to overdose this morning but they got her just in time. I'm on my way right now to try to talk to her, to find out what she knows. What's *your* victim's family like?"

"Riche and not exactly nouveau, I'd say. Got that old San Francisco money smell about them. Sur-

prised, shocked, but not overly expressive or re-
morseful, at least not in public. Very self-contained
and not too happy, I would say, at having to meet
with the common man, as in 'cop.' "

"I know the type," I told him. "Moving in some
rare, pure atmosphere above the rest of us and all of
that. Unfortunately, death's a leveler and they're
going to have to see a whole lot more of us before
we're through."

I hung up and gave the news to Carl and Steve,
then headed out the door and for the hospital.

CHAPTER TEN

She was lying there, still and small and wan against the whiteness of the sheets. Her eyes were closed, shadowed by dark circles just beneath them, and her fragile, childlike hands lay palm down along her sides.

Patti Burke, sitting in an armchair near the window, jerked her head up as I entered.

"How is she?" I asked, nodding toward the bed.

"Just coming out of it. Weak, dazed, depressed, but able to talk a *little* bit. I think the major questioning had better wait till later on."

I approached the bed and gently touched the sleeping woman. Her eyelids fluttered and she looked at me with a flat, unfocused stare.

"Wanda," I began, starting to bend toward her, but just then a large and bustling nurse burst into the room, waving her hands back and forth in front of her like some traffic officer at a busy intersection.

"Enough of that," she stormed. "I told this one

here there's to be no questioning till the poor wee thing is strong enough, so don't you go annoying her."

The brogue came through thick and larded and I wondered which county she was from.

"You're Scots-Irish, aren't you?" I asked her. "I recognize the accent because I'm that background myself. Although I wasn't born there, just heard it from my kin who visited my parents when they were living."

She softened and began to beam.

"That I am and proud of it. From north of Belfast along the Antrim road. Where do yours hail from dearie?"

"County Donegal," I said. "That's in the Free State, I know, but they were originally Scots-Irish farmers from the lowlands east of Glasgow."

"Well, now, what do you know about that?" She bustled back and forth across the room, tucking in the sheet around her patient, placing her hand across the Brighton woman's forehead to feel how warm or cold she was. "And here we all end up in this big old California valley a million miles from home."

"Look," I said to her as Patti covered her mouth to hide a smile, "a dreadful thing has happened to this young person and that's why she tried to take her life. Her little baby was found murdered this past weekend and I've got to talk to her, to try to get some clues that might help us catch the killer. I respect your judgment, but do you think I could have just a few moments with her now?"

The nurse's eyes sprang open.

"She's the mother of that precious wee one tossed out in the dump? I didn't know . . . Well, dearie, if you're kind and gentle and only ask a couple of the most important questions. Then you can come back later on, you know."

The arms had ceased their waving back and forth and the rotund feisty figure in the ample nurse's white had melted into amiable docility.

"Thank you. I promise I won't tire her out. I'll leave within five minutes."

Satisfied, the woman gave my arm a little pat and began to leave the room.

"Murdering wee babies," she muttered, as much to herself as to any one of us. "They ought to be strung up with sticks of dynamite jammed up their asses. You do what you have to do to catch them!" And she disappeared into the hall.

Once again I approached the bed. Wanda was staring at me but this time the eyes held a focus they'd lacked before. I drew up a chair and sat down beside her.

"You're going to be all right," I told her, "and you have a lot to live for. You're a pretty, kind girl and you were a good mother to your Lucy. You must not destroy someone so worthwhile. And *we* need you, we need you to help us find who killed your baby and your friend. You, perhaps more than anybody else, hold the key to the solving of these brutal killings, because you knew both of them. You have a job to do, Wanda. Please stay with us for your baby's sake if for no other reason right now."

I sensed I had to get down to basics, to give her the most direct and simple, yet compelling reason not to take her life. Idealistic platitudes sometimes sounded fine, but I believed a more grounded, common-sense approach was needed here. The stick that reached straight out for her to grab and save herself.

I saw a change flash through her eyes and she became even more focused and alert.

"I never thought of it like that," she said weakly. "I never thought that I could still help Lucy."

"Well, you can." I bunched the covers carefully around her neck. "You're needed very much. I'm going to ask you some questions now. Please stop me if I'm tiring you. I can always come back later."

"No, no," Wanda said in protest. "I may answer slowly but I want to do it now."

"First of all, what was your relationship with Meryl Masters?"

She struggled to raise up slightly on the pillow, then fell back, and I placed a restraining hand across her chest.

"Friends, close friends for several years, though we hadn't seen each other in some time."

"Why did you leave Lucy with her this weekend,

Wanda?" As I spoke, I saw the faintest flush of color begin to come back into her cheeks.

"Because my parents didn't know about my baby. They're very religious, very conservative and old-fashioned, and it was bad enough that I was living with Sonny out of wedlock but to have a baby when I wasn't married *was not* acceptable."

"And so?" I asked gently.

"So I decided to finally tell them because she *was* their grandchild, after all, and they had to know sometime, but I didn't want to bust right in on them with Lucy in my arms. I wanted to tell them quietly, by myself, and ease them into it so I went alone. They live in Bodega Bay, on the coast north of San Francisco, so I drove here, dropped off my baby, then went on up there?"

"How did it go?" I asked. "Were they understanding?"

Wanda gulped and shook her head. Tears streamed down her cheeks and dropped onto the pillow as she lay in choked silence, moving her head slowly back and forth.

"No," she finally answered as she squeezed her eyes shut tight, "no, they weren't. They called me a worthless whore and told me not to ever bring my bastard baby up there. They kicked me out. In the name of God, they said."

"Oh, my dear." I slowly stroked her shaking shoulder. Patti moved to the far side of the bed and smoothed her hair back from her forehead. "They were wrong, so very, very wrong. I cannot believe that any God would approve of what they did to you."

"Maybe He would," she gulped. "Maybe I *am* a whore. I was taught different, I knew right from wrong. I used to be such a good, good girl. Always knew my Scriptures, always perfect Sunday School attendance, always the little angel He'd have wanted me to be. I sinned when I left my parents, sinned when I left the church, and now I pay the price. I see it all so clearly. Now I pay the price."

My mouth dropped open, shocked at the flagellation this helpless woman heaped upon herself.

"No, Wanda, that's not true. Were you not taught that God's a loving God, one who forgives the creatures He created?"

"Nooooooo," she shuddered, rolling the word way out. "My mama and my daddy's church doesn't believe one bit in that. God is hell and fire and brimstone and He punishes transgressors."

"But you must've come to some decision, moved from that church's circle, sometime ago," I protested. "Why are you still so influenced by what it says?"

"Because it was what my parents taught me, the earliest thing I knew. They ground it in me day and night, they and all the brethren. I say I don't believe it and I try not to, too—how could anyone call Lucy a bastard?—but that's all I ever learned, all I ever knew, and I cannot shake that feeling, can't help thinking maybe they were right."

The imprints on one's childhood, I thought sadly, are marks which always will remain. Common sense and intellect can try to deal with them, to rationalize and reason them away. But often they're too strong and live deep in one's emotions no matter what the mind might say.

We sat quietly for several minutes, distant murmuring hospital sounds the only thing to touch the silence.

"How did you meet Meryl?" I asked, still wondering at the odd pairing of the San Francisco sophisticate and this guileless girl lying here in front of me.

"In Lodi," Wanda answered, naming a town several hours driving time north of San Madera. "She was working in the county social services office there and I was waiting tables at a restaurant. I needed help at one time and she became my case worker. I know it sounds strange but we seemed to hit it off. She was everything I wanted to be—so clever and so pretty and always knowing just what to do—and she said she'd have fun teaching me how to be like her." She paused a moment, then said ruefully, "But I guess it didn't work."

"You are who you are, Wanda," I told her. "There was never any need to try to be like Meryl, just to be yourself. Why did the two of you drift apart?" Maybe, I thought, Masters had tired of her little Pygmalion game and had dropped Wanda in boredom.

"Oh, just this and that, you know. She moved down here and I moved to Vegas with Sonny. She didn't even know about the baby till I called her asking her to keep Lucy for the weekend."

"Why was that?" I asked curious. "If you'd been such good pals I'd have thought you'd have sent a birth announcement, even if you didn't usually write."

Wanda ran her tongue across her lips.

"Because, you see, Meryl used to go with my guy, with Sonny. She was dating him, in fact, when she and I first met, and even though she'd long since broken off with him by the time he and I got together, I wasn't sure how she'd take it if she knew I was living with him now."

Wanda gave a little cough and I handed her a glass of water. She took small sips, then gave it back to me and I placed it on the table, trying hard to take in what I'd just heard.

If I'd been surprised at stylish cool Meryl Masters befriending unworldly little Wanda, then the thought of Masters and tough ex-con Sonny Mitchell totally floored me. The coarse and the smooth—burlap and satin, raw wool and silk. Did her rich polish demand a bit of the rough-and-tumble from time to time? I'd known girls like that, girls who walked on the wild side because it made them feel an edge they craved and couldn't get any other way.

"If Meryl was through with Sonny, why'd you

think she'd mind the two of you had gotten to-gether?" I asked Wanda.

She gave another little cough. I hoped I wasn't pushing her too hard but her color was still good and there was a lot I had to know.

"Because she could be funny like that. Even if she'd tossed something out, she wouldn't want any-one else to have it. So I just thought it best she didn't know. Except I needed her this weekend—there was no one else I could leave my baby with—so I finally had to tell her."

"Was she angry?" I asked curiously. "What was her response?"

"Didn't seem so, just surprised. But it wasn't Mer-yl's way to get angry right up front. She'd let you know later on when you weren't expecting it. Not that she was mean or anything. Just funny little ways about her sometimes."

"Wanda, we've so far been unable to get in touch with Sonny. Do you know where he might be reached?"

"Nooooo . . ." her voice dragged. "Truth is, we haven't been getting along too well lately. He felt the baby was a drag, he felt I was starting to be a drag. And you know," she cried out, suddenly animated, "Lucy looks just like him. Blond hair, brown eyes, even the dimple. You'd think he'd like her better." She paused. "But he *was* still there when I left Vegas."

Suddenly a choking fit consumed her and the hefty nurse stuck her head around the door.

"Maybe it's time to wrap it up now, dearie," she said to me in obvious concern. Not even our new-found common background was going to keep her from tending to her patient.

"No!" Wanda barked vehemently, and I was surprised at her sudden strength. "Leave her! It's important. The only way to help my baby. I just choked on a little spit. I'm doing fine." She reached for the water glass herself and began to drink.

Reluctantly the brogue withdrew and moved on down the hall.

"This may be hurtful, Wanda, but I have to know," I went on, after she'd drunk half a glass of water and laid back against the pillow. "How did Sonny take being dumped by Meryl Masters and do you think he in any way still cares for her?"

The fragile girl winced slightly, pressing her lips together as if in pain.

"He didn't like it. He didn't like being thrown over by anyone, no matter who she was. But I think he was also a little bit in awe of Meryl—couldn't understand how, or really believe, he'd ever attracted a classy woman such as her—so he didn't make too much of a fuss. As for caring . . ." Again her voice trailed off, then she rallied. "I really don't think so. I really, truly think he'd gotten her clean out of his system."

"And, of course, he had you to make him forget her," I ventured.

"Yes, he had me." Wanda momentarily brightened. "Of *course* he forgot about her when things were good between us."

Stated with bravado, slightly false perhaps, but strong enough to make her feel momentarily good about the situation. Had she often compared herself to Meryl, I wondered, and asked herself if Sonny found her wanting? Probably about a hundred times a day.

I've got to wrap it up, I thought. I can't push her to the limits of her strength. But I still needed to know a few important things.

"Wanda, when you got to Meryl's, did you notice anything unusual? In her manner, her behavior, the surroundings? And was anyone else there with her or did she tell you she was expecting someone?"

The blond girl quickly shook her head.

"She was fine. Laughing, joking, even holding Lucy and twirling her around. And she said she'd planned a quiet weekend, just the two of them doing things together."

"What about the front door? Do you recall if you locked it behind you when you left there Monday morning?"

She tried to think, wrinkling up her forehead.

"I honestly don't know. I used the key to open it—Meryl'd lent me one in case I got back real late Sunday night—and I may've popped the latch, then slammed it shut behind me without locking it again. Is it important?"

"Maybe, maybe not," I told her. "The door was open when we got there. We didn't know if someone else had come in after you or if you were the one who left it that way. It's just a small point now. Don't concern yourself about it."

I drew closer to the bed and looked into her eyes "Wanda, do you have any idea, any idea at all no matter how very small, who might've killed your baby and your friend?"

"No," she answered with a little cry. "It had to be a burglar—someone who broke in to steal—because no one who knew them could've done it."

She, in her innocence, might believe that, but I knew better. I knew no one had come to rob, to plunder the belongings of another, for no clue existed that began to point in that direction. I knew the facts and I knew my own deep feeling. That another, different, far more deadly motive existed for these gruesome killings.

Once again I tucked the sheets around her, then I rose to go.

"You've helped us, Wanda," I told her softly, "you've helped us get a start. By telling us about relationships, by telling us that Meryl was alone and acting normal. You may not see the importance in all of this, but trust me, it *is* important. Now rest and gain your strength because I'll need you in the future. I'll need to talk to you again, so you can help me catch your baby's killer."

She nodded gratefully, dropped her head back on the pillow, and closed her eyes.

"Stay with her," I said to Patti, "comfort her and let her rest. I'll be in touch later. Right now I've got to get on back. Stockton's coming down," and I left that clean calm room with its ravaged lost young soul and walked swiftly down the antiseptic hallway.

A common denominator, I thought as I drove back, a common denominator turning up already. Sonny Mitchell, a violent ex-convict on parole, knew both victims . . . perhaps the only other person in the entire world besides Wanda who did so. Not just his infant daughter with whom he'd lived, but also the adult victim, Meryl Masters, who'd resided several hundred miles away.

The first had caused a disruption in his life he didn't want; the second had tossed him out like one of last year's fashions. And he could not be found.

I mustn't make too much of this, I warned myself, but after all, it had leaped right up and stared me in the face. Keep it in mind, I cautioned, but don't get overly excited. Let's see what turns up when you reach the station.

And then I left that thought alone and turned to face another. Irrational though it seemed, I was beginning to dislike my adult victim. I was starting to catch little glimpses here and there that led me to believe she'd not been a thoughtful person but one who enjoyed playing with other people's feelings. Nothing definite, nothing definitive, but a hunch I had, based only on flimsy whimsy in my mind.

Leave it alone, I lectured to myself, you really know nothing about the woman yet. After all, Wanda Brighton had called her her friend and had seemingly adored her, and for all I knew, she'd truly cared for Sonny Mitchell but broke it off because she'd realized it could never work. Then look at her job. A selfless occupation if ever there was one, especially for a rich young girl from San Francisco.

Yet the logic sounded hollow and I was still left with a feeling of extreme distaste for Meryl Masters.

Not that it mattered one little bit. Whether I loved her or hated her, the investigation would still go forward the exact same way—hard-charging and meticulous in all its aspects. It was just that I usually felt such empathy for my victims that I surprised myself with this strange new feeling.

I glanced up and realized I was close to Tommy's school, and purposely detoured several blocks just to see if I could spot him on the playground. I'd take any chance I got to catch a glimpse of him, for he made my heart glad and refreshed my spirit. I peered eagerly through the chain-link fence as I cruised slowly past, but the field was empty save for several younger boys.

Tommy, I thought as I drove away. Was he really doing okay with the divorce or were little telltale signs of some distress already surfacing that I could not pick up on—distress that in later months would build and grow and suddenly erupt into disaster?

He seems fine, I thought. We talk an awful lot and he seems just fine to me, but you never know. And then I recalled what Mrs. Miller had said to me—"hardly ever mentions his dad"—and how I'd wondered if that was good or bad. I knew he looked forward to his times with Jonathan, like the upcoming Cub Scout dinner, and came back from them happy and smiling. But in between visits, it was true, he'd stopped talking about his father very much. Was this normal? Was it not?

Just keep on talking to him, I counseled, and any problems he has he'll let out. Keep the avenues of communication open and let him know you love him and you're there for him, then it can't help but turn out right.

I flicked on my favorite sixties' rock station and began to tap a rhythm on my knee. And see about those drum lessons, for the two of you.

I looked ahead of me and saw the mountains in the distance—the blue and purple craggy peaks now capped with winter whiteness that surrounded this fertile valley that I lived in. The sight of them, so towering and so permanent, never failed to give me strength and impart a feeling of calmness and serenity.

At times when problems seemed to overwhelm me, as they sometimes do with every one of us, I'd drive out beyond the city, out among the farms and patchwork fields, and watch the sun cast shadows on those mountains of the High Sierras as it moved slowly down their roughened sides and across the valley floor toward the ocean and the coastal range a hundred miles away.

I'd gaze at them in the deepening twilight, watching as their crevices grew dark and dusky and their bare rock backbones caught glints of pink and gold. And I'd return refreshed, rejuvenated, and ready to go on again.

I wheeled into the station lot and parked between another gray detective car and a beat-up black-and-white. San Madera was a little city—in many ways just a bucolic overgrown town—and while our police department was adequate for our needs, it was tiny by big-city standards. We had our share of rapes and robberies and murders, but neighbors still said hello to neighbors and many left their doors unlocked at night.

Across the lot I saw a tall, dark-haired young officer loading cartons into a civilian car. He was out of uniform but I recognized him and called a loud hello. He'd helped me out last year, while doing his probation, by supplying a vital clue early on in the investigation of a missing child.

"Pete, what's happening?" I asked. "You moving out or something?"

I was only joking so when he nodded in the affirmative my jaw dropped open in surprise.

"I'm not up to it, Detective Harrod," he told me bitterly. "I pulled the pin this morning and handed it to personnel. I didn't know what I was coming into. I just wanted to help people with their problems but the citizens, they wanna kick you in the back just as much as crooks do."

"Won't you reconsider?" I begged him. "From all reports, you're a good cop, the kind who *can* make a difference. I know it's tough but surely the rewards are there."

"What rewards?" he asked derisively, slamming down the trunk lid. "I just came off a domestic violence call earlier today and before it ended the two of them, the husband *and* the wife, had turned against me, calling me 'pig bastard' and spitting up and down my uniform. It happens all the time."

I stood in sorry silence, little left to say. I'd seen it time and time again—brave probationers full of heart and courage marching through the Academy gates, only to be brought up short by life.

Powered by high ideals, they'd come to aid mankind but then they'd meet the real true world and find you *cannot* always make a difference, no matter what they say. They'd learn that often friend resembles foe on the tough and cold mean streets, and that's when disillusionment set in and didn't usually go away.

A wearing, thankless job as a citizenry demands you risk your life but won't pay you back with its support, never mind respect.

"I'm sorry, Pete," I told him, "terribly, terribly sorry. Good luck to you in whatever you decide to do."

"I'm going into farming," he responded. "My uncle has a spread five miles out of town. My wife will be happier and now maybe want to have some kids." He paused, dejected, and looked down at his shoes. It wasn't easy giving up a dream.

"You'll find you'll miss it, you know, and then you can come back."

"No, Detective, I won't miss it," he answered me. "I'll miss the promise of what I thought it was." And he climbed behind the wheel and drove away.

"Screw it," I murmured quietly as I walked upstairs, "another good one gone." And then I set aside my thoughts of Pete and walked inside and upstairs to the squad room. I tossed my coat behind my chair, then glanced around to see who else was there. Pretty empty. They must all be in court or in the field doing legwork. About the only soul I saw was Dan Kent, a young detective who'd worked with me on several homicides and was now assigned to robbery.

I looked at him and saw an unfamiliar worn look that belied the number of his years. He usually glowed with a fresh-scrubbed bright vitality fitting to a fellow in his late twenties with a lovely wife, a brand-new baby boy, and a job he loved to do. Usually, that is, except for the trying time last fall when his dad had fallen ill.

"What is it, Danny?" I asked, going to his desk. "Is everything okay?" The dad, a Chicago cop, had recovered from his heart trouble and was back at work last I'd heard, but my first thought was there'd been a relapse.

He raised his eyes and looked at me—weary, dull, defeated. His mouth sagged slightly at the corners. He reached out and yanked a chair toward him, motioned to it, and I sat down.

"Rena," he said in one word, pulling at his lip. Then, "She's started up again, about my being a cop. She wants to leave me."

Males in Kent's family suffered a history of early deaths from heart disease and when his dad had been hospitalized, I knew she'd put pressure on Dan to quit the force, fearing the stress so prevalent in our work would take its toll on him and hasten the fatal attack she was certain lay in his future.

But he loved his job far too much to do that, and the last I'd heard, they'd called an uneasy truce and I thought no more about it.

"I'm sorry, Dan," I told him quietly. "Do you think she'll follow through?"

"I'm scared as hell she will, Kate"—he jammed his fingers roughly through his hair—"and I just don't know what to do about it. I love her, love my baby, but I love my job as well."

"What would you do if she walked out?"

He thought a moment, pressing his lips tight together and staring bleakly at the wall.

"I'd wait awhile and pray she'd come back," he answered, "and if she didn't I'd give up the force. She means too much to me to live too long without her."

"But how would you survive?" I asked, honestly concerned. "It would tear you apart to stop doing this, Dan. I know how it is. Being a cop isn't an easy thing to walk away from at any time, but especially when you don't want to go. Leaving it behind will rip at you and eat at you and turn you into someone other than yourself."

I thought of the rookie I'd just left in the parking lot. I didn't think his good-byes were going to be the snap he thought they'd be.

"I haven't looked that far ahead, Kate," he answered me, his eyes filled with misery. "I just can't speculate because I'm hoping some miracle will happen and we can work it out."

"What about the women in your family?" I asked him. "They've lived their lives being married to cops and somehow they're managing to deal with it. Couldn't they talk to Rena, somehow point her to the way to go?"

"Uh-uh," he told me, adamantly shaking his dark

head. "All their families were filled with cops, too—they were practically teethed on the department—and she feels like an outsider on that matter and believes they can't relate to her and understand how she's feeling. She thinks they'd think she's silly or a sissy."

Suddenly he swung around and looked at me, a gleam of hope lighting up his eye.

"Look, Kate, maybe *you* could talk to her. Maybe you could explain what it's like to be a cop, why it's so hard to walk away from. And maybe reassure her stress doesn't get to all of us and that I've learned to handle it when I feel it coming." His boyish face pleaded with me to try to make things right.

I didn't have to hesitate. I knew I wasn't the right one for the job.

"It wouldn't work, Dan," I said reluctantly. "The last one she'd want to hear it from would be another cop. I'm the enemy to her and she wouldn't want to listen."

He let his breath out in a futile puff and lightly banged the desk.

"I guess you're right, damn it. Kate, I just don't know what to do."

"There is no easy answer, Dan," I told him. "This job, or rather my estranged husband's reaction to it, broke up my marriage, too." Although, I reflected wryly to myself, that wasn't all that it had been about. Control, domination, had entered in there, too.

"Not going to happen, Kate," he told me, his lips set firmly. "Somehow I'll balance this all out."

I knew the odds he faced in finding a happy solution but I wasn't going to take away his hope. Maybe, after all, he'd have more success than I.

"Good luck, then, Danny." I gave his shoulder an encouraging little squeeze. "And come talk to me anytime you want to."

"So that's the long and short of it," Mungers finished saying, then wiped some luncheon sandwich crumbs from around his mouth. "No prints at Rimerton except the adult victim's, no evidence of anything unusual inside the Mazda. But then, of course, we expected that, didn't we? I mean, about the car. We're pretty sure the killer used his own vehicle to transport the bodies."

I leaned back against the desk, looking at him skeptically.

"Doesn't something strike you as odd, Carl? You mean Wanda never touched anything inside the condo when she dropped her baby off and no earlier visitor left an imprint of his finger pads?"

"Sure it's odd," he readily agreed, "but remember what I told you. The lab boys said only the big pieces of furniture on the first floor, as well as the doors and doorjambs, bore no prints at all. The victim's were found throughout the second floor and in obscure places on the first, such as picture framings and the like."

"So what does this suggest to you?" I asked. I already knew the conclusions I drew from it but I wanted to see if Carl concurred.

"One, there were no earlier visitors; two, Wanda handed the baby directly to Masters and left without touching anything; and three, the killer either touched nothing or entered wearing gloves and never took them off, maybe not even while he did the murders. Or . . ."

"Or?" I prompted. "Or what?"

"Or, and I think this is what most likely happened, the murderer *did* touch items throughout the first floor but only major items—those that'd normally sit right up front in a visitor's face, like the tables and the chair arms.

"And then, after the killings but before he removed the bodies, he went around and wiped them off. It was probably pretty easy to remember where he'd put his fingers. There probably *were* some prints of Wanda's, too, but they got obliterated in the process."

I listened, nodding enthusiastically.

"That the way I see it, too, and if we're right, that of course brings us to something else. Our murderer, I'd say, didn't enter that condo with the clear intent to kill our victims. If that'd been the case, he'd either have gone in gloved or been careful not to let his fingers come in contact with a surface from which any prints could be lifted. I think this indicates the killings were probably not premeditated but sprang spontaneously from a sudden rage of some sort."

"I think you're right, and there's something else we can speculate, too," Carl continued, a toothpick bobbing from his mouth. "Here he's got two bodies on his hands, yet he takes the time to go around carefully wiping off his prints—remember, he didn't miss a single one—before he removes his victims.

"It's not as if he knew he had all the time in the world. A neighbor could've come and rung the doorbell, a previously invited guest could've shown up. So I'd say our killer is cautious, cool, and clearheaded. A person not easily given to panic in a normally panic-driven situation."

Although we couldn't know for sure if we were right, I thought we'd drawn a pretty accurate picture of what'd gone on at 4608 Rimerton last Friday evening as well as sketched an on-spot profile of our killer's personality. Our lunch hour hadn't been wasted. Brainstorming, as well as hard evidence, was invaluable in solving any crime.

"Who was the primary target, Kate?" Carl asked me next. "Or do you think the two of them were equally marked for death?"

"No, no way," I answered. "I believe the killer wanted to do away with Meryl Masters and Lucy was only incidental, probably because she just happened to be there."

"Happened to be there or was starting to raise a

ruckus. Maybe that's what the tape was for. To shut her up till he removed her."

"Maybe," I answered, straightening up and reaching for a donut from Carl's plate. But if that's the case, I thought bitterly to myself, why'd he have to beat her up and bruise her?

CHAPTER ELEVEN

The resemblance was remarkable. When the Stockton detectives walked through the squad-room door later on that afternoon, my eyes shot immediately to the taller of the two and I thought I was looking at Steve Darrow.

Dark-haired, hefty, and broad-shouldered, it was Darrow all over again. I didn't see the flashing grin or cocky wise-guy eyes, but I sensed that they were there, waiting to be shown.

Spare me, I thought silently to myself, let the likeness just be superficial and stop at that.

"Detective Harrod?" The shorter one advanced, holding out his hand. "I'm Robert Harris, Stockton Homicide, and this is my partner, Charlie Rhoads."

I sized him up, liking what I saw. Serious but not overbearing, friendly but not trying to be your best buddy when you weren't even looking for one. And there was something else, too. An unexpected quickening of the heart I hadn't felt in ages. Frowning, I pushed it away and made introductions all around. The visitors began to draw up chairs.

"No," I stopped them, "let's go down the hall. there's a little room there where we can be more private."

I led the way and the other four followed, and when we reached the room I motioned to them to take seats around the circular table.

"First thing we need to do is to bring each other up-to-date on anything that's occurred since we last spoke. What about on your side?"

Harris pushed back slightly from the table and began to speak. He had a trim brown mustache set below a straight firm nose and clear sharp eyes that eagled in on you when you got within his range. I'd hate to be a suspect sitting opposite him, I thought.

"Nothing new except the bit about the fingernails," he started. "We learned this just before we started out. Meryl Masters had no skin caught beneath her nails, which is unusual in a strangling case, so she either didn't put up much of a struggle or else her killer was clothed in such a way she couldn't reach his flesh. What about down here?"

I filled them in on Wanda Brighton's story about why she'd left Lucy in San Madera, as well as the findings about the car and the scarcity of prints at Rimerton. Rhoads pulled out a cigarette and lit it, then saw my look and quickly stubbed it out. Smoking in the workplace had been outlawed for quite some time now.

"You're absolutely certain Brighton, not Masters, is the mother of the child?" Rhoads asked pointedly, setting his elbows on the table and hunching forward.

I saw Darrow watching him and wondered if he'd noticed the resemblance.

"Well, I haven't seen a birth certificate, if that's what you mean. I've only got her word for it. But why would she make up a story like that? She claims the baby's hers, she's got photos of it in her wallet, and she tried to kill herself because that baby's dead. What does that sound like to you?"

"Sorry," Rhoads mumbled. "It just seems odd the killer would take out two people who weren't connected to each other, under the circumstances in which they were killed."

"Damn right," Mungers interjected, "we were thinking the same thing ourselves. A street robbery, sure, or a jealous husband walking in on his shacked-up wife and lover, but not two unrelated people in a condo, especially when burglary or robbery was not a factor.

"Where's the motive? The reason you kill Meryl Masters cannot be the same reason you kill Lucy because the two of them weren't tied together. They weren't a unit, they hadn't even seen each other till the other night. I was thinkin' maybe he killed the baby by accident, hushing her up while he did Meryl, but, God, the bruises on that little thing. Now I'm not so sure.

"You just feel like murdering two people, no matter who they are, so you knock upon a door and kill whoever you find behind it just for kicks? I don't buy it. There's more to it than that, but I'm damned if I can put it all together."

"Look," I said, after Carl had finished and slumped back in his chair, "I don't want to make too much of this but there *was* a connection. Not directly between Meryl and Lucy but through a person they both knew, a person other than Wanda Brighton. Turns out the baby's father, who's not married to the Brighton woman, used to date Meryl Masters several years ago. I gather she threw him over and he wasn't any too happy about it. We're trying now to locate him in Vegas, but so far we've been unsuccessful."

"Wait a minute," Darrow interjected. "You say this joker holds a grudge for three–four years and only now gets around to acting on it? And takes out his own baby, too? I don't think so. If you've got a beef with a dolly you straighten it out long before that or else you forget about it and move on. At least that's the way a real man works."

I looked across the table and saw Harris watching amusedly. Instantly I found myself wondering how he treated "dollies," then scolded myself for wandering away from business. I channeled my attention toward his reply.

"Oh, I don't know about that," the Stockton detective countered. "I had a homicide once where the guy waited six years to even up the score."

Darrow frowned, settling back into his seat while Mungers got the coffeepot and made the rounds, filling up our cups. I noticed his stomach didn't seem quite as sloppy today and wondered if he'd lost some weight or just tucked it more tightly into his belt.

"Who's the father anyway?" Charlie Rhoads asked casually, sipping at the brew and narrowing his eyes as the fiery liquid bit his lips. I'd bet they made it every bit as hot in Stockton. I hadn't seen a cop house yet where the coffee didn't feel like lava.

Mungers picked up Mitchell's rap sheet, held it at the top between two fingers, and let the rest of it free-fall to the table.

"One of our finer citizens," he said sarcastically. "A guy who's done time all over California and Nevada. Hey, Steve, maybe that's why he waited so long to settle an old score. He'd been in the joint before and couldn't take care of business until now."

My eyes scanned Rhoads's flushed face as he began to read the rap sheet. I wanted to see his reaction as he took in the lengthy list of robberies, assaults, burglaries, and carjacks. Not your everyday father-of-the-victim, that's for sure.

He never got beyond the top. I saw his eyes widen and his fingers clench the page until his knuckles whitened. He looked at Bobby Harris and then he looked at me.

"Son of a bitch! Alvin 'Sonny' Mitchell," he drawled out, drumming his fingers up and down against the table. "Sonny boy. We're old, old friends, the two of us. You mean *this* scum is the father of the murdered baby and the Brighton woman is the mother?"

"You got it right," I told him. "That's the mismatched set of parents. She's a naive unworldly little thing, sweet as she can be, and he's a violent criminal long past rehabilitation. Between them they produced a baby girl, destined to live less than five months on this earth before some callous bastard smothered her to death."

"She smothered, then?" Rhoads shot me a quick glance. "That's the official cause of death?"

"Right," I said. "As Carl mentioned, she was badly bruised, as if from a kicking or a beating, but she died because her mouth and nose were taped. I'll turn our files over to the two of you later on today, so you can read the details of the case."

I was wondering if I'd been wrong about him after all. I hadn't seen a flashing grin yet, nor a cocky wise-guy eye. Darrow couldn't have gone this long without showing at least one or the other to a new acquaintance.

"Look here," Rhoads went on, running his finger down the sheet, then pausing at an entry. "Here we are. Four years ago in Stockton, a jewelry store robbery, owner wopped across the head and nearly killed. That's mine and I also managed to tie him into two earlier robberies in the area. He did some time for those, but whaddya know, folks, this is California and cons are out before their victims even heal."

"Amen," Darrow exclaimed, slapping his hand down on the table, "we've all been through it, Charlie. Damn judges, damn DAs. Fuckin' liberal hand-holders." The tiny crescent scar showed white against the redness of his face.

"What do *you* think, Detective?" Harris, who'd sat quietly for the past few minutes, turned to me and looked straight into my eyes. "Do you have a hunch, a gut feeling about all of this?"

I sipped my coffee slowly and peered at him across the rim. Courteous, low-key, yet undeniably firm. I liked his style and felt I could easily work with him. And there was no denying I felt something else besides. That unfamiliar pounding that'd first occurred only minutes before.

Damn it, I thought, I do not need this complication in my life.

"No, no I don't," I said, forcing myself to stare right back at him, my eyes giving nothing away. "Except that this was no ordinary crime, no crime that the killer blundered into and committed among strangers. Forceful passions were at work here and there *is* a connection between Meryl Masters and Lucy Brighton, if only we can find it."

"We have, right here—Sonny Mitchell. You said so yourself," Rhoads snorted.

"Yes, and we need to talk with him. But I'm saying if that doesn't pan out, I strongly feel there's something else, and we probably won't solve our crime until we find it."

I suggested they toss their cups and ride out with us to 4608 Rimerton and then on to the Dumpster. I wanted them to see the murder scene themselves and also the spot where Lucy's body had been found, so they could flesh out the crimes that up till now we'd just been painting verbally.

"What're your plans?" I asked Harris as the two of us walked down the hall together. "Can you stay a few days?"

"Up to you," he answered. "We don't want to interfere. Somehow it made sense to come down here, at least till we got the jurisdictional thing sorted out, but we don't want to hang on unnecessarily and interfere with your investigation."

"As far as jurisdiction goes," I told him, "I know Lucy was murdered here and I'd bet Meryl Masters was, too. Right now I'm treating 4608 Rimerton as the murder scene because there's no evidence to the contrary and the two victims were last seen at that location.

"True, our killer could've abducted them from the condo and murdered them in his car, maybe even transported Masters to your town and strangled her up there, but I don't think so. According to your report, postmortem lividity indicates she'd lain in a different position than the one in which you found her for at least several hours after death. As if she'd been on her back in a van or car moving north from our town up to Stockton.

"No, they're our homicides, little doubt about it, but one dead body *was* found in your woods and there's a lot of work to do, so if you'd care to stick around, you're more than welcome."

He nodded in acceptance. He wasn't going to fight over jurisdiction because the evidence was all too strong that these two deaths were San Madera occurrences. The place where the victim is killed, not the spot where she is later found, determines which agency takes control.

Besides, in real life it's not like in the movies, departments fighting to get the case for their own. Too often, light manpower, tight budgets, and heavy caseloads make a force glad someone else can legitimately take a case off their hands or, at the very least, help out.

Harris smiled and held the door for me when we reached the car.

Quaint, I thought. Nice but quaint. He doesn't have to do that when we're on duty. Feeling a little skittish because of my earlier unexpected feelings, I made sure I stepped wide so I wouldn't brush against his hand.

"We've got a little lull in Stockton homicides right now," he said, his eyes crinkling at the corners, "and this case interests me. Besides, as you just pointed out, our woods were involved, if only as a drop point. Charlie and I'd be glad to give an assist. Right up front, he's got an 'in,' if you can call it that, with Sonny Mitchell, so why not turn us loose on that?"

"Fine," I answered, pulling out of the space and following the car containing the other three. "When we get back to the station, we'll put our heads together and divvy up the work."

We rode in silence for a moment. Then, making conversation, I asked about the drive down.

"Great till we got to your neck of the woods," Harris answered. "The tule fog set in about twenty miles north of here and I thought we'd either get lost or rear-ended before we reached San Madera. Fortunately it thinned before too long."

Tule fog, a thick treacherous mist rising from the ground, plagues the Big Valley during the winter months and into early spring. Dense, moist, and white, and as bad as any London pea soup, it sometimes reduces visibility to only several feet or inches, causing freeway pileups and shutting down life in general till it dissipates.

"You have much experience with it?" I asked, smiling the secure seasoned smile of a native used to such things. "It can be a killer this time of year."

"Not in a very long time," Harris answered. "We don't have that critter down in LA and that's where I was till fairly recently."

"LAPD?" I asked, surprised. "I just assumed you'd been with Stockton most of your career."

"No, that's Charlie," Harris told me. "He's been with our department nearly twenty years, ever since we got out of the service. Like him, I'm originally *from* Stockton, but unlike him, I chose to go south."

"Why did you leave LA?" I asked. "I hear a lot of cops are quitting down there nowadays because of morale problems. Was that it?"

"No," he answered, staring out the window. "It's a long and complicated story, but it wasn't that." I found I wished I'd never asked.

"Okay," I said, glad of a chance to change the subject, "here we are," and I pointed at Meryl Masters's town house. "Here is where it all began, sometime last Friday night."

We walked around the condo, letting Stockton look and poke and search where they desired. The air hung still and stale around us and set a mood of silent emptiness, as if the heart and soul inside those rooms had taken leave and passed on by.

How quickly a deserted space loses the aura of habitability, I thought. It's as if, without a human touch to pump it up, it falls flat and collapses all around itself.

"What about the personal belongings?" Harris asked. "Find anything there?"

"We've got her phone and address books downtown," I answered, "and we're starting to go through them, but she didn't keep a diary or anything explicit of that sort that'd help us out. Sometime tomorrow one of us will come back here and go through every drawer again, look again in every corner, and"—I motioned toward a bookshelf in the corner—"leaf through every page in every one of those, in case she's hidden something in between them."

"Photo albums?" Harris queried thoughtfully. "Find any of those?"

"Not albums, no," Steve answered, "but several batches of loose snapshots. Scenery, cars, girlfriends, stuff like that. Nothing that jumps right out to follow up on."

As they spoke, I wandered toward the bookcase, my eyes perusing titles. I saw a mix of current bestsellers, some thin-leafed poetry volumes, several manuals on social services procedure.

Suddenly I spied a book that looked different from the rest, slipped in between two glossy-covered novels. Its dark and plain binding and the fact that it was pushed deeper toward the bookcase back had made it difficult to see.

Curious, I pulled it out and found myself staring at a photo album. The one we said we hadn't found. I carried it to a nearby armchair, sat down, and started leafing through it, seeing pictures laid out on soft black paper with an adherent clear plastic overlay.

I saw the usual shots of family gatherings around

a Christmas tree, what I guessed were friends or relatives in various poses, picnics at some rocky beach.
The earliest dates on the photos' edges, imprinted by
the developer, went back nearly ten years, with the
last page bearing last year's date.

She must not have been much of a photography
enthusiast, I thought, if it took her a decade to fill
up an album. I imagined the bunch of loose snaps
we'd found earlier would've eventually found their
way into a second book, when Masters had finally
gotten around to buying one.

I continued leafing through—page by page, front
to back—glancing at the pictures. I heard footsteps
overhead and knew the other four were upstairs
now, going through the victim's bedroom.

I turned a page midway through the volume, then
suddenly stopped, staring at the ragged edges facing
me. An entire leaf, which would've held six pictures,
had been roughly torn out. I checked the continuity
of the dates. The missing photos had been made
three years ago.

Just about to call the others, to tell them what I'd
found, my eye happened to fall on the dark green
carpet next to the bookcase and I thought I saw a
tiny scrap of something lying there.

At any other time I'd have ignored it, but because
I'd just seen the jagged edges in the album, I bent
and picked it up and peered at it. Sure enough, it
appeared to be a piece of the same paper that composed the book of photos.

Drawing in my breath, stifling any hope for fear of letdown, I tried to fit it like a puzzle piece along the torn edge protruding from the spine. Working top to bottom, I got halfway down when it slid easily into place like a hand into the right-size glove.

"Carl, Steve, get down here," I called as I rushed into the hallway, and they came barreling down the staircase, followed by the other two.

"Look at this," I cried triumphantly, holding out the album for all of them to see. "An entire page was ripped from here, probably within the past few days. I found a remnant from it lying on the carpet next to the bookcase, in an area where a vacuum or sweeper could easily suck it up. I doubt Meryl Masters didn't clean her house, so that's why I say 'past few days.' And I'll go even further. I'll say probably Friday night."

We dropped down to the floor in a little circle, examining the photo album. Harris sat across from me while Charlie Rhoads squeezed himself in close beside me. The page immediately before the missing one showed only springtime photos of a brand-new Mazda while the next was filled with scenes from the High Sierras in the fall and wintertime.

"What was on this page that made it so very important to our killer?" I asked the others, tapping at the torn edge. "His own picture or something else? What was here that made him stop long enough after the murders to search for it and rip it out? What was Meryl Masters involved in three years ago last summer? Find that out and we'll find the key."

We trooped back to the station and found a call waiting from Las Vegas PD. Sonny Mitchell still was nowhere to be found.

"Want we issue a bulletin for him now?" the sergeant asked.

"Negative," I replied. "Not at this point. There's nothing to tie him to any crime. We just want to inform him of his daughter's death."

I heard Rhoads muttering behind me, and I gathered he was displeased with my decision.

"Tell me about his vehicle," I said to the Vegas sergeant. "Is it still at the rented house?"

"No, it's not. He drives a black-and-chrome Harley—an '83 Low Rider—and it's not been there since we started checking. We also dropped by the motorcycle shop where he allegedly works. They said they haven't seen him in several days, but you know how bikers are, sticking up and covering for each other."

I hung up and turned toward the others, but Rhoads picked up the ball before I'd even thrown it.

"Lemme at him," he declared. "I know one or two things about the habits of ol' Sonny Mitchell and I stand a good chance of tracking him down. He's a vicious stone-cold bastard who wouldn't have blinked an eyelid at these murders. Punish Meryl, rid himself of unwanted baby baggage, all in one fell swoop."

I thought him overly enthusiastic about the proba-
bility of Mitchell being the killer, but it was an avenue that had to be explored so why not turn him
loose on it?

"Go for it," I told him, "he's all yours. But keep
in close touch and fill me in on what's happening.
We can't go off like vigilantes here."

I was afraid at first I'd spoken out of turn. That
he'd take offense at my pulling rank, especially since
he'd given no indication he *wouldn't* report to me. It
was just a fear I had, maybe because I wasn't used
to working with him, that'd made me speak out. A
fear he'd run off and do his own thing.

"Never." Rhoads raised his hands in mock surren-
der and cracked a grin, showing even white teeth
below his deep brown eyes. "You'll know about everything I do."

"Look," I said as we all gathered again around the
table, "I think it makes sense, as long as you guys
are willing to help out, if we dole out the work as it
comes along, rather than saying 'Stockton takes one
victim and San Madera takes the other.' If a lead
needs following up, whoever's available will go out
on it. Agreed?"

"Sure," Harris answered readily. "Works better
that way. Creates a better flow of resources."

Just as with jurisdiction, the partner situation in
real cop life isn't always as shown on TV.

Often, but by no means always, you'll team up

with the same guy day after day in patrol. But at the divisional detective level, one person will be in charge of each particular case, yes, just as I was heading up the Brighton-Masters matter, but that cop will use all the men at his table interchangeably to help him track down the clues.

One day Darrow might be with me, the next day Rhoads, depending upon availability. And sometimes Carl and Harris might go off together. On a complicated case this size, with not one but two victims (and dumped in widely different locations at that), the more manpower one can get, the better. Another reason I was glad Stockton was sticking around.

"Okay," I said, "let's deal with what needs doing now. Charlie wants Sonny and he's got him, so why don't I concentrate on talking to Meryl Masters's employers and family and the rest of you can get on to her neighbors and any friends you might find, as well as canvass the gas stations and convenience stores along Route 99—that's the most likely road the killer would've taken from here to Stockton woods. Talk to the Highway Patrol and appeal to any motorists who might've been traveling north last Friday night."

"What're we looking for?" Darrow asked. "We don't even have a vehicle description." Always appearance-conscious, he smoothed his hair behind an ear. Never know when a female might be passing.

"We're looking for anything unusual, anything out of the ordinary that might've aroused suspicion. It's a long shot but we've got to do it."

We jotted down some file notes, then pushed back from the table and went our separate ways, five probes sent out to catch a killer. What would we bring back, I wondered, and would it be enough to do the job? Enough to send that killer to his death cell?

The long face told me something was very wrong. I'd driven home, anxious to spend a quiet evening relaxing and being with my son, but the moment I walked in the door I took one look at Tommy and knew there was a problem here that needed dealing with right now.

He sat on the rug before the fireplace, his blond hair pressed against the deep black tufts of Molly's fur. His arms hugged the animal tightly, and when I approached he glanced up and I saw his lip begin to tremble.

"Tommy, what's the matter?" I asked, dropping down beside him and taking him into my arms. The fire crackled close beside us, its glow bathing us in soft warm light, and I moved a little closer to it, drawing from its comfort.

"Nothing, Mom," he mumbled, pressing tight against my chest. Mrs. Miller passed the doorway, and looking up, my eyes met hers and she gave a helpless little shrug.

"Tommy"—I pushed him gently back from me and held him at arm's length—"we promised always to be honest with each other, remember? We vowed to share our feelings and not keep things bottled up. We're on our own now, you and me, and we need to be able to depend upon each other and help each other out. Please tell me what's troubling you."

"This Friday night . . ." he began, then choked and couldn't get the remainder of the words out. "This Friday night," he tried again, "Dad can't take me to the father-son dinner at Cub Scouts. He called and he won't be able to take me."

"Why not?" I asked, stunned. "What did he say?"

"That something else had come up," he blurted out vehemently, "something with his work." He shuddered in my arms. "I wish things were different. I wish you and he had gotten along better and weren't getting a divorce, then he'd be going with me. He wouldn't be forgetting me."

Sobs racked his little body and again he pressed his head tight against my chest, making a burrowing motion as if he longed to hide. Molly, sensing as dogs do that something was amiss, crowded in against us and began to lick my cheek.

I stared, unseeing, at the wall across the room. In all the months following the separation, Tommy had seemed to accept the events that had happened, accept the explanations given. Calmly, with few questions, without undue grief. I recalled how I'd reflected he was coping okay.

But then I also recalled how, this very afternoon, I'd wondered if perhaps he bore some hidden distress, internalized a worry or a sadness that, unknown to me, bothered him from time to time.

Now I had my answer. A barrier to the smooth transition from a child with a father in the house to a child without had surfaced and placed itself squarely in the way. Was it permanent, I wondered, or could I somehow make it disappear so my son could continue his adjustment unhindered?

"Tommy, listen to me. I know it's hard not to have your dad here, but he's not forgotten you. This could've happened even if he were still living in this house. But that doesn't make you any less upset and I know that. I cannot tell you it's all right, don't worry about a little dinner, because that's not recognizing and respecting your pain.

"What I *can* do is tell you that I know it hurts and that I love you, that there may be times like this but they will pass. They'll hurt when they do happen but they'll be over quickly, and then you'll be right back on track again, doing the things you love to do."

I rocked him back and forth, kissing him lightly on the head and thinking of what he'd said about the divorce.

"I, too, wish things were perfect, but they never are. Not for you, not for me, not for anyone. We can only do the best with what we've got and realize we never can have everything."

I pushed him back again and looked deep into his eyes.

"Are you going to be okay with this thing?" I asked. "Do you accept anything of what I say?"

I must've looked worried—and, indeed, I could feel my brow furrowing—for he watched me solemnly for a moment, then broke into a sudden grin.

"You look funny, Mom. All frowsy and fussed, not the way you usually look." It was as if a weight had lifted from his shoulders and a light had flicked on inside of him, causing a radiance to spread across his face.

"I love you, Mom," he went on. "I understand. I'll be okay. But thanks for letting me tell you that it hurt. Just telling you makes it a little better."

"I'm always here for you, Tommy," I assured him, "you know that. I'll always listen to you when you want to talk, and you're right. Just the act of talking, of sharing, often makes the pain more bearable."

"But why is that, Mom?" he asked me, wondering. "Nothing's changed about the reason I was crying."

"Because you let someone else help you carry the load," I told him, "and even though the load itself didn't change, that's what made it seem a whole lot lighter."

We scrambled to our feet, the dog getting twisted up between us, and headed in for dinner. I could smell the warm rich scent of roast and gravy wafting through the air.

"I'll tell you what." I laid a hand on Tommy's shoulder, stopping him as we passed through the hall. "We'll do something special Friday night, you and me. It won't take the place of that dinner, but it'll be fun and it'll keep us busy. How about it?"

"What?" he asked, intrigued, peering at me curiously.

"I don't know yet," I admitted, "but trust me. It'll be something a-okay."

He broke into a grin, throwing out his palm, and we did a high-five as we waltzed into the dining room.

I'd made him feel better, I reflected as I pulled back my chair, but why had Jon let him down so badly? And all the bad feelings about my marriage flooded forward and memories I'd been trying to bury rose quickly up.

Relationships with men do not work for me, I thought. They've caused me so much bitterness and pain. And remembering my unbidden interest in the detective from Stockton, I vowed those feelings would be squelched before they had any chance to root.

Not worth the trouble, I told myself. Not worth risking getting burned again.

CHAPTER TWELVE

I wanted to know so much but I couldn't learn it all right now. I'd have to probe a little here, prod a little there, drawing from numerous different sources till the facts came together and began to jell.

For starters, what was an up-class girl like Meryl doing working in a scrubby county social services office? How had she met Alvin "Sonny" Mitchell and how long had they been a couple? *Could* Mitchell have killed Meryl and his own tiny pink-skinned daughter while in a murderous rage that seized him and drove him into frenzy?

I headed out the door and straight for Mariposa Hospital, for I had a hunch Wanda Brighton could add some more to what she'd already told me. I parked my car, pulled my collar till it stood up straight, and watched my breath come out in misty puffs. I'd never known a winter as cold as this one.

Entering the room, I saw Wanda sitting up in bed, chatting with Patti Burke. Her color had continued to improve and her eyes, while reflecting pain and sadness, were brighter than they'd been the day before.

"They tell me you're being released tomorrow," I said to her, placing a hand lightly on her shoulder. "What will you do then?"

Her expression sobered and her mouth began to droop. She smoothed her fine, fair hair with her palm before she answered.

"I'll take my poor baby girl and go back to Vegas," she began, now scratching at the sheet with short square nails devoid of any polish. "I'll bury her there . . ." Her lips began to tremble and she quickly bent her head. "And I'll search for Sonny. Though maybe he'll be home by then."

"You wouldn't take Lucy to Bodega Bay?" I asked, my voice scarcely above a whisper. "Maybe your parents would act different now, because of the circumstances."

Wanda shook her head so wildly her hair swirled out on either side.

"No, never! I know they wouldn't change their minds, not even now, and I will not take the chance that they would reject and dishonor Lucy when I went to bury her. I'm taking her to Vegas."

"Wanda," I said softly, drawing up a chair, "tell me how Meryl Masters met Sonny in the first place and how long they were together."

She jerked her head up and stared at me, questions filling her eyes.

"Why do you care about Meryl and Sonny?" she asked. "That was over a long, long time ago."

"I just need to know," I said, revealing nothing. "Will you help me out?"

"I told you I was one of Meryl's cases up in Lodi. Well, Sonny's younger sister was a client, too. Her husband beat her up and kicked her out and she needed help. She had four kids and no way to feed them.

"Anyway, one day Meryl visited Joanie at the place she'd found for her to stay and Sonny dropped by while she was there and they hit it off. He'd just gotten out of prison . . ." She stopped short. "Did you know about that?" she asked guiltily. "Or did I give something away?"

"I know all about Sonny," I informed her. "He's led a very active life."

"He's different now," Wanda proclaimed adamantly, thrusting out her chin. "He's trying hard—he's going straight this time."

"That may be," I murmured, although I deeply doubted it. "I certainly hope so. Let's get back to him and Meryl—how long did their relationship last?"

"Let's see . . ." said Wanda, squinting as she thought, "probably six months or so."

"Why did it end?" I asked. "Do you know?"

"I think she just got tired of him," the young girl told me. "Meryl could be like that. She'd grow bored with a person on a moment's notice, drop them, and never look back. And then there was the other guy. Maybe that had something to do with it, too."

"What other guy? A new boyfriend?"

"Yes, someone she took up with not long after she dropped Sonny. Actually, I think for a while there she was seeing both of them together, though one didn't know about the other."

"And who might he have been?" I asked.

"Dunno," Wanda answered, staring vacantly in front of her. "Meryl could be like *that*, too. Close-mouthed and secretive. If she didn't want you to know something, you weren't going to know it."

"But why wouldn't she have told you her new guy's name?" I asked curiously. "After all, the two of you were friends."

Wanda shook her head as if she'd tried unsuccessfully to puzzle that one out herself.

"You know, I think it was probably because she liked to have secrets just for the sake of having secrets, whether they were important ones or not."

I sat in silence for a moment, getting ready to walk on eggs and trying to find the lightest way to do it. I knew, regardless of how I said it, I was going to upset her.

"Wanda," I began carefully, "you told me Sonny found the baby to be a 'drag.' Did she annoy him very much, did he ever strike her?"

The girl looked at me and began to cry, burying her head between her hands.

"Wanda, tell me."

"He would've liked her eventually," she wailed. "Oh, I know he would've, when he'd been with her a little longer!"

"Did he ever hurt her?" I repeated, visions of dark ugly bruises on the soft smooth baby skin pounding at my brain.

"Only once, maybe twice. When he'd been drinking and she was crying far too much. He can get real stormy when he's drunk and he raised his hand and slapped her."

"Honey"—my voice was low and even as I bent slowly toward her—"do you think it possible that Sonny could've killed your baby?" I drew my breath in and watched while she took in my words.

"My God," she cried, raising wide shocked eyes to look at me. "No, no. He never could've done that! He never would have, no matter what!"

I sat back against my chair and stared at Wanda Brighton. Which of two things was she telling me? I wondered. What she honestly believed or a lie she wished desperately to be the truth?

"It's happened, Kate. She's gone." Kent caught my arm as I came into the room. "Rena moved out last night and took the baby with her."

"Oh, no, Dan. Where did she go and what did she say before she left?" I kicked a pebble to one side as I listened sadly to his news.

"To her mom's. Said she needed to get away awhile to think things over."

Though Dan was from Chicago, he'd married a San Madera girl, which meant Rena was still close by in town. At least they still circulated within the same orbit, a fact that, it seemed to me, might make reconciliation easier than if she'd become a faceless voice at the end of a long-distance phone line thousands of miles away.

"She didn't mention divorce, then?"

"No, thank God. Only wanting time to get her bearings, to figure out what she'll do next."

"What're you going to do, Danny?" I stared into his worried face. The pallor of his skin, the deadness of his eyes, told me he hadn't slept too much last night.

"Just like I said before, Kate. I'm going to wait awhile but if she won't come back, I'm going to quit the force. I cannot bear to live without her."

"I'm sorry, kiddo," I whispered softly, "truly, truly sorry. But I can't think of a single thing to help you work it out. Just know that I'm here for you when you need a friendly ear, but I can't give you any magic answer."

And feeling helpless and absolutely ineffectual, I turned around and slowly walked away.

"Kate, come over here, there's something you should know about."

Mungers, standing by the coffee maker, waved me toward him as I came into the room. I broke my stride, veered in his direction, and poured myself a cup of brew while he began to talk.

"Steve and I went on out to Rimerton to nose around the neighbors. Some of them weren't home, some of them knew nothing—not even the time of day, I'd say—but that elderly gentleman living to the right of Masters's town house turned out to be a gold mine."

"You mean the one who put us on to the Mazda?"

"The same, a Mr. William Ford. I think he spends most of his time in or near his unit, so he's normally well versed on what goes on with his neighbors. And keenly interested, too, if I'm not mistaken. He told us Meryl Masters had a visitor Friday morning about ten o'clock—apparently she didn't go to work that day, or if she did, she went in late—and the visit wasn't pleasant. It ended in a shouting match between the two of them, Masters and her guest, and a door banging shut when that guest finally left."

"Male or female?" I asked as I slowly sipped my coffee. For all I cared, the drink could've been milk or plain water. I was totally absorbed with what Carl was saying.

"Male, the old man told us, and also that he'd noticed him at the town house at least once before."

"Look," I said to Carl, "I'm on my way down to county social services and I go right past the town house. Mind if I drop by and see this helpful soul myself?"

"Not at all. I've given you the gist of what we learned but go ahead and get it firsthand."

Usually I delegated authority well, I thought, believing that someone who didn't do that ended up wasting other people's talents and accomplishing only about a tenth of what was out there waiting to be done. But here, as I'd told Carl, I was passing by Rimerton anyway and I had a hankering to hear this story from the man himself.

I swallowed the remainder of the coffee in one gulp, checked my desk for messages and new reports, then began to make my way across the room. Little had come in from patrol the night before and I was thankful. When I became immersed in a complex case such as this double homicide, I preferred to give it my full, unshared attention.

So lost was I in my thoughts that I almost collided with Robert Harris coming through the doorway.

"Sorry, Harris," I apologized, sidestepping so he could enter. Then I had a sudden thought. Remembering my resolution of last night, I told myself it was strictly business.

"Look, Bobby, I'm riding down to social services to poke around in your victim's background. Want to come along?" Since Stockton was giving us an assist on this thing, I reasoned, I might as well get to know them.

"Sure thing, Kate," he answered, and again I saw the crinkle start around his eyes. But something else, a certain seriousness, showed there, too. "Charlie's off chasing Sonny Mitchell so I'm on my own. I was just sticking my head in to touch bases, then get on with my investigations."

Does it bother him working for a woman? I wondered as we walked together down the hall. It didn't seem to—not up front, at least—but who knew what he was really thinking? Maybe I'd ask him someday, when I got to know him better.

And then I startled and surprised myself as I listened to me start to talk out loud about a subject I'd planned to leave alone.

"Does it matter to you that I'm female?" I ventured as we approached the car. "I mean, I don't know what your situation is in Stockton but I felt maybe you'd never worked before for a woman."

As soon as the words left my mouth, I felt ill at ease and awkward and I longed to snatch them back.

"Of course it matters," Harris told me in an amused tone. "It makes all the difference. I really appreciate it when a person is a female and I'm glad that you are."

He was toying with me, though in a kindly way, and embarrassed and feeling foolish, my face warmed and blushed.

"I meant professionally," I stammered, sorely wishing I'd kept quiet. "I hope you don't mind my running the show."

I took the corner too quickly and his body swayed briefly and brushed against mine. It was as if an electric current had shot through me. I glanced quickly at him as he regained his balance and saw him, his face tight, staring straight ahead.

"Well, it's your department," Harris answered, and his voice, normally so level, was now thick and husky. "If it wasn't you, it'd be Darrow or Mungers and that's just how it should be. Charlie and I are only visitors so we'll work under whoever's in charge in your town." He paused. "But aside from that, no, it doesn't bother me that you're a woman. You had to be good to get where you are now and that's all that really matters."

We rode in silence for a moment, then braked to let a group of school kids march across the street.

"Sorry I brought that business up," I told him contritely. "Usually it doesn't even enter my mind. I hope I didn't make you feel awkward." Again I felt the color in my face begin to rise.

Oh, leave it alone, Katharine, I moaned angrily to myself. Every time you open up your mouth, you make it worse.

Harris swung his head slowly toward me. His face had lost its tightness, and again, I saw a bemused expression. When he spoke, his voice was normal.

"It didn't bother me, Detective Harrod, in any way. Obviously it was something you wanted very much to say and so you said it."

Instead of feeling better, I felt worse, like a small child who's been patted on the head and put gently in its place. I squirmed in my seat like some rattled schoolgirl and tried to focus on the case. If I got back into a familiar groove, I'd regain my balance and start acting like myself again.

"Has Rhoads made headway in his search for Sonny Mitchell?" I asked, breaking the verbal rut that I was in.

"He's got some leads, he thinks. He's working on the theory Sonny might be back in California, probably at his old stomping grounds up north. Charlie made a few phone calls when he got in last night and one or two of them made him get pretty excited."

"When he got in?" I asked. "Where'd he been? I thought the two of you were going out to dinner."

"Didn't end up that way," Harris answered. "I went on back to the hotel but he downed a few beers with Darrow. The two of them seem to hit it off pretty well together."

Lord, I thought wryly to myself, remembering my thoughts when I'd first spotted Rhoads. They looked alike, drank side by side, and got along okay enough to share some laughs—try to tell me now they weren't two of a kind. Still, I'd keep an open mind till I knew Charlie better. I didn't really want to think he was as lightweight and as shallow as Steve Darrow.

We pulled up in the parking lot behind the condos

and made our way to the front door of William Ford. One push of the bell brought a face staring from behind a curtain, and in several moments the door itself swung slowly open and that same face peered cautiously around its leading edge.

"Mr. Ford," I began, "we met on Monday, when you were kind enough to tell us about Meryl Masters's car. I understand you now can tell us something else. About some sort of argument between Masters and a stranger last Friday morning."

"That's right," he said, obviously delighted to be of help. He swung the door wide open and waved us into his tidy quarters.

"Come sit down, just like those other fellas did this morning."

I imagined he enjoyed the break in his routine and didn't mind if he had to repeat the same story several times.

"Tell me about the incident," I said to him when I was settled in a deep soft chair.

"All right," the frail man answered, pushing up his steel-rimmed glasses tight against his nose. "I was looking out the window about nine-thirty or so—getting the sun, so to speak, because it rises on this side of the building and warms up the living room—and I saw this fella coming up the path. Walking at a brisk clip, too. Course that coulda been because he was so cold.

"Anyway, he disappeared inside 4608—I know

that because I heard the door open and then shut—
and he stayed inside for nearly half an hour."

Ford began to cough, took out a large green handkerchief and gave his nose a hearty blow, then continued his story.

"Right around ten o'clock I heard the front door
open and a woman's voice, very angry, telling him
to go away and not come back. Then the man's voice
answered. Ugly and harsh, I thought, but I couldn't
make out everything he said. And then I saw him
hurry down the steps, never looking back, and the
door slammed so hard I thought it'd spring right off
its hinges."

Harris moved forward in his chair, his arm resting
lightly on his knee.

"Do you remember the exact words Masters
used?" he asked.

Mr. Ford squinted, pursed his lips, and looked up
toward the ceiling.

"They weren't pretty," he answered slowly. "Not
very ladylike, I'll tell you that. She yelled, 'Screw
you, Jack. Get the fuck away from me and stay
away!' " He shot me a hasty glance in apparent
embarrassment.

"And what *could* you understand from his reply?"

The sun streamed across the patterned carpet,
highlighting Ford's worn leather slippers. As I
watched, he began to shuffle his feet back and forth
against the rug, struggling to recall the moment.

"Just something like 'Meryl dear,' " he finally answered. "That's all that I remember hearing, but he uttered it very sarcastically."

"And you don't know who this man is?" I asked.

"No, I don't, but like I told the other officers, I've seen him here at least one time before. No yelling and screaming then, though. At least, not so I could hear."

"How long ago was that?"

"I'd say sometime last fall or summer. See, I'm a student of human nature and I never forget a face. That's how I recognized him last Friday."

"Can you describe this man, sir?" I asked him.

"Sure. Probably thirty-five to forty, maybe five-ten or so, swarthy with dark hair and a little beak nose. His face is sort of round and fleshy with almond-shaped eyes, and his body's got a little too much weight on it for its height. He looks kind of soft and pudgy."

"How was he dressed?"

"Gray business suit. Blue overcoat on top of it."

"And you're absolutely certain Meryl Masters called him 'Jack'?"

"Oh, yes, definitely," Ford answered. "She screamed that at him when he was hopping down the steps, and it made me think of that old nursery rhyme, 'Jack Be Nimble, Jack Be Quick.' "

We thanked him and took our leave. As we went down the walk, I turned and saw him watching from the window.

"Well, we know one thing for sure," I said to Bobby Harris. "Whoever that morning caller was, it definitely was *not* Sonny Mitchell. Not unless he'd dyed his hair and shrunk down several inches."

They gaped at us as if we'd posed a foolish question. Meryl Masters's coworkers stood around Harris and myself in that squat, depressing county social services building and let their mouths hang open when we asked if they knew who might've killed their colleague.

"Did she ever mention any enemies?" I swung my eyes from one of them to the other, watching their expressions. In unison, they shook their heads back and forth in firm denial.

"All right," I told them, "I'll want to speak with several of you individually. The rest of you know where to find me if you remember anything that might be helpful."

Meryl's supervisor, a lean balding man named Scotty Hansen, had been able to supply few details about his dead employee, except to say she'd not come into work on Friday and that she'd kept pretty much to herself and handled her cases like a true professional.

"She didn't mix," he told us, "but if I had to pick any persons she talked with more than others, I'd have to say Janet Horrocks at the desk next to her and, for some reason or other, the file clerk, Steven Brownfeld."

Now, after dismissing the other workers, we called the Horrocks woman into an empty office Hansen had told us we could use.

Tall and thin and endlessly chain-smoking, she glided into a chair and crossed her legs, letting the top one swing back and forth, back and forth, in nervous agitation.

"How well did you know Meryl?" I asked. "You sat right next to her. Surely the two of you talked personal from time to time."

"Yes, we talked," the skinny woman agreed, "but only superficially. Meryl stayed very tight-mouthed. Closed and to herself. We'd have a few laughs together, sure, and sometimes she'd voice an opinion or other, but I never felt I could really get to know her. She kept you at arm's length. She'd let you see just so much of her and no more."

The Horrocks woman tilted back her head and blew a puff of smoke across the room. Harris and I ducked our heads, and I gave a little cough.

"Sorry," she apologized. "Filthy habit, got to give it up. But not right now. All this stuff unnerves me."

"I gather she might have not told you, but did you ever have reason to believe Meryl was involved with anyone? Did you ever know her to even date?"

"Not date," Janet Horrocks answered, "not in the usual way, no. Oh, she could've done, but if so, she never let on about it. Like I told you, when she walked in here to work, she left her other life outside.

"But a couple of years ago, starting right after she came here, there *was* someone. I only know this because sometimes there'd be phone calls, like to set up a rendezvous or something, and I couldn't help but overhear. This went on for quite some time, maybe all the way up to a year or so ago, and then it abruptly stopped."

"You say 'rendezvous,'" Harris interjected. "Do you mean something different from just setting up a date?"

"Yes," the Horrocks woman answered. "I got the impression this person, whoever he was—I never heard a name—was coming in from out of town and wanted to know if Meryl would be available."

"But you never saw anyone pick her up after work and you never saw a photo of a boyfriend on her desk?"

"Never. And I knew better than to ask about the calls."

I'd already queried Hansen about Meryl's caseload but thought I'd probe Horrocks about it, too.

"Did Meryl have problems with any of her clients?" I began. "You get quite a mixed bag of people looking for assistance and I imagine occasionally there's the rough one who's dissatisfied he can't get more from the system and might be prone to take it out on one of you."

"Uh-uh," Horrocks stated with finality. "Meryl never had any trouble along those lines. It seemed she always lucked out. She had a load of pussycats for clients and they adored her. And if there'd been any troublemakers, she'd have sweet-talked them out of it. She was a good social worker, no doubt about it, even if she wasn't very social with any of us."

I placed my foot on the rung of Bobby's chair and, looking at the Horrocks woman, began to muse.

"I just don't get it," I puzzled out loud. "I don't get why a girl like Meryl Masters, from a wealthy family in the Bay Area, would end up in social services. It doesn't seem quite her style. She doesn't strike me as a bleeding heart who'd sacrifice herself for the starving masses."

Horrocks lighted up another cigarette and began to laugh.

"She *did* talk a little about that to me once," the woman said. "I think she took this job as a short-time lark, in order to annoy her kin, and when she saw just how much it did that—how aghast they were at the thought of their little girl getting down and rolling with the dirties—well, then, she just kept on at it. To devil them, you know."

"But why?" I asked. "Why would she want to shock and upset them?"

"Dunno, I'm sure," Janet Horrocks answered. "Why do any of us do the things we do? I can only guess that Meryl held some sort of grudge against her snotty blue-blood family and liked to get their goat because of it. She had a few good laughs about their shock from time to time."

The Horrocks woman departed in a cloud of smoke and Steven Brownfeld entered the room to take his turn.

"Who was Meryl Masters?" I asked. "Did you know her well?"

Brownfeld, a lanky, red-haired fellow in his twenties, gave a start and stared at me. I noticed his left eye wandered slightly. I also noticed he looked scared.

"She was a social worker," he stammered, and despite the coolness of the day, I saw his brow begin to sweat.

"But what was she like?" I insisted. "I understand she befriended you so I thought you might know her somewhat better than the rest."

"No, not really. It's true we'd chat a little from time to time but about nothing heavy, just about the weather and the like." Brownfeld bit his lower lip and started looking toward the ceiling.

"Oh," I said, arching my eyebrows, "your boss seemed to think you were more like a special friend."

"No, I wasn't. I can't really tell you anything about Meryl. Why would she confide in me anyway? I'm just a little file clerk." Brownfeld took out a handkerchief and wiped his brow. He bent slightly toward me and I saw a string of pale brown freckles splashed across his milky skin.

"Our mistake, then," I told him. "We were informed otherwise."

The young man rose, hooking his right foot around a chair leg and nearly toppling it. After righting it, he hastily left the room.

"Well, what do you make of that?" Harris asked me. "Is he just nervous or is he hiding something?"

"Could be either," I told him, "but we're not going to forget about it."

We searched Meryl Masters's desk but found nothing that would help us. It contained no personal items other than a lipstick and a comb, just folder after bulging folder of her cases.

"Let's hit the road," I told Harris. "I think we've milked this place pretty dry."

We'd walked outside and turned the corner when I heard someone call out my name, and I spun around and saw a young clerk-typist staring at me pleadingly.

"Detective Harrod, do you have a minute?" she asked breathlessly. "I couldn't say anything in there because it might just be dumb and not mean anything, but I *do* know something maybe you should know."

"Of course, honey," I told her reassuringly and drew her toward a bus bench. The three of us sat down, as the wind blew cold around us, and Bette Marne began to unburden herself.

"It just seemed peculiar, that's all, like I didn't know what she'd be doing out there."

"Out where, Miss Marne? Take your time and start at the beginning. We've got the whole morning if you like."

"I live out the San Luis Road," she said, naming a lonely country byway running toward the mountains six or seven miles from town, "and sometimes I'd see Meryl Masters driving out that road and sometimes driving back. Well, what was she doing out there? I'd wonder. I mean, it's off the beaten track and all. I just thought it strange . . ." Her voice trailed off and she looked up at us sheepishly.

"Maybe she was enjoying the scenery," I offered, thinking this was really no big deal. "We all take rides in the country to appreciate the scenery."

"But on rainy days?" the girl protested. "I'd even see her there some rainy days."

Harris cleared his throat. "No, that was no joyride, I'd say. Masters had a destination and a purpose and wasn't just looking at some trees and leaves. Is there anything else you can tell us about these occurrences, Miss Marne? Were they always on the same day or same time of day?"

"Always on a weekend, sometimes morning, sometimes afternoon. And you know where Burnt Creek Road comes into the San Luis one? Well, I never saw her past that point. I never saw her on the other side of Burnt Creek, where San Luis keeps on running toward the mountains."

"Buy you a cup of coffee," Harris offered as we headed toward the car. I turned toward him and saw that he was looking at me steadily.

"It's free back at the station," I reminded him, looking at him with a smile, hoping he'd override my protest.

"Sure it is, but let's buy one anyway." He motioned toward a nearby snack shop. "We can sit around and chew over what we've learned." And shortly we were seated, one across from the other, in a corner booth with two steaming mugs in front of us.

"I don't care for her, you know," I volunteered as I slowly stirred the coffee to start cooling it.

I wondered if he'd think me foolish to have formed this personal sort of judgment on the dead. There was, after all, a difference between saying one hadn't been a nice person and saying you didn't like her. The first was an objective opinion, the second subjective and emotionally involved.

"Who?" Bobby asked, pouring cream into his cup. "That young girl we just talked to?"

"No, Meryl Masters. Maybe it sounds silly but I began getting a dislike for her after talking to poor Wanda Brighton, and the feeling built today. I think she was an unkind person. A person who was a user, and a manipulator who liked to play with other people's lives."

Harris didn't laugh or chide me for my negative assessment. Instead he looked thoughtful as he added more cream.

"That's good, you know," he told me. "If you can

look behind the words that people give you and find a deeper, fuller portrait of the one they're talking about, then you can get to know that person better. And often when you get to know him, you can find the pointers to the reason for his—or in this case, her—murder."

"You don't think I'm petty, then, passing judgment like that?"

"Not at all. I think you're a smart cop using your instincts and your intuition."

"What do you think's out San Luis Road?" I asked, changing the subject. "Another one of Meryl's little secrets?"

"Maybe the same one," Harris answered. "Maybe that's where the rendezvous took place. How shall we go about finding out?"

"I know the area," I told him. "It's mostly farm-land and the houses are few and far between. It's not like everyone's sitting right up on the road watching cars go by, so we're going to be up against it to get our answers.

"I think we'll take a picture of the Mazda and a photo of the victim and work our way door to door and hope. That's really all that we can do. First time I have a chance, though, I'm going to ride out that road just looking at the mailboxes, to see if any name connected to this case pops up on one."

We both knew this whole San Luis Road thing could be a bunch of nothing—an innocent little foray to see a pal out in the country—but on the other hand, it could be the most important secret in Meryl Masters's life. We had to know.

"Steve's running down her friends through that address book we found," I told him. "Could be he'll find one of them lives out by Burnt Creek Road. If so, that'll put a close to it. If not, we'll try to uncover the big attraction."

We sat in comfortable silence for several moments, sipping the coffee that had now cooled down. The waitress passed by with refills and heated it up again.

"And 'Jack'! Who's Jack?" Harris muttered. "And what were the two of them fighting about on the very day she was murdered?"

"Maybe the family will know," I said, "when we get around to talking with them. It'll be right at the top of my list of questions but don't expect too much. I'll bet they were pretty much in the dark about a lot in their daughter's life."

"You're going to talk to them by phone? You don't want to visit them in person?" Harris gave a little frown.

"I do. I think a couple of us ought to go to San Francisco. I'm just calling them to tell them we'll be coming up."

I believed in face-to-face encounters whenever possible, especially with the principals in a homicide investigation. Nuances in phrases could be lost, expressions left unseen, if you failed to make the personal contact.

I turned toward the window, then gave a little start. A young boy had walked by, and at first glance I'd thought that it was Tommy.

"What's the matter?" Harris asked, noticing the strange expression on my face. "Seen a 'most wanted'?"

"No, nothing like that. I thought it was my son but it was only someone who resembled him."

"How many children do you have, Katharine?" Harris asked casually. He didn't look at me. Just looked down at his cup while he stirred his coffee.

"Only one. He's nine." I smiled. "We're going to take drum lessons together."

Harris put his head back and laughed a hearty laugh.

"I think that's great! And what's your husband going to do? Play the trumpet or the saxophone?"

I heard a slight tension enter his voice as he again lowered his eyes and went back to stirring.

"There is no husband," I replied, sobering. "Our divorce will be final in several months." I reflected on the lengthy marriage and the bitter ending to it all, but "It just didn't work out" was all I said.

"Nor did mine," Bobby volunteered, and now he was looking straight at me, eyes serious and intent. "That's one reason why I left LA. I needed a change of scenery."

"Children?" I asked cautiously, and I felt a warmth of intimacy begin to spread through me.

"None. Fortunately for them, unfortunately for me. At least you have a son you can delight in."

"Yes, but sometimes it's tough," I confided, feeling so at ease in this man's presence. "Oh, I don't mean him. I mean because of the problems Jon and I have forced on him." My thoughts filled with remembrance of the coming Cub Scout dinner. "Sometimes he has a hard time dealing with the situation and I worry it will overwhelm him."

"Was your husband a cop?"

His voice was low and even but a certain tension was still there.

"No, an architect."

Abruptly my mind snapped back to the business at hand, and I got out some cash to pay the bill.

"My treat, Katharine." Harris took the check from me and when our hands brushed, he didn't pull quickly back, just let the brush pass casually by as if it were so natural. "Even though I'm the guest in town, this one's on me."

CHAPTER THIRTEEN

I saw him running down the sidewalk, weaving in and out, shoving people right and left. And then I saw a hurtling, speeding bike ridden by a youngster collide with Carl and send him crashing to the ground.

We braked so fast the car rocked backward on its shocks, and both of us spilled out the doors and ran to him. He was sitting now, having drawn up from his sprawled position, clutching his knee with one large hand while his usually inexpressive face contorted in pain. As I reached him, he took out his radio with the other hand and began to put out a broadcast:

"Two-eleven purse snatch, eleven hundred block Dexter. Male white, five-eight, one hundred thirty pounds, approximately sixteen years of age, black coat, blue jeans, heading eastbound on foot from the location. Property taken was a brown leather shoulder bag."

He completed the broadcast, groaned, and shoved the radio back into his pocket, causing several toothpicks to leap out on the cement.

"Carl, are you hurt bad?" I knelt beside him and looked into his face. The pale blue eyes were filled with pain.

"Christ, Kate," he moaned in obvious distress. "I've twisted the whole thing around. The knee's wrenched and the ankle feels as if it's broken." His huge frame hunched across the useless appendage.

"Get an ambulance," I called to Bobby, "he can't walk out of here."

Carl leaned against me as a crowd gathered and stared down at him. His eyes dulled with the pain's intensity, and he grabbed my arm and held it hard.

"I was just having a sandwich down at Marty's," he forced out, "when I glanced up and saw this juvie grab some old lady's purse. So off I went and now I've really screwed this thing up good." He gestured to his knee. "What a time to do it, too, when we've got so much on our plate."

My dear friend, my partner. I hated to see the suffering he was feeling. At least there was one hurt I could relieve.

"We'll keep you right up to speed on everything, Carl—don't worry about that. And we'll use your brain. You can analyze what we've got and tell us where to go with it. As far as legwork is concerned, we got lucky. We got Stockton."

I heard the wail of the ambulance drawing closer, and in a moment it screeched to a halt at curbside and two white-coated men approached Carl with a stretcher. I watched as they lowered him onto it and then I squeezed his shoulder as they carried him away. I'd seen the odd twist of that ankle and I knew about smashed knees. I had a feeling he was going to be gone a long, long time.

The forgotten victim, I thought as I drove home, that's what Lucy has become. In the days following the IDing of the bodies, our focus had shifted full force to Meryl Masters, with little mention of the poor dead baby.

Usually this term is used when describing the avalanche of sympathetic attention often focused on the perpetrator of a crime and the few crumbs of thought thrown to his hapless target, but I meant something else. Here, Lucy had lost the limelight not to the killer but to the murdered woman. Meryl Masters had become the dominant victim.

The reasons for this fact were clear. Lucy had no background—only four short months on earth—but Meryl had been here for nearly thirty years. Long enough to have made many enemies and gotten into many twisted situations that could've easily spawned her death.

We felt, therefore, that it was in Meryl's past that we'd find the missing parts to lead us to the killer of *both* victims.

"But you're *not* forgotten," I murmured, tightly clasping the steering wheel. "You're in my heart and in my mind, and everything I do to get closer to this murderer, I do for you. For I cannot forget how you looked that awful night."

I knew the others felt the same way, too, even though we rarely spoke of her. I know cops, and I knew that each of us was looking for justice for Lucy, even though we only spoke of Meryl.

Again, I pictured the little body with its bruises and the tape across its mouth, and again the same question came back to nag at me. Why remove the tape across the baby's nose?

That had puzzled me from the beginning and it puzzled me now. Had the murderer taken pity and decided to allow her a little air? Had it somehow been ripped off accidentally? Or was there some other, entirely different reason for the absence of that length of silver sealer? And if I knew the answer, would I see a clue to catch a killer?

I sighed, perplexed, and put the picture from my mind. I could drive myself mad if I dwelled on it for very long.

I walked inside the house and heard the phone begin to ring. Mrs. Miller, coming through the hallway, rushed to answer it while I put down my things.

"It's Mr. Harrod," she whispered as she clutched the receiver to her chest. "Do you want to talk with him right now?"

"Darn right I do," and I reached out for the receiver. I'd tried to phone him, to find out why he'd broken his date with Tommy, but he'd always been out, then not returned my calls.

"Hello, Katharine," he said formally. "I'm finally getting back to you. Sorry I couldn't do so earlier." Smooth, breezy, unruffled.

"Is it true you're not taking Tommy to the father-son dinner?" I asked. "He said you'd called him and told him no."

"He's right, Kate, I can't. Hated like hell to let him down but there's a meeting I've got to keep that night. Only time this client is going to be in town."

"But it's also the only time this special banquet is going to take place this year. He's awfully disappointed. Are you sure you can't make it?" I was pleading for my son's sake, for I well recalled his pain of the other evening.

"Can't, Kate, absolutely not." Jon didn't even sound concerned. "He'll get over it." He paused, then gave the subtle jab. "After all, *I* don't let him down that often."

I let his implication pass without any fuss—I was too far along with my life to engage any longer in his tiresome verbal bouts—and sadly I hung up the phone. I'd hoped to gain some good news to hold out to Tommy but all I'd ended up with was the reaffirming of a dreadful disappointment.

*   *   *

"I missed him by a minute!" Rhoads shouted. "He left Bishop early this morning, after rummaging around in some of his old haunts there for a day or two."

"How do you know this?" I asked, listening intently to what he said.

"Contacts, that's how. Calling in a favor. And it paid off even if I'm just a little late because now I know where he's heading and I can wait and roust him there."

Rhoads's large face was flushed and his brown eyes sparkled. He looked enormously pleased with himself at what he'd turned up.

"And where would that be?" I asked curiously.

"Up around Lodi, I'll bet you anything. That's where he was hanging out when I busted him for that robbery four years ago. He's got kin in the area as well as a lot of scumbag friends. And look at this"—Charlie pointed to a map—"here's Vegas, here's Bishop, here's Lodi. One straight line from southeast to northwest."

"Do you think you'll find him at his sister's?"

Rhoads did a double take, drawing in his chin and staring at me with wide-open eyes.

"How do you know about the sister?"

"Wanda told me," I answered. "I think her name's Joanie, if I'm not mistaken."

"Joanie, that's right," Rhoads agreed. "Joanie Creighton, a dreary mousy blonde who keeps pop-

ping out kids by that old man of hers without a way
to feed them. He beats her up, sends her packing,
back she comes. Whammy, she's pregnant again."
Charlie slammed his fist into his palm for sound
effects.

I couldn't help but smile. Even though his appraisal of the poor sad woman was deprecating and
sarcastic, Rhoads's manner of delivery was both
charged and colorful. Filled with fervor by his hunt
for Sonny Mitchell, he was like a little kid bursting
full of energy, imbued with an endearing quality that
began to draw me to him despite myself. An endearing quality cocky Steve Darrow would never
have.

"And what will you do with him when you find
him?" I asked, not without some concern. "To us,
he's just the father of a murdered baby, no more,
no less."

"Come on, Detective," Rhoads said mockingly but
without the unkindly edge that drives a needle home,
"you don't really believe that now, do you? I know
this rat like the back of my own hand and I think
there's a damn good chance he killed both of them.
Sure, I'm going to turn him inside-out and shake him
till I'm otherwise convinced."

"Well, make sure you have probable cause first,
okay? Take it easy till you have good reason to believe he isn't leveling with you. We don't want to go
harassing the wrong man even if it *is* Sonny
Mitchell."

"My wish is your command, O boss," Rhoads clowned, and then, realizing he'd turned around the words, he began to laugh and I laughed with him. Suddenly, as if a shade dropped down, he stopped and a shot of something painful filled his eyes, then quickly disappeared.

Strange, I thought. I wonder whatever brought that look on.

"Hey, Kate, this address book's a fizzle." Darrow lumbered into the room and dropped the little leather volume on my desk as if he wanted to be rid of it. "Half the numbers are no longer working and the people I talked to at the remaining ones haven't got a clue as to what could've happened to the Masters woman."

"What kind of people did you find?" I asked. "Male, female, young, old?"

"Female mainly. Girls about her own age. And isn't that a little odd? A good-looking babe like her without a pony in the stable. You'd think there'd be randy studs rutting all around."

I saw Rhoads stiffen slightly as he listened to his beer buddy run his mouth. He obviously disapproved of Darrow's coarse talk about the dead—feeling, I imagined, that it showed disrespect—and I found myself admiring him for his old-fashioned values. The more I saw of this man, the more I liked him, and I felt I'd been very wrong in my initial judgment of him. The resemblance between Rhoads and Darrow seemed to stop right beneath the skin.

"What did the females tell you?" I asked, picking up the little book and flipping through it. I was sure Steve had thoroughly enjoyed his assignment and hoped he'd behaved himself so that no complaints would be forthcoming. He'd come on strong with an unappreciative woman witness last summer and she'd screamed to the lieutenant. Darrow was slapped with a "conduct unbecoming" judgment and taken off the homicide table for a while.

"The girls were more like casual acquaintances, not real friends," Steve informed me, lightly stroking at his scar. "Masters didn't seem like a person who let other people come too close to her. Or if she did, she memorized their numbers and didn't write them down in there. The chicks I talked to all seemed to have a very superficial relationship with her—a lunch here, a movie there, but no girlie-girlie chatter."

Darrow cracked his gum while he watched me studying the address book. Rhoads came around the other side and perused the pages with me. I caught the smell of stale tobacco on his breath and moved a little bit away. A nonsmoker for some time now, I found such odors vastly unappealing.

I, too, noticed the lack of male names and thought it curious. I'd hoped, of course, that Steve would've located Mr. Wonderful from out of town—the mysterious paramour Janet Horrocks had told us about—but no such luck.

"Tell me," I asked, "did any of these phone numbers belong to someone living out the San Luis Road or in that area? Maybe near Burnt Creek?"

"Nah," Darrow answered. "All here in town except for a couple of San Fran numbers. Guess that's the family so I left them for you."

Interesting, I thought. She drives out that country road a lot and yet she doesn't list the number in her book. What gives?

"Did you check out every one of these?" I asked.

"Every one except two or three that didn't answer, even though I called back several times. I've put little red dots beside the no-shows—see," and Darrow pointed to several tiny crimson pencil marks. "I'll keep calling those until I get them."

"No, leave the book with me," I told him. "I'll follow up on them. You get on with the Highway Patrol and checking out the stores on 99. How's that coming, by the way?"

"I'm going back up there today," Steve informed me, flicking a fleck of dust off his Gucci loafers. "No luck yet but I'm far from finished. Wanna ride along, Charlie?"

"Sure thing," Rhoads answered, the eager little boy bursting forth. "By the time we're finished there, ol' Sonny ought to be in Lodi."

"B.S.," I said out loud, "who's B.S. and why those unfortunate initials instead of the person's whole name?" I was looking at the dainty script handwriting in the address book and wondering about an entry that bore one of Darrow's red dots.

I wasn't sure how long ago Steve had tried to reach this party, so I picked up the phone and dialed. It rang several times and then I heard the click of an answering machine and a male voice told me he couldn't take my call right now but please leave name and number.

The voice did not identify itself and was neither high-pitched nor low—more of a tenor than anything else, I'd say—and I could tell little about the age of the man from its sound.

I hung up without leaving any message, deciding I'd try later on today. After all, it was possible the person worked, which would explain his absence now and also make it likely he'd be home later.

I dialed the other dotted numbers and was rewarded by finding two girls who were at home. No, they both said, they'd not been close to Meryl, not privy to any of her secrets, could not tell me if she was involved with any fellow or if there'd been someone in her life who wished her dead.

I closed the little leather book. It'd all been checked out now, except for Mr. Two Initials, and his turn would come.

I leaned back and thought about Rhoads and Harris and how glad I was they were working with us.

Especially Harris. I wasn't kidding myself about that. The two fitted in easily, bringing no friction to the team and besides, they certainly came in handy. I'd talked to Carl this morning and found my feeling had been right. He was going to be laid up for several weeks or maybe months. The ankle was indeed broken and the fall had aggravated an old knee injury. Cartilage had been torn and the whole thing badly wrenched.

I'd pictured him lying in his small sparse bachelor apartment and asked him was there anything he needed.

No, he'd told me, Sandy was looking out for him. She'd drop by at lunchtime as well as after work to tend to him, and following surgery on the knee tomorrow she'd be at the hospital to take him home.

I'd seen the apartment only once or twice but remembered it as being sterile and impersonal, much like a hotel room. I found myself wondering if Sandy would add any bright personal touches to give the place a little bit of flavor and kind of hoped she would.

Harris walked in and tossed his coat across the chair. He'd caught me in my reverie and began to tease, the kindly smiling eyes meeting mine. This time the slight tension, the hint of things unspoken, was absent and I found I felt a letdown, a sense of disappointment.

"Were you plotting out your next move or just

daydreaming, Katharine? I don't often see you sitting still."

"Well, truth be told, a little bit of both." I began to tap a rhythm on my desk.

"Getting started early on your drumming?" Harris joked. "I've got a friend who's a drummer in the Stockton PD band and he's always practicing the beat, no matter where he is. Drives you crazy sometimes if you're with him. Slaps his palms on the dashboard of the car, the countertop when you're eating lunch, even on his own thighs when nothing else will do."

"Is that really true?" I asked in wonderment.

"Sure, that's what drummers do. They're always practicing the beat."

I'd thought till now that the only practice would take place on a drum itself with a set of sticks, but suddenly I saw the sense of keeping time with just your hands whenever you had the chance and it appealed to me enormously.

"Oh, that frees you up a lot, makes it all a lot more flexible," I said joyfully, eager for the whole experience. "But tell me, what does your friend do during stakeouts? Thump then, too?"

"No," Harris answered seriously, "I believe he cuts it out at times like that."

"Do you play an instrument, Bobby?" I asked him, gathering up my hair, then letting it fall down and running my fingers through it absentmindedly. I found I wanted to know much more about him.

"Not really, I always thought I'd like to try the saxophone, but I haven't gotten around to it. Sailing's my thing, my great escape. To get out on the water with just yourself and the sound of the wind rushing by. Well, there's nothing like it to soothe the soul."

He'd been standing but now he eased his body onto the outside corner of my desk, his right leg on the floor, his left leg swinging free. I felt a sudden heat sweep through me. I was keenly aware of his closeness. "Tell me, Kate, how'd you get interested in drums, of all things? That's not usually the instrument of choice."

"Rock 'n' roll," I answered. "I love rock 'n' roll. Its soul and its vitality. Jackie Wilson, Ben E. King, the Stones, the whole Motown sound. And I love the drums because they're the timekeepers. They set the foundation for the whole band to play on and that appeals to me.

"Besides," I went on, now getting really enthusiastic about it, "it's challenging and fascinating to think of all of your appendages working at one time but doing different things. The right foot on the bass, the left one on the high hat, the right hand on the cymbals and the other on the snare."

In my mind's eye, I saw myself playing like Charlie Watts, the drummer for the Rolling Stones, and lost in my fantasy, I slid forward to my chair edge in high excitement. I looked up to find Harris watching quietly, an amused smile showing on his face, and realizing my own face was flushed and my eyes sparkling, I withdrew into quick embarrassment.

"No, no," he protested, "don't feel awkward about it. I think it's wonderful when someone holds such passion for something and dares to give it a try."

I relaxed, my discomfort quickly fading, and swinging back to business, pointed to the address book.

"This has all been checked out, with negative results, except for one set of initials that I'm going to work on tonight. What about tomorrow for the visit to the Masters family in San Francisco? Would you be free to ride up there with me then?"

I spoke briskly but my heart waited for his answer. Stop it, you silly girl, I chided myself. You don't want any of this, remember?

"Sure thing," he said, "and if there's enough time on the way back we can head up to Stockton so I can show you where Meryl's body was discovered."

"I'd like that, Bobby," I said approvingly. "It always seems to help me if I can get the total picture, see where everything took place. I like to be able later on to sit and visualize it all as I'm wondering were to go next."

I shoved the address book into my purse, grabbed my coat, and said good-bye. I was dying to do a little legwork on the area down San Luis Road so I decided I'd ride on out there now and look for familiar names on mailboxes. If none turned up, I'd go on home and try to contact B.S. later.

The day was winter clear, the mountains standing large and firm in sharp relief against the sky. At this time of year, their crevices assumed a darker look— deep purple, almost black—than lent them by the paler shades of summer.

Wide fields lay on either hand beside the road, close-cropped and barren for the most part except for random patches of cold-weather crops showing rich and radiant green. Here and there a dried-up tumbleweed pressed against a split-rail fence or nestled near a gateway.

Driving slowly, I checked the mailbox name at the end of each long driveway leading from a far-off farmhouse to this lonely two-lane road. None sounded the least bit familiar in relation to this case.

In the distance, to the right, I saw a long and towering stand of eucalyptus and knew they flanked both sides of Burnt Creek Road. According to the Marne girl, she'd never seen Masters driving past that point, but suppose Meryl had turned up Burnt Creek itself because her destination lay out there? I decided to explore a little father and swung the car hard right.

Here, the houses sat closer to the road. Instead of large wide spreads, these people seemed to farm much smaller plots, probably just an acre or so. I'd guess they were probably tenants or workers who resided in outbuildings on the sprawling acreage of a landlord living up another of those long straight drives.

Here again I saw no boxes with familiar names, and after several miles of searching I turned back. I'd hoped for something, sure, but I'd known all along it was a long shot. Well, I'd just follow my original plan and call B.S. tonight.

And find out what? I wondered. That the person didn't even live out this way or, if he did, was just another casual friend who could tell me nothing?

But why those two initials and what was it they meant? I couldn't get away from those nagging questions and I had to know the answers. Until I did, that entry in that little leather book would eat at me and bother me like some stone left unturned

I turned my head and watched the fields slip by, brown and green and gold and shadowed by the sun moving slowly to the west. Soon I saw the city lights and, driving toward them, left the countryside behind.

I pulled into my drive and cut the motor, suddenly tired and craving peace and quiet and comfort. I smiled, looking forward to these pleasures, but first I'd give B.S. another ring.

CHAPTER FOURTEEN

We got an early start, heading north on 99 while the sun still lay behind the eastern mountains. Swirls of pink preceding it announced that it was coming, and after we'd been riding only half an hour, we saw it like some brilliant golden coin rising up from the horizon.

"He never answered," I told Harris, sipping on the coffee we'd picked up at the convenience store, "I was listening to the darn machine again. Maybe he was late getting home from work, maybe he's gone out of town. At any rate I'll try again when I return. Right now, I'm looking forward to seeing what we dig up in San Francisco."

The steam from the contents of the foam containers caused the inside of the windshield to mist up. I reached to wipe it off, then hunkered down in my seat, drawing my coat cozily around me and holding the coffee close to my chin so that its steam would settle on my face instead.

We'd decided Bobby would drive up and I'd drive back, so I had nothing to do now but watch the scenery and have a little chat.

"You and Charlie go back a long way, don't you?" I asked by way of making conversation.

"Sure do, but how do you know that?"

"You said earlier you were both from Stockton and you seem easy in each other's company. Sort of fit like hand and glove, as if you've not only worked together for a while but understand and like each other, too."

Harris laughed. I loved the sound. Low and throaty with an unconscious sexiness woven through its chords.

"If you ever leave police work, Katharine Harrod, you can go into psychology. You've hit it right on the mark."

I laughed along with him. "What do you mean, 'go into,' Bobby? Don't you know that's what we cops already are or better be? Psychologist of the first order?"

The road ran straight before us and the early-morning traffic was minimal. Harris settled back and draped one arm across the steering wheel while controlling it with the other. He seemed perfectly at ease with me, but like a brother with a sister, and I felt a disappointment. I found I wanted more.

"Let me tell you something about Charlie Rhoads," he said companionably, as if he were looking for-

ward to talking about his partner. "He's the best
friend a guy could ever have. Charlie and I grew up
together, went through school together, into the service together. He was always there for me when I
needed him—always, without exception. You couldn't
ask for a truer friend than that."

I listened to his impassioned words and decided
to make my confession.

"You know, I was prepared to dislike Charlie
when I first saw him. You've not been around us
enough to know this yet, but Steve Darrow and I
aren't on the best of terms. It doesn't affect our working relations, and in many ways, he's a good detective, but personally he rubs me the wrong way.
When Charlie walked into the room, I saw Darrow
all over again—big, blustery, smart-assed, and smart-
mouthed—but I was wrong."

"What do you think of Charlie now?" Harris
asked, peering at me intently as if my opinion really
mattered to him.

"I think he's a big puppy dog." I grinned. "He's
got a way about him that makes you can't help but
like."

"I'm glad," Harris answered. "There's the physical
resemblance, sure—that can't be denied—but if
Steve's the way you say he is, then Charlie's certainly
not like that."

He paused, reading a road sign advertising a restaurant twenty miles or so ahead. If I read his

thoughts correctly, he, like me, was thinking about some breakfast.

"Charlie's a hearty fellow, much more outgoing than me," he continued, "but he's got a depth and seriousness to him that lie just beneath the surface. Sometimes, in fact, I think he takes things a bit *too* seriously, is too prone to dwell on them till they adversely affect him."

I instantly recalled that strange look of pain I'd seen flash through Charlie's eyes and felt I knew what Harris was talking about. I'd known people like that, including my own husband. People who internalized their problems and let them tear them down.

"What about his personal life?" I asked, suddenly very curious about the man. "Is he married? Was he ever?"

"Ah, there's another story," Harris answered with a smile. "He's married, that's for sure, and to my high school sweetheart. But don't worry," he added hastily, "it caused no problem between us. Jane and I had broken up long before Charlie started dating her. I still care deeply for her but only as a friend. A sister, really. And I wish the very best for her."

As the last words rolled from his mouth, I saw Bobby's eyes reflect a momentary bleakness and I wondered what it meant.

None of your business, really, I counseled quietly to myself. Don't even ask. But I couldn't help the pang of jealousy I felt.

I turned, looking out the window and watching gas stations and convenience stores pass by. Route 99. The road we theorized Meryl Masters's body was transported on, the road that so far had yielded no clues.

Rhoads and Darrow had called in late yesterday to say they hadn't found a single soul who'd noticed anything suspicious last Friday night. They'd posted flyers at the various service centers asking for information vital to the case, so we still might get a hit, but as of now, ground zero. The Highway Patrol, for their part, also reported nothing unusual occurring on any of their watches that evening.

"If only this road could talk," I said to Bobby. "She came along here, I know she did, right along these spots we're passing over. It's agonizing to think we can't re-create the scene and get our answers."

"I know the frustration, Kate," he answered, "I feel it, too. I was at the spot where her body was finally dumped and I can't re-create *that* scene, much as I can taste my wish to do so."

We turned off 99, heading west, and before long a restaurant built in handsome Spanish style appeared before us.

"How about it, pardner?" Harris said. "Are you ready for some breakfast?" And he turned to me and our eyes quickly locked, serious, questioning, exploring. I saw a muscle tighten in his cheek and I felt my own face begin to flush.

"Sure thing," I answered quickly, stumbling to break the moment. "I think I could eat the whole enchilada."

The house sat on a tall bluff overlooking the Pacific, just west of the city itself. Large and square and made of granite, it projected an aura of austere grandeur. A long drive, flanked by rows of ficus trees trimmed like big round balls, led to the massive front door.

"I think I'd prefer a cozy little cottage myself," I said to Harris. "I doubt I could make myself at home in here."

We stepped out of the car and heard the cold ocean waves slapping hard against the rocks. In the distance, far out on the horizon, I saw a freighter or a tanker making its way farther north.

We walked into a high-domed portico and rang the bell. Long moments passed before a stiff-backed, bland-faced butler answered and with clear, precise words told us the Masterses were expecting us.

We followed him and he led us into a surprisingly cheery drawing room, where muted lights glowed on richly patined wood and a crackling fire burned brightly in the fireplace.

A man and woman, probably in their sixties, rose to meet us. He wore well-tailored slacks, a shirt with lightweight vest, a dark blue coat that set off his tan and the whiteness of his hair. His agility and compact frame spoke of a body encompassing a strength uncommon to its age.

She, as svelte as he was trim, was dressed in pleated skirt and matching sweater set with a strand of pearls encircling her neck. Her hair, carefully styled and falling close around her face, framed fierce eyes that fixed on me and never wavered. She held a teacup poodle in her arms and lightly stroked its fur.

The two of them together—their dress, their style, their carriage—spoke of old money, breeding, and conservatism.

Bobby led the way.

"Mr. and Mrs. Masters? I'm Detective Harris—we met when you came up to Stockton—and this is Detective Katharine Harrod of San Madera Homicide in the city where your daughter resided."

We shook hands all around and Masters asked me if a pipe would bother me. I said no and he lighted up, puffing quickly at first to get it going.

"My condolences about your daughter," I told the two of them. "May we sit down? We've got some questions we'd like to ask you about Meryl."

Mrs. Masters waved us to two seats close to the blazing fire and they settled themselves on an opposite sofa.

"What kind of person was she?" I began. "I know she was your daughter and you must have loved her dearly, but how did you see her as a person, if you can separate the two?"

"As a willful, spiteful girl who delighted in tormenting us and turning our lives upside-down," the woman answered quickly. "That was what Meryl was!"

"Now, DeeDee," her husband interjected, "you can't keep on like that, not now. Meryl may have been difficult but she's no longer with us, so let's remember the better times."

"No, Harold," Mrs. Masters protested, her fierce eyes filled with fire. "I will not pretend Meryl was other than she was—these people want to know and I shall tell them."

"What exactly did she do to upset you?" Harris asked.

"Everything. If you wanted her to go one way, she would purposely go the other. Pure, unadulterated contrariness just to devil us. And she reveled in it. It seemed to delight her to cause an upset, to humiliate and distress us."

DeeDee Masters stroked her pearls.

"That silly job, for instance. That demeaning dirty job dealing with all those filthy people. People the likes of which Meryl had never been raised around.

"First of all, she didn't *have* to work. She had her grandfather's money, the allowance he left her. She could've been a member of the League and lived the sort of life she was cut out for, but no, she had to go and take some welfare type of work to bring us all shame."

"Perhaps Meryl worked because she loved her job," I suggested, astounded at the vehemence I was hearing. "Many consider that type of work extremely worthy of respect and I understand she was very good at what she did."

"Don't you kid yourself," the mother continued. "Meryl did that work because she knew it annoyed us. It was her little game, playing with us, pushing something disagreeable into our face. 'What's your son doing now? Is your daughter settled yet?' These are the kinds of questions people ask and most parents can give such lovely answers. But not us. We either kept quiet or had to make excuses, like it was just some phase she was going through."

"But why, if what you say is true, would Meryl want to upset you? Did she hold some sort of grudge against you, and if so, for what?"

Harold Masters laid his hand on his wife's knee and leaned forward.

"No grudge that I know of, Detective. It was just that Meryl was always an obstinate child. My wife's right. It really did seem she got some sort of perverse pleasure out of rocking the boat and she'd do so, then laugh at us when she saw our upset. She had this notion, too, that the family was too conservative, too bound in silly tradition, and she liked to flaunt her contempt, thumb her nose at it."

"Oh, we loved our daughter, don't misunderstand." Mrs. Masters hurried to set the record straight. "After all, one does love one's child, doesn't one? It's just that there wasn't too much in common."

She kissed the little poodle on its head, then murmured something to it in the dotty tone some people use with infants.

"Does that explain why you weren't certain whether or not Meryl had had a child? I understand when Detective Harris met with you in Stockton you were ambiguous on the subject."

"Oh, of *course* we knew she'd never had a baby!" DeeDee Masters waved her hand through the air, scoffing at the idea. "Even for Meryl, that would've been going a bit too far. No, that was just to indicate anything was possible with Meryl because she was so secretive and left us so much out of her life. After she reached twenty-one, we knew very little about her, except what she wanted us to know. Like about that wretched job!"

"So you wouldn't be able to tell us about any male friends?" I ventured. "Especially those she was serious with?"

Masters chuckled, smoothing his white hair back with the flat of his hand.

"Absolutely not, Detective. Meryl would never let us get a look at any of her fellas. Not that I'm sure we'd have wanted to, I can tell you."

"Then you wouldn't know who Jack is, or a friend with the initials B.S.?"

The parents looked at each other, eyebrows arched,

and shrugged their shoulders. The poodle began to struggle and Mrs. Masters set the dog upon the floor.

"Jack, B.S.? That means nothing to us."

I glanced around the room, noting the gleaming cut glass and the texture of the Persian rugs lying on the wide-board floor. What must it have been like to have grown up in such a house, I wondered, among such riches? I could only imagine, for neither I nor my friends came from a similar background.

I reflected on the estrangements between Wanda, Meryl, and their respective set of parents. In both cases, but for different reasons, the mothers and fathers had cut their children off. Wanda's because she wouldn't adhere to their narrow religious discipline, Meryl's because she was a renegade who wouldn't toe their upper-crust social lines.

Had this, perhaps, been why these two women were drawn together to form such an unlikely friendship? Because their backgrounds shared the common denominator of being cast out by their parents?

So much lost for so very little, I thought sadly. Precious relationships destroyed because of rigid, unbending beliefs. The chance to know a child and watch her grow to adulthood and well beyond tossed aside for petty differences because the parents would not let go, refused to relinquish control and take joy in whatever path their children chose to follow.

I thought of my own parents, killed in an accident when I was just fourteen, and how they'd never had that chance to see me grow, to watch me make mistakes and then finally find myself, to know their only grandchild, Tommy. And how they'd never have squandered the time we would've had together if they'd only had the chance.

But was I wrong? Might they have been the same as Meryl's and Wanda's parents once I'd tried to spread my wings, and judge me by a certain set of standards, then find me wanting?

No, I assured myself with confidence, for I remembered them well enough, recalled the kindness of their ways, to know that they'd have loved me unconditionally throughout their days.

And there was the waste, I told myself bitterly. That these parents of Meryl and Wanda had been alive to have the chance for a relationship and then had chosen to throw it away.

"Your daughter's effects will be turned over to you," Harris was saying. "When going through them, please alert us to anything you find that might be of help to us."

Mrs. Masters frowned, as if in displeasure, and drew herself up extremely straight. Her eagle eyes fixed on some point beyond Bobby. Again she picked up the dog and began fussing with its fur.

"To tell you the truth, Detective, I'm not sure when we'll pick those things up. Or whether I *will* go through them. Quite frankly, they don't interest me all that much."

Harris and I exchanged glances, then we both looked down at our shoes. I had only one question left.

"Is there anyone else in San Francisco who could possibly give us information about your daughter?" I asked.

In unison, the Masterses shook their heads.

"If there is, it wouldn't be anyone *we'd* know," the mother responded. "Meryl would pop in about twice a year for family gatherings—probably because they gave her a chance to put on her little act and get things stirred up again—and then she'd return to her own world apart from the rest of us."

We rose and Mr. Masters indicated he'd see us to the door.

"Why would a girl cause such disruption in a family?" he asked in obvious bewilderment. "Look at all this"—he waved his hand toward the paneled wood, the long and winding staircase, the massive crystal chandelier—"this was the world she came from, the world she could've had, but she willfully estranged herself from it. Oh, she'd have gotten the money one day, if she'd behaved herself, but she could've enjoyed all this now. I just don't fathom it."

My head jerked up and I focused on Masters.

"Am I to understand you cut Meryl out of your will?"

"Oh, no, Detective, she was still the primary beneficiary. We had a son who died several years ago in a boating accident and that left Meryl as our only child. No, I meant if she didn't do anything worse in coming years than that idiotic job—anything besides that that would further disgrace the family— we'd have left it to her. If our daughter had swung out too far, naturally we'd have disinherited her. And why not? The choice, after all, would've been hers."

He turned to us and peered into our faces.

"You're smart people, Detectives. Can *you* tell me why Meryl would've acted the way she did?"

"Why?" I repeated. "I don't know why a person would do that, Mr. Masters. Some would say because they're crying out for something that's missing in their life, for a type of attention they never felt they could get. Only you and your wife and Meryl would know if that's the truth here."

The bland-faced butler opened up the door and Bobby and I stepped out and got into our car.

"Let's get going," I said hurriedly, "to a place where there's heart and soul and a bit of warmth for other than a dog."

"Don't you think it's odd they never asked?" I looked across at Bobby while the waitress set down my sandwich.

"You mean 'whodunit'? Exactly right."

We'd stopped for lunch at a coffee shop not far from the cliff house, fueling up for the drive to Stockton and the longer drive back home. The electric moments that had sparked between us earlier had now been pushed underground and we were just two cops discussing business. But I knew that they had happened. And that the spark had not emanated just from me.

"No probing at all, no questions like did we have any clues—the sort of questions other victims' parents always ask. Just the old sad song about how Meryl had done them wrong." I skinned off a piece of crust from my sandwich and ate it by itself.

"Well, they aren't exactly grieving, at least not in the conventional sense," Harris offered. "And it may be they're not grieving at all. It's more like she was one of their possessions rather than a real-flesh child."

"Did you notice his build?" I asked. "He's in great shape for his age. Suppose he went to visit Meryl, maybe to try to talk some sense into her, and he stumbled in on her and the child and thought, despite what his wife said, that she'd had a baby of her own. And then he went crazy and killed the two of them. Out of rage and to save his own precious name."

"You're forgetting, Kate. The wife's the one who's so passionate about all of this. Mr. Masters is low-key."

"Out front, you're right, but obviously they're in tune with their appraisal of, and their feelings toward, their daughter. It's possible there's a fire within him that he doesn't show, but pushed to it, he'd take care of business if he had to. And I think physically, he's well equipped to do so."

Harris pushed his chicken salad around his plate. That's funny, I thought. I have it in a sandwich, he has it on a dish, but we both like it, whatever way it comes.

"It's possible, of course it's possible. How many cases have you and I both handled where a person kills to protect their position and their precious name?"

I thought of one at least, but I didn't answer, just raised my brows and nodded up and down.

We finished up, paid the check, and got back into the car. The bridge across the bay hung sweetly to our left, a fragile magic necklace between the city and the northern land. I viewed the tall, straight buildings, the vast expanse of water with the mist collecting in small clouds upon it, the green and rolling hills that stretched beyond.

"Look, Bobby," I said, "just look at that." And both of us, even though we'd seen it many times before, slowed the car and gazed like we were tourists.

"And they wonder why we live here," he said. "They wonder why we live here after quakes and fires and floods. We live here, not just because it's a place of beauty, but because it holds out the promise and nourishes the soul. I wake up every morning believing anything is possible, anything I want to do *can* be done. It's a tough state to leave, Katharine. How can you easily leave a place that makes you feel like that?"

"You see it that way, too?" I asked, smiling broadly. "I've never understood why anyone would want to live in any other spot on earth."

The city rolled away behind us and we headed east, then north, for the ninety-minute drive to Stockton. "Would you mind dropping by the station?" Harris asked. "I've kept in touch by phone but I'd like to physically sort out what's lying on my desk."

"Not at all," I told him. "Besides, I'm curious to see where you hang out. How are they doing without you, by the way?"

"Luckily nothing big has broken," he replied, "but even if it had, we'd be covered. We've got a bunch of good investigators working under us—eager beavers building up experience who can handle most anything that comes along."

We reached the city limits and I glanced around with interest. It was a long time since I'd been to Stockton and I saw a trim little metropolis, probably about twice the size of San Madera, with neat frame houses standing in straight rows.

"Did you grow up near here?" I asked, turning to Bobby. "You and your friend Charlie?"

"No," he answered, "on the other side of town.

My home's no longer standing. Charlie's is still there but gotten all run-down. Changing neighborhoods, same as any other place."

We pulled into a parking lot nearly identical to ours down south, and the two of us strode into the brick one-story building. It was early afternoon and most of the desks in the detective squad room were empty, their occupants out in the field.

Harris stopped beside a broad dark one and started thumbing through the papers lying on it. Peering at them from behind his shoulder, I saw they were the usual batch of preliminary investigation reports, follow-up investigations, and dispositions from the courts.

My eyes began to wander across the rest of the desktop. No photos, no personal touches of any kind, just more orderly stacks of books and papers. Nothing to give me a clue to the private life this man had.

"Okay, Katharine," he said, "just let me have a look at Charlie's pile and we'll be on our way."

We walked to the adjoining desk, a total contrast to Bobby's neat one. It looked as if everything upon it had been dumped there from an upturned basket, then never sorted out. Sticking up and peeking through the flurry of the papers was a family photo showing a sweet-faced blond-haired woman and two little girls.

I was bending forward to get a better look when I heard Bobby give a whistle. Jerking up my head, I saw him check his watch while holding a scratch pad sheet between his fingers.

" 'Hear you're lookin' for me, man. Well, fuck off,' " he began to read aloud. " 'There's nuthin' we have to talk about, you and me. You're not gonna pull your shit with me again.'

"One guess as to who this little love note is from," Harris said, handing it to me. "A message loud and clear from Sonny boy himself. It came in about a quarter hour ago so I doubt it's been passed on to Charlie yet. Damn, where's Helen?"

He swung his head back and forth around the room and finally spied a portly black-haired woman come through a door and settle herself heavily behind a secretary's desk.

"Helen," he called out, "I just stopped by to check on things and found this note on Charlie's desk. Are you the one who took it?"

"From Mr. Foulmouth? Oh, yes," she said, drawing back in mock disgust. "I wanted to wash my mouth and my ears out with soap."

"Did he identify himself or say where he was calling from?"

"No. Told me Rhoads would know who he was and to take down exactly what he said, as he said it. And he wouldn't give me his whereabouts, although I asked him. I'm pretty sure it wasn't long distance, though, but these days you can't really tell."

"Any background noise, anything distinctive?"

"No, Detective." The heavy woman took a deep breath, causing her chest to heave slowly up, then down. "No other sound than his lovely voice."

"It's time to ring up Charlie," I said, reaching for the phone. "I know he feels stymied because he hasn't tracked down Sonny yet. He expected to have him located by this time."

Darrow answered, then handed the receiver to Rhoads.

"Son of a bitch," he growled when he heard the news, "I'll take care of him. No, I haven't gotten a definite make on him yet but I know he's up in Lodi. That's why he's calling me, don't you see?—because the slime I got in touch with there told him I was looking for him."

"What do you want to do, Charlie?" I asked. "Come on up north and try to rout him out?"

"Give me a day or two more working from this end. There's a lot down here I need to stay on top of, and besides, I have a hunch there's going to be a phone call I can make this weekend that'll let me know exactly where the bastard is."

We hung up and left the building, on our way to the lonely crime scene in the woods.

"There's not much love lost between those two, is there?" I commented as we climbed into the car.

"You got that right," Harris agreed. "Charlie's really got a bee in his bonnet about Mitchell and it sounds like Sonny remembers him awfully well."

"You weren't working here when he busted him before," I stated. "Does he talk about it very much?"

"Nope, never heard him mention Sonny Mitchell before that poor baby died."

The houses started thinning, becoming farther apart as we left the heart of town and once again drew near the outskirts. I felt tense, on edge, anticipatory but in a taut way about finally viewing the spot where the Masters woman had lain stripped and dead. Harris pulled up beside a vacant lot and motioned to the brush and pines.

"Let's go."

I walked across the barren ground, glancing left and right. I saw the houses closest to this open space and recalled that while one occupant had seen some car lights, none could offer any sort of vehicle description.

We reached the end of the short spare grass and Bobby reached forward and began to part the brush.

"Right there," he said, and I stared down at a patch of twigs and fallen leaves that looked little different from any other.

I felt a chill go down my spine as I looked slowly all around—at the spot itself, the empty lot, the tall still trees, the thick unruly brush that once had held her. I pictured the darkness of that Friday night at midnight and my mind's eyes saw a stealthy figure carrying a dead woman across his shoulders, stuffing her in among some scrub, then beating a retreat to his waiting vehicle and slipping silently away.

"You might never have found her," I said, my eyes meeting Bobby's, "if it hadn't been for that eager dog. Or she could've lain here hidden for some months."

"Right," he answered, "because there was certainly nothing farther out on this lot to indicate foul play had taken place in here. In fact, the whole crime scene was one of the cleanest we'd ever come across."

"Just like the condo at Rimerton," I murmured. "Not a clue left anywhere behind."

We started walking quietly across the lot, returning to the car. I gave a final backward glance at the brush and tall thick pines.

"So this is where she lay alone for nearly three full days," I offered, "and that pair of twisted sisters down in San Francisco can't even ask if we've got any thought who did it."

I slid behind the wheel, Bobby got in on the other side, and we started driving back to San Madera.

"I saw that picture on Charlie's desk," I said. "Is that the woman you were talking about? The one who was your high school sweetheart?"

"That's her, that's Jane. And their two little girls. She's a wonderful person and a great wife and mother. I wish he could see that. See how lucky he is and appreciate what he's got."

Startled, I looked at him and saw his face held the same bleak look I'd seen on the drive north.

"How do you mean?" I asked quietly.

Harris bit his lower lip, as if deciding whether to go on.

"It bothers me, Kate," he said finally, "it bothers me a lot because I love that woman dearly and I love Charlie, too. But he's been seeing someone else— some other woman living out of town—off and on for some time now. I knew nothing about it till I moved up here, but then it became apparent. He'd disappear occasionally, and one day when I asked where it was he'd gone, he admitted he was having an affair."

"Is it serious," I asked, "or is he just playing around for fun?"

"I don't know," Bobby answered wearily. "We don't talk about it much because he knows I disapprove because of my love for Jane. I think he slacked off this woman for a while, but now he's back to her again. Just last night he told me he was going to see her for a couple of hours. I guess he *had* to bring it up with me in case you needed him in a hurry."

What a mess, I thought. I was sick of broken marriages. Of all the sorrow and duplicity, the sad and wounded hearts. Why couldn't life turn out to be a fairy tale more often than it did?

"Does his wife know?" I asked.

"I think she suspects but I doubt she's got proof. I'm certain she knows *something's* wrong, though, and it kills me to see the way she is sometimes. Remote, distracted, not the bubbly girl I used to know.

I've asked her if she'd like to talk but she shakes her head and says everything's okay.''

"Probably because her husband is your best friend," I pointed out, "and she doesn't want you upset in any way."

Harris shifted in his seat and cleared his throat several times, seeming uncomfortable. Finally he turned toward me, his expression slightly sheepish.

"Look, I didn't mean to talk like this, Kate. It's really Charlie's private business and I was out of line confiding in you. The thing's been on my mind and when you mentioned Jane, it just started spilling out."

"Don't worry about it," I assured him, "this won't go any further. You needed someone to talk to and I'm glad that I was here."

We changed the subject, chatting comfortably about the case, about the threat of tule fog, about mindless little bits of this and that.

As we neared the first bright city lights I realized I didn't want this ride to end, I wished it could go on forever.

But you don't, I cried, angry at myself. You know you really do not want involvement. Not now, maybe not ever. This is just a passing fancy, a momentary attraction that soon will go away. And I felt the conflict within me, pulling this way, pulling that.

CHAPTER FIFTEEN

I focused on the day ahead, determined to solve
the mystery of B.S. I'd dialed the number earlier
this morning and was rewarded with neither real
voice nor machine. It'd simply rung and rung till
finally I'd hung up.

And I focused on the nighttime, too, smiling as I
thought of the surprise in store for Tommy. He'd
looked at me at breakfast and informed me, "Mom,
it's Friday," and I'd known what he meant.

"It certainly is," I answered with a laughing voice,
"and you and I go on a special date right after
work."

"Where to?" he begged, pulling at my sleeve.
"C'mon and tell me."

"I won't reveal a thing, kiddo, except you're gonna
love it!"

Then I'd asked him something I'd been wondering
about, ever since the other day when he'd told me
Jon couldn't take him to the dinner.

"Tommy, what did you mean about your dad 'forgetting' you? He didn't 'forget' to take you out tonight. Something unexpected came up."

My son sat silent for a moment, his blond head bowed.

"I mean, sometimes when I'm at his house now he doesn't pay attention to me like he used to. It's not fun like it was at first. He does a lot of grown-up things and not things with me. He forgets me, like I'm not that important. Like he did about tonight."

I hugged him to me, verbally reassuring him, but what did I really know? What did I know about what went on when he went to visit Jon?

When I reached the station, I headed for the phone again. I waved hello to Darrow and the others but concentrated totally on lifting that receiver. Perhaps a little of my haste came from a desire to hide a slight embarrassment over my thoughts about Harris on the ride last night.

Of course he couldn't know what I'd been thinking but that didn't stop me from feeling that he did. You know how, if you dream about someone, you guiltily believe that person can somehow get inside your mind and find out all about it? Well, I felt like that. Exposed.

I glanced at Dan across the room and saw him raise his eyes in a faraway unfocused stare. He spoke occasionally with Rena on the phone but nothing had changed from the night she'd left. The impasse continued and, I knew, pulled at him and dragged him down.

"Damn it!" The explosion sounded off suddenly as Kent slammed his fist down on the desk. His normally even-tempered face was dark with anger and his eyes were now sharply focused.

Quickly I hung up the phone and rose and went to him.

"What's happened, Dan?"

"I missed the filing date on Cannon," he told me tightly, "and now they're gonna kick him loose."

Once a suspect's been arrested and booked, we've got a forty-eight-hour window in which to take the case to the DA to file charges. If we miss our deadline, the perpetrator walks.

"Who's Cannon and how did that happen?" I asked, stunned that Kent had let the window close. Sloppiness or negligence had never marked his work.

"He's a suspect in a holdup over on Alvarado several months ago, and I made the case the other day, picked him up in a bar he hangs out in, and had him cold. And then, I don't know"—he waved his hands helplessly—"the time went by and it just slipped my mind till now, when suddenly it hit me. Christ, Kate, I've never done anything like that before!"

I saw his anguished face as tears filled his eyes.

"It's Rena, isn't it?" I asked. "You're all messed up because she left you."

"Of course it's Rena," he answered despairingly.

"I miss her, I miss the child. I can't think of anything else. I can't concentrate on what I'm doing. It's just all a blur."

"Look," I said, alarm filling my voice, "you've got to pull yourself together. Missing a filing's bad enough but it pales against losing your concentration on the street. If you start to make a bust and lose your focus while it's going down, you're also going to lose your life. You're placing yourself in a very dangerous situation."

"I know, Kate, I know. But please don't worry. I don't want you to have to have me on your mind. Somehow I'm going to get it all together."

Sure you are, I thought grimly as I watched him, but can you do it before it's way too late?

I walked back to my desk and reached for the receiver, picking up where I'd left off before Dan's outburst.

Again the phone rang while I tapped my foot quickly, not really expecting an answer. Suddenly I heard a clatter as it was jerked off of its cradle and a male voice gave a tentative hello.

"Hello," I responded, and identified myself. "I believe you were a friend of Meryl Masters."

The line went quiet, except for the sound of faint breathing.

"Hello?" I ventured.

"I don't know anyone by that name," the voice finally answered. "You must be mistaken."

"Are your initials B.S.? Your number's in her phone book. Why would it be there if she didn't know you?"

"My initials aren't B.S. and I don't know anyone with those initials either. Just don't bother me."

"Wait a minute," I implored, "please tell me your name so we can get this sorted out. A woman's dead and we're trying to piece her life together. I feel you could be of help to us if you'll just let me have a few minutes of your time."

"No," the voice told me, faltering and starting to become high-pitched, "I didn't know her."

"Do you live near Burnt . . ." I began but then I heard the phone slam down. I hung up and dialed again but no one answered, not even the machine.

"Who's free?" I called. "I want to take Meryl's photo and the color picture of her car out to San Luis Road."

Rhoads started toward me, then dropped back and waved his hand.

"I can help you out in an hour or so, but I'm waiting for a tip right now."

Darrow grabbed his coat and gun.

"Let's go, Katie baby. I'll help you do your door-knocking."

Planning as we drove, we decided we'd stop first at the houses closest to the road, which meant those built on Burnt Creek itself. The chance of anyone from the homes at the ends of those long driveways having seen Meryl Masters or her car seemed remote to me, unless she'd passed by as they collected letters from the mailbox.

"How're you doing on your own, babe?" Darrow asked suddenly, his mouth curving into a smirk. "Need a visit from the man?"

He rarely got personal with me, knowing it would lead him nowhere, but every once in a while he simply couldn't resist.

"Doing fine, Steve," I answered airily, quelling the spirited reaction he desired. "As a matter of fact, I find I don't need visits from any one of you."

"Oh, Miss Independence, well excuuuse me! But better keep my number handy just in case you change your mind."

"It's handy," I told him, "but the only time I'll be calling is when we've got a body. Besides, you know I'm really not your type. I can count at least to ten and even tie my shoes."

We parked in the first driveway after we'd made the right turn off San Luis and walked together to a frame one-story house. A spotted dog, tethered by a rope to a wooden porch post, lolled lazily in the sun, not even bothering to bark at our approach.

We knocked loudly and a few seconds later the front door opened and a bespectacled woman with stringy unkempt hair stared at us and asked us what we wanted. Wary and suspicious, she requested our IDs before we could even offer to pull them out.

"We've got a picture of a woman and a car," I told her, when she'd finally relaxed and invited us inside. "We'd like to know if you've ever seen either in the area."

She took the photos, one in either hand, and looked at them for just a moment. Then, catching Steve and me off-guard, she stated matter-of-factly she'd seen that car many times, parked near the third house down the road.

"Sporty little thing," the woman told us. "Can't help but notice it go by. Sticks out among the pickups and the Jeeps."

"Who lives there?" I asked, still astounded at the way our luck had run. I'd expected several hours of knocking, possibly with no good results.

"Don't know," she answered, "it's a rental. Actually, where that car usually parks is by a little garage apartment in the rear."

We thanked her and she smoothed her wandering hair behind her ear and led us to the door. She showed no curiosity about our questions, just bent to pat the dog, then said good-bye.

Steve and I stood and looked at each other for a second. I could feel my eyes twinkle as I told him, "Let's go see who lives there." I was more than ready for an encounter with Mr. B.S.

We walked down the road, beneath the tall broad canopy of eucalyptus, turned in at the third drive-way, and continued to a little flight of stairs leading to a door above a two-car garage. I'd checked out the mailbox as we'd passed. No name, only a number.

"He may not be home," Darrow pointed out. "If he's a workingman, this is the wrong time to catch him."

"But he was home earlier this morning," I protested. "Maybe he's got a cold today."

We climbed the steps and I rapped sharply on the door. I could swear I heard shuffling behind it but it didn't open. I rapped again, even harder, and this time a thin nervous voice asked who it was.

"San Madera Homicide," I answered. "We'd like to speak with you a moment."

I listened carefully and thought I heard a groan, and then the door swung slowly open and I saw him standing there, the lanky red-haired youth from county social services.

"You!" I said, unable to contain my surprise. "What are *you* doing here?" I could feel Darrow staring at me, wondering where I'd lost my command presence.

"I live here," the youth answered, his head hanging down, his feet shifting in monotonous rhythm.

"I know your name is Steven Brownfeld," I told him, "but are you also B.S.?"

He nodded his head miserably.

"May we come in, kid?" Darrow pushed his way past him into the small apartment. "I think we need to get some things straightened out."

I followed him and glanced around me. The place was furnished with a mishmash of Salvation Army and Goodwill and was none too neat. Several cheap reproductions hung crookedly upon the walls and a framed photograph of Meryl Masters stood on a table.

"You didn't know her well," I murmured, "or so you told us."

Steven Brownfeld collapsed into a chair, his shaking hand stroking his forehead. Once again, as in the office, sweat began to form along his brow.

"What was your relationship to Meryl?" I asked, wondering whether his answer would be anywhere close to the truth.

"I was her cousin," the boy wailed, raking his fingertips on the covering of the chair, "her third cousin!"

Whatever I'd expected to hear, it certainly wasn't this.

"But why the secrecy? Why all the effort to avoid us?"

"Because no one at the office knew who I was—she wanted it that way. See, she and I have always hit it off, even though I was a good bit younger than her. We were both oddballs in the family and so we gravitated toward each other. When I lost my job, she felt sorry for me and she told me she'd get me a little position down here but we'd have to keep it quiet."

"And why was that?"

"Because she was scared the family might find out and that'd never do. They'd skin her alive."

"I don't understand," I said, puzzled. "Meryl worked at social services herself. Why would they be mad if you did, too?"

I glanced at Darrow, sitting quiet and listening. He'd figured out I knew a whole lot more here than he did and was content to let me carry the ball. No hot-shotting or stealing the lead today.

"Because that would've been pushing it too far and she couldn't risk that," Brownfeld answered. "It was bad enough that *she* worked there but if it became known she'd brought in one more family member, that would've tipped the seesaw. See, Meryl liked to push things to the limit but not go one bit further."

"Why was she so careful not to cross the line?" I asked him as I got up and walked across the room. I stopped by Masters's picture and picked it up, studying it. "What would've happened if the limit had been broken?"

"She'd have lost her inheritance," the boy explained, "and she wasn't going to take any chances on that. Meryl was a renegade but she'd never go so far as to lose her comfort. She liked to stir things up but she'd never, ever risk that."

The game player, I thought, walking back to my chair with the photo, always the game player.

"What about the B.S.? What does that stand for?"

"Just my initials gone backward," he responded, "just another of Meryl's little jokes. She always teased me about how backward they stood for bullshit, so she called me B.S."

"Even in her address book?" I asked incredulously. "Even there where no one could see?"

"I guess so," Brownfeld answered. "Meryl just being secretive again. It gave her some sort of kick to do things like that. I think it even gave her a kick just to know I was working at social services, even if she couldn't risk teasing the family with that."

"But why, after her death, didn't you come forward? Why hide your relationship with her then?" Darrow, having sorted out the situation, leaned forward, asking the question.

"Oh, well . . . it would've just been too embarrassing," the boy explained plaintively. I thought he was going to cry. "I was caught in a lie and I just thought it easier to keep my mouth shut about it."

"So," I began, "now that we've got this tangle worked out, maybe you can be of some use to us after all. Do you know if Masters was seeing anyone, especially someone from out of town?"

Brownfeld shook his head quickly.

"Meryl would never have told me anything about that. She'd never have shared that sort of thing with me."

I should've known better than to expect a good

answer. The boy was right. Miss Secrets would've kept that all to herself.

I held little hope for the next question either, but regardless, I had to ask.

"What about Jack? Do you know any Jack she might've known? Pudgy, swarthy, beaklike nose?"

"Oh, God." Brownfeld nearly doubled over with laughter. Concerned, I thought his nervousness had led him to a fit. "Your description, it's so perfect," he cried, then started choking. "That's exactly what he's like! That's Jack Benson, Meryl's first cousin. Her mother's sister's child."

I frowned, recalling a recent denial.

"Why didn't Meryl's parents give me that answer when I asked them about him?"

"Because they didn't know who you were talking about. DeeDee and Harold and all the older family members use only 'John.' "

At last I was on the right path, I exalted. A confused, mixed-up mess was turning into one that fed me much-needed information.

"How did the two of them get along, he and Meryl? Like sweet kissing cousins?"

"Oh, hardly," Brownfeld chortled, "they couldn't stand each other. See, if anything had happened to Meryl . . ." He paused, realizing what he'd just said, "Or if she'd fallen into disfavor, Jack would've been the one to inherit.

"He was always lurking about—she told me that

much because she thought it hilarious—trying to catch her out in a bad situation, trying to get the goods on her so he could expose and discredit her to DeeDee and Harold. But she was too clever for him and it just never happened."

I thought of manipulative Meryl, of the two twisted sisters by the sea, of skulking devilish Jack, and I slowly shook my head. What a family of misfits!

"I've got to ask you, Steven. Where were you last Friday night—the night your cousin was killed?"

"I was right next door," he answered immediately, motioning toward the house at the front of the lot. "They had me in for dinner and to watch TV all evening. They're home now, want to ask them?"

"No"—I held up my hand—"it won't be necessary."

He glanced at the photo of Meryl, which I still held in my hands.

"She was special," he said, in obvious adoration. "So gorgeous, so self-assured, so very self-possessed. She was always on the outside—on purpose, I know—and I was there, too, though *I* didn't mean to be. I think I amused her and she pitied me, though in a kindly sort of way."

Brownfeld didn't seem the least bit dismayed by his unflattering appraisal of their relationship.

"Were you very much in love with her?" I asked.

Startled, he stared at me and started blushing.

"She was wonderful," he moaned, and tears began to fill his eyes. "No one could ever hold a candle to her, not even come close. Please find out who did this to her. Find it out for her . . . and for me."

The flash of red and chrome danced before his eyes, big and bright and spanking new, shining from the showcase window.

I'd covered Tommy's face as we approached the store and then, when we stood precisely in front of it, I took my hand away and let him see the glory of it all.

"Drums!" he cried, his eyes popping wide, his mouth falling open. "Oh, Mom, they're beautiful!"

He stepped forward and touched the plate glass with his hand, as if he wished to burst right through it and reach that gleaming set. It reminded me of him on Christmas morning, when he'd run into the room, then stand and stare in awe at the tree and all the presents.

"Can we go inside, Mom? Please?"

"You betcha," I answered. "This is the surprise. This is what we're going to do. We're going to see about buying a drum set."

"The whole set? For our very own? Wow!"

"Yes," I told him, "and I've already lined up somewhere to take lessons."

The pleasure apparent on Tommy's face let me know my "something a-okay" for Friday night had fulfilled his greatest expectations. And looking at all those handsome drums around me, I was excited as a little kid myself. How to know what to get, I thought, how to know which one to choose.

I watched as several other patrons strode up to drums and started testing them with confidence, playing fast staccato with their sticks. It certainly seemed *they* knew what they were doing. A salesman approached, offering his help, and I felt here was my salvation.

"We're beginning drummers," I began, "my son and myself. Actually, we haven't started taking lessons yet but we will soon. We'd like to get some drums but don't know what we need."

"You'll need the basic kit, ma'am, and I would recommend a medium quality, not top of the line. There's time for that later. Also wood, choose wood over metal. Makes all the difference in the sound. Richer, more resonance."

"I'm lost," I told him, "what's the basic kit?" I knew professional drummers—those persons who made their living at it—used more than a single instrument, but I'd always thought those of us just starting out could get away with one drum and add others as we went along.

"That would be the snare, the bass, the floor tom, and two rack toms. And, of course, you should have a cymbal and a hi-hat."

My God, I thought, what are we getting into here? Was this guy being straight or trying to hustle us?

I looked at Tommy and saw the pleading in his eyes, pleading based on well-founded fear this all might be too much for his mother to agree to. I glanced around me at the drums arranged in sets of red and blue and pearl, gleaming with their bright chrome hardware, and I knew I felt as Tommy felt— we had to have them.

"What would such a thing cost?" I asked, thinking at the worst maybe several hundred dollars.

"You can go upward of two thousand, ma'am, and even far beyond. But I've got several kits in the one-thousand-dollar range that would suit the two of you just fine."

My heart fell hard inside me. I could actually feel the heaviness descend. I'd had no idea, no idea at all. Damn it, I should've done some research before launching this excursion.

"Tommy"—I bent down to him—"let's go outside and talk."

The salesman saw my hesitation and guessed what might be coming. I'd like to think the downcast looks on both our faces touched his heart.

"Look," he said, "I've got a set over here for just nine hundred dollars. The drums are a little smaller size than usual—more like a jazz kit than a regular set—but it should do the two of you just fine. It's mahogany and beech covered with the plastic and I'll even throw in a cymbal and a hi-hat."

He led us to a corner of the room, and standing

there in front of us was the sweetest set I'd ever seen, deep red with brilliant chrome and just the right size to suit us.

"Ahhhhh," I heard my son exclaim, and he squeezed my arm. "Mom, it's beautiful."

Suddenly the money didn't matter. I'd find it somewhere and find some way to justify it. I was like a teen buying his first car—I just had to have this set.

"Shall we get it?" I asked my son, knowing I'd now crossed the line and could not think of going back.

"Oh, yes," he breathed, "it's wonderful. Can we take it home tonight?"

I looked questioningly at the salesman, wondering how I'd fit it all into my car.

"I can break it down for you," he reassured me. "Unless your vehicle's extra tiny, it should all fit just fine."

Happily we watched him disassemble that sweet shining set and help us stow it in the trunk and behind the seats.

"How about a special hamburger at Marty's?" I asked Tommy, naming a favorite coffee shop. "And then one of his super duper shakes?"

Ordinarily he'd have jumped at the offer but tonight he hesitated and I knew he just wanted to get those drums home.

"Come on," I urged, "we'll have all night for them.

It'll be fun, and besides, we need to eat or we won't have energy to play."

"Okay," he agreed, and I guessed his tastebuds had been teased by mention of the juicy burger and the thick rich shake, "but suppose somebody steals them while we're away?"

"We'll park right out front," I told him, "and sit where we can see the car, and on top of that, I'll throw an old blanket over them to hide them."

We entered Marty's and soon were eating heartily and chattering about our drums.

This is so much fun, I thought suddenly to myself, trying out new things, following interests I've often thought about but never got around to doing. And once again I became acutely aware of how my life was opening up. Of my growing sense of freedom, my growing sense of happiness.

We finished up, paid the bill, and walked out arm-in-arm. The car was there and the drums were, too. Right where we'd left them, undisturbed by anyone.

We went on home and played with our new toy till I feared the neighbors might be calling. Then, filled with joyous contentment, we tumbled into bed. The father-son dinner had never once been mentioned. The drums had loudly, noisily, happily filled the void.

I'd invited them all in for brunch, thinking it'd be a nice gesture toward our visitors from Stockton.

Thinking, too, it'd be another chance to see Bobby Harris. I'd asked them if they wanted to go on home for the weekend but they'd both declined, saying they preferred to work from here. Charlie, especially, seemed anxious to stay down, explaining he was expecting that call about Sonny Mitchell and didn't want to chance missing it by being on the road.

"I've left your number, Kate," he told me cheerily as we gathered 'round the table. "Hope you don't mind."

Even Carl had joined us, hobbling in on crutches. He looked drawn and in pain, and I felt the conviviality and the hashing over of the case would give him the boost he needed.

Tommy, of course, was delighted to gain an audience for the drums and ran to them and started beating, calling out, "Look what Mom and I got last night." I told him maybe later but not right now. Not everyone loved the drums like us.

We finished up the frothy cheese-filled omelets, then passed around another plate of Mrs. Miller's biscuits. I got up and poured the fresh-brewed coffee, replenishing our cups a second or third time, and then we pushed back a little from the table, crossed our legs, and started throwing thoughts around.

"I still don't understand about the tape," I said, picking up a biscuit crumb and absentmindedly eating it. "Why seal the baby's mouth and nose, then rip it off the nostrils later? It just doesn't make sense."

"I've got a theory about that," Carl told us, obviously glad to be a part of things. "We found the mouth tape clean of prints, right? Well, it's not too easy to put a strip on without fingerprinting it. Not easy, that is, unless you've covered up your hands.

"I figure maybe the killer didn't think of this at first and slapped the tape on bare-handed. When he realized he'd printed it he tore it off, then cut a new strip and used something to protect himself while he applied it."

"But why not retape the nose?" I asked.

"Because maybe he decided by that time he didn't need it—he suspected Lucy was already dead—but just in case she wasn't, he didn't want to take a chance on leaving the main orifice open in case she cried so he resealed the mouth."

"That makes a lot of sense." Harris nodded in agreement. "Which means that somewhere there's a piece of duct tape that carries the killer's prints."

"If it's not been compacted in a sanitation truck," I offered wryly.

Charlie, taking out a cigarette and tapping it against his hand, listened to us without comment. He seemed somewhat distracted and I guessed he was thinking of his hoped-for call from Lodi. I still had my doubts about Sonny as a suspect but I agreed with Rhoads that he had to be questioned.

I knew he had gone AWOL as far as Wanda was

concerned. I'd phoned her when she got back to Vegas and she'd told me she'd come home to an empty house—bike gone, clothes gone, cash gone, along with whatever else he could carry in his saddlebags.

Whether this was proof of guilt or just a result of dissatisfaction with domesticity remained to be seen. At any rate, she'd promised to call if Mitchell returned and as yet I hadn't heard from her.

"Kate, bring them up to speed on yesterday," Darrow urged smoothly, getting up and stretching. He'd seemed low-key from the start this morning, less willing to try to bait me, and I wondered if the fact he was a guest in my own home brought out his nicer side.

"Ah, yes, the mysterious Jack," I said, and filled them in on both Steven "B.S." Brownfeld and the lurking cousin.

"The boy told us this guy goes out of town a lot, and sure enough, when we phoned him we got his service and learned he'll be away till Monday. We didn't leave a message. We'll just contact him fresh next week and go from there."

"Where's he live?" Carl asked. "Here in San Madera?"

"No, in Merced," I told him, naming a town about halfway between here and Stockton.

"Well, look at that," Rhoads interjected. "He's positioned just right for the dumping. One hour south of home, then two hours north, then back to base. Throws all the dirty work away from him."

I nodded approvingly. "It's certainly something to consider. We'll see what the new heir says when we talk to him."

"The new heir? How do you mean?" Carl asked.

"Well, if Brownfeld's correct and Benson was next in line to inherit after Meryl, then he's just moved up to the head of the line."

The phone rang shrilly and Charlie's head swung quickly toward the sound. In a moment Mrs. Miller came into the dining room to tell him he had a call. He punched Darrow lightly on the shoulder, as if to say "wish me luck," and left the room. The rest of us chatted desultorily but all our thoughts were on Rhoads and what he'd come back with. It didn't take long to find out.

"Bingo!" he cheered, his face animated, his eyes sparkling bright. "That was my snitch up in Lodi and it's going down just like I hoped it would. There's motorcycle racing tomorrow on a track outside of town. Mitchell's planning to be there . . . and so am I."

"Good work, Charlie," I praised him, "I'll ride up there with you. Maybe one of you two can go along, in case we have to spread out and work the crowd?"

I kept my voice level as I looked at both Steve and Harris, trying not to show who I wished would make the ride. It worked out just right. Bobby volunteered immediately and Darrow begged off, citing a "prior commitment" while giving me a wink.

Rhoads didn't look too happy. "Look, Kate," he protested, "I don't really need backup. I can handle him myself."

"It's policy," I told him, "and good working procedure as well. At least one man, better off with two, so we'll drive to Lodi with you."

"Fine with me, then," he agreed, and rose up from the table. "If you'll excuse me, now that I've had my phone call, I *will* go out of town for a couple of hours. Got to see someone up in Merced."

"*There* again!" I joked. "Another suspect besides the lurking cousin?" and just as soon as I'd spoken, I could've bitten off my tongue. It must be his lady friend, I thought, and catching Bobby's eye I knew I'd been right.

"No, Kate, not a suspect," Charlie answered. "A person far, far nicer than that." And though he was going to a rendezvous with a lover, I saw a mix of anguish and futility pass across his face.

I don't believe he's taking this affair lightly, I thought with dawning realization. Unlike playboy Darrow, he's not acting the part of rake and stud. I think he probably hates what this is doing to his marriage but cannot break away from this other woman.

And even though Charlie Rhoads was an admitted philanderer, my heart softened toward him and his predicament. He was just a human being, after all, and vulnerable to foibles like the rest of us. And one of those foibles had caught him in a trap.

Or maybe, I thought, going one step farther as I searched the closet for the coats, maybe his marriage isn't all that it's cracked up to be but he won't leave her. Bobby's so blinded by his teenage memories of Jane that perhaps he might not see if she's not an easy person to live with.

Whichever theory was correct, I believed one thing was certain. Charlie Rhoads's situation brought him only grief—it did not make him a happy man.

I distributed the coats and the other three departed amid profuse thanks and rubbings of their stomachs, but Harris lingered, hanging back a little.

"Kate, there's a great jazz group playing downtown tonight and I wondered if you'd care to go." He stopped, seeming suddenly ill at ease. "I hope I'm not out of line by asking," he stumbled, "or that I seem unprofessional." He looked straight at me, his eyes filled with concern. And something else.

I'd been taken off-guard, never really having expected he'd ask me for a date, but I quickly recovered.

"Of course, Bobby, I'd like that very much." And I felt my face begin to glow and my heart start to pound.

Don't be silly, I reprimanded myself, we're just two colleagues going to a show. But the feeling of excited pleasure didn't stop.

*   *   *

I spent the afternoon working out some details of the case, banging on the drums with Tommy, and thinking about tonight. I'd start getting ready right after dinner, I decided. Harris was picking me up at eight and I wanted to allow myself time to get dressed at a leisurely pace—no rush, no hurry.

When the table had been cleared, I went upstairs and ran my bath. Deep, hot, lots of bubbles. I soaked lazily for a while, then toweled off, put on my clothes, carefully applied my makeup, and brushed out my hair. Checking myself out in the mirror when I'd finished, I noted a new sparkle in my eyes, a healthy flush on my cheeks. Even my step seemed to spring as I walked across the hall.

I sought out Tommy and found him playing with the dog, the two of them rolling on the floor beside the drums.

"Hi, kiddo, I'm going to be going out for a little while this evening, to hear some music with a friend. I'll be home after you're in bed but I won't be late."

"Who with? Karen?" he asked happily, referring to the journalist friend Darrow had played with for a while, then dumped when the game got old.

"No, honey, one of those detectives who was at the brunch today. One of the men down from Stockton."

Tommy's eyes narrowed and his face grew still and serious.

"Which one, Mom? The big one?"

"No, the other man. The shorter one with the mustache."

"Is it like a date?" he asked, staring at me.

"Not a date, not really. Nothing romantic about it. Just two friends going to hear some music."

"But he's not Dad," my son protested.

"No, he's not," I said. "I don't go out with Dad anymore, you know that."

"I *do* know that," he insisted, rapidly stroking the dog, "but I didn't think you went out with anybody else, either!"

I'd never thought ahead to this time, the time I'd spend a social evening with a man—perhaps because I'd had no inkling it would come around so soon— so I'd never wondered what Tommy's reaction might be and how to prepare for that reaction.

"Look, honey, it's okay." I dropped to my knees and my hand rubbed circles on his shoulders. "I'm just going to hear some jazz with a fellow I work with. No big deal."

Tommy considered my words, then dropped his head and shrugged.

"Okay, Mom," he said, still not sounding overly happy. "It just seemed sort of strange at first. Like, you haven't done it before."

"I understand," I told him, rising to my feet, "I understand how you feel and I'm glad you talked to me about it. Any better now?" He nodded, but only halfheartedly.

The bell rang promptly at eight and I opened up the door, feeling expectant but also slightly awkward. It'd been a long time since I'd gone out with any man other than my husband.

He was standing on the steps, his eyes smiling, the skin crinkling at the corners, and immediately I felt at ease. It's going to be all right, I thought, and hoped I looked all right in my tailored velvet slacks and cream silk blouse.

The group was one I hadn't heard before, playing in a cozy little club on the other side of town, and though not a jazz fan, I found myself enjoying their music. We had several drinks, nursing them along, and when the music ended, Bobby asked me if I'd like to get a late-night snack at a restaurant just down the street.

We walked companionably along, our shoulders and arms occasionally brushing, then left the cold crisp air and turned into the restaurant, choosing a quiet booth near the back.

"Katharine, I don't mean to pry," Bobby told me when our order had arrived, "but you'd mentioned, I thought, that your divorce would soon be final. Did I misunderstand you?"

"No, no, you didn't," I answered, and I felt my heart start to quicken. "In the spring, that's when it will all be over."

And then the words, once I'd started, began to tumble out. I found I longed to talk.

"At first I couldn't believe it was going to end, wanted badly for us to work it out. But when I finally saw there was no hope of things mending, I found I wanted it to be over as quickly as it could. I filed late last fall and the six months waiting period will end in May."

"Do you want to tell me what happened?" he asked quietly, and I sensed a sincere concern.

I nodded quickly, wanting to confide, and again the words gushed forth.

"For nearly sixteen years, Bobby, I thought I had a happy marriage but suddenly last spring he ordered me to choose between my job and him. When I protested, he refused to try to work it out. He couldn't see that what I did was just as much a part of me—a part that I'd be lost without—as loving him and Tommy, so he walked away."

"Do you have regrets, Kate?" I saw him watching me intently.

"Regrets? Of course I have regrets. Regrets that a family and a marriage died. But do I still love him, feel I want him back? No, absolutely not." I shook my head and tossed my loose hair back.

"How does your son take it?" Bobby asked curiously. "Has he adjusted?"

"On balance, okay, I think, but he doesn't talk too much about it even though I try to draw him out. And I think he's beginning to feel Jon's ignoring him, not paying attention like he used to, and that's so odd, you know"—and now I leaned forward eagerly as the words continued spilling out—"because Jon made such a big deal about fighting for custody of Tommy but when he lost, instead of appealing, again he just turned around and walked away."

"Maybe the fight itself was the thing, Kate," Bobby suggested. "Maybe the struggle wasn't about Tommy at all."

I looked up quickly, looked deep into his concerned eyes, startled at his quick perception.

"You're so right, you know," I murmured, "because he tried to pretend the breakup, too, was about Tommy and my feelings for him, then he admitted he was using our son just as a screen." And I remembered that awful night last spring when the truth had finally come tumbling out.

I was silent for a moment, then I looked at Bobby and began to smile. I leaned back, feeling much relieved, then suddenly, to my surprise, I reached across the table and began to pat his hand.

"Thank you, Bobby, for making me talk about it. I feel so much better now."

He smiled at me—that kind, warm smile—and put his hand on top of mine. Let it linger briefly, then withdrew it as I quickly withdrew mine.

"You know, Katharine," he began, "talking always helps. My ex-wife and I also split up under very bitter circumstances. Ours was definitely not what you'd call an 'amicable divorce.' I came home from work one day and found her in our bed with one of my best buddies. Not as close a friend as Charlie but a buddy nonetheless. My partner, someone I felt I could trust and depend on.

"Turned out it wasn't just an indiscretion, a little one-night stand. It'd been going on between them for quite some time. They'd been deceiving me and I never knew it till I saw it with my own two eyes.

"It knocked the wind out of me and I had to leave LA. I couldn't stand to see her or him—and I saw *him* nearly every single day—or all the places where we used to go, because it tore at me and reminded me of the long-gone times when things were good between us."

He paused and drank a glass of water.

"Anyway, I came on up to Stockton and my old 'brother,' Charlie Rhoads, helped me out as always. He encouraged me to talk to him about it. At any hour, on any day, just whenever I felt it was over-whelming me. And I did. He—he and Jane, too, for that matter—got me through it and out the other side. Talking may not change the fact but it surely helps you heal faster."

"I know that, Bobby," I told him when he'd fin-ished, "that's what I'm always telling Tommy. But still I didn't mean to burden you with all of this. You asked a simple question and you opened up the dam."

"No burden, Kate, please believe that. I'll always

be here to listen to you." Inwardly I blushed with pleasure and allowed myself the luxury of believing he wouldn't speak like that to everyone—he was talking just to me.

"You're a good friend, Bobby," I told him, longing to say more but still fighting my feelings, "and Charlie's a good friend, too. I'm lucky to have you and you're lucky to have him."

"I know how fortunate *I* am," he said jokingly, "but I'm not too sure about the other." We sat in silence for a moment, then he started talking again.

"Remember I told you earlier you could depend on Charlie, that he'd never let you down? Well, that wasn't just idle talk or hyperbole, it was the truth. You see, Charlie saved my life once and risked his own life in the process. For that, I'll owe him till the day I die."

"My God, were you shot at?" I asked, trying to recall recent police shootings in Stockton and coming up empty.

"No, nothing like that. It was back when we were in the service. We were both on a covert mission to South America—Charlie's was more covert than mine—and one night a member of the 'opposition' snuck up behind me and was about to jump me with a knife. Charlie apparently had been tailing him— just routine, never thinking it'd have anything to do with me—and then he came around a corner and saw that I was just about to meet my end."

"What did he do?" I asked, enthralled, cupping my chin between my hands and leaning far across the table. Bobby's eyes stared past me as he relived the scene.

"He killed him," he told me matter-of-factly, "Charlie killed him just in time." He paused, looking down. "Heck, Kate, he pretty much obliterated the guy!"

CHAPTER SIXTEEN

We couldn't spot him anywhere, though we'd split up and searched the hurly-burly crowd for nearly half an hour. Finally, we had to admit the emptiness of our efforts. For whatever rhyme or reason, our partner was nowhere to be found.

Rhoads had told Bobby late last night he'd drive north alone because he wished to leave at daybreak and drop by and see his kids before pursuing Mitchell.

"You come on up later," he'd said, "and meet me at the gate at ten. That'll give the crowd time to build, and we won't stick out like three sore thumbs."

So Harris had picked me up right after breakfast and the two of us drove up together, chatting about the mellow sound of the jazz the night before, the coming encounter with Lucy's father, the way the tule fog had disappeared. We got personal only once.

"Still feeling better from our talk last night?" he asked when we'd been driving nearly half an hour.

"Yes, Bobby," I answered quickly, touched by his concern. "It's kind of you to ask."

"It's not just kindness," he assured me quietly. He did not elaborate, just kept on driving, concentrating on the road ahead, and I dared not counter, "What, then?"

We easily found the dirt track where the meet was being held, parked in a dusty unpaved lot filled with bikes and trucks, then tried to make our way toward the gate to rendezvous with Charlie.

It wasn't easy. The crowd, though not that large, was already slightly rowdy, and buxom hard-faced girls and hairy fatty men in grimy tank tops pushed and shoved and jostled as we walked. We used our elbows to try to gain some space but it was a constant effort.

Once inside the gates we stepped aside to wait for Rhoads. When he failed to show in fifteen minutes, we split up and began to search the crowd, thinking maybe he'd come early, spotted Sonny, then started tailing him. Now Harris and I were right back where we'd started. Standing at the gate, wondering what to do.

"I phoned Jane," he informed me, "and she said Charlie dropped in around eight this morning, stayed about an hour, then left to come on over here. Unless he's had an accident, God forbid, he should've arrived at the track well ahead of us, so where is he now?"

"Did you look over there?" I asked, pointing toward some portable toilets and concession stands set up across the field. "Maybe he had to relieve himself or followed Mitchell somewhere 'round back of those tables."

Harris shrugged. "You've got a point. Might as well check them out, too."

We walked around the top end of the oval track, heading toward a row of big green plastic johns. Beside us, motorcycles were revving up, ready to begin their dirt runs. The noise of the exhausts sputtered and sparked the air around us, and at one point I put my fingers in my ears.

We waited outside the toilets but no one went either in or out, except the odd biker or his tattooed girlfriend. The food stands, too, were far from busy, with many of the concessionaires just starting to set up for the rush for beer and hot dogs that would come much later. Set well back from the track, the noise level was much lower here, and I could actually hear the twitter of some birds sitting on the branches of a nearby tree.

Suddenly, though, I began to hear the sounds of something else. Angry voices muted slightly, as if dampened by some material surrounding them.

I glanced swiftly at Bobby, to see if he heard them, too, but he was still intent on staring at the toilets. I peered between two booths and saw a low square shed, built of graying aged wood and leaning slightly to the left, set fifty feet or so deeper in the field. Perhaps once used for storage, it now looked abandoned.

As I studied it, eyes narrowed, I caught the sounds again—this time rising high, then falling, then rising up again.

"Bobby, listen!" I nudged his arm urgently. "Someone's inside that building over there."

He cocked his ear and immediately heard the muffled sounds himself.

"Come on," he called, and hurriedly we moved behind the booths and toward the shed. As we drew within six feet of it, a large rough voice yelled out, "You don't know shit, Daddy!" then this was followed by another noise, a deep dull thud as if one object had impacted strongly on another. Seeing no entrance on the end or on the side closest to me, I raced to the opposing wall, where several flimsy wooden planks hung loosely off a hinge.

His back was to me and his large frame filled the door, and before I could yell out, Charlie Rhoads brought his fist up high, then slammed it down in front of him.

Shoving him aside, I pushed my way into the small dim space and saw a man lying on the bare-plank floor, bleeding profusely from the nose and mouth. As I neared him, he began to rise, a great raging hulking male stumbling to his feet. Rhoads raised his fist again and I slapped it down, demanding,

"What's going on here?" He swung his dark eyes toward me and I couldn't miss the blazing fury.

"What the hell, Charlie . . . ?" Harris murmured, a shaken, baffled look laid across his face.

"He's got a knife, goddammit," Rhoads barked at us. "He's got a knife and he was gonna use it!"

"Damn right I've got a knife," his opponent volunteered, dabbing at his nostrils as he leaned against the wall. He glared at me and I saw the blondish hair, the large brown eyes, the deep firm dimple in the cheek, and I knew we'd caught up with Sonny Mitchell. "I've got it but I never touched it. This pig pounced on me when I had nothin' in my hand. He was gonna try to beat the shit outta me. Look here!" and Mitchell began reaching toward his pocket.

"Hands up!" I yelled. "Keep them away from your body. Up against the wall and spread 'em!"

"Fuck it!" Mitchell screamed, but he grudgingly complied. Harris began to pat him down and shortly withdrew a long thin blade from a leather sheath near his back pocket.

"A bit above the legal limit, I'd say," Bobby told him, "and also in violation of parole." He began to slap the cuffs on.

"But I didn't take it out!" Sonny bellowed, banging his open hand against the wall. "He's lying. I never touched the goddamn knife!"

Rhoads moved forward threateningly and I pushed him back. "The hell you didn't," he yelled across my shoulder. "I saw the blade."

By this time a small crowd had gathered outside the shed, and suddenly two deputies from the county sheriff's department pushed their way forward. We explained the situation and handed the arrestee over to them, for booking on the carrying of the knife and the parole violation.

As they prepared to lead him away, Mitchell spat at Rhoads and curled his dark unshaven lip.

"You thought you'd do me like you did the last time, pig, but your two fellow oinkers showed up and queered the deal. Too bad, fat-ass copper!"

The crowd parted and the deputies took Mitchell to the car. I turned to Charlie.

"What happened in there?" I asked quietly.

"He had a knife. I know he had a knife. I saw the blade."

"But we found it secured in its holder."

"I don't know how he got it back in there, Kate, I swear I don't. I saw it flash. He was going to stab me."

"This makes no sense, Charlie. If that's true, why didn't you draw your gun? Why lash in the direction of an unsheathed blade with your bare hand?"

Rhoads crumpled and tears began to fill his eyes.

"I *knew* he had a knife. He's a biker and a certain type of biker always has a knife. But you're right, I hit him for another reason. I hit him because I lost it and I wanted to smash the shit right out of that fuckin' slime. All I could see was that little baby, that pathetic little baby that he murdered."

"But we don't know that," I protested angrily. "We've got no cause to believe Sonny killed his daughter."

"He did, Kate, he did," Charlie insisted, "and I'm just on the verge of proving it. I've got someone who's just about agreed to squeal."

Furious, I drew in my breath and stared at him.

"You and I are riding back together and I'll hear about it then, but let me say this much right now. As long as you're on my watch, you *do not*, repeat *do not*, assault a suspect. You follow procedure, you do it by the book. Is that thoroughly and completely understood?"

Rhoads nodded and hung his head contritely, looking at the ground.

"I'm a good cop, Kate, but when I saw him, it pushed me past the limit. Christ, that little baby . . . No, Kate, it will not ever happen again. Not on your watch, not on any other. This I swear to God."

He threw his head upward from his cell bench and glared at us. His mouth and nose showed puffiness but the blood had been washed away. Despite the scowl held by his face, I could plainly see the face of Lucy.

Rhoads and Harris moved quietly to the side and I took the lead.

"We need to talk with you," I said, "about your little daughter. When did you last see her?"

"The kid?" Mitchell looked surprised. "When Wanda took her away from Vegas. That's when I thought it'd be a good time to scamper. Sick and tired of all that daddy crap, wanted to hit the road again."

He hawked up some phlegm from deep down in his throat and spat against the concrete, then studied the tattoos that ran up and down his arm.

"Well, you won't have to worry about that 'daddy crap' anymore, Sonny," I told him, neither roughly nor especially gently. "I'm sorry to have to tell you your daughter's dead." I watched closely for his reaction.

"Dead?" His mouth dropped open but I saw no tears. "The hell you say 'dead'! What're you talkin' about?"

"Do you know a woman named Meryl Masters, Sonny?"

"Meryl? Shit, what is this? Yeah, I usta know her. Not for some time now, though."

"What was your relationship with her?"

"She was a fuck now and then," he growled. "What's it to you?"

"I think she might've been a little more than that," I ventured, "and I think she dumped you and you didn't like it."

I studied him, waiting for his answer, and I sensed beneath the dirt and grime the presence of the animal magnetism that had attracted Masters.

"Bull balls, lady. She didn't mean Jim Dandy to me."

"Where were you a week ago last Friday night?"

"Whoa, whoa, whoa," Sonny interjected. "Let's slow down a moment here. Let's get back to the kid. How'd she die? Wanda fail to burp her and she choked?"

I felt revulsion for this creature and a deep full sadness for little Lucy. I began to shake and almost thought my voice would crack with anger as I began to speak again.

"Maybe *you* can tell us that, Mitchell," Charlie intervened, but I waved him back. I doubted the rapport between him and Sonny would be such as to produce a fruitful interrogation.

"Your daughter was smothered under unknown circumstances. Meryl Masters was also killed, but in a different manner. We have reason to believe the same person did them both. Now I ask you again. Where were you a week ago last Friday night?"

"Let me see . . ." Mitchell screwed his face up. "Well, I'll tell you, copper, that's gonna be real easy. I was playing poker with all my buddies down at Sandy's Bar, just like I do about every Friday night."

"What's the owner's name?" I asked, getting out my pad.

"Sandy. Sandy something or other. And he's the bartender, too. He was there all evening. He'll tell you true. Him and me had a little bet going on a blonde across the room."

"What kind of bet?" I asked.

"Whether she'd leave with Johnny Run that night or not. I collected. Turned out she did."

"We'll check this out," Harris told him, "and get back to you. But don't bother to hold your breath."

"Yeah, well, *you* get back to me—you or lady piglet—but keep Psycho away from me." Mitchell jerked his head toward Rhoads, whose facial muscles tightened till they stood out in knots along his jaw.

I stood up to go, making sure Charlie was the first to exit, with Bobby and me following behind. I turned around at the cell door and looked once again at Mitchell. I found it difficult to believe that anyone, no matter how hard they were, could go untouched by the murder of their own child.

"She was a lovely little girl, Sonny," I told him quietly. "You were very lucky to have had her."

He took my words and twisted them, layering them with tawdry cheapness.

"All girls are lovely," he wisecracked with a wink, "and Sonny Mitchell's always lucky when it comes to having them."

Disgusted, I turned and walked away.

"Tell me why you started tailing him without us," I ordered Rhoads as soon as we'd left the jail and hit the main road south. Harris was driving the other car back home, giving me the chance for my much-desired private chat with Charlie.

"I got there early, Kate, and almost as soon as I walked up, I spotted him getting off his bike. He headed immediately for the can and I tailed him, staying well back, fully intending to wait for you two before approaching him. He went on in and did his business and when he came back out, I suddenly felt I couldn't lose the opportunity to talk with him."

Charlie shifted in his seat till he was facing me, his eyes reflecting both bleakness and humility. He knew he'd screwed up royally and was hoping he could justify it. I saw him pull out a cigarette, then hesitate as he put it in his mouth.

"No, go ahead," I told him, and rolled my window down. Gratefully he lit it and drew deeply to his lungs.

"I saw the shed and thought that'd be a good place for a little talk, so we went back there. I was just starting to question him and then I . . . Well, Kate, like I told you, I just lost it. I kept thinking of that helpless baby and the misery of a man who killed her, and it was as if a big cloud of rage came over me, and I found myself balling up my fist and reaching out and striking him."

"So it's true you saw no knife."

Charlie heaved a great big sigh, blowing smoke across the car.

"I guessed he had one—like I said, they all do—but no, I didn't see it."

I stayed silent for a moment, watching wide flat

fields flash by, and I felt an empathy for him begin to grow in me. I understood what he was saying, I knew just what he meant. The department manuals, all clear and clean and orderly, lay out in vivid black and white how you must treat a suspect. It all seems so right, so easy to follow to the letter.

But then you get out there on the street and the ball game changes. You're just human, after all, and you learn that despite your training, you have limits just like anybody else. And sometimes those limits are pushed to the very edge of their endurance, and the simplicity of those manuals' words don't seem to cover complex situations. No, no doubt about it, it's no easy thing to be a cop.

"But control, Charlie, control. You've got to be able to keep it or there's no difference between them and us. Surely you believe that."

Even though I understood his feelings, I could not appear to condone his use of violence.

"Of course I believe it," he insisted, "but you must know what it's like. You must've had some time in your long career when you, too, were pushed too hard and maybe went too far. I'd say it happens to most of us sooner or later."

He'd hit home, bringing back memories of that case last spring when I'd almost crossed a line I'd never thought I'd even draw close to. Rhoads was probably right. We all face that line at some point or another.

"Do you honestly believe it won't happen again?"
I asked, concerned about his future role in this case.

"Absolutely, Kate, it was an aberration," he assured me, his handsome face looking more relaxed.
"The urge is gone now—totally out of my system.
And maybe it wasn't all Sonny Mitchell anyway."

This last was uttered very low, so that I could
hardly catch it.

"What do you mean?" I asked, bending toward
him. "What else possibly could it be?"

Charlie turned his head toward the passenger window and sat silent for a moment before answering.

"My life's a little complicated right now," he told
me finally. "I don't want to talk too much about it
but my marriage has been cracking for some time.
There's a woman that I'm seeing, a woman that I
care for deeply, but I'm still hoping I can work it out
with Jane.

"This other woman, though, just yesterday, told
me to choose one of them or the other, and so today
I'm all torn up inside. I'll get it sorted out soon—I've
got to—but right now I feel like shattered bits and
pieces of the whole."

Ah, I thought, the girlfriend in Merced, where
Rhoads was heading after brunch. Instead of a long
and loving evening, he'd walked into the demands
of an ugly ultimatum.

"Whew," I told him, "you do have a load on you!
Do you need some time off? Would a break from
work refresh you?"

"No, Kate, hell no. Work is my salvation—I lose myself in it—and I already told you there won't be any more incidents like today."

I believed him and felt a great relief. And also felt a sympathy for Charlie and his messed-up life, for who knew who was to blame? I was going to let his crack at Sonny Mitchell slide right now. Keep the matter in abeyance, hidden from the brass, till I'd given it a little more objective thought.

"Let's get back to the case," I told him, and I felt as if the air in the car had suddenly cleared and gotten lighter. "You said something about a snitch who's going to squeal?"

"Yeah," Charlie said excitedly, "a guy who indicated to me Sonny told him he'd done the job. Trouble is he's only *indicated*. I can't get him to come totally clean yet, but I will."

"Is he reliable, your snitch?" I asked skeptically, knowing the moral quality of a good many of these people.

"I can count on him, I feel I can count on him," Charlie answered. "It'll give us leverage with Sonny anyway."

"Well, when he's ready, bring him in and let me listen," I advised, not getting overly excited. "In the meantime, we've got to check out the alibi in Vegas."

"Yeah, a bunch of jailbirds cooking up a story for another," Rhoads countered with disdain. "What do you expect them to say? Of course they'll back him up."

Something pulled at me, then suddenly I remembered.

"What did Mitchell mean back there when he said you were going to do him like you did the last time?"

"Oh, just a bunch of bull," Charlie answered off-handedly. "Running off his mouth the way they all do. It's cheap ex-con talk, Kate. You should be used to it by now."

I hadn't seen her in a long while—she'd been out of town on stories and I'd been up to my ears in crime—but shortly after I got home from Lodi, Karen Windall knocked loudly on my door.

I'd just kicked off my shoes, thrown my clothes aside, and slipped into a housecoat. It'd been a long and tiring day, and the idea of some quiet and a relaxing vodka-soda was awfully appealing.

When I heard the knock I grimaced and my first impulse was to let it go away, but when I opened up the door and saw who was standing there, my face broke into a smile and I welcomed her on in.

"Hello, stranger," I told her delightedly. "I was wondering if I'd ever see you again."

"Heck, yes," she responded. "You know we always circle around to each other even if it takes a long, long time. Us single gals can't lose touch. We've got to stick together in this sad male-dominated world."

Male domination was one of Karen's favorite topics and came up often in conversation. Having been burned untold times by members of the opposite sex—most recently Steve Darrow—she was always swearing there'd never be another. Until the next time, that is.

A tall, lithe blonde who wore her tailored clothes like a model from a magazine, she projected an image of total self-assurance. But I knew better. I knew inside she was bruised and vulnerable, just like all the rest of us.

"Hey, hey, what's this?" she chortled, pointing to the drum set. "Is that Tommy's?"

"It's mine *and* Tommy's," I said proudly, enjoying her reaction, "and our lessons start this coming week."

"Rock 'n' roller!" she proclaimed, a look of utter and complete astonishment showing on her face. "I can't believe it! I'll have to do a feature story on the rockin' cop."

"Laugh all you will, Karen, it's going to be a lot of fun. And aren't they just beautiful?" I stroked the drums admiringly.

She looked at me and shook her head, then took the scotch and soda I handed her and sat down on the sofa.

"You're starting to enjoy yourself, aren't you,

Kate?" she asked seriously. "You've lost that harried bitter look you wore so often in the fall and summer."

"Yes," I answered eagerly, "yes, I am. Life's starting to be fun again. There's so much to explore, so much new to do, and I feel a great big boundless energy to get my hands on all of it and try to take it on."

"You're a wonder woman, you know that?" Karen told me, sipping slowly at her drink. "You've gone through hell with that husband of yours and now you're working a rough, demanding job and raising a growing boy all by yourself. And all the while having the best time of your life. I've gotta hand it to you. I don't know how you do it."

I hated talk like this, hated being called a strong woman. I never viewed myself as such. Just as an average person like many others, trying to get by. Funny, I thought, how you see yourself and how others see you.

"I do it just like we all do," I responded, trying to make short shrift of this conversation. "By taking it day by day, facing each bump as it comes, and handling it the best way I can. No more, no less."

She nodded reflectively, then sat quietly for a moment enjoying her drink. I knew the wheels were spinning inside her head, though, and that soon something would come popping out. Karen was never silent for long.

"Who's that stud who looks like Darrow?" she suddenly queried, fulfilling my expectations. "I saw him down at the station and couldn't believe my eyes. I thought it was the man himself."

"You're talking about Charlie Rhoads," I told her, "currently on loan from Stockton, and yes, the resemblance certainly is striking. But I wouldn't think of getting involved if I were you. He's married."

"Wasn't thinking of it, just wondering who he was. One that looks like that is enough for any girl, and I've already had my turn. By the way, I saw Steve the other day but we didn't exchange any words."

"He told me," I answered. "Downstairs at the station, when you picked up the daily occurrence sheets."

Karen frowned.

"No, that's not when I meant. It was earlier than that. I saw him about two weeks ago, before that woman was murdered, walking near the Rimerton apartments where she lived. Hey"—she gave a sudden snort—"maybe he was banging her, too."

"Not funny, Karen," I told her. "He was probably on some follow-up investigation or maybe even seeing a male buddy. I know he sometimes hangs out with the other sex, too."

She swung her head toward me and looked at me piercingly.

"Are *you* seeing anyone, Kate? That's about all that's missing from your life, even though I say 'who needs it?' "

"No, no I'm not," I replied, wanting to keep the jazz evening a secret. It was mine alone to remember and savor, and not something I cared to share. Besides, if I told her about it, she'd refuse to leave it alone. She'd hound me for details about the relationship's progress—if, indeed, it ever progressed—for weeks, maybe months, to come.

"Well, it's probably just as well," she said caustically. "They only complicate things. Look at me and the sorry mess I've allowed men to make of my life. And it's little better at work, as you well know. I've got this new guy on the crime desk who still thinks women belong in the kitchen.

"Thank God for those sexual harassment laws. Sometimes I just love to push his face into it when he starts going too far, 'cause he knows he can't go one teeny bit further without getting in serious trouble."

"I don't play that game, Karen," I told her, swallowing the rest of my drink. "I just try to do my job and let the small stuff roll off my back. I find that if I act as if I belong, and don't fuss and holler to get what I want just because I'm a woman, the guys then forget I'm female and accept me at my own assessment."

"Each to his own, Kate." Karen grinned at me. "I still like to rub them around in it."

We both stretched our arms above our heads, yawning, then decided to call it a night. We walked to the door and I opened it quickly for Molly, who was waiting to dart out for her final run.

"Keep in touch, Kate," Karen admonished, "and I'll try to do better, too."

She gave a quick wave, then drove off in her little red sports car, while I strolled out into the yard and watched Molly sniff the close-clipped grass.

CHAPTER SEVENTEEN

"I've got him, Kate, that squeal I told you about," Rhoads called out excitedly. Bobby, Steve, and I raised our heads as he came hurriedly across the room, slapping his hand against his thigh. "Damn it, I knew he'd come around. He finally admitted Mitchell confessed to him he'd done the job. Killed Meryl from jealousy, says the baby was an accident."

Harris rose to his feet, his eyes glowing with relief and pride.

"Well done, Charlie," he said, and clapped his partner on the shoulder.

"Who is this guy?" I asked. "And what's his relationship with Sonny?"

"They did time together down at Men's Colony," he answered, naming a prison near San Luis Obispo, "but Jerry's not a big-time felon, no heavy-duty physical stuff. Lighter crimes like theft and receiving stolen property. They used to pal around a lot up near Lodi and Sonny looked him up last week when he got into town."

"Where you got him?" Darrow asked, starting to dial a number.

"He's coming in at ten, to tell you what he's already spilled to me. Jerry Edgar's his name."

"I'll listen to him," I said, still, for some reason, mentally dragging my feet on this thing, "but we're still trying to check out Mitchell's alibi. No one answers yet at Sandy's Bar but it should open up by noon."

"Screw the 'alibi' "—Rhoads held up his two index fingers, indicating quotes—"I told you before all his biker buddies are going to lie for him."

"Hey, Kate," Darrow called out from his desk, "I just phoned up to Merced and Jack Benson is now due in this afternoon. Contacted his service to pick up his messages this morning and told them he'd be back in town by one."

"Fine," I told him. "We'll wait till he gets settled, then pay him a little visit. That'll work out just right. Jerry at ten and Jackie Boy in early afternoon."

I looked at Rhoads, fiddling with some papers at his desk, saw his beaming, glowing face, and thought how sure he was he'd nailed Sonny Mitchell and how very pleased he was with himself about it. And well he should be if it was true.

God, I thought, I wish I could hold half his optimism. I'd love to wrap this one up and put it far away and see the killer brought to justice. But caution made me take a wait-and-see attitude, perhaps because I'd been let down so often in the past.

At ten to ten, Rhoads rose and walked across the squad room to go downstairs and meet his snitch. I toyed with some pencils in a holder and wondered if maybe, after all, we were on the right track.

The photo, I thought—the photograph ripped from Meryl's album—certainly pointed that way. If Sonny was indeed the killer, it'd be entirely logical for him to have torn it out if it was a picture that, to the inquiring eye, would forge an immediate connection between him and Meryl.

And really, I reasoned, letting my mind play along, would Jack Benson rip out such a photo? As the dead woman's cousin, wouldn't people *expect* to find him in any album she might have, and because such a snapshot would arouse no suspicion, wouldn't he leave it intact?

But—and this remained a real possibility—suppose the missing item had nothing to do with the murders, had been destroyed for some other reason entirely?

Damn it, stop it, I scolded myself, or you'll drive yourself into a fit. Of course it's connected and if you can discover what happened to it or the tape, you'll discover who murdered your victims.

I glanced up and saw Bobby watching me, and when our eyes met, he got up and walked over.

"Would you like to have dinner tonight, Katharine?'' he asked. ''That is, if nothing's breaking with the case.''

I felt myself blushing and spied Darrow gawking, a wide grin spread across his broad face. I lowered my voice so he wouldn't hear what I answered.

''I'd like that very much, Bobby.'' I tried to speak smoothly but the words seemed to come out in small jerks and chokes.

''We'll talk later, then, when we see how it's going.''

A clatter near the doorway caught my ear and I looked up to see Rhoads and a much smaller man stooping over, then straightening up, before coming toward me. Edgars—for that was surely who this person must be—had brushed clumsily against a trash can while entering the room and sent it crashing over.

I stared at him, trying to size him up, and I saw a thin slight figure, possibly thirty-five years of age, with mousy hair and a gray pallor to his cheeks. His mouth was small, one of the smallest and roundest mouths I'd ever seen. Whenever he opened it slightly, it immediately sprang into the shape of an ''O.'' I was reminded of a lone Cheerio spilled out on a table.

Distinctive though the mouth was, it was the eyes that most caught my attention. Oval in shape, light blue in color, they darted uncomfortably from here to there to here again. The reason for this darting was nerves, I was sure, but I also felt they could wander through shiftiness.

All in all, I well knew the type. Amazing, I thought, how so many crooks resemble each other. The petty thieves are of one sort—small and evasive like this one and exuding an air of defeat—while the felons are tough guys like Sonny, roaring out on their cycles and staring with cell-hardened eyes.

Of course there were good reasons for this sameness, I decided. They'd spent a lot of time in each other's company—and don't they say a wife grows to resemble her husband, and vice versa, after many years of togetherness?—and they'd all attended the same "school."

"Jerry, this is Detective Harrod," Rhoads began heartily. "She'll be sitting in with us so you can tell her what you told me. Detective Harrod, Jerry Edgars. He's been a real help."

I smiled, extending my hand, and suggested we move to the small private room down the hall. I motioned to Darrow to join us but indicated Bobby should remain behind. I wanted one of my own men with us but I didn't want the snitch to feel overwhelmed by the company.

Edgars, after mumbling hello, said nothing further as we left the room and moved down the hallway. He kept his eyes toward the ground, and his feet seemed to shuffle rather than walk properly along. He was certainly no eager-beaver witness, I decided, and put his attitude down to his fingering his friend.

"All right," I said when we were all seated and

comfortable, "suppose you tell me now what you told Detective Rhoads."

Edgars looked up and I saw his eyes start to water. He put his hand to his mouth and coughed.

"Go ahead, Jerry," Charlie urged. "Remember what we talked about. How you'll find it hard to live with yourself if you let him get away with these killings."

"I saw Sonny last week and he told me he offed that woman and the baby." Edgars hung his head again. I waited. He remained quiet.

"I'll need to know more than that," I told him. "I'll need to know where, when, and why. And exactly what it was he said to you."

The squeal took a deep breath and began speaking in a monotone, staring straight ahead at some far-off point between me and Darrow.

"It was last Thursday evening. Sonny had just gotten into town and we were having a bunch of beers up at the Shovelhead outside of Lodi. Him and me, our paths have been crossing for quite a long time now, but I hadn't seen him since he moved to Vegas, not till the other night. Well, anyway, Sonny seemed real down, like he'd got a load on his mind."

Edgars paused to wipe a trembling hand across his brow. I waited, without urging him, till he was ready to begin again.

"Soon he switched from beer to hard stuff, and after he'd knocked back a few, the conversation stopped and I asked him what was wrong. It wasn't like ol' Sonny to get all weird that way. That's when he told me he'd knocked off some broad down south, and a baby, too, though that was accidental."

I drew in my breath, not yet daring to believe I could rely on this witness.

"Did Mitchell say why he did it?" Steve asked, hunching forward in his chair.

"Uh, jealousy, he said it was jealousy. She was an old girlfriend and she was balling somebody else."

"Why would that bother him if she was just an ex?"

Edgars glanced up, his mouth hanging open, his eyes shifting rapidly around.

"I dunno. That's just what he told me."

"How did he kill them?"

"Strangled her, I don't know about the baby."

"Are you willing to testify to this in court?" I asked.

The snitch shot a quick glance at Charlie and nervously licked his lips.

"Uh, yeah," he said, dropping his eyes.

I jerked my head toward the door, indicating Rhoads and Darrow should leave.

"I'd like a few moments alone with Mr. Edgars," I advised.

Steve started to go immediately but Rhoads frowned and drew me aside.

"I think the witness might be a little more comfortable, a little more willing to talk, with me here, Kate."

"It'll be all right, Charlie," I assured him, "go on."

The two left and Edgars and I were alone.

"Water, Jerry," I offered, "or could I get you some coffee?"

"No, not," he stammered, "but would it be okay if I lit up a smoke? I'd really love having a smoke."

"Of course," I said sweetly, preparing myself for the big cloud of pollution that soon would fill that small room.

"Tell me, why didn't you come to us before, Jerry?" I began smoothly. "Why wait till now, and then so reluctantly?"

"Because he's my friend—Sonny's my pal—so I couldn't."

"But murder's a heinous crime," I counseled, "especially the killing of a four-month-old baby. *You've* never been involved in anything like that, probably never will be. *You'd* draw the line. So what friendship was worth shielding a killer, especially a killer who's just a beer buddy, not a *close* friend?"

Edgars shook his head miserably.

"I just didn't want to," he moaned.

"Then what made you change your mind?" I asked softly. "Conscience begin to take over?"

"Somethin' like that," he whispered.

"Jerry," I asked, watching him closely, "did anyone put any pressure on you to come to us with your story?" I had to go gently, could not use strong phrases like "finger your friend," in case the witness felt guilty and ran.

"No, no one did, I swear it!"

I still was uneasy, laden with skepticism. True, few snitches like squealing on one of their pals but this guy was feeling no joy at all. And Sonny and he had just been beer drinkers together, not bosom buddies till death did them part.

I'd take his tale, sure, but I'd be glad when Sandy's Bar opened and I could get the alibi story all sorted out. I stared at Edgars, watching him pull on the cigarette with his little "O" mouth. Perfect for smoke rings, I thought, and hoped I'd not see one.

"What did Sonny look like when you saw him that night? Short hair or long, bruises or not?"

The snitch stared back.

"Sorta short and thick, like he usually wears it. No bruises that I noticed, no." He paused. Then, "You don't believe me, do you? You think I didn't see him at all. Well, I did. I drank beer with him."

"But did he confess to you?" I persisted. "Did he really spill his guts about doing those killings?"

"But how'd I know otherwise?" Edgars protested. "How'd I know what to say?"

"The papers. The papers all over the state gave the murders good play."

Edgars began to squirm in his seat, muttering and mumbling. Again, he put his hand to his head.

"I can't do this," I heard, "I can't do this."

"Why not, Jerry. If it's the truth, why not?"

"I can't, I've changed my mind. Not to Sonny. He told me nuthin'," and Edgars leaped up, knocking over his chair.

"Sit down, let's talk about it," I advised him. "If Sonny *did* confess to you, you'll be protected and you'll feel a lot better having told the truth. You did the right thing to come forward."

"No, I can't," he cried plaintively. "I want out of here. It was a mistake to come."

He banged the table with his fist, in apparent disgust with either his weakness or his lie.

I pulled the knob and Edgars stumbled into the hallway. When he saw Charlie waiting near the squad-room door, he pushed right past him, calling, "I can't do it, Rhoads. You'll have to roust out someone else. I can't do it." And the scared, miserable little man fled the building.

I looked at Charlie. His mouth was hanging open in shock and disbelief.

"What happened? What went wrong? I knew I shoulda stayed. Kate, what the hell went on in there?"

"He changed his mind, pure and simple. For whatever reason, Edgars changed his mind. If he didn't have the guts to stick it out with us for thirty minutes, he'd never go the distance in the courts. Better to find that out now than a whole lot further down the line."

"You didn't handle him right, Kate. You must've scared him off. He was okay with me." Rhoads was livid.

"Look, Charlie, I know how disappointed you are but I handled him right. And I repeat—if he couldn't stand my questions, how do you think he'd do with the defense? Anyway"—I clapped him on the shoulder—"if Sonny's alibi holds up, Edgars's story won't matter. We'll know it was all a lie. We'll know he fibbed for some reason or another, maybe just a desire to please. Or did you offer him something? What did you offer him anyway?"

"I offered him nothing. He owed me from times in the past."

"You know, we can still use him as leverage if Sandy's Bar doesn't check out. We can tell Mitchell one of his buddies came to us, tattling that he'd confessed. *He'll* know he didn't, but he might think we're believing this snitch, and it'll scare him and stir him up some, maybe make him start saying things better kept quiet. First things first, though. I'm calling Sandy's."

I dialed the Vegas number and, after several rings, a deep male voice answered. I asked to speak with Sandy, the voice said, "This is he," and we chatted pleasantly for several minutes. I depressed the button, then dialed another Vegas number and talked about the same amount of time. Satisfied in one way, deeply dissatisfied in another, I hung up and called my squad over.

"Sonny Mitchell's alibi stands. Sandy Reston swears he was there all that Friday evening. Knows it was that night because of the bet about the blonde and Johnny Run. Johnny got out of jail on Friday morning and was tossed back in by Saturday night."

"Well, sure," Rhoads spat out sarcastically, "I told you he'd stick up for Sonny. I predicted that. That man's word's a bunch of crap."

"No, it's not," I told him. "My second call was to the sergeant in Las Vegas. He told me that while Sandy's clientele may leave a lot to be desired, the man himself is honest as they come—he'd accept as purest gold anything he said."

She'd crossed my mind several times, but in all truth, I'd been too preoccupied with other things to give much thought to Wanda Brighton. After I'd spoken with her briefly when she'd arrived in Vegas, she'd fast-faded from my mind.

I picked up the phone and called her. A thin, high voice answered after several rings.

"Wanda? It's Katharine Harrod, the detective from San Madera. I wanted to know how you were doing."

"All right." A pause. "No, not all right. Alone."

"Sonny's not come back?" I didn't think so but he might've done and she'd not dared to phone me.

"He isn't coming back. I know that."

I heard her clear her throat, then give a little snuffle. I wondered why she'd never called to see if we were making progress. It was as if she'd read my mind.

"I knew you'd get in touch with me if you had anything to say," she told me placidly. "But you won't, will you? You won't ever find the fiend who killed my baby."

"We *will*, Wanda," I assured her. "It takes time but we surely will." I felt futile, helpless, as my words of empty meaning rang out along the lines.

"I buried her, you know," she told me, and I pictured her, small and frail and lonely, standing by that sorry grave. "I buried her and no one came. Not Sonny, not Mom and Dad, not anyone. And now I'm all alone."

She sounded hopeless, deflated, as if all the strength of life had fled. The suicide attempt sprang quickly to my mind and frantically I scoured my thoughts to try to find some way to reach her.

"Wanda, you must not let go," I told her. "You must believe that someday you will find someone who cares, someone with whom you can share a life. You are such a young, young girl with such hard experiences behind you, but life can be sweet, too, oh, so sweet, and I beg you to hold on till that sweetness comes your way."

The phone went silent for a moment and I wondered if I'd lost her. Then a stronger voice took over as she began to speak.

"They want me back at my old job," Wanda told

me quickly. "They say there's a good chance I could advance."

"What did you do, Wanda?" I asked her. "Before the baby came."

"I was a desk clerk at one of the hotels on the Strip," she said. "I got off welfare and was working doing checking in and checking out. But just before Lucy was born I got some computer training and now they say I can qualify real soon for better work back in the office."

"Go for it, Wanda," I told her enthusiastically. "Grab on to that chance and ride it for all it's worth. Go forward with your life!"

"Am I supposed to forget Lucy?" the young girl asked me. "Because I can never do that."

"Of course you're not supposed to forget your baby," I told her, still surprised at her simplicity and naiveté. "That would be a wrong, impossible thing to do. You're supposed to love her precious memory, to cherish the moments you had with her, and then rise above your sad, sad loss and fashion a worthwhile life for you, the baby's mother. Live each day in such a way you'd make Lucy proud of you."

Dear God, I thought, please let me somehow get through to her. Let my simple rah-rah words give her something to hold on to. It was so hard, I knew, to reach a person in despair and sometimes words were all we had to work with. But words can carry power.

I heard her give a deep, fast sigh, as if she were standing tall and gathering herself together.

"I'm going to do that," she told me with finality. "I'm going to remember what you said and live each day for Lucy. I'm going to take that job and be the best that I can be."

She'd found a branch to grasp, a rope to draw her to a shore of hope and out of a lake of deep despair.

But would it last? I wondered sadly as I finally hung up. Would Wanda's upbeat mood continue to sustain her? Or would hopelessness take over and lead to pills again?

I saw her pushing the cart down the grocery store aisle and suddenly I knew I was going to try to talk to her. Maybe I *was* the enemy and she wouldn't listen to me but someone had to try to help Dan and I didn't see anyone else rushing to the fore.

I'd met Rena Kent several times, at division Christmas parties and once or twice when she'd dropped by the station, but I didn't know her well. A slim, pretty woman with coal-black hair and a pleasant face, she'd always struck me as a girl any man would be happy to have as his wife.

I maneuvered my cart close to hers and waited till she set some little jars in the basket, beside a fat-faced baby holding up its fist.

"Hi, Rena, how're you doing? It's been a little while."

She glanced up quickly and a wary look crossed her face. She's wondering if I know, I thought. Wondering what I'm thinking. She smiled shyly.

"Hi, Katharine. It's good to see you."

"Look," I said, speaking softly so other shoppers wouldn't hear, "I'm real glad I ran into you. I know about the separation and I wondered if I could come and talk with you sometime real soon."

She frowned and began to shake her head, her hand going to her jet-black curls. I rushed ahead before she could shut me out.

"I'm not trying to be a busybody, Rena, but Dan's in agony and I can't think you're not suffering, too. I care about both of you very much and there're one or two things I'd like to say if we could chat for just several moments."

She looked straight at me and I saw the pain and misery in her eyes.

"It's none of your business, Katharine," she told me bluntly, but her voice began to break.

"Please, Rena, it can't do any harm."

She stroked the baby's fine-haired curls, considering.

"All right," she finally said reluctantly, "but you can't talk me into anything. You can't understand my position because you're on the other side. I know how I feel and why I feel that way. It's got nothing to do with not loving Dan. It's got to do with living."

"Still, I'd like to visit for a little while."

"Sure, how about later on this afternoon? The baby will be sleeping then." And she gave me directions to her mother's house on the other side of town, then we wheeled our carts away.

CHAPTER EIGHTEEN

"It doesn't look as if he needs the money," Steve observed as we pulled up behind the silver Jaguar in the drive of Benson's small but tasteful house, "but I guess you can never get too filthy rich."

"Catch the license plate," I said, signaling with my head. "A bit pretentious, what?"

Darrow squinted at the personalized California tag and gave a hoot. " 'JACQUES!' You'd think he'd feel a little foolish riding around with that."

We'd driven up together, leaving Rhoads and Harris pursuing other leads. Since Steve had been my partner when the Brownfeld kid had told us all about Meryl's cousin, I'd decided to take him with me to Merced.

"So what's the drill, tough or sweet?" he asked as we walked up a path laid with random bricks and flanked by tiny, well-trimmed shrubs.

"Depends on him, doesn't it," I countered, "and what he's got to say. All we know right now is that he and Meryl fought that morning, eleven hours or more before the murders. If he was so steamed, then why not do her then, while in the heat of rage and passion? And why Lucy? Why would Benson kill the baby?"

"Maybe the thing with Meryl started eating at him," Darrow answered, "and during the day he decided she'd have to go. Besides, there was the advantage of working under cover of darkness. As for the little girl, I just don't know."

I rang the bell, a pretty pearlized affair set within a thin brass rim. Shortly the door swung inward and Jack Benson stood there staring, his almond eyes popped open dark and round and shiny like two huckleberries on a bush.

I had no doubt that this was he, for the man exactly fitted William Ford's description. Swarthy, pudgy, little nose curving like a parrot's beak. I recalled how my recitation of those features had sent Steve Brownfeld soaring into fits of laughter.

"Mr. Benson? We're Detectives Harrod and Darrow of the San Madera Police Department. We'd like to speak with you about your cousin's death."

"Come in, I've been expecting you," he answered. "Aunt DeeDee and Uncle Harold said you'd called on them. Poor Meryl. Have you any idea who did it?"

Benson, talking with his hands, led us to a stylish living room while keeping up the chatter.

"We tried to contact you last week," I told him, "but you were out of town. Why didn't you give us a ring if you knew we wanted to see you?"

"Oh, well," he flustered, "I wasn't really sure. I just thought I'd hear from you. I mean, I didn't *know*, but now you're here, I'm not surprised."

We settled on a sofa and two chairs, and I noticed how the plumpness of his calves protruded between his sock tops and the bottom of his pants. He had an oily feeling all about him, even though I couldn't physically detect the glisten.

" 'Poor Meryl,' " I started, harking back to his own words, " 'poor Meryl' indeed. No, I'm afraid we're not too far along with the solving of the case so we thought maybe you could help us."

"In any way, Detective, in any way." Benson laid his hands along the chair arms and waited for my questions.

"Did your cousin have any enemies you know of?"

"Enemies? No, though if I were you I'd be looking in the area of that silly social service job she had. Harold and DeeDee feel the same way, too. You run up against a bunch of off-beat types in that line of work, and I personally believe one of them took a dislike to her and decided to remove her.

"Or maybe it started out as robbery and then went badly wrong. They must've sensed or known she was many cuts above them and figured she owned lots of goods worth stealing."

"No, it wasn't robbery, Mr. Benson," Darrow told him. "We've completely ruled that out."

"Well, look at her list of clients. I'm still sure you'll find the answer there."

"How did you get along with your cousin, Mr. Benson?" I asked, ignoring his suggestion. "Were you close?"

"Oh, I thought the world of her," he answered with exaggerated gestures, "and I was devastated when she died. Meryl could be a little headstrong and independent—like with that shameful low-class job—but looking at the bigger picture, she was certainly a wonderful human being."

"When did you last see her?" I asked him softly, riveting on his eyes as I spoke. They revealed nothing as he responded.

"Oh, not for some time, Detective. You must understand that though we were close relatives, we *did* live fairly far apart. Sometimes weeks or even months would pass without our seeing each other. And then when we did, it was usually at some family gathering, not just the two of us alone."

Again he waved his hands in front of him, as if swiping at some flies.

"So you didn't see Meryl on the day she died?"

The oval eyes popped wide again and stared at me. I saw uneasiness, maybe fear, creep in.

"Of course I didn't. I just told you."

"Mr. Benson, we've got a witness who's prepared

to swear he saw you leaving Meryl's town house at ten o'clock on the morning of the day she died, and another witness who'll swear you hated Meryl and were always trying to discredit her and paint her in a bad light with her parents.''

"And why would I do that?" he parried, suddenly extremely wary.

"Because with Meryl out of the way, you'd inherit all the Masterses' money. Isn't that correct?"

He licked his lips, beginning to perspire.

"I don't know the terms of Harold's and DeeDee's wills," he said, "it would be crass to ask."

"I think you *do* know the terms," I told him, "or *think* you do, at least. But answer my question about the Friday morning visit."

Benson squirmed in the velveteen-upholstered chair as his face turned deep and brilliant red.

"I saw her," he admitted, his voice dropping to a whisper. "I feel like such a fool. I was wrong to lie."

"Why did you, then," Darrow interjected, "especially if you've got nothing to hide?"

"I wanted to stay out of it. I just thought it'd be simpler if you thought I wasn't there. I mean, I knew it couldn't have any bearing on the case."

"You're wrong, it could. Tell us what the two of you talked about that morning. You see, something Meryl told you *might* have some bearing on what happened later, yet you maybe wouldn't recognize that fact."

"Nothing special, we talked of nothing special. I was just passing through town and thought I'd drop in to say hello. Didn't really expect to find her home but she said she'd taken the day off to do some catching up around the condo."

"Did she mention expecting any visitors that night?"

Benson paused, then shook his head.

"No, she said nothing of that sort. We just had some coffee, chatted about little things, and then I left."

"And there was an argument," I stated matter-of-factly.

Benson gave a start.

"No, no argument. Who told you that?"

"The same person who told us that you'd been there. This individual overheard a verbal altercation loud and clear, out on the steps as you were leaving. Would you please tell us what that was all about?"

"That old nosey parker next door, that's who's been telling you these tales," Benson huffed and puffed. "Has nothing better to do all day but listen to the comings and the goings."

"Be that as it may, what were you two arguing about?"

"Oh, nothing, really. He wasted his time on that one. I was just trying to persuade her, for the one hundredth time, to give up that foolish job. DeeDee and Harold, they're getting up in years, and the family didn't like it, you know."

Right, I thought, I'm sure that's it. What really happened was you thought you'd catch her in it a little deeper and take your tale right home to aunt and uncle.

"And that was it, then?" I said aloud.

He nodded vigorously.

"Well, you must've made her pretty angry. I understand she told you to screw yourself, and get the fuck away from her and stay away."

My use of the vulgarities flustered him, and again he began to blush.

"Well, Meryl could be like that," Benson explained shakily. "I don't like to speak ill of the dead, but Meryl could get very overheated, very nasty, at the slightest opportunity. It meant nothing, it was just her way."

Unnerved though he was, I could see he was going to let us have only *his* version of the disagreement.

"Mr. Benson, please tell us where you were on Friday night—the night Meryl Masters was murdered."

He visibly relaxed and his face began to brighten.

"If that's what all of this is about, Detective, I only wish you'd asked me earlier. I was eating dinner with Aunt DeeDee and Uncle Harold at their house in San Francisco."

He got up, strode confidently to the phone, and lifted the receiver. Jumping quickly to my feet, I followed him, not prepared to let him speak to them before I got a chance to ask the question.

"No, no, Detective, I won't alert them." Benson was as cool and smooth as a ripened cucumber now that he saw the direction this was heading. "I'm just helping out. Dialing the number for you."

I took the phone, and after several rings a voice answered, "Masters residence." I ID'd myself and asked to speak with either the master or the mistress.

After waiting several minutes, I heard the approaching tap of heels upon a hardwood floor, then DeeDee Masters asked how she could help me.

"Do you recall where you were the evening of your daughter's death, and who, if anyone, was with you? . . . All right, and what time was that—when did dinner start and when did it end? . . . And, Mrs. Masters, you're certain of the day? . . . I see. Well, thank you very much."

"He may have hated her, but for sure, he's not the one who killed her," I told Darrow as we headed down the highway. "Unless Harold and DeeDee are lying, he, too, has got a cast-iron alibi."

"They *are* certain of the date?" Steve inquired insistently.

"Absolutely. When I asked Mrs. Masters the same question, she shot back, 'Wouldn't you recall what you were doing the day your daughter died?' I guess, even if she had a strange relationship with Meryl, she's right. Said 'John' came for cocktails at seven and lingered after dinner for some bridge. Didn't leave till somewhere around eleven-thirty.

"But, Steve, you know something?"—my mouth narrowed and I slapped my palm against my thigh—"he was frightened when he saw us and relieved when we left, yet he had an airtight alibi for Meryl Masters's murder. I think Jack Benson's got something to fear from us, all right, but I don't think it's got anything to do with his cousin's killing."

He didn't answer and I glanced over at him, wondering if he'd heard. I saw him staring straight ahead, eyes fixed on the road in front of him.

He seemed preoccupied, intense, unlike his usual wisecracking self. I'd noticed it to some degree on the drive up to Merced but on our return home the mood seemed to have deepened. I didn't ask him what was wrong. I didn't want him prying into *my* life so I wasn't going to pry into his.

Then suddenly I saw Darrow's hands tighten on the steering wheel and his darkly handsome face became ugly, lips set in a sneer that bared his straight white teeth.

"Fuck it!" I heard him mutter underneath his breath, and I could ignore him no longer.

"What's wrong, Steve?" I asked, turning in my seat to face him. "Anything you'd care to talk about?"

We'd always worked well together on a case once we got down to business but because in our spare time our relationship had usually been more adversarial than friendly I now found it odd to speak to him this way.

"Hell, no," he answered in a lilting singsong voice. "Nothing ol' Stevie boy can't handle."

Just as you like, I thought. I'll keep my nose out of it. Didn't really want to know anyway.

We drove several miles in silence, the humming of the tires and the swooshing of the passing cars the only sounds I heard. Then Darrow began rapping softly on the steering wheel. I glanced quickly over and saw his left hand balled up into a fist that he brought up and down, up and down against the firmness of the plastic.

"C'mon, Steve, what gives?" I asked. I found that, after all, I wanted to know. I couldn't ride all the way to San Madera with the rapping and the cursing going on and no accompanying explanation.

His head swung around and he looked at me with steely eyes that seemed to stab right through me.

"Oh, you women," he said with sarcasm. "My brother's dumping his two-timin' stinkin' wife. Has to. She's half-drunk all the time and bringing home God knows what disease. Leaves him with two young kids to raise but there's no other choice, is there?"

I hadn't even known he had a brother, much less one in a hapless marriage.

"I'm sorry, Steve," I told him, wondering why he was taking his brother's troubles so very personally.

"Sorry, hell," he raged. "Women are always sorry. Women are always cheap drunken tramps. Oh, not all, not all. I take that back. Somewhere in this god-

forsaken world there must be one or two good-girl
Virgin Marys. I'd like to believe that, I really would.
But most of the so-called fair sex are whoring
rubbish.''

His face darkened even deeper and now his eyes
focused on some point ahead. In the three or four
years I'd worked with him, I'd never seen him like
this before, running out of control, letting his guard
down to reveal a deeply personal side.

"My mother was the same way. Did just the same
stuff to my father that my brother's getting now.
Stinking drunk, falling down, slipping out and sleeping all around. Leaving that good hardworking man
to get us up and change the diapers and wipe a
snotty nose.''

He was yelling now, hands gripping the wheel
ever tighter as the words tumbled from his throat. I
sat mesmerized, drawn by the unexpected look behind a curtain I'd never even known was there.

Shallow Steve Darrow, I'd always thought. Mr. La-
dies' Man. A good enough detective but a wisecracking smart-assed one-liner where the women
were concerned. Before today I hadn't wanted to
know any more than that. I still wasn't sure I did
now.

"He took it all he could and then he told her to
get out. And she did. Walked right out on him and
me and my little baby brother and never once looked
back. Just another dolly in a long, long line of trol-
lops. And that line just keeps on coming.''

His voice was filled with bitterness and his words growled out in rounded spat-out phrasing.

I knew he'd been married once and that that marriage hadn't lasted very long, and now I thought I knew the reason why. And the reason he kept a string of women like a stableful of ponies, unable or unwilling to build a deep relationship with anyone. He'd been deeply hurt a long, long time ago and he couldn't start to trust, he couldn't give respect where none existed.

Then just as suddenly as it'd started, Steve's anger stopped, jerked back inside him where I couldn't see it anymore. He relaxed his grip, shifted uncomfortably in his seat, and cleared his throat several times. I sensed discomfiture, embarrassment, and I was sure he was berating himself for having revealed so much to me.

"It's all right, Steve," I told him softly. "It's all right to talk about it." I don't think I'd ever spoken to him in that tone before.

"Don't give it another thought, dolly," he wise-cracked at me. "You gals just can get to a man sometimes." And he gave a wink and snapped the subject closed.

But I'd seen behind the curtain and I'd not soon forget. I'd been given a whole new perspective on Steve Darrow.

"I know you're scared, Rena," I began, settling into the comfy sofa in her parents' den, "but is that fear so paramount it dwarfs all the goodness in your life, robs you of the joys you share? And do you think by leaving Dan you'll take that fear away? For you won't.

"As long as you love him, whether you're with him or not, you'll be concerned about his well-being. Walking out will never change that fact, so why not stay and try to work it out? If you love him—and I know you do—can you not strive to come to terms with your fear and salvage your marriage?"

She shook her head bleakly.

"You don't understand. It's dreadful, it overwhelms me. And I'm not imagining things, Katharine. There's his family history. Men in his family die early from heart trouble and stress only hastens those deaths. And you know being a cop's an awfully stressful job."

"I don't deny that," I answered, "but Dan handles work stress very well. What he doesn't handle easily is the situation he's in now with you. He's torn apart and it's telling on him. He's letting down on the way he's taking care of business and I'm scared he's going to put himself at risk. He missed a filing deadline on a suspect the other day because he wasn't paying close attention. I'm worried next time he'll get careless when he's on a bust and the crook will seize the upper hand."

"Then why doesn't he give it up? Why doesn't he just quit?" she asked, searching my eyes deeply for an answer. "That way we'd both be happy, and he'd live longer, too."

"It's not that simple, Rena. Being a cop is not an easy thing to leave. It's not like a lot of other jobs that require no emotional commitment. If you ask Dan to give it up you're asking him to leave a part of himself behind. The very qualities that made you fall in love with him are those that made him want to be an officer. His need to do this job is so deeply ingrained in him that it cannot be separated from him without wounding him, leaving him half a person."

"I don't understand," she told me with bewilderment. "Other people make career changes and it works out just fine."

"Let me try to explain a little better," I began. Upstairs I heard the low whimper of the waking baby and then a soothing voice, probably that of Rena's mother, comforting him. "People are drawn to some professions solely because they love the work itself and they want to do it well. Carpenters, for instance, take pride in honing their craftsmanship to a fine perfection but they usually tend to look at their work objectively and dispassionately, without emotional involvement.

"Certain other professions, however, draw people who not only love the work but who engage in it because of selfless humanitarian reasons. And law enforcement is one of those. People who become cops are usually highly idealistic. They want to help others and they believe they *can* make a difference and bring fairness and justice to their fellow man. When you're asked to leave all that behind, you feel you're not only giving up the job you love but you're deserting those people you long ago swore to help. The emotional tie between a cop and his work is just too deep to easily say good-bye."

My mind moved backward as I talked and I saw myself as a young probationer thinking I could save the world. I hadn't, of course, but I felt I'd done some good, made some difference. Some few, like the young cop who'd just quit, became discouraged, it's true, but most would continue to struggle, to fight the good fight for all their working days.

I glanced at Kent's wife and saw that she was watching me intently. I decided to get a little personal, in order to better try to make my point.

"My soon-to-be-ex asked me to give it up, Rena, but I couldn't do it. Because I knew that if I did I'd never be myself again, I'd be only an empty husk of the woman I'd once been."

Her lips parted as she listened, then she spoke.

"I never knew . . . never looked at it like that before. I never fully perceived how very much might be involved. I feel so stupid. I should've known more, should've better understood the depth of his commitment."

"You can't blame yourself, Rena," I told her.

"You're not a cop, you never felt the call. It's not an easy thing to understand if you're on the outside looking in. But trust me. If Dan gives it up, it'll be like cutting off his arm or leg."

She nodded slowly but confusion filled her face.

"I understand, Katharine, but I still don't know what to do about it. I'm scared, scared to death, and your words still don't fix that."

"Rena, he is who he is and you can't change that fact nor would you ever really want to. There is no easy answer but maybe I can suggest a few things that might help. Try to get a new perspective and work on keeping it. See, believe, and understand that Dan's is not a deliberate decision to go against your wishes. He is helpless to change the way he feels, to change the essence of the man he is.

"Accept that fact, then put it behind you and get on with your life. Make the most of what the two of you have together and look to the future with hope. Don't dwell on your worries. When you find them creeping in, get busy with the baby, with a hobby, with work you can get absorbed in. Stress the positive and let your fears slide far away."

"If only I could, Katharine," she told me sadly. "I don't know if I'm a strong enough person to do that."

"Maybe not alone, Rena," I responded, "but with the help of others it could work. Are you aware of the Spousal Support Group with the department?"

Puzzled, she shook her head.

"It's a group of husbands and wives of police officers. They lend support in times of trouble and they
get together to talk out their fears, the very fears that
you have. They're there for each other, reaching out
to help the members build positive, constructive lives
with their families. Here, let me give you this." And
I scribbled a sergeant's wife's name and number on
a scrap of paper.

Slowly, still bewildered and dejected, she reached
out and took it.

"I don't know, Kate, I just don't know. Right now I
can't imagine anyone making me feel alright. But
maybe I'll call. Maybe I *can* change. I know your
words today made me look at everything from another way around."

"Try it, Rena," I urged her. "Try it for you and for
Danny and the baby. I care about you all and I truly
believe you can work it out. You've got nothing to
lose and all the world to gain."

"I will, I probably will," she said with sudden decision. "God knows, I love him, Kate, with all my
heart and I can't bear the thought of life without
him." Her voice choked and she gave a little sob.

"Funny," I told her, rising to go, "he said much
the same thing about you."

I dropped by Carl's apartment, to see him before
I went on home to change for dinner, and was star-

tled by the difference in his looks between Saturday and today.

Whereas he'd left the brunch in an upbeat jovial mood, I now found my partner lying back against the pillows, despondency spread across his face. He momentarily brightened when I came walking in, but after several minutes his face again lost its fervor.

Glancing around the little rooms, I saw a whiskey bottle on the kitchen counter. Carl had always been a man who enjoyed a drink—but never more than one or two and never while on duty. Granted, he wasn't working now but I was still surprised to see Old Grand-Dad standing beside a glass at five o'clock on a winter afternoon.

I looked closely at my friend. At his tousled untrimmed hair and day's growth of beard, at the hopelessness within his eyes.

The stereotype cannot be happening here, I told myself, alarmed. Cop can't work, becomes depressed, starts turning to the bottle.

"How's Sandy?" I inquired, wondering if her absence was part of the explanation. "She been by today?"

"Nah," he answered, stretching. "She's sick. Got the flu or something. She'll be here tomorrow, though. Said it's not real serious."

I sat down on the corner of the sofa and brought him up-to-date on everything that'd happened with Sonny and with Jack.

"Charlie was so certain it was Mitchell," I explained, "and now he's bitterly disappointed. I've got to admit I pinned my hopes on Benson, but another letdown there. Momentarily, Carl, we're stymied. If you get those brain cells working overtime, let me know which way to go."

I got up, rummaged till I found the instant coffee, and made a cup for each of us.

"Harris, the other cop," Carl began as I handed him the mug and he reached up to take it. "He seems like a real straight guy. I mean, not that Rhoads isn't, but Bobby's got something extra about him."

Caught off-guard, I didn't know what to say, so I just nodded and murmured, "Yes, it seems so."

Turned out, Carl wasn't just making small talk, he was on a calculated fishing expedition.

"Is anything going on there, Kate? I couldn't help but notice the way he looked at you that morning at the brunch."

I felt myself begin to blush, then wondered why. This was my old buddy, Carl, who knew me pretty much as well as I knew myself and who'd helped me through one tough time after another . . . just as I, in mutual support, had always been there for him to lean on. If I confided in him now, he'd be a quiet and sensitive ally, not prone to poking and prying like Karen Windall.

"I don't know, Carl," I answered honestly. "We went out to hear some jazz that night and we're having dinner together this evening. I don't know what I feel. Yes, I'm attracted to him, both physically and emotionally, but it's all moving much too fast. It came on me unawares, when I wasn't looking for it, and I'm scared, I don't know how to handle it. I've not dated anyone since Jon and I broke up, you know that."

"Has Harris said anything direct to you about his feelings?"

"No, nothing. There've been some looks, some touches, but then other times he acts real casual, as if I wasn't there." I paused, then gave a little laugh. "Could be, you know, there's nothing to it—that he's just looking for someone to pass the time with while he's down from Stockton. Could be you and I are jumping the gun, old pal, reading too much into a simple dinner date."

"No, Kate, I don't think so," Carl told me, "I've got a pretty good instinct about things like that. My advice to you is to relax and take it as it comes. If this relationship develops into something special, there's nothing wrong with that, so don't sweat it and get all uptight. Has Tommy noticed anything yet?"

"Ah, yes, and there's a little problem there. He's trying to accept my dating but I know it bothers him. And I feel slightly guilty about that, even though I know I shouldn't."

"You're right, you shouldn't, and always remember that." Carl pulled himself up straighter on the sofa, and I noticed how the color had flowed back into his face, how the despondent stare had vanished. My visit, the sharing of my problems, were doing him some good.

"Tommy's a smart kid and he'll accept all of this as time goes by. There may be some rough patches at first but he'll get used to it and hopefully even like it. Harris, after all, seems like a decent sort of man—one that little boys would take to."

I spied a vase of red and yellow blossoms sitting on a table and guessed the records clerk had added this bright and homey touch on her last visit before she caught the flu.

"And what about *your* love life, Carl?" I asked. "Have you gotten any closer to making a decision about Sandy?"

He sighed, reclining on the pillow. "There's been a little complication there," he admitted. "Lila's trying to get back into the picture."

Lila—a high-flying fancy woman—had walked out on Carl many years before, but I'd always seriously doubted he'd ever gotten over her. Though I didn't know her well, I knew that she was trouble, always keeping Carl's life stirred up, never letting it have a smooth uncomplicated surface.

"You wouldn't take her back, would you?" I asked, aghast. "You've walked that road before and you know it leads you nowhere."

"No, Kate, I wouldn't," he assured me. "This old man knows when he's well off. Nope, it's just with her putting on her sweet routine again, it makes it kind of tough to concentrate on someone else."

"Sandy's a fine woman, Carl," I lectured, "and I believe the two of you would be awfully good for one another. Take my advice and start concentrating pretty hard."

Nothing could ever be simple and straightforward, I began grousing to myself. Not my murders, not my life, not Carl's romantic forays. And then I had to stop and laugh out loud.

"We're pretty good at playing Ann Landers to each other, pal," I told him, "and I think we've given each other some pretty good advice. Tell you what. I'll take yours and you take mine, and we'll both turn out all right."

I clapped him on the shoulder, said I'd speak to him the following day, then got up to go.

As I walked toward the door, I saw a framed photo of a police officer standing on a shelf near a window and I stopped to peer at it. Something about the broad face, the clear blue eyes, struck me as familiar.

"Who's this, Carl?" I asked.

He paused a moment, then said softly, "My dad."

"Your dad?" My surprise leaped right out as I turned to stare at him. "You never told me your father was cop. Like Kent's. You and Kent both had cops for dads."

In all the years I'd known him—and they'd been quite a few with many hard and shared experiences—Carl Mungers had never told me this till now. I knew he, like myself, had been raised on a spread outside of town but I'd always thought his mother was a teacher and his father tilled the soil.

"I don't talk too much about it, Kate," he told me, his eyes locked warily on mine as if he held some fear.

"Here? Was it here in San Madera?" I peered again at the photo and thought I recognized the uniform the force had worn several decades ago.

"Yeah, but he didn't make it through academy. He was canned."

"I'm sorry, Carl," I told him, embarrassed for him because he seemed uncomfortable. In fact, I felt a little bit uncomfortable myself. "The physical can be pretty rough. God knows, I never thought I'd get over that six-foot wall myself."

"It wasn't that, Kate," he told me sadly, and his voice dropped several octaves lower. "He was cut because some woman, some jealous girl he used to date, accused him of rape. There was nothing to it, groundless from the start. She was a spiteful troublemaker angry because he'd left her for my mother. The investigation came up empty, no charges were ever filed.

"But though my dad was cleared of that woman's accusations, the department was going through one of its periodic super-sensitive PR periods and he was terminated one month prior to graduation. He'd gotten his uniform, his badge, he'd almost made it through. Kate, it broke his heart."

"Oh, Carl." I flung my hands out futilely.

"But how could *you* become a cop, then?" I finally asked. "I'd have thought you'd hate the lot of us so much you'd want to stay far, far away."

"Because *he* still loved it, Kate, despite what the department did to him, so I wanted to make it up to him, to go on in his stead. I wanted to be the best copper ever and show them what a Mungers could do. I wanted to make the old man proud of me and let him live his hopes and dreams through me."

"And he did, didn't he, Carl?" I asked, thinking of the flawless professional sitting here before me.

"Yes, he did, Kate. He died a happy man just by watching me do my work. The stories I'd tell him, the busts we'd share. He lived for the times I'd drop by and we'd talk shop. But you know what?" And Carl looked at me with a twinkle in his eye. "A funny thing happened somewhere along the line. I took up the work for him but ended up loving it myself."

As soon as I walked through the door, the sound enveloped me—the banging, rapping sound of Tommy at the drums. Our first lesson was tomorrow evening, and I thought how eagerly the two of us were anticipating the event.

"Hey, kiddo," I called loudly, "I need to talk with you a minute."

Laying down the sticks, he scampered over and I put my arms around him and hugged him to me, then started smoothing back his hair.

We dropped down on the rug, talking about school, about the coming lesson, about the burrs caught in Molly's fur. Then I told him, "I'm going to sit and visit with you while you and Mrs. Miller have your dinner, but around seven o'clock I'm going out with my friend, Detective Harris. Like the last time, I'll look in on you when I get home."

Tommy drew back and stared at me.

"That same man again, Mom?"

"Yes, the same one. He's a nice person and we have a lot in common. Anyway," I added lamely, "he'll be going back up north real soon."

"And then you won't see him anymore?" Tommy asked happily.

"Not necessarily. I'd hope I could always keep his friendship, but no, I certainly wouldn't see him as often as I'm doing now." I took his face with both my hands. "Tommy, there's nothing to be afraid of, darling. You will always have my love, my time, and my attention."

He scooted back off to the drums and I went upstairs to get ready. Precisely at seven, the front bell rang, and again I opened up the door and welcomed Bobby.

He smiled at me but went directly to my son, who was hanging back near the archway to the den.

"I brought you something," Harris said, a twinkle in his eye, and he extended a long thin object wrapped in tissue.

Tommy took the packet gingerly and began unwrapping it, and shortly a pair of brushes and a set of drumsticks sporting fat round knobs fell out upon the floor. Eagerly, he bent and scooped them up, grinning with delight.

"Every serious drummer should have more than one set of sticks," Bobby told him lightly, "and before long, you'll be needing those little brushes, too, for the subtle swishing sounds."

Eyes shining, my son made his way to the brand-new set, sat down upon the stool, and began to do his strokes. Although he called good-bye, I doubt he even heard the front door close behind us.

CHAPTER NINETEEN

He laid the clipping on my desk, jabbing at it with his finger.

"Take a look at this," Rhoads told me, excitement lighting up his voice.

I glanced down and saw a photo of a little baby, a baby very much like Lucy Brighton, and above the picture I saw a headline with words that made my hair stand up on end—"Cops Question Paroled Child Molester About Baby's Killing."

Another infant—another sweet lost soul like Wanda's little girl—had fallen prey to another monster.

I went to the beginning and read the story slowly. A six-month-old baby boy had been found strangled with a nylon cord and dumped in a vacant lot near a playground in Visalia, a city one hundred miles farther to the south. Police in that city were questioning one Lester Farnham, a molester recently released from jail and seen by several witnesses in the area where the body had been found.

I felt bitter phlegm begin to fill my throat and I thought that I would vomit, as the words brought back with vivid detail the scene of finding Lucy's body.

"My God," I said, "it's terrible. Another little child."

"Yes, Kate, it's awful," Charlie answered, "but there's a point to why I'm showing this to you, it's not just a ghoulish gesture. Read down a little farther."

I quickly scanned the words, trying to find what Rhoads wanted me to see, and then I saw it. Lester Farnham had been born and raised in San Madera and, before being sent to prison, had lived close to Meryl Masters's Rimerton address.

"Interesting," I told him, "but what're you saying here? Do you believe there's a connection with our case?"

"He does babies, that's what. He molests them and sometimes, like down in Visalia, he kills them. And he knows the area and our crime scene, probably still has friends he visits there. He could've seen the Brighton child being dropped at Meryl's town house and decided to have a go at her."

"Lucy wasn't molested," I pointed out, "and the detectives down south are only *questioning* Farnham about the killing, they're not charging him yet. All this guy is guilty of is molestation at some time in the past. I doubt he fits into our murders here."

"Look, Kate," Rhoads urged, banging his fist lightly on the desk, "I really think we should dig into this a little further. I've already spoken to the cops in Visalia, and they're willing to let us have a go at him."

"On what basis, Charlie? Why not pick up every convicted molester in the state and interrogate them all? There's absolutely no evidence to show Farnham was anywhere near San Madera at any time since he got out of prison. The paper even says he's been living in Visalia since his parole several months ago."

"Let's go ask him where he was that Friday night. At least let's go ask him, Kate."

I leaned back, considering. I liked eager beavers but Rhoads was starting to wear me out. Still, he might have a point here.

Suppose the suspect had been hanging around his old haunts that Friday night and got a hankering to stroke a baby. Suppose he'd watched Wanda carry Lucy into Meryl's, then leave without her? Suppose he already knew Meryl lived alone, and thought maybe he'd go in and she'd be asleep and Lucy would be all his to touch and torment?

Somehow he'd gained entry, but instead of finding Masters soundly sleeping, he'd found her wide awake and in the way. And then it had all started going wrong in a cacophony of messy missteps, and he'd panicked, killing them both.

I shook my head, still not happy, but I had to admit the scenario held possibilities.

"Tell you what, Charlie," I conceded, "let's see what Visalia does with him and then we'll make our decision. Let's see if they think he could be a killer or not before we make the trip. If they charge him, we'll take a drive, but if they kick him loose we'll forget about it. Because—and I go back to this—because at this point he's a known molester, no more, no less, and Lucy, thank God, was never touched."

Rhoads arched his eyebrows unhappily, as if to say he thought I was wrong in holding back, but he accepted my decision and lumbered on back to his desk. I wondered if the turmoil of his personal life had settled down any in the last two days, if he'd come any closer to satisfying the Merced woman's ultimatum, but I didn't want to get involved so I wasn't going to ask him.

I saw Steve enter the room and heave his gunbelt on his desk. He'd not had much to say to me this morning and I imagined that despite his earlier wisecrack about not giving it another thought, he now felt deeply embarrassed about his outburst.

Parents, I reflected, how truly deeply they affect our lives, even into adulthood, even when we didn't always know them for that long or in a kind and loving way.

Steve's alcoholic mother, Carl's dad who'd failed to be a cop, Wanda's and Meryl's judgmental mothers and fathers. All had marked their children and helped to shape the path that they would take.

I got up, walked to the john, then came back and sat down at my desk. Picking up some paperwork, my gaze wandered across the room and I saw an odd thing—Charlie Rhoads with his head in his hands as if steeped in sorrow. The Merced mess, I thought, and despite my earlier resolve to stay out of it, I almost rose and went to him. Before I could push my chair back, though, his head snapped up and he now looked composed and normal.

A hand pressed lightly on my shoulder and I gave a little jump, then looked up into the smiling eyes of Bobby Harris. I hadn't seen him since he'd left me late last night, after lingering over coffee in my den for several hours following our return from dinner.

"What's up, Kate? Anything happening?"

I started to tell him about Charlie's bright idea when Rhoads ambled over, lighting up a cigarette. Though I'd not smoked for some time now, I well knew how that urge acted, remembering how the intensity of working a tough case would make me crave the physical act itself of inhaling and exhaling. Just the drawing in, the letting out, relaxed and satisfied, never mind the taste and the beneficial nicotine. I let him go this time, didn't remind him the rules said not to smoke.

"Visalia just called back," he said, glancing at both me and Bobby. "They've just released Farnham. Not enough evidence to hold him. But, Kate, I still think we should ride down there. The detectives told me

they let him go only because they don't have enough
to charge him. That off the record, they still believe
he might've done the crime."

Why not, I asked myself, why not? Rhoads's instincts about Mitchell had proved all wrong, but
who's to say he wouldn't do better here? At least
he, unlike the rest of us right now, had hustled up
a suspect.

"Okay, Charlie, find out where he lives and let's
go talk to him. I'll admit it's maybe worth a try."

"I've already got the address, Kate," he answered
jauntily. "Want to leave right now?"

"No," I answered, "we'll go first thing in the
morning, there's a few things I need to clean up here.
But why don't you run his rap sheet so we can start
to know this joker."

I picked up the phone, dialed the social services
number, and asked to speak with Brownfeld.

"So you made it in through all that fog?" I cheerily
greeted him. "Tell me, do you know any reason your
cousin Jack might have to fear police? Could he be
involved in anything illegal, do you think?"

Brownfeld began to chuckle, completely at ease,
and I was glad I'd gained his trust. I remembered
the scared rabbit who'd met Harris and myself at the
downtown office and then later at his apartment out
on Burnt Creek Road.

"I wouldn't be at all surprised if he did a lot of
things on the shady side," he told me, "but what

they are, I wouldn't know. If *you* find out anything, please tell me. After the way he tried to trip up Meryl, I'd love to see old Jack exposed in front of Aunt DeeDee and Uncle Harold."

"What's his business anyway," I inquired, "or does he just live off his money?"

"He dabbles a little in fine art, I think. Says he's got a shop somewhere in Merced. That's why he goes out of town a lot—supposed to be on buying trips— but I don't really know how serious he is about it."

As I was putting down the phone, Rhoads walked up and laid Farnham's rap sheet in front of me. I peered at it and saw it was shorter than I'd expected. Just the vital statistics of the subject himself and the entry that he'd been convicted of two counts of child molestation a little more than five years ago.

"Hmmmm, male white, thirty years of age, five-nine, one hundred thirty-five pounds, brown hair, blue eyes," I read aloud. "He's younger than I thought he'd be. Somehow I expected a man around forty-five or fifty. What do you know about these crimes, Charlie? Were they done here in San Madera?"

"Nope," he answered, "they weren't. They were done down in Tulare. He had some relatives living there and seems when he'd go to visit them, he'd diddle the neighbor's five-year-old and then his own cousin's baby after it was born.

"Was caught one day when the cousin walked in

on him and found him with his mouth down on the infant, and after word got out, the kid next door told her mommy that Uncle Lester—that's what she called him, though they weren't related—used to put his hands up her panties and make her do nasty things to his wee-wee."

"One baby, one little girl," I mused. "There's quite a difference between an infant and a five-year-old. One can be made to participate, no matter how reluctantly, while the other just lies there and takes it. Apparently either way appealed to Farnham." I looked at Charlie. "Did Visalia tell you anything about the guy? Is he full of bluff, in denial, what?"

"They said he's a nervous Nellie who pisses in his pants several times a day. Tears, sobs, protestations of innocence, the lot."

"Why don't you run over to his old area," I suggested, "and see if you can turn up anyone who maybe used to know him. And could tell you if Lester was seen around here the weekend before last."

"Rollin', boss," Charlie told me, and gave me a mock salute before he grabbed his coat and gun and headed out the door.

I worked a little longer, then wound it up and started home. As I drove along I felt my face begin to brighten. Tuesday night and time to learn to beat those drums at last!

"We'll be doing mainly stickwork for the first few months," the instructor told us, "but today I want to show you what you're working up to, where you're heading. Who wants to lead off?"

I gestured to Tommy to go sit before the set, I'd take second turn. We'd decided to share a couple of lessons, then switch to individual half hours later on.

"No, Mom," he protested, suddenly shy, "you go. I'll watch and then I'll know how to do it."

I positioned myself before the drums, feeling awkward and bewildered . . . and also feeling a tingle of excitement run through me. I took a stick in either hand, the teacher helping me to set my fingers just so around them, and looked down at the little snare standing there in front of me.

"We'll start with the four-four beat," he said, "the basic rock 'n' roll beat—and you count it one, two, three, four. Say the numbers out loud, and on each of them I want you to strike the cymbal with your right-hand stick but on the one- and three-count also depress your bass drum pedal, and on the two- and four-count hit the snare with the stick in your left hand. Got it? Go slow and don't be afraid."

I shot a glance at Tommy, and knew by his parted lips and gleaming eyes that he was completely captivated by what was happening.

Tentatively I began mouthing the numbers and banging at the cymbal and the drums. At first everything became confusion as I felt my way along, with the snare getting four hits instead of two and the bass sometimes being left out altogether, but gradually I started feeling the rhythm and began to play, and my heart lifted and my spirits soared. Who cared that I was only doing beginner's work? I was keeping the beat and that was all that mattered.

Soon the music took me over and I lost myself completely in it as it led me to a higher plane. A plane where I could fly above the frenzied terror of the morning, the disappointment of the afternoon, leaving them behind as my concentration riveted on the instruments before me.

"All right, trade places," the instructor finally shouted, and quickly I handed off the sticks to Tommy, crying, "You try it now. It's so much fun!"

For fifteen minutes we alternated at the set, and then the instructor brought out a little round practice pad and showed us how to do our stickwork.

"Forget the bass and cymbal for a while," he told us. "That was just so you could see your goal. I want you to concentrate now on developing your hand movements. Do single strokes, double strokes, triplets. Like so." And he demonstrated with a speed of such rapidity that I thought we were in the midst of an artillery barrage.

"Those are some of your rudiments," he explained. "It's important you master your rudiments, and it's these three you should practice between now and next time. Later on, we'll move into flams and paradiddles."

So much to learn, I thought, but I was not discouraged. I would master it, and one day I'd actually be able to play along with my beloved rock 'n' roll instead of just humming and tapping my foot to keep the beat.

The lesson ended, and exhilarated, we gathered up our sticks and music books and left the studio.

"That was great, Mom," Tommy said, pressing up against me. "Let's go home and do some more."

"Maybe we should do our drumming in our heads," I answered gently, hoping not to break his joyful mood. "I doubt the neighbors would appreciate a late-night serenade."

I put our car away and we went inside and lovingly caressed our shiny set, then walked upstairs and got undressed for bed.

What will tomorrow bring? I wondered as I climbed beneath the sheets. Another wild-goose chase or is Rhoads right on-line with Lester Farnham?

CHAPTER TWENTY

"Did you find anyone who knew him?" I asked as we headed toward Visalia.

"Yeah, several people," Rhoads responded, hunching forward in his seat. "Or knew who he was anyway. Said Lester was a loner, a queer off-beat duck that no one 'specially wanted to get close to. Figures, doesn't it, a guy who'd do a thing like that?"

"And what about anyone who'd seen him lately? Any luck there, Charlie?"

He scrunched his face up and made a little sucking sound. "Nah, no luck there. But that doesn't mean diddly squat, Kate. He coulda come and gone and no one seen him."

"But what would he've been doing here," I persisted, "if he wasn't visiting someone? It's a long drive from Visalia just to take a gander at your old neighborhood."

"I think I probably missed the one he came to see. The one other weirdo like himself who might've been his friend. It was just bad luck I didn't run across him, but I'm sure he's out there somewhere. There's no way I found everybody Lester knew up here."

He took out a cigarette, looked at it, then stuck it up behind his ear.

I still was not convinced this was a trip we should be making, but since Charlie seemed so determined I'd ride on down there with him. If Farnham *did* turn out to be a viable suspect, it'd be best if there were two of us around. Standard operating procedures in case the subject suddenly got rough. A good practice, too, to have two pairs of ears to take in what he said.

The air was crisp and clear, the heavy fog of yesterday having failed to rise from the ground this morning. It could change like that in this valley in the winter. One day dense and misty with the cloaking whitish vapor, the next, star-spangled bright with sun that blazed with golden brilliance.

We slowed down as we reached the Visalia city limits, and Rhoads pulled out the street map and the address for Farnham the local PD had given him. His mother's address, really. They'd told Charlie he'd moved in with her right after his release.

"Next right, then hang a left," he instructed as we looked out around us. The streets in this area were a mixture of apartment houses and single-family dwellings. The sort of blocks where the houses had come first, then gradually given way to the demands for urban density.

"There it is," I said, pointing to a small frame bungalow with a green asphalt shingle roof and crimson bougainvillea growing over the tiny porch roof above its door.

We parked out front and walked quickly up the walk, and I noticed that though the place showed signs of seeing better days, its lawn was neatly clipped, its screens and shutters tightly set in place, unlike those of so many of its neighbors.

"Think the mother's home," I asked, "or did Visalia say she worked?"

"They didn't, and I guess maybe so. There's laundry flapping in the back that probably was put out not too long ago. The colors look too deep to be really dry."

We rang the bell and waited, and soon the door creaked open and a tall, gray-haired woman looked at us suspiciously. I saw the well-lined face devoid of makeup, the hands with blunt-clipped nails and coarse red skin, and I knew here was a person who'd lived no life of luxury, who'd made no weekly visits to the salon.

"Yes, what is it?" she asked peremptorily.

"We're detectives from San Madera Police Department," I informed her. "Is your son, Lester, at home?"

"What do you want with him?" she cried angrily. "That other lot just finished with him and now you two come along. He's done his time. Isn't he to have peace even now?"

"No, ma'am, he's not," Charlie answered. "Not until we get a few things sorted out."

"What kind of things?"

"May we see Lester, please? You know we're not going to go away."

Reluctantly the woman swung the door farther open and motioned to us to come inside.

"I'll go get him," she said churlishly, and walked toward a closed door off the hallway near the house's rear. I saw her push it forward, go inside, then shut it softly behind her. We waited, and after several minutes it opened up again and a scared wimpish-looking man with sallow skin and rimless glasses walked out and stared at us with eyes as round as coins. I saw his brownish hair was thinning and his face was marked with acne scars across the cheeks and chin.

"Lester Farnham?" I began. "We'd like to talk with you."

"What about?" he squeaked. "I've just come from those other cops and they were satisfied. They let me go."

"It's about another matter, Lester," Charlie told him. "Where were you a week ago last Friday night?"

"I can tell you that," his mother butted in, and I held up my hand and stopped the conversation.

"Ma'am, it'd be better if you waited in another room. We'd appreciate speaking with your son alone."

"It's okay, Mother," Farnham told her shakily, and she walked through the house and into the backyard.

"About that evening, Lester. Where were you?" Charlie gave his chair a tug, inching it closer to the man.

"I . . . I don't know, I really don't. The days and nights all seem to run together ever since I left the joint. Same ol', same ol'. Nothing ever different."

"Except when you drove up to San Madera, maybe to see someone in your old neighborhood."

"I never did"—the frightened man held up both hands as if to ward us off—"but even if I had, so what?"

"So what?" Charlie repeated harshly. "You saw a tiny baby being carried into a building, that's so what. And your filthy prick got hard and you just had to touch her, had to put your stinking dirty hands all over her, till you were hot enough to jerk off there against her little body."

"You're crazy!" Lester cried, and I saw the fear that filled his eyes. "I never went near San Madera, not once since I got out." He licked his lips frantically, then began to chew the lower one, and I noticed the large brown mole that grew beside it.

"Come on, Lester, you guys never change. They claim they work wonders on you down there in Atascadero, but they can't purge it from your systems. You sick shits just live to see the day you're sprung so you can find and do another child."

I shot a glance at Charlie, to warn him to go slow, but he was heated up and kept on charging.

"It's not true," Farnham whimpered, twisting his hands together till the knuckles whitened. "I don't have the urges anymore. Honest to God, I do not have them."

"What would you say if I told you one of your old buddies up our way saw you near the baby's house that night. Would positively state you were not only in San Madera but were also right out there where that same baby was killed?"

"They'd be crazy," Lester wailed, "and anyway, I don't know anyone there anymore. Please, please leave me alone. Please don't do this to me."

I saw the frantic wildness of his eyes, and despite myself, I felt sorry for him. Guilty or innocent—and I was definitely starting to believe the latter—Farnham was a pathetic creature.

"Come on, Lester," Charlie prodded, "make it easy on yourself. Tell us all about it and it'll be over before you know it. We understand. We know you have a sickness and you're not responsible for what you do."

"No, I'm cured, I'm okay now," and Farnham began to cry.

"Charlie, let's go outside a moment," I interrupted. He shook his head, waved me off, and opened his mouth again. I stepped in before his words came out.

"Lester, do you have a job?" I asked him softly.

"Job? Oh . . ." The man seemed bewildered, and again he began to twist his hands. "Oh, yes, I wash the dishes in a burger place downtown. It's only part-time, though. Wait a minute. Oh, wait a minute." Farnham's eyes darted back and forth as hope began to flood them. "I don't usually work nights, but I subbed for a guy who was sick one weekend evening not too long ago. It could've been that Friday night you're talking about. I'm not really sure but it could've been."

"Who's your boss, Lester?" I asked. "And what's the address of the place?"

"Mr. Tally, and it's Shorty's Burgers down near Fifth and Main."

"We'll be in touch," I told him, and motioned to Charlie to come along.

"Don't you think we coulda leaned on him a little longer?" he asked as we were getting in the car. "I was just starting to get him going."

"I think your style was pretty rough," I told him bluntly, "and if the guy is dirty, we might've gotten a lot more out of him by going easy. I know the type. Hard-charging doesn't work."

"Oh, the white gloves approach," Rhoads answered haughtily. "Well, I tend to disagree."

"There's no evidence, Charlie," I responded. "Nothing we've found out so far indicates the man had anything to do with our two murders. And if his boss can clear him, then that puts a finish to it."

"There's another alibi pulled right out of a hat," he scoffed. "You think it's going to stand up and salute?"

We found the pocket restaurant near a downtown corner and went inside and asked for Mr. Tally. A waitress pointed to a tubby round-faced man pushing grease off some burners with a spatula. We identified ourselves and asked him if he kept time cards for his employees.

He did, he said, but all the papers for the week in question were at home in the office where he got his payroll ready. Without telling him why we wished to know, we asked if he'd check to see if Lester Farnham had worked a week ago last Friday night, and to give us a ring to let us know the answer.

"Be glad to," Tally assured us. "Okay if I wait to do it till I get home this evening, then ring you up tomorrow?"

"Absolutely," I told him.

"Uhhh, he's not in any trouble, is he?" the boss inquired, wrinkling his brow.

"Just a routine inquiry," I answered, "nothing more."

"So let's head for home," I said once we got outside, "and forget Lester Farnham till Tally phones us with his answer."

"And if it's negative? If Farnham didn't work that night and we know he's lying?"

"We wouldn't know that, would we, Charlie? The man himself said he wasn't certain of the day, just *thought* he might've been working then. But if Tally says he wasn't, then try to round up some more peo-

ple Farnham knew in San Madera, to see if they spotted him that night. Or find someone down here who
knows him, in case he dished with them and let
something vital slip."

Frankly, I thought we were beating a dead horse
here—grabbing a name out of the paper and forcing
it to run. I had an instinct for these things, born from
years of hands-on experience, and that instinct told
me we didn't have our man.

But Rhoads held this notion about Farnham and I
had no other suspects to offer in his place, so we'd
see it to its end. Which, I thought as I headed toward
the freeway, would probably come tomorrow, with
Mr. Tally's call.

The smile bathed his face like summer sunshine.

"Rena came back to me," he said. "She moved in
last night."

"Oh, Dan," I cried with relief, "I'm so glad."

"I know about the visit, Kate, about the talk you
had. I can't do enough to thank you, can't tell you
how I feel."

I blushed, then waved him off.

"She was ready to listen, Dan. And to look at
things in a way she'd never thought to look at them
before. I didn't work a miracle, I just led her where
she really wanted to go."

"Whatever, it's you I'm thanking anyway," he told
me. "She's going to that support group, too. Says it

makes the world of difference to have people like herself to talk to."

I squeezed his shoulder and, my eyes a little moist, walked on over to my desk. Other people's happiness made me sweetly happy, too.

It might've ended there, but it didn't. Shortly afterward a small bouquet of flowers arrived, accompanied by a dainty scripted note.

"Thank you, Katharine," the writing said, "for giving me my family and my life." I looked at it, deeply touched, then tucked Rena Kent's grateful words in a private corner of my desk.

My curiosity was up. I'd gotten a peak into a side of Darrow he'd not revealed before, that day we were driving home after questioning Jack Benson, and now I wanted to know a little more. Just because it intrigued me.

What kind of life did a man so burned by women manage to lead for himself? I realized I didn't even know where he lived. Had never even cared to know up till now. All I'd ever needed was a beeper number to call when a homicide came in.

I looked up his address in the Rolodex. Out of the division and somewhere in the East End, an area known for the mobility of its tenants rather than for permanence and stability. Probably one of those swinging singles condo complexes that'd mushroomed in the area several years ago.

I'd take a quick drive-by look, then be on my way. I just felt a need to see where Steve went home to every night, a need to flesh him out a bit inside my mind. I'd been seeing him as a one-dimensional playboy and now I wanted a little more than that.

I drove past the boxlike concrete structures, then, to my surprise, turned onto a street of small well-tended homes, each sitting in the middle of its individual plot. I spied Darrow's house almost immediately, mainly by recognizing the red Corvette standing out in front.

It was a tidy little cottage, painted a deep cream with bright blue shutters and four steps mounting to the doorway. Ruffled curtains were pulled back at each of several windows and when the sun struck the panes they flashed brightly in their cleanness.

A caramel cat stretched languidly along a porch step and as I cruised slowly past, Darrow himself came out the door, knelt and picked the kitty up, then laid a kiss gently on its head.

I passed on by, not wanting to be seen, then turned at the end of the block, waited several moments, then drove back by.

Steve was on his hands and knees now, carefully trimming an ivy topiary that grew beside a flower bed bordering the lawn. A bag of fertilizer and several garden tools lay on the smoothly trimmed grass beside him and I guessed when he'd finished shaping the plant, he'd spade some of the bag's contents around his other trees and shrubs.

As I drove slowly off I tossed a backward glance and saw him step back from the topiary to survey his work. It must've pleased him for a little smile spread across his face.

I shook my head in wonderment. I'd never have guessed the playboy had this side to him. Little cottage, loving cat, well-tended garden that obviously gave him pleasure to nurture and sustain. If you'd asked me before my drive, I'd have told you Steve Darrow wouldn't know a daisy from a dahlia and spent his off-time hustling women instead of digging in the soil.

Which just goes to show, I thought, what you've always known but sometimes do forget. Everyone has several sides, not just the one they choose to show you. Nothing, no one, is ever simple nor are they crystal-clear.

We sat close together on the sofa, comfortable in each other's presence. I refilled his cup, then turned to face him slightly, tucking my blue-jeaned leg beneath me. What I had to say wasn't easy because it was bound to touch on tender feelings, so I picked and chose among the words, trying to find those that fitted best.

"Bobby, I know you think the world of Charlie Rhoads, but has his behavior ever struck you as odd when you've been working with him?"

Harris stared at me, crinkling smiling eyes suddenly dead-serious and eagle-sharp.

"How do you mean, Kate?"

"Well, like the business with Sonny Mitchell. He was way out of line to strike him. He just lost it. We talked about it on the way back down here and he admitted he should never have touched the suspect. And then there was this morning's visit to wimpy little Lester Farnham. Rhoads plunged in and charged and tried to mow the man down. No cool, controlled interrogation there."

Harris compressed his lips and stared off into space. After several moments of silence, he swung his head around and looked at me.

"I've noticed things, yes," he conceded. "Little things, and only lately, maybe in the past few months. But you're right. There's a harshness, a volatility, about him that didn't used to be there. And something else, too, something I can't quite put my finger on. A strangeness of some sort."

"Could it have to do with this other woman?" I asked. "The woman in Merced? He told me about her, you know. Told me she'd given him an ultimatum."

"He told you?" Harris asked, surprised. "I wouldn't have expected him to do that. He's usually very closemouthed about her."

"Well, I think that's probably what's bringing on this odd behavior," I concluded, "and your friend had better get the mess straightened out before he goes off the deep end."

"I think he'll resolve it when we return to Stockton," Bobby offered. "If his lover has, indeed, told him to make a choice, well, when he's living with Jane again on a daily basis he'll be forced to come to some decision. When he's down here, away from both of them, it's easier to think he can have his cake and eat it, too."

"Would that be anytime soon? Going back to Stockton, I mean." I asked the question, but I didn't want to hear the answer, and I focused on a loose thread on the sofa rather than look directly into Bobby's eyes.

"Soon, Kate, yes. The brass called down while you were gone, said they couldn't spare us for longer than a couple more days—said Masters was really San Madera's case. We knew when we came here we couldn't stay indefinitely. The hope was we'd catch the killer within the first forty-eight hours."

"I understand," I told him brightly, but my heart had grown heavy. "We're just grateful for the help you've given us. And who knows? You say a few more days? Well, we might get lucky and wrap it up by then."

I walked him to the door, and as we reached it, he turned to me and quickly took me in his arms. Eagerly, tightly. I felt a wave of warmth engulf us and I clung to him with a ferocity that surprised me.

"Katharine," he murmured, his mouth pressed against my hair, "I have feelings for you that I did not expect to have. Feelings that I've tried to fight, that I've not had for any woman for a long time."

"I, too," I stumbled, conflicting emotions still warring deep within me. "I have those feelings, too, but, Bobby, it's so soon, so sudden. I don't . . ."

"We'll go slow," he whispered, "we won't rush anything. We won't let haste spoil whatever this is that's happening."

He drew me even closer, and then I looked into his eyes and he bent down and kissed me, and now I wished the moment would never ever end. But it did, and Bobby quickly walked through the door and pulled it shut behind him. And I stood there, in wonder, and laid my fingers on my lips.

He stirred his spoon around and around in the oatmeal dish, making lots of circles but picking up no food.

"Why're you stirring it, Tommy?" I asked him. "Is it too hot? Here, add some cream."

He slowly shook his head and kept his eyes locked on the cereal.

"Hey, what's wrong, kiddo?" I put my hands on both his shoulders and turned him toward me.

"You kissed that man, Mom. I saw you kiss that man." And he threw down the spoon and ran from the table.

Mrs. Miller, turning from the sink, looked at me in pity, then rolled her eyes toward the ceiling. I went after him, and found him on the sofa, curled into a ball.

"Tommy, there's nothing wrong with what I did," I told him, wondering how in the world he'd seen. I'd believed him sound asleep in his bed upstairs throughout Bobby's visit.

"You said he was your friend," he pouted accusingly, "but you kissed him on the mouth. I don't kiss my friends but you kissed him."

"This is a different kind of friend," I explained, wishing it could be easier. "It's different with a man and a woman than it is with boys and girls. And when two adults enjoy each other's company, it's okay to kiss."

"You'll get a baby," Tommy told me. "Martha says you get a baby when you kiss."

"Honey," I said in consternation, "Martha's wrong. That is not how a baby starts. You know that. Your daddy and you have talked about how a woman becomes pregnant, and so have you and I."

"Well, a kiss starts it anyway," my son stubbornly insisted, "even if more happens after that."

You've got a point, I thought wryly to myself, but out loud I told him, "There's going to be no baby, I assure you. But, Tommy, I'll be honest with you, there may be more kissing. Mr. Harris and I find we care for one another, just as I care for you only nowhere near as much."

"Will you marry him, Mom?" Tommy asked fearfully, looking up into my eyes. "Will he move in here with us?"

"Let me tell you something, kiddo," I began, and I dragged him onto my lap. I didn't care if he was nine years old and becoming a "little man," I wanted to hold him like a toddler. "There'll be no marriage, no moving in, nothing like that, I promise you. At least not anytime soon.

"But one day, Tommy, one day in the future I might get married again—if not to Mr. Harris, then to someone else—and if I did, we'd talk it all over well in advance. There'd be no sudden changes, no surprises. You would always know exactly what's going on. Okay?"

"Okay, Mom." He leaned up and kissed me. "I guess sometimes you're lonely. I guess sometimes you need a friend." He looked toward the set of sticks and brushes Bobby had given him. "And Mr. Harris seems like sort of a nice man for you to have around."

"Look, Kate, I've gotta run up to Merced for an hour or so this morning," Charlie told me. "I should be back by noon. If that's okay with you, that is. If you don't need me here."

"Go right ahead," I answered coolly, thinking to myself, Do what you want, you're not on *my* payroll. I was still less than satisfied about the Farnham business.

Darrow watched him go and arched his eyebrows. "A sick puppy, I'd say. Too bad he can't handle his women the way some of us studs do."

I ignored him, picking up the phone. There was something I was dying to find out.

The voice answered "Merced Homicide," and I identified myself and told them I wanted to satisfy a little idle curiosity.

"You've got a citizen up there named Jack Benson, and I'm wondering if he's maybe involved in something he shouldn't be. A relative got murdered down here, and when we questioned him, he acted like a scared rabbit and it wasn't because of his cousin's death. He's no longer a suspect in the homicide— he's been cleared of that—but I feel something else is going on."

I gave Benson's particulars to the fellow on the other end of the line.

"No, he's got no rap sheet," I answered in response to his question. "We checked on that early on in the investigation."

He told me the name meant nothing to him, but he'd ask around and call me back. Within minutes, the phone rang and I picked it up, confident I'd be speaking to Merced PD.

"This is Mr. Tally," I heard instead. "Mr. Tally from the burger shop down in Visalia. Look, I pulled those time cards you asked about and, sure enough, Lester Farnham covered for another guy a week ago last Friday night. Came on at four, went off at twelve."

"No possibility of error?"

"Oh, no. I'm absolutely certain he was working on that day and time."

Rhoads wouldn't be happy to hear this news, I reflected, then realized that even though I'd never seriously considered Farnham a suspect, I was feeling a letdown now that he'd been cleared.

Damn it, I thought, every road we walk down leads to a dead end. I want a change of luck, I want to crack this wall we're facing, I want to find the monster who strangled Meryl and killed that little baby. Please let me soon see a viable suspect in these murders.

The phone jangled again, and this time it was Merced.

"You're in luck," the voice told me. "I threw the name around and one of our guys on theft picked it up. Says Benson's suspected of fencing stolen art-work. Part of some sophisticated little ring up here we've just not been able to crack. Uses his store as a legitimate front, but most of his work is dirty. He may suspect we're on to him, but as I said, we've not been able to nail him yet."

So that was it. That was why "Jacques" with the silver Jag had squirmed and squiggled the day we'd gone up to see him. He'd tried to get some dirt on his dead cousin while all the time he was involved in a game that would make DeeDee's and Harold's hair stand up on end. I wondered if they'd checked their own art collection lately and noticed anything was missing.

Well, well, I thought, leaning back and smiling to myself, if Merced can finally close in on him and his dirty little ring, the family reputation will take a harder slam than any Meryl ever dealt it.

Harris came in, walking jauntily across the room, and when our eyes met, we smiled and I gave a little wave. A feeling of warm happiness surged through me, and I found myself reliving that moment at the door.

And then my mind filled with thoughts of Tommy, and I hoped I'd handled things all right. Always talk to him, I counseled, always explain what's going on and make him part of it. That's the only way anything will work.

I was rising from my desk when my phone rang once again, and I snatched it up, wondering who it could be now. As I grasped the receiver, the sound of raucous, high-pitched sobbing exploded in my ear.

"Hello, who is it?" I yelled into the phone, hoping an authoritative voice would calm the person down. Soon some words forced their way in between the sobs, and I listened closely and heard . . . "killed" . . . "son" . . . "murderer!"

"Who is this?" I begged. "Please get hold of yourself and tell me who this is and what is wrong."

"You killed him!" a woman screamed. "You

hounded and harassed him till he couldn't take it anymore. And now he's dead and he never did a thing. Not this time he didn't."

"Who're you talking about, who's dead?" I asked, though I was beginning to get an awful feeling I knew the answer.

"Lester Farnham, that's who's dead. He jumped off the freeway overpass last night, right into the path of an eighteen-wheeler. He was torn to pieces, lady, torn to shreds. Only little bits were left. My son, oh, my son . . ." And the sobbing began all over again.

"Mrs. Farnham, I'm sorry—truly, truly sorry—but whatever happened to Lester had nothing to do with us. We weren't going to arrest him any more than Visalia police arrested him because I found out this morning his alibi checked out."

"Then why couldn't you have waited for that information before you came hounding him again? Why'd you have to send that devil down last night to terrorize my son? I blame you, too. You're the boss lady, that's what it says on this card you left here yesterday. And the moment that cop left, Lester went straight out the door and I never saw him again. No note, nothing, just his car parked by the overpass and two witnesses who saw him jump."

A sick feeling began welling up in me, and I felt my skin grow cold.

"Mrs. Farnham, I didn't send anyone down to talk

to your son last night. There must be some mistake. The person must've been from Visalia PD.''

"No, he wasn't," she screamed at me. "You know well he wasn't. You're just trying to get off the hook now, with your denials. It was that bastard that was here with you yesterday. The big man with the dark eyes and ruddy face and stinking cigarette breath."

"Please believe me, Mrs. Farnham, when I say I sent no one. I don't know what you're talking about, I need you to tell me exactly what happened." My stomach started churning with the fear of what I was going to hear.

"He came in at eight o'clock and made me leave the room, just like before. He got Lester alone and backed him into a corner and laid his arm across his chest. I know this because I was peeking out the bedroom door. Then he sat him down and yelled into my poor son's face. Awful things, dreadful things, and called him names I'd never heard before.

"And then he started talking quieter but still in a threatening tone. I heard him say, 'Faggot, you better confess or I'll slap you into prison, where every other inmate will ram you up your stinking ass—you won't last two seconds.' He talked like that to *my* son, in *my* house."

"I'm sorry, Mrs. Farnham, please tell me what happened next."

"Lester was crying and begging, and I tried to intervene but that devil threatened me and told me to get back in the room and stay there. I was terrified, I thought that he might hit me, so I did just what he said.

"Then finally he left, and I ran out and found Lester slumped down on the floor, crying in the corner just like he used to do when he was a little boy. And then he got up and pushed me aside and ran out of the house, and I heard the car start up and saw him drive away. And I never saw my son again."

Mrs. Farnham broke down in fresh weeping, and it took her several moments before she could begin to speak.

"He made mistakes but he *was* my son and I loved him," she moaned. "He'd paid for what he did and wouldn't do it anymore. And you murdered him"— and now her voice rose in a crescendo and she began to scream—"you murdered him as sure as if you'd stabbed him with a knife. And I hate the both of you! May the two of you rot in stinking hell!"

She slammed the phone down and I sat there, stunned. I glanced across at Bobby and at Darrow, but decided not to say a word. I'd keep this conversation to myself till after I'd gone one-on-one. I checked my watch. Two more hours till showdown.

CHAPTER TWENTY-ONE

I was waiting for him when he walked into the room.

"Charlie, let's get a cup of coffee and go down the hall."

"Sure, boss lady, what's up?" His face held a look of total innocence, but I sensed that a slight wariness had crept into his manner.

"Let's get our coffee and talk about it there."

He shrugged his big shoulders, and we moved toward the door. I saw Darrow watching us quietly, a puzzled look spread across his face.

We filled our cups, then walked down the hall and into the little room. I shut the door and turned around and faced him.

"Charlie, where were you last night?"

"Why, boss? I thought my own time was my own."

"Not when you're on department business, it's not."

He threw his hands up, and I couldn't read the gesture.

"Did someone say something bad about me, Katharine?"

"Look, Rhoads, I don't know why all the fencing. Mrs. Farnham phoned this morning."

"Ah, so that's it." His face broke into a great big grin, and I saw he was going to try to bluff it through. "Was she complaining about anything in particular?"

"She told me about your visit there last night, the way you came down heavy on her son. You were wrong, Charlie. You didn't clear it with me, you didn't inform anyone you were going. And you know why? Because you knew damn well I wouldn't have authorized it, so you snuck off behind my back."

Again he threw his hands up, and this time he seemed to be saying, What's all the fuss about?

"Look, I know this guy is dirty and I just wanted to have another go at him. I didn't try to sneak around on you. The idea just came to me on the spur of the moment and I hit the road. I *know* it's not proper procedure, but hell, Kate, sometimes you cannot always go by the book. You gotta act when you gotta act."

"Like with Sonny Mitchell?"

"I thought we already talked about that. I told you I had my reasons."

"So what did you find out, Charlie, in your second chat with Mr. Farnham? Did you get him to confess?"

"No, not yet, but I laid a little groundwork. Once I find the creep who can place him near the scene that Friday night, he'll start to spill his guts."

"Charlie, there is no such person, he doesn't exist. Farnham's boss called me this morning and his alibi checks out. And there's another reason the man won't spill his guts, Charlie, the most important reason of all. Lester Farnham's dead, crushed and shredded by an eighteen-wheeler. He plunged off a freeway overpass right after you left him last night."

Rhoads's mouth dropped open and he looked at me, astonished.

"The hell you say!"

"That's right, it's true. I verified it with the Highway Patrol after the mother's phone call."

"Are you saying I'm the cause of it, Kate? Are you saying that piece of slime jumped because I talked to him? Because if you are, that's not fair. It had nothing to do with me. He jumped because, alibi or no alibi, he was guilty as sin and he knew it."

"We may never really know why Lester killed himself, Charlie, but it wasn't because he was guilty. It could've been because of the renewed police presence in his life, in which your interrogation was the final straw. It could've been because he wasn't making it on the outside—no friends, poor-paying job, days and nights, as he put it, all seeming to run together. Or it could've been because he was basically an unstable individual who'd have committed suicide sooner or later.

"But there is one thing I *do* know, and that is that I can no longer have you on my team. You ignored procedure, you went against my direct orders to clear your moves with me, and in this specific instance, you went behind my back to tear apart an individual you knew I wanted left alone. Our styles don't mix, Charlie, and I will not stand for insubordination, so, as of now, you're going home."

He sat there as if I'd punched the wind out of him.

"No, Kate, please, Kate, let me stay. This'll never happen again, I swear it. I need this case, I need to stay close to it. I've got to catch the bastard who did that to that woman and that little girl. Give me one more chance. Please!"

"Sorry, Rhoads, I've had it up to here. You'll hurt the effort if I let you stay. I won't say a word to Stockton unless I'm asked, but I want you out of here right now."

He looked at me and saw the firm resolve set upon my face, and knowing any further protest was futile, he shoved back his chair and left the room.

"I had to do it, Bobby. Surely you can see I had no choice."

"I'm just stunned, Kate, stunned that it happened. I'd never have thought Charlie would be thrown off a case."

By the bleakness of his look, I knew I'd hit him hard.

"If it were one of my own men, I'd try to work it out with him, either by a serious chewing out or some days off. But I have no obligation to Charlie and I don't want him around here anymore. He had one warning with Sonny Mitchell and he didn't take it. He's a loose cannon rolling in my field."

We were sitting in the back booth at Marty's, where we'd gone at lunchtime so I could apprise Bobby of the situation. I was wolfing down my sandwich but he barely touched his omelet, just pushed it around his plate.

"You think I was wrong," I fumed, when he gave no response.

"Maybe you could've cut him some slack, Kate," he offered finally. "Charlie's a real hard-charger and he's gung ho on this case. Maybe it's like he said. He got the notion on the spur of the moment and took off without calling, without even thinking to call, 'cause he was all fired up. Wrong procedurally, yes, but not bad enough to merit what you did."

I drew in my breath in frustration and smacked my hand down on the table.

"You feel like that because he's your friend, Bobby, your long-time friend from years gone by. But you didn't see him with Farnham earlier. Like I told you last night, he was riding rough where he had no need to, he was on the verge of running out of control. And because I saw that performance, it's easy for me to believe he went down there again and drove that man right past the edge.

"No, Bobby, no question in my mind. You can work with Rhoads in Stockton but I can't work with him down here."

Harris pushed his plate aside but continued sipping at his coffee.

"Look, Kate, I respect your decision," he told me. "No matter how I feel about Charlie, I respect your rights and your reasons for doing what you did. This is a professional issue and I will not take sides. And if I *did* take sides, it would come between me and him or between me and you, and I could not bear for either thing to happen. So I'm just going to let it drop."

I felt a great weight lift from me as the tangled webs I'd stepped in suddenly loosened and let me go, but then I looked at Bobby's face and saw the sadness mirrored there for what had happened to his friend.

"This pains me, too, Bobby, I want you to know that. This isn't easy for me, not something I liked to have to do." I paused a moment, picking out my words. "To tell you the truth, it's one hell of a mess that I'd like to forget about as soon as possible and I truly hope you can do the same."

And we smiled as the serious mood was broken, and reached across the table and clasped each other's hands.

"You're sure he's married, Kate?" she asked. "Because I was seriously thinking of going after him.

There's something about that type, I guess, that just appeals to me. They'll be my downfall yet."

"Yes, he's well married, Karen," I told her, "and otherwise involved as well. I don't really think you want to get involved with Charlie Rhoads. Besides, I thought you said one like that was enough for any girl and you'd had your turn."

"I did, but every time I see him, I can't help remembering what it was like with Steve, and I keep thinking maybe he's the same, just not as big a prick."

I was back in Marty's, in the same booth where I'd eaten lunch, drinking yet more coffee, this time with Karen.

I'd run into her in the lobby on my way out this afternoon, and she'd asked if I wanted to grab a cup before heading home. I'd said sure, why not? We're always seeing each other on the run, why break the habit?

"Well, you're out of luck anyway, kid," I told her, "he's no longer with us. He's returning to home base up north."

Karen arched her eyebrows in surprise and ran her hand across her fine blond hair.

"But I saw him just this morning," she protested. "Passed him on the road. In fact, it was that sighting that started all the hots building up again."

"Ah, yes," I answered, "he was going to Merced. It was after he returned at noon that he decided to go on back to Stockton."

"No, no," she said, "not on the way to Merced. He'd have taken 99 due north and I passed him driving out the San Luis Road."

"What time was this?" I asked quickly.

"Around ten-thirty. I was out there digging around an old crime scene for a color story. Remember the Barnett family killings? Well, the son who did it is being paroled real soon."

I didn't hear the rest of her words, only the part about the time. Smack dab in the middle of the three-hour period Rhoads had supposedly been up north. Only this meant he'd never gone at all.

If she'd passed him shortly after nine, then he'd probably delayed his start awhile, killing time on a country road, or if she'd spotted him close to twelve, then he'd likely returned to our area earlier than planned and, for some reason, had elected not to come directly to the station.

But if Karen had seen him in midmorning, as she claimed she had, there was no way possible he could've made the hour-long trip north and still been back by noon.

"You're sure it was Charlie?" I asked casually, looking down and stirring my coffee. "It couldn't have been Darrow?"

"You've got to be kidding, Kate! I may've mixed them up at first but I'd never mistake that hunk now that I've seen a lot more of him. And we passed within a stone's throw of each other. I'd have had to be blind not to recognize him."

"Did *he* see *you*?"

"Don't think so. He was looking straight ahead. But, then," she whined, "he never seems to notice me even when I'm right under his nose."

Why the lie, I wondered, and why San Luis Road? That country byway kept popping up in my investigation and yet it had yielded very little. Only the true identity of Steven Brownfeld and the lead he'd given us on Benson, but both of those had proved dead ends.

And then an awful thought occurred to me and I hurriedly picked up the bill and told Karen I had to get on home. We said good-bye and I watched her drive out of sight, then darted to a phone, put in some coins, and dialed a number. I checked my watch—still time enough, I hoped. My workday ended earlier than the average person's so maybe I still could catch him in. I was in luck, and relief flooded through me.

"Steven, this is Katharine Harrod. Tell me, have you been at work all day? . . . Since nine a.m.? . . . Thank you very much . . . No, no, nothing, not to worry, I'll explain to you some other time. But listen, do me a favor—if any of my detectives calls on you, tell him you were told to check with me before talking with him, then *do* give me a ring . . . Right . . . Good-bye."

I was certain now I knew why Charlie had driven out San Luis Road. He'd been beelining his way to

Steven Brownfeld, to roust him the same way he'd rousted Farnham. But he hadn't found him home, and now that he'd been tossed off the team I doubted he'd try making further contact. Still though, just in case he did, I was glad I'd seen the danger and cautioned Brownfeld.

Thank God, I thought, that I caught it in time. Thank God I canned that screwup before he had a chance to lay heavy on another blameless person in the Masters-Brighton murders. It was a good thing Brownfeld hadn't been at home, and also a good thing I'd found out about Farnham when I did. Otherwise I'd have continued on with Charlie.

But then, as I drove home, something else occurred to me. Suppose there'd been a different reason Rhoads had canceled out Merced and driven to that country road?

Nah, I said, stop deviling yourself, there's none other that it could have been. And besides, what does it even matter now? He's gone.

There's something wrong here, I thought—very, very wrong about the whole damn thing—but for the life of me I can't see what it is.

I was sitting in the den, a pad and pencil on my lap, making one of the lists I inevitably end up making at some point in every case. Usually, like now, when I've become frustrated in its solving and think if I can only jot things down, I'll get a clearer view of what I've missed.

And then a feeling started growing in me, a certain feeling that someone innocently connected to this case could tell me something that would help me. And further, that the only reason they'd not so far done so was simply that I'd failed to ask them or they'd failed to realize its importance.

I began studying my list to find the missing link, looking at the names of everyone we'd talked to, reading scrawls about their alibis and attitudes. But minutes later, despite pouring over it intensively, I'd still made little progress.

My son came in, sat down, and started banging on the drums, and my first reaction was one of irritation at the sound and interruption.

Oh, mellow out, I scolded, go pick up those sticks yourself and take the edge off of your attitude. Getting all uptight isn't going to help you any.

But instead, I picked up the list and read it off again. "Brownfeld, check, Benson, check, Farnham, check." And then I stopped, staring at two names, as a sudden thought ascended. Suppose the roots for the reason for the murders lay somewhere back in that time in Lodi when Sonny and Wanda—the only known links between my victims—were seeing Masters on an almost daily basis?

I felt the pair themselves had given me all they could about the case, but consider Mitchell's sister, the one Wanda'd told me had been Masters's client? Since she'd interacted with all three of them—and had known Meryl not only as her social worker but also as her brother's lover—had she perhaps picked up on something during those months when all their paths had crissed and crossed? Something that would shed a gleam of light on the murk I was staring into now?

I decided I'd look her up tomorrow but I wasn't getting too excited. I had to admit what I was doing was taking a desperate stab, with little real hope she knew anything important. But what the heck. I wasn't making any progress anyway so I might as well try all the stabs I could, just in case one poked a hole in a cache that held a clue.

I'd drive to Lodi early in the morning. No need taking Steve or Bobby, I'd do it on my own. Just two women sitting down together, to chat about some people whose lives had intertwined several years ago.

Joanie Creighton hadn't been too hard to find. I'd rung up Lodi detectives and asked if they knew where Mitchell's sister lived, and they'd told me they sure did. Although she herself had never been in trouble, her brother was so well known in the area her address was entered in his file, listed as a likely place to find him when the cops needed to go look.

I drove to the aged apartment building in a commercial part of town and climbed the stairs to a second floor that reeked of stale cooking and other smells I didn't care to put a name to.

I knocked on the door of 205 and a gangly child with bare feet and missing upper teeth gawked at me while I asked to see his mother. Nodding silently, he pulled the door wide open, watched me walk inside, then ran off to tell Creighton a lady cop was waiting.

She came boiling in all full of herself, looking for a fight—standing in the middle of the floor shaking her finger at me and washing me all over with her angry eyes.

"Damn cops," she cried, "giving my brother all that trouble! What is it you want now?"

If she'd used a little of this feisty attitude on her husband, I reflected, he might've laid off beating her and she'd not have ended up out on the street.

"Mrs. Creighton," I began, bending to retrieve a pink curler she'd just shaken from her head, "I'm not here about Sonny, I'm here about the murders of Meryl Masters and your niece. I hope I'll get your cooperation because I imagine you cared about them very much and want to see their killer caught."

The steam went out of her a little, and she settled her slight frame far forward on a chair. I couldn't help but notice the resemblance to Sonny—and to little Lucy, too. The blond hair, the deep brown eyes, the dimple in the cheek, were there and all in place.

"The baby, yes . . ." she said, and put her hand up to her face as her eyes began to water. "What an awful thing to do to a precious child. You know, I never saw her, never got to see her, didn't ever have the chance. But Wanda sent a picture. Dear sweet little thing, she looked just like Sonny."

"You're right," I answered softly, "she surely did."

"You saw her?" the woman asked, surprised. "Did you . . . ? Were you . . . ?"

"Yes, I took care of her after she was found, I was the first detective on the scene, and I saw that she was handled properly."

And the memory of that night in that filthy pockmarked parking lot flew full into my mind, and I could almost smell the stinking greasy smells, could almost feel the lightness of the little body lying on the green plaid shirt. Lucy, the forgotten victim . . .

I pushed the scene away and concentrated on her words.

"Thank you, then," she was saying. "No matter you're a cop, I must thank you gratefully for that."

I nodded and glanced around the shabby unit, noting the scratched woodwork and the broken toys lying on the floor, and I thought how tough so many people have it, so often through no fault of their own. And yet they don't give up—just keep on living, keep on fighting to survive.

"Does social services still help you out?" I asked.

"Not now," Mrs. Creighton answered proudly. "I've go a job waitressing at night, and between that and the cleaning I do in this building here, we can just make out. My sister watches this lot while I work"—she waved her hand at the three small children sitting on the floor—"and sometimes gives them hand-me-downs from her own brood."

"But earlier, maybe several years ago, you *did* get help, didn't you, and Meryl Masters was your social worker?"

"Yes I did, more than once. The old man was beating me up regular back then and throwing me on the street, and the kids were just babies and I couldn't get no work. She took good care of me. She knew how to get the most benefits and was kind besides."

A wave of surprise swept through me as this worn woman called her "kind." Apparently Meryl's approach to her clients had differed from her approach to her friends, lacking deception and duplicity and marked by obvious caring and concern. Perhaps they'd touched a part of her she'd not known she possessed.

"Meryl used to date your brother, Mrs. Creighton, before he took up with Wanda. Because you knew all three of them during that period, maybe you saw or heard something that would shed some light on the tragedy that happened later. There's a missing piece I need to find but I'm not seeing it, so I thought maybe you could help me out. Do you know who else besides Wanda and your brother Masters was involved with at that time?"

"No, miss, I don't." The woman looked positively

deflated. "I was hoping you'd ask something I could tell you because I thought an awful lot of her. She never ever put on airs with me, just helped me out, like I already told you."

"But surely in all your dealings with her, especially on the personal side, you learned something about the broader scope of her life?"

"No, Detective, I didn't. Ms. Masters—I never could get used to addressing her as Meryl—kept things to herself. I think Sonny even had a hard time getting close to her . . . and he was sleeping with her, imagine that!"

Mrs. Creighton's hostility toward cops had dropped completely, and now it was like girlfriend gossip time. She moved even closer to the chair edge, if that was possible, and leaned toward me intently.

"Why do you think both of them were killed, Detective? Why would someone want to harm that precious child?"

I sighed and shook my head.

"To be truthful, Mrs. Creighton, it's got us puzzled, too. We're certain Meryl was the primary target, but we're not sure at all if Lucy was killed because she was Lucy or because she just happened to be there at the time."

I rose, getting ready to leave that cheerless apartment, and reflected how I'd wasted a whole morning on this trip. But it'd been a good idea, I consoled myself. Even if it hadn't produced, it'd been a good idea.

"I'm really sorry, miss, I sure wish I could help," she said, ruffling a toddler's hair. "Ms. Masters and my own niece, my own flesh and blood. I'd give anything to be able to tell you a clue that'd help you catch their killer."

"It's all right," I assured her, stroking the toddler's hair myself, "it was just a thought. It's not your fault that you didn't know the woman better."

Silence followed while we started walking toward the door.

"I guess you've already asked him," Mrs. Creighton stated matter-of-factly. "I guess he couldn't help you out or you wouldn't be here with me."

"Who do you mean?" I said, turning toward her. "If you mean Sonny, no, he couldn't help us."

"Not Sonny, no. I already told you Sonny couldn't get that close to her. I mean that cop that punched my brother out last Sunday, the one who banged him up and sent him to the joint. He was always hanging around Ms. Masters's desk when I used to go to see her. He was always there, always talking, always taking up her time."

I didn't even get into the car, just stood there leaning up against it, shaken by the knowledge I'd just gained. Rhoads had known Masters all along, had known her and never said a word. And by his silence had laid a lie upon the case and hindered the investigation. Why? And what link had bound the two of them together?

And then the pieces started falling down and fitting and I saw a picture I'd not seen before, angled from a different slant and full and rich with meaning.

Rhoads had gotten on the case and started racing like a madman, pointing fingers right and left. He'd pushed Sonny in our face and beat him up, hounded Farnham till he'd jumped off a bridge, then tried to get to Steven Brownfeld. He'd run ahead of us, run outside the lines, acting like a gung-ho roughhouse cop out to lead the pack.

I'd thought he was a screwup, but I was now convinced the reasons for his actions lay much deeper. I believed Rhoads was on a mission and had to reach the killer first, not so he could be a shining star but so he could deal with him in his own way. Cruelly and brutally, in order to force out a confession.

I had no proof of this so I couldn't challenge him with my suspicions. But I *did* have the strength of my convictions, based on what I'd learned coupled with the plain pattern of his actions, and I knew somehow he must be stopped before he harmed somebody else.

For, if I was right, being thrown off the case wouldn't deter Charlie. He'd keep on digging, keep on searching on the sly, till he zeroed in on the one he believed had murdered Masters. He might even return to those we'd already talked to, to give a final

shake and tug at them before moving on to someone else.

I pondered all of this up front but down below,
the underlying platforms of my mind kept circling
around the biggest teaser. Why had Rhoads not told
us he'd known Masters and why did he care enough
to break the rules so he could catch her killer?

I reached the freeway and started heading home.
I had to talk to someone, but to whom? I couldn't
go to Bobby, not right now, and I didn't especially
want to involve Steve. Why even ask, I thought, you
know just where you're going—he'll help you out,
he'll show you what to do.

The bourbon bottle had been put away and the
cheeks were free of whiskers. I looked at him and
saw a brighter, fitter Carl than the one I'd left the
other day.

"I need to talk with you," I said, and leaning on
his cane, he stepped aside and waved me in.

"You got something, Kate?" he asked eagerly.
"Something on the Masters-Brighton case?"

"Yes and no," I told him with reluctance. "It's got
no bearing on who the killer is, but it's definitely got
a lot to do with the investigation."

Carl threw his cane aside and eased down on the
sofa, but I began pacing back and forth across the
floor. My nerves were jangled, my mind in turmoil,
for I'd never faced this type of situation before.

"Charlie Rhoads knew Meryl Masters," I told him bluntly. "Apparently knew her very well and never told us. I've just learned this from Mitchell's sister up in Lodi. She dropped it sort of casually, as if she thought I'd known all along."

Carl, whose deadpan face usually never gave away his feelings, shot his eyes wide open and dropped his jaw and stared.

"Say what?"

"That's right, and I've no doubt it's true. My source knows Charlie well by sight and gave no indication she was lying. And that's far from all."

I told him about Rhoads's off-the-wall pursuit of Lester Farnham, how he'd been seen by Karen on the road to Brownfeld's, and reminded him of the way he'd punched Sonny at the track.

"I think he's out to find the killer first and beat him till he forces a confession, and the fact he's off the case isn't going to stop him."

"How do you mean, 'off the case'?"

"I let him go after I learned how he'd handled Farnham. He'd gone out-of-bounds again and I couldn't work with that kind of cop. Until today, I'd thought his actions were just gung-ho cowboy craziness, but now I'm sure they're deadly and calculated, with one specific purpose in mind—to step outside the law to deal with Masters's killer."

Carl pursed his lips and stared at me, then got up and hobbled to the stove to boil some water. He filled the silver kettle and set it on the burner, then turned around and faced me.

"What makes you think he's going to be content wringing out a confession?" he asked me slowly. "What makes you think he'll stop at that? Why wouldn't he go all the way?"

My eyes locked with his as the horror of his words flooded through my mind, and now it was my turn to drop my mouth wide open.

"My God," I whispered, staring. "My God, I never thought of that, I never followed that far through. I've been so blind. Of course you're right. And the only reason he's not done it before now is that he's not been really sure he's found the killer."

"And it gets worse, Kate," Carl continued, spooning out the coffee. "Suppose Rhoads tracks down a person he believes to be the murderer but who's really not, who's just another innocent he's misjudged. But because he's anxious and frustrated by that time, his decision-making's shot and he rushes in and bangs them. And they're dead but they never had a thing to do with either killing."

"What would you do in my shoes, Carl? How would you approach it?"

"If you confront him, he'll deny your suspicions about his game plan, that's for sure, but if you at least tell him those suspicions, the fact someone's on to him could make him lay off and leave it.

"I don't see how he could deny knowing Masters,

though, for you're on far more solid ground there. You've got a wit you feel's reliable, plus I imagine the shock of what you know might make him give himself away when you decide to hit him with it. And then he'll have to come clean and tell you what it's all about."

"I'm going up to Stockton, then, to talk with him," I told Carl as he handed me my cup. "I'll take Steve or Bobby with me and confront him." I stopped short as a sudden thought began to hit me. "My God, Bobby! Carl, Charlie's been his best friend since childhood, he saved Bobby's life when they were in the service. Harris loves Charlie like a brother and I don't know how I'm going to break this to him."

"Be prepared for denial, Kate," he advised me. "He isn't going to want to see it and he's going to be real angry at the person bringing him the news. Not only is Rhoads his closest friend, he's his partner, too, and now you're going to tell him you think he's dirty. Put yourself in his place. Suppose it was you, with someone telling you that same thing about me."

I nodded in agreement, hating the task ahead.

"I'm leaving now," I told him. "I want to track down Bobby and get that over with, at least. I'll tell you, I'd give anything not to have to do it."

"You're afraid it'll mess things up between you, aren't you?" Carl asked softly.

"Yes," I answered truthfully. "Yes, damn it, yes I

am. I'm scared to death because he's already upset
about Rhoads's dismissal, and besides, I don't want
to see him hurt. But the chips will have to fall, Carl.
I'll just have to let them fall."

And then my mind returned to the giant puzzler.
Why had Rhoads hidden his relationship with Meryl
and what exactly had that relationship been?

"As to why the secret, I've got no clue," Carl told
me frankly, "unless right from the start Rhoads knew
he was going to operate alone. The relationship itself? Who knows, but I'll tell you this for sure. Whatever it was, it must've been pretty deep."

He walked me to the door, and just before we
reached it I felt his large hand lay heavy on my arm.
I turned to him and saw a sheepish grin begin to fill
his face.

"I took your advice the other day," he told me,
watching my expression. "I started concentrating
hard on Sandy and we had a little talk that night. I
think the two of us are getting married, maybe in
the spring."

I threw my arms around him and squeezed him
tight, delighted at the news I was hearing. That explained the absence of the whiskey and the whiskers.
He was at peace now, and a happy man.

"I'm so glad for both of you," I told him. "It's the
best news I've heard in a long time. You can't help
but know I've been hoping this would happen."

He returned the hug and saw me out the door.

"Hang in there, Kate," he told me, giving me a big thumbs-up. "It'll be real tough but just hang in there."

"I will," I answered slowly, frowning at the prospect of the unpleasant work ahead. "And, Carl, you hurry and come back to work. You don't know how much I've missed you."

And I walked away and down the stairs, on my way to tell a man the friend he loved was running on a rampage.

CHAPTER TWENTY-TWO

I found him in the squad room, cleaning out his desk. As I approached he looked at me, and when he smiled I saw the familiar crinkles start to form around his eyes.

"I got the call this morning," Bobby told me. "Stockton says it's time to come on home. I've stalled them off until tomorrow but then I've got to follow Charlie."

"Bobby, about Charlie," I began, but he held up his hand as if to say he didn't want to hear it.

"Kate, that's over. I told you so when we had coffee. You did what you had to do and I respect that fact. What we need to talk about is you and me. I'm going back but I want to keep on seeing you and I hope you feel the same way about me. Will you have dinner with me tonight, then maybe take a quiet drive somewhere, so we can discuss some things about the two of us?"

He broke my heart and I sat down heavily, sick with the sorrow I was going to unload on him.

"Bobby, I need to ask you several questions, questions about the case. I'll explain why *after* I hear your answers. It's important I don't tell you till then. Who responded first to the Stockton crime scene, you or Charlie Rhoads?"

"I did," he answered, obviously surprised. "I took the call at the station, then phoned Charlie and got him out of bed. I drove to the lot and viewed the body, and he showed up a short time later. Why?"

"What was his reaction when he saw the victim?"

"Somber, serious, same as me. Same as you or Steve when you respond to a homicide."

"Did he indicate he'd ever seen the corpse before?"

"No, Kate, he didn't." Harris was becoming agitated. "In fact, he specifically told me later he'd never seen her around town before we found her in the woods that day."

I pulled my chair a little closer, and bent forward and laid my hand across his knee.

"Bobby, Charlie Rhoads knew Meryl Masters when she lived in Lodi. He'd turn up at her work on a pretty regular basis."

Astonishment consumed him and he stared at me.

"I don't believe it," he exclaimed, "I just don't believe it. There must be some mistake." The crinkles had left the corners of his eyes and his skin looked pale and taut.

"Bobby, Sonny Mitchell's sister was a client of Masters's for many months. She'd drop by and see her pretty often when she received assistance. I drove up to talk to Joanie Creighton this morning, simply because I was frustrated with the case and wanted to leave no stone unturned, and out of the blue she told me Charlie used to hang around Meryl all the time.

"She knew who he was because she'd seen him when he'd busted Sonny for robbery, and then often after that in court. It was around that same time that both she and Rhoads were turning up at the social services office, so his face was real fresh in her mind."

"But she's Mitchell's sister," Harris cried indignantly. "How can you believe a word she says?"

"You can tell about a person, Bobby, you know that. The woman wasn't lying. Besides, she didn't make a big deal about it, just sort of dropped it as an aside. I could tell by her expression she didn't know what she was throwing out. In fact, I believe she thought I already knew."

He looked at me and shook his head.

"But why, Kate, why would he keep it to himself?"

"I think I know why, Bobby, but you're not going to like it."

"Try me."

"Because he cared enough about Meryl, for whatever reason, to want revenge on whoever killed her. And I think he believes he's the one to deal out the eye-for-eye."

"Meaning?"

"Meaning Mitchell and Farnham weren't aberrations. Charlie's going to keep on tracking the murderer on his own, then when he finds him, kill him himself."

Bobby pushed back quickly from the desk and stood up straight, holding both his hands high in front of him and shaking his head rapidly back and forth.

"No, Kate, no. You're way off base there. You're talking about a dirty cop, about a guy Charlie Rhoads could never be. You don't know him like I do or you'd never say that to me."

"How well *do* you know Rhoads?" I asked quietly. "Bobby, please listen to me and consider what I'm saying. How well do you really know your friend Charlie Rhoads?"

"Since childhood. I've told you. In high school, in the service, now in Stockton."

"Your relationship spans a lot of years, Bobby, but you've kept in touch, not actually been with him, for a lot of that time. People change, as we both so well know, and sometimes those closest to them are the very last to see, especially if there've been long periods when they've been away from them."

He sat down woodenly in his seat and rubbed his hand across his head.

"There's got to be a logical explanation," he murmured slowly. "If what you say is true—the part about him knowing Masters, I mean—then there's got to be a logical explanation. But all the rest is crap, Kate, pure and simple crap!"

I let that pass and honed in on the first thing that he'd said.

"Let's get that explanation, then, Bobby. Let's ride up to Stockton and put it straight to Charlie. It's time to get this thing sorted out."

He blew out his breath, his mouth pushing forward, his cheeks hollowing, as he did so. He looked at me and I saw the bleakness in his eyes.

"He's not there, Kate. When the lieutenant called this morning he told me Charlie had gotten into some sort of fracas with a suspect as soon as he arrived. He's on temporary suspension, pending an internal investigation of possible use of excessive force."

The mountains lay far off to our right as we rode out of San Madera, tall and cold and dark against the winter sky. I looked at them and longed for springtime, when the harsher colors of this landscape would yield to lush and verdant ones, and the air would hang like pale blue gauze against the distant peaks.

"I know this must be tough for you, Bobby, so let me put it to him. After all, I'm the one who dug this up about Masters and I'm the one who has the theory about what he's up to now."

"That's okay with me, Kate. I'm still dubious about all of this, as you know. Of course I'll back you up if it starts looking like you're right, that goes without even saying, but I'd really prefer it be your show."

We spoke without emotion, just two cops working on a case. Any sparks existing between us had been dulled, at least momentarily, by the seriousness of the business at hand.

We were heading for Point Reyes, a narrow strip of land jutting into the sea across the bay from San Francisco. Lying north-northwest, it was very nearly a part of the mainland, separated from it only by the narrow finger of water called Tomales Bay that dug its way in near the top and ran like a silver sliver back down toward the city.

"He's at the cabin," Harris had told me, after trying to contact Rhoads at home. "Jane said he stormed in from the station, threw a few things in a bag, then left right away. She's upset, she doesn't know what's happening, but she thought it best not to try going with him. She knows Charlie. He's best left alone when he's like that."

"Where's the cabin?" I asked. "And is it his?"

"Yeah. It's a weekend place he's had for years. Just a little rustic, two-room affair up north in a stand of trees near the ocean."

"Let's keep him company," I said, and now we were on our way.

Except I wanted to make one stop first.

"Bobby, something's been bothering me, something about Charlie Rhoads and Sonny. I've got a strong feeling he may've used excessive force on him before. I mean, prior to the time he punched him out in Lodi. If we drop by your station first, is there anyone you could talk to, any way you could get into his package, to find out if my feeling's right?"

"What good would that do?" he responded truculently.

"If it turns out to be true, then it shows the present pattern of behavior was established some time ago and is now growing. It shows there's a violence in the man that's no longer easily contained."

I spoke softly, looking straight ahead, well aware how hard my words were hitting Bobby. Again, just as I'd done back in the squad room, I gently laid my hand atop his knee.

"Bobby, if this is true, we need to know it."

"I've heard no mention of it since I came back from LA, but I guess I could ask around." He spoke slowly, reluctantly, and I knew he hated the job he had to do, as much as I'd hated confronting him after leaving Carl.

"And there's something else, as long as we're in the area. I'd like to try to get in touch with that snitch, Jerry Edgars. I've got a feeling there's something wrong there, too. Do you know where he hangs out, how to contact him?"

"No, I don't," Bobby answered, "but I'm sure the guys on vice can fill me in."

We reached Stockton and pulled into the station lot, then made our way to the detective squad room.

"Get me my address and I'll be out of here while you work on that other project," I told him, "then we'll meet back here in several hours. We can probably still make Point Reyes sometime late tonight."

I waited by his desk while he talked with a motley crew over at a corner table. Scruffy, bearded, wearing torn denims and baggy shirts, they were typical of any vice unit at any city police department in the country. Shortly, he began walking back toward me.

"They say Edgars can be found most afternoons hanging out at Tootie's or one of the other bars on Main Street. That is, when he's not in Lodi, giving his business over there."

"Thanks, Bobby, I'll be back by five. If I haven't found him by then, I'll just hang it up till another time."

I drove to a seedy part of town where bars and pool halls vied for space, standing with flashing neon signs amid the grime. Even with all the dancing lights, Tootie's sprang out at me from the crowd, with the pair of winking shining eyes that rolled around the middle of each "O."

I parked the car and strolled inside—casually, coolly, trying not to look too much like a cop. I imagined my cover was blown by just about everyone inside, though. This'd be a real tough crowd to fool.

I saw him right away, small frame hunched over

a beer halfway down the bar. Luckily no one was sitting near, and I slid up on the stool beside him. He turned to me, just as you'd do to see who your neighbor is, and I saw a strange look pass through his eyes, as if he knew he'd seen me before but wasn't quite sure where.

"Jerry Edgars?" I said quietly. "I met with you down in San Madera. Is there somewhere private we can talk?"

He started, and I thought he'd jump right off his stool as recognition flooded in and he remembered who I was.

"Jesus," he stammered, "I've got nothing more to say. I told you that day . . ." His small mouth began forming "O"'s again, as round as the ones in Tootie's sign.

"Let's sit in that booth over there." I nodded toward an empty one just opposite us. "What I've got to talk to you about is just between you and me."

Edgars shot a scared-rabbit look around the room, then picked up his beer and followed me across the floor.

"Look," I said when we'd settled in, "I meant it that our talk would go no further. This isn't about busting someone, it's about me trying to get some understanding. Okay?"

"Okay." He nodded miserably, still glancing all around.

"That day you came down to see me, you told us

Sonny Mitchell confessed to you about the murders, then you ran from the station, wouldn't stay to back it up. Why did you scamper off like that?"

Edgars licked his lips and began to wipe his brow.

"Because I couldn't get Sonny in trouble," he whispered.

"But if he killed that little baby, don't you think he deserved to be in trouble? You were afraid of him, weren't you? I think that was it."

The snitch paused, gulping nervously at his beer.

"No, not Sonny. I weren't never afraid of him. And he didn't kill the baby."

"I don't get it." I leaned across the table and looked into his face. His shifty little eyes lit on mine, then quickly flitted off from one side to the other. "If you're his friend, why'd you try to frame him when now you say he didn't do it?"

"I can't tell you," he whimpered. "He'll kill me if I do."

"No, this is between you and me. The person you're afraid of will never know we talked. Why would Sonny kill you?"

"Not Sonny . . ." Edgars bit his lip and I smelled his beer breath waft across the table. "Look, miss, you're different from the other cops. You treated me just fine that day in San Madera. Are you really leveling with me now? About not telling, I mean?"

"Absolutely," I assured him. "Trust me."

"It's the other one I'm scared of. The big cop who

got me down there in the first place. You know, Detective Rhoads.''

"Why are you afraid of him?" I asked quietly, signaling to the bartender to bring another beer.

"Because it was all a lie, and if he finds out I'm
squealing he'll send me straight back to the joint, just
like he threatened in the first place.''

I covered his shaking hand with mine, then gave
it a little pat.

"He won't find out, I promise you. Now tell me
the whole story.''

Edgars began sipping the fresh beer, then wiped
the froth off his lips with the back of one hand.

"I believe you," he said, finally looking me straight
in the eye, "and it's almost a relief to get this off my
chest. I never did feel good about what I was doing
to ol' Sonny.''

"So go ahead, then.''

"I'd snitched for Rhoads for years but never, ever
lied for him. Then he came to me one day and gave
me this story he wanted me to tell the cops in San
Madera about Sonny. How he'd confessed to me he'd
done those murders. But there was no truth to it. I
never even saw Mitchell the night I was supposed to
have been hangin' out with him.''

"Why did you agree to do it, then? Why didn't
you tell Rhoads to take a hike?''

Edgars balled up his fist and began giving little
bangs on the tabletop to punctuate his words.

"Because he told me if I didn't do just what he said, he'd throw me back in jail—me and my brother, too, who's just down from the joint."

"And you believed him?"

"Hell, yes, lady, I believed him," Edgars snorted. "I know Detective Rhoads and I never doubted for a minute if I didn't at least *try* doing what he asked, he'd toss the two of us right back inside the can."

"He tried to frame him, Bobby. When he couldn't get him any other way, he tried to manufacture evidence. That's why Jerry Edgars ran out on us that day. Weasel that he is, even he couldn't go through with something like that."

Harris sat quietly, listening to me closely. We'd waited till we got into the car and headed out of Stockton before starting to talk.

"But it's just his word against Charlie's," he protested stubbornly.

"Look at the facts, Bobby. It turned out Mitchell had a solid alibi so why would he confess to something he didn't do? And the snitch certainly wasn't trying to bring glory on himself—I've rarely seen a more reluctant witness."

We drove silently for several minutes, and when he didn't speak, I began to draw him out.

"What went on with you, Bobby? Anything worth mentioning?"

He slammed his hand down on the dash, uncharacteristically losing control.

"Damn it, yes, Kate, you were right. I talked to an old sergeant there, talking like I already knew, and he alluded to the fact Charlie had been disciplined with suspension and salary loss three or four years back when he busted Sonny for that robbery. Apparently roughed him up way beyond the call."

"Did the sergeant go into any detail?"

"No. Remember, he thought I was already aware. Just said a couple of things to make me know it was pretty bad."

I didn't press him. I didn't need to know how bad. All I'd wanted was to have my suspicions verified that it had happened.

"What do you make of all this, Bobby?" I wanted to hear the opinion he'd formed for himself, now that he'd heard more evidence firsthand.

"If it's true, Kate, then my friend has changed. Or maybe I never really knew him like I thought." Bobby stared straight ahead at the darkening light coming through the windshield.

"But maybe you *did* know him and just refused to accept what you knew because you loved him so very much. Like that time in the service when he saved your life. What was the word you used for what he did? 'Obliterate' the man?"

He slumped down in his seat.

"Yeah, it was pretty terrifying. Not just taking care of business but going far beyond. If the MPs hadn't happened on the scene, the guy would've been minced dog meat."

"But he was dealing with a person who'd tried to kill his best friend. Maybe that accounted for the extreme reaction." I was playing devil's advocate here but it was a role I had to take.

"No, Kate, no. It went well beyond that. I knew that at the time and I pushed it far away. But I never forgot about it, it always stayed with me. There was something present in him that day—a rage, a cruelty—that frightened me and that I'd never seen in him before. Like I said, the rest of us wouldn't have handled it that way."

"And you never saw him like that again?"

"No, but you gotta remember, I went straight down to LA from the service. As you pointed out earlier, in recent years Charlie and I haven't really been around each other that much."

"There're some people like that, you know," I told him. "People who have to settle everything with an atomic bomb. Shrinks say it's sometimes learned behavior from their childhood—they've seen a parent discipline with whacks instead of words—or else it grows from rage caused by feelings of inferiority or helplessness, resulting in an inability to properly control a situation. And so the person reaches a quick flashpoint and erupts in one big bang. Like Charlie did with that guy in the service. Like Charlie did with Sonny Mitchell."

He didn't answer me and I looked out the window. We were nearing San Francisco now, the twinkling lights bright and sharp in the clearness of the night. It was a rare evening in this city to see a sky unobscured by fog, and looking around me as I drove, I reveled in the sight.

"Bobby," I said, turning off at the exit to the Golden Gate Bridge, "remember the other night when you came over? Right after Rhoads and I had gone to Farnham? I asked you then if you'd noticed any odd behavior recently by Charlie, and you conceded yes, 'little things,' or something to that effect. I think you've been more aware than you think that some disturbing changes might be going on with your friend."

He didn't look at me, just stared through the window, and I wondered at first if he'd even heard what I'd said.

"You're right, Kate," he finally responded with a sigh. "I can look over the year I've been in Stockton and see certain things I've not faced up to before. Things that go farther back, even, than the past several months. A remark here, a move there, all slightly off-kilter.

"But I'll tell you this"—and his voice rose and his tone was defiant—"even knowing what I know now, I've still got to hear it from Charlie. I've got to hear it from him that he knew Meryl Masters and he's chasing the suspects. I've still got to go in there believing we're wrong and letting him tell us we're right. Because that's not been proven yet—we're only speculating—and I at least owe him that much."

I recognized his cry for just what it was. The loyal friend standing by his buddy and holding to the desperate hope we'd been wrong.

"I understand, Bobby," I consoled him, "and I'd feel the same way in your shoes."

We glanced at our watches and saw the time had passed far quicker than we'd thought. It was nearly eight o'clock, leaving us with at least another two-hour drive to Charlie's cabin. Though the mileage wasn't so great, the Point Reyes road was a narrow, twisting, climbing affair that demanded low speeds and careful steering to avoid a sudden plunge into the ocean.

"How about stopping for the night and going on in early tomorrow?" Harris asked. "Personally, I think it'd be better all the way around to do this in the daylight, when everything's bright and clear."

"I agree," I said, though somewhat reluctantly. Now on the charge, I was anxious for the confrontation to begin, but I also desired daylight to get a firm grasp on the unfamiliar surroundings. "Do you want to cross the bridge, then get a motel in Corte Madera and start out first thing in the morning?"

"Sounds the best way to me, Kate. It'll give us a chance to refresh ourselves so we'll have all our wits about us."

We checked into a wood-and-glass two-story structure and took two rooms on the second floor.

"Looks like we're going to get to have that dinner

after all," Harris said wryly, "though not quite under the circumstances I first had in mind. Want to get settled, then meet in the restaurant at nine?"

I was nervous because I didn't know what he was going to ask of me, what sort of commitment he was going to want me to make. I knew I didn't want to lose Bobby Harris, but I also knew I was not yet ready to get heavily involved.

I'd given a lot of thought to the situation since that long embrace and kiss at my front door. And I'd come to some decisions, decisions that were right for me. I could only hope he'd not ask more than I'd found I was willing to give.

I freshened up my face and smoothed down my wrinkled clothes. We'd left in such a hurry I'd stopped by the house just long enough to throw a few things in a bag, then hug and kiss Tommy good-bye. I'd worn jeans and a jacket and packed no fancy date dresses for tonight.

I walked into the restaurant promptly at nine, and he was there waiting for me. As I saw him turn toward me, my heart did a flip and I could feel my eyes start dancing. Strangely, when we were in close contact on a case, my feelings toward him became strictly business, sublimated and suppressed by the work we were both doing. But once alone with him in a casual setting, my emotions began flooding in, consuming me with their intensity.

The hostess seated us in a green banquette along the far wall and we sat awkwardly for a moment, both pretending to study the menu.

Like school kids on a first date, I thought suddenly. Now that we know we're going to talk seriously, we find we're both ill at ease.

I decided to break the ice that had suddenly formed, so we could relax once again, and the easiest way to do that was to return to the case.

"Bobby, I'm going on the assumption Charlie *did* know Meryl, and my mind's been turning over as to what their relationship could have been. Do you think it's possible they were ever lovers?"

He considered for a moment, toying with his fork.

"If it's true he knew her, and I only say 'if,' no, I don't think so. From what I've gathered, he became involved with this woman from Merced around that time, and as we know, she's still very much on the scene. I don't think there was anyone before and there's certainly been no one else since."

"Then why the extreme passion about Masters's death?" I murmured.

"Katharine." He suddenly reached across and took my hand. "We need to have that talk because I won't be down in San Madera much longer. And whatever happens tomorrow, I'll return only long enough to finish clearing out my things and then I'll be gone.

"But I can't lose you. It's strange to think all this

strong feeling could come up in just the past several days, but that's what's happened and I find I do not want to leave you."

I looked at him, at that dear face I'd grown to know so well, and I covered his hand with mine.

"I feel the same way, Bobby," I whispered huskily, "about not wanting you to go. This also has come on me so unexpectedly and yet I, too, have no doubts of my feelings. But I am not ready for any sort of commitment right now, and if this is what you're asking for, I'm sorry, I cannot give it. Remember what we talked about? About going slow? I'm afraid that's what I must do."

He leaned back, looking disappointed, but then his next words surprised me.

"I know we should, and we will. It's just my getting ready to move away that gives me this urgency to finalize something with you. Something that probably needs time to grow a bit more."

"Look," I said frankly, exposing more than I'd intended to show, "there are times I think I'm falling in love, but I know it's not true, it's too soon. I've been badly burned and I'm not ready to trust a man, any man, just yet. Besides, I'm just beginning to explore the new world I've been thrust into in the past year, and after a lumpy start, I find I'm enjoying it and want to keep on."

I paused, considering my next words.

"No, 'enjoying' doesn't say it enough. Embracing

it, loving it, wanting to gulp it all down, if that doesn't make it sound silly. I'm being on my own, trying new things, and I want to do more of all that before making another commitment."

"You're throwing me out for the drums?" he asked, smiling.

"Not throwing out, but, yes, like the drums. They represent just what I'm talking about. Exploring, trying things out, setting a pace just for me. My life is opening up just now. Even Jon, the one impediment, has finally faded away."

"So what are you saying, Katharine? What part do I play in this life?"

"A big part, Bobby. Oh, I hope a very big part. I want to see you as much as I can, but I'm not ready just now for more. Can you believe how deeply I care and still accept what I'm saying?"

I looked deeply, anxiously, into his eyes, hoping I wasn't gambling a good thing away. But I knew, regardless of that chance, this was what I must do.

"We'll just take it from there, then," he answered slowly, "and I won't pressure you for more. But know this. I intend to be with you whenever I can, whenever *you* want to see me."

My heart filled with my happiness, a deep reverberating happiness I felt I hadn't known in years.

"I'd hoped it'd be no other way, Bobby Harris," I told him as my voice rang with joy. "I believe we'd waste something wonderful if we started drifting apart."

He slid along the circular seat till we sat side by side, and we stayed that way while we ordered and ate and ended the meal, pressing warmly together, whispering small words.

CHAPTER TWENTY-THREE

"Any ideas on how we're going to approach this?" I asked as we picked up the Point Reyes road. "He's not exactly going to be happy to see me."

Bobby kept his eyes on the twists and turns as he considered our strategy.

"I think we've got to trade on our relationship," he answered. "That is, if you don't mind. We've got to tell him we've realized there's something meaningful between us and we've ridden up to share the news with him. It's a cheap shot at what we've got together, Kate, I don't deny that, but I'm convinced it's the best way to make it work."

"I don't mind," I told him, "because we've got to get this thing settled. And it's just like any other police procedure. You play the best cards you hold in order to achieve your goal. Besides, this *is* just what you'd do anyway, isn't it, Bobby? Take your new best girl to meet your long-time friend?"

He grimaced, and I hoped he hadn't thought my words were flippant, but we were plotting our moves now and it all had to be laid out.

"Of course, Kate, it's right in character. That's just how I'd act and that's why he's going to be relaxed and believe us."

Mentally, I compared the difference between Bobby's attitude as we'd left San Madera—"I'd really prefer it be your show"—and his feelings now, acting as equal partner. The information we'd dug up in Stockton had obviously impacted on his mind. Still, I knew he hurt.

"Bobby, I've said this before but I've got to say it again because I care. I know how tough this is for you, and if there were any way I could make things different, I would."

"It's tough, yes, but I know this much now. Something needs sorting out here. And when I'm on a case, personal feelings can't enter into it. And they won't."

I tucked my leg up under me for better comfort. We'd both dressed casually, in jeans, open shirts, and running shoes. The story we'd give Charlie was that we were on an outing.

We swung out toward the ocean, with the crashing winter water on our left and towering Mt. Tamalpais to our right. The scenery was awesome, and despite the serious nature of our trip, I found it difficult to take my eyes off the vista around me.

"So shall we just ease into the bit about Masters or confront him with it shortly after we arrive?" As I spoke, I watched a seagull swoop across a golden field and dive at the craggy grayish rocks along the coast.

"Let's play it by ear, Kate. I can probably get a better handle on his mood than you. When I sense the time is right, we'll do it."

"And if he denies it, as we expect him to?"

"If Mitchell's sister was right, there'll have been other people who knew about their relationship besides her, and you can start to dig them out."

"But not you?" I asked. "You wouldn't pursue this, would you?"

Harris hunched over the wheel, concentrating on the road.

"No, Kate, I wouldn't, not even as your reluctant partner. If Charlie denies knowing Meryl, that's it for me. I'm for sure going to take his word against some convict's sister's. And anyway, remember, I'm off the case after today."

"Fair enough," I answered. "Let's hope we both come away from that cabin satisfied."

The road now climbed and curved, then suddenly it descended in sets of twisting "S"s and we were on the flat, entering the village of Point Reyes Station.

"The cabin's further on," Bobby told me. "We'll pass the turnoff to the Point itself, then continue five or six miles more on this road."

I settled back, alone with my own thoughts, and watched the beauty of the wooded flatlands and the sparkling water rushing past. And I wondered what Bobby was really feeling about the possibility of a cop gone wrong.

Because even though Rhoads was no close friend of mine, though at one point I'd certainly grown to like him, I found the fact he'd betrayed the trust, broken the union, hard to understand or live with. He'd concealed his involvement with a victim and was now following his own vendetta, and that went against the grain in a very hard, hard way.

So if I, who'd only been a short-time friend, now felt this bitter sickness at the staining of the badge, then how must Bobby feel? I could only imagine.

Suddenly a narrow finger of water appeared on my right, and not far across it, I saw the mainland. It was so close I felt I could take a stone and throw it and land it on its shore, and I marveled at how, for many miles, it would be made to keep its distance by just this liquid sliver.

"That's Tomales Bay," Bobby said, pointing. "Just a little farther and we're there." He shifted uneasily in his seat, staring straight ahead.

Abruptly the road curved a little, and then it settled back and ran straight ahead toward a stand of thick dark trees towering on the left.

"Here we are." Bobby nodded toward a narrow track leading through a field, then disappearing into the denseness of the forest. And the car swung off the asphalt and, in a cloud of whirling dust, began heading for the cabin.

I saw him first, coming out the door, a cigarette dangling from his lips. He halted at the sight of us, surprise spread across his face, and stood stock still, on the first step from the top, while we parked the car beneath a tree.

"Charlie," Harris called out, "how're ya doin', fella?"

We got out of the car and started walking toward him, toward the tiny cabin nestled in a clearing in the woods.

"Hi, Charlie," I greeted him. "I hope you don't mind I'm here."

"I could care . . ." he muttered, shrugging his big shoulders, then asked, "What the hell's with the two of you anyway? Driving all the way up here?"

His face held a wariness I could not define, yet I was certain of its presence. He came down off the steps, threw his arms around Bobby, then looked at me.

"Come to stick it in me once again, boss lady? Is that the reason for the trip?"

"No way, Charlie," Harris intervened. "The weekend's coming up and we took an extra day, headed up this way for a little outing, and decided to drop in on you. I talked with Jane before we left. She told me you were at the cabin."

"Yeah, more chickenshit behavior by the brass. Come on inside, I'll tell you all about it. But first, what's this about a little trip? You two an item on the social side?"

His dark eyes moved from me to Bobby, and as I watched, Rhoads's face became more florid. Several times, he reached up and ran his fingers through his hair.

"I know we caught you off-guard, Charlie, but as long as we were in the area we wanted to give you the good news. Kate and I have started seeing each other, yes, and nothing's going to change when I return to Stockton."

"Well, look at that!" Rhoads clapped Bobby on the shoulder. "If you'd asked me about her yesterday, I'd've said 'forget it,' but that's all past now, I've got other things on my mind. Jane tell you I got suspended?"

"No," Harris answered truthfully, "not Jane. I heard it from the lieutenant when I phoned the station."

We'd entered a cozy living room with a fireplace at one end that contained some crackling logs. The smoky warmth felt good, and I sat in an armchair close to it while Rhoads and Harris settled on a worn sofa not far off. Beside me, a little table held an ashtray overflowing with stale butts.

"So what's this about the suspension, Charlie? What went on?"

"A bunch of crock." Rhoads's face darkened. "I'm just back on the job and I make this bust. You know Wade, that guy we had the warrant out on for the ADW? Well, I bring him in just fine but then he starts squirreling all around and I've got to calm him down, and the next thing you know he's squealing I tried to choke-hold him and I'm off the job. Bullshit!"

"Did you?" Bobby asked, playing at being funny. Rhoads snorted.

"Whaddya think? Hell, no. I know better."

I didn't know if it was the influence of the outdoor atmosphere or the casualness of the situation or something else entirely, but Charlie seemed different from when I'd known him before—louder, rougher, not as reachable, and definitely edgier and more intense. Despite his heartiness, he seemed to be laying on a bluff that kept us from reaching through to him. I wondered if maybe he'd been drinking, but I couldn't catch the smell of liquor, even though I tried.

At least he doesn't resent my being here, I thought. That'll make this job a whole lot easier. And I wondered when Bobby would decide to make the move.

"I'm glad to see the two of you," Rhoads was saying, "I really am. I came up here to be alone but I'm glad the two of you dropped in. My old buddy and his girl . . ."

I saw Bobby shoot an uneasy glance at him and wondered if he'd picked up on the same strangeness

I'd observed. Why is he acting this way, I thought, not like his usual easygoing self? Somehow I doubted the suspension was the cause. He'd never put up a false front between him and Bobby over that.

"Look, you'll stay for lunch, won't you?" Charlie asked. "I'd like you to. I'm gonna run to the store just down the road and get a couple of six-packs and some steaks. We'll just put 'em on the grill and have ourselves a time."

"Sounds good to me," Harris told him. "Want us to come with you?"

"Hell, no, I won't be more than half an hour. Stay by the fire or take a walk outside. There's a little path that goes through the woods just 'round the back."

We watched him get into his dark blue van and drive out the narrow track, and I asked Bobby, "Which one will it be?"

"How about that walk?" he said. "I'd like to stretch my legs. You going to be warm enough?"

"Maybe too warm," I told him, putting down my jacket. "Even though it's winter, I always heat up when I walk. I'll just grab this shirt of Charlie's. I'm sure he wouldn't mind." And I picked up a heavy woolen shirt from a hook behind the door and draped it loosely across my shoulders.

"How do you think it's going?" I asked Bobby as, hand-in-hand, we started through the woods. "He certainly doesn't seem to resent my presence."

"No, that part's doing fine," he answered, reaching

out to hold a bough back from my face. "But he's different somehow. Not relaxed, not easy, even though he pretends to be."

"So you've noticed," I responded. "I wondered if it was just my imagination or if it was real. If I didn't know better, I'd think he'd been drinking or doing drugs."

"No, Charlie's not been drinking and I'd bet he's never done a drug in his entire life. It's something but it's definitely not either one of those."

We strolled comfortably along, and as a slight wind came up, I pulled Charlie's shirt from my shoulders and slipped it on.

"Look, I'm going to jog ahead a little," Bobby told me. "If I remember right, there's a rise just down a bit that gives a good view of the ocean. If it's where I think it is, we'll continue on, but if it's any farther we'd best turn back to the cabin because Charlie'll soon be there."

I watched him running down the path, and again a warmth and longing filled my being. I was so lucky, I thought, so very lucky to have found this man. And to have found that he was willing to go slow.

I meandered along, my mind playing with the possibilities of what would happen in the cabin, and I felt the heightened anticipation I always feel when I'm closing in for a climax. For, one way or another, this thing about Rhoads and Masters was going to be resolved.

Suddenly the wind picked up and I began to shiver. Maybe we should just go straight back, I thought, and see the ocean some other day. I pulled the shirt tight around my chest, then jammed my hands deep into the pockets.

The fingers of my left went clear down to the bottom, but the fingers of the right touched some crumpled mass like a napkin or discarded note. Curious, as anyone would be, I clasped the object and withdrew it, and when it was free of the material I turned my hand and spread my fingers out.

And there, lying in the bottom of my palm, was a balled-up twisted piece of silver tape.

I looked at it and winced. Ever since the night I'd first seen Lucy, I'd avoided tape of any sort. I stuffed the wad back into the pocket where I'd found it. Probably some old binding from an ancient project he'd meant to throw away.

And then my fingers closed around it once again— lightly, slowly—and my breath suddenly left me as a thought, awful in its import, ran swiftly through my mind.

Suppose I'd worked it out all wrong. Suppose the puzzle pieces had fallen down but never really fitted because I'd put them all together backward and seen a picture that wasn't really there.

I'd believed Charlie was trying to avenge Meryl's murder by tracking down her killer and dealing justice out himself, but all along I could've been so very wrong. He could've instead been trying to find a scapegoat—Sonny Mitchell, the Farnham man, anyone—to draw the heat far from himself. Himself. The murderer of Meryl Masters and that hapless dimpled baby, Lucy Brighton.

I heard footsteps and looked up and saw Bobby jogging back.

"It's too far," he called, "let's turn around. He'll be coming back soon."

Slowly I started walking toward him, looking steadily at the ground so he wouldn't see my strange expression. I didn't want to share this yet, didn't dare to say a word till I was very sure. After all, a wad of tape's not that uncommon. We strolled slowly to the cabin and I forced myself to joke and smile.

Once inside, Bobby left to use the bathroom and I quickly ran from room to room. I knew what I was looking for—the ripped-out page from Meryl Masters's photo album—for the tape and page were all that'd been carried from the murder scene besides the victims' bodies and if I'd already found the tape, shouldn't the pictures be there, too?

At this point I should've had a search warrant. I knew that but the urgency to know right then, to find out the truth immediately, completely overwhelmed me.

I turned out the trash can in the kitchen, theorizing he'd probably have thrown it away, but found only garbage and miscellaneous debris. I dashed outside to the large green canister standing near the door, grabbed a stick from nearby on the ground, and started poking through it.

Beer cans, fast food wrappers, a newspaper or two. And then, sticking out from underneath a longish piece of cardboard, I saw a flat piece of paper and the corner of a photograph. Slowly I withdrew it and found myself staring at the missing page from Meryl Masters's album.

Five pictures under plastic looked up at me. Shots of Meryl with Steven Brownfeld, Meryl with girls I didn't know, a handsome collie running on a beach. But where the sixth and final picture should've lain there was only a blank space, as if someone had removed it.

I dashed back inside, the photo sheet held close behind me, and started going through the drawers. I heard the toilet flush and then the water at the sink begin to run, and I knew Bobby wold be joining me soon.

The living room yielded nothing and I darted to the kitchen and hurriedly pulled out each drawer.

Knives, spoons, can openers, the usual jumble such drawers always hold. And then I fingered through a set of dish towels. And saw a single photograph lying deep between the folds.

I pulled it out and stared at it. A smiling Charlie Rhoads with his arm around Meryl Masters, standing near a stream. He'd had to keep it. Even though incriminating, he couldn't bear throwing it away.

I heard footsteps behind me and Bobby came into the room. Silently I held my hand out, the photo plainly visible. Then I laid the tape and the plastic album holder on the kitchen counter.

"I found the tape in the pocket," I said, "the pocket of Charlie's shirt. The rest I found right here, in the drawer and in the trash."

The import of my words hit him immediately and he sank down into a chair.

"Oh, my God," he moaned, burying his face between his hands. "Oh, my God, Charlie, why?"

I went to him and put my arms around him and held him to me tight. I could feel the sobs that racked his body, and my own tears began to rise.

"It's all there in plain sight," I told him sadly. "It was always there but we were just too blind to see— pointing fingers at other people, attempting to frame Sonny, his professed 'need' to stay on the case when I dismissed him. He wasn't trying to get the jump on us, as we once thought. He had to make sure he knew what was going on so *we* wouldn't get the jump on him and finger him as the killer."

Bobby finally raised his head, tears streaming down his face.

"That's why he didn't go ahead and remove the ones he tried to paint as suspects. It wasn't because he concluded they hadn't done it, Kate, it was because he badly needed them, needed someone we'd arrest instead of him. And he was going to keep on searching till he found that soul and brought him in and had him charged."

I pressed close to him, laying my hand along his thigh.

"I figured that out, too, Bobby, and that's why I say we've been so blind."

"But why, Kate?" he anguished. "It doesn't make any sense."

I heaved a sigh and felt the sadness seeping through me—the sadness at a friendship lost, the sadness at a cop gone bad.

"It doesn't have to make sense to be real, Bobby, always remember that. And I'm afraid this is very real indeed."

And then, as if we needed more, the final clincher fell in place and locked the puzzle down.

"We wondered why the crime scenes were so clean," I mused, "both Meryl's and Lucy's. As antiseptic as if they'd been scrubbed down. Good luck? Maybe in one but certainly not in two. Only a pro would know how to leave a scene like that, a pro like a seasoned cop. Like Charlie."

Other memories rushed in, too—memories of acts that at the time meant nothing. Like the way Rhoads had crowded in beside me at Meryl's condo when I started going through the album. To make sure he'd made no mistake and overlooked a picture that should've been removed.

"Are you ready?" Bobby asked. "Ready to face him?"

"Are *you* is more to the point? Do you want a few more minutes or do you want me to call up Steve? We could hang around with Charlie after lunch and Darrow could be here in several hours. We wouldn't have to make our move till then."

"No, Kate, I'll be fine. I don't want Darrow, it's important I handle this myself. Don't worry, once we're face-to-face he'll be just like any other suspect."

"Okay, kiddo," I told him as he started getting to his feet, "if that's the way you feel, we'll do it."

The van pulled up and found us standing near the driveway.

"Enjoy your walk, kids?" he called out. "I've got some great steaks here. Let's go in and have a brew."

I glanced at Bobby, and we climbed the steps and followed Rhoads inside.

We waited till he'd fired up the grill and the three of us were lounging by the crackling logs before I started.

"It's odd, you know," I said, sipping slowly from the can, "that you never saw Meryl before her death. You went back and forth to Lodi fairly often, she was a highly attractive woman, and she was involved with your quarry, Sonny Mitchell. Strange your paths had never crossed."

My eyes strayed casually toward Charlie, and I saw an open face of innocence. A bluff, I thought, well feigned to keep me off the scent.

"Well, that's the way it goes, I guess," Rhoads replied. "There's an awful lot of people in that city."

"You're saying you never met her, then?" I laid the question down quietly and set my beer aside. The time for sipping was over.

The wariness I'd seen earlier crept back into his face.

"Hell, no. What're you playing at anyway? If I'd ever seen the dame, I'd have said so right up front."

"Funny." I put a puzzled frown upon my face. "I ran into someone who said she'd seen you with Meryl a number of times at her office, no mistake."

"Crazy." He wasn't giving anything away but I saw a tightening of his facial muscles. "I guess I'd remember that if it had happened."

"So you never met her?" I asked, continuing to watch him casually.

"Not that I know of, no. Hell, I guess I could've seen her, passed her by, you know, just the same as Bobby could've done. Or yourself, even, if you'd come up to Lodi."

"Charlie, I'm afraid it's a whole lot more than that." Bobby rose and draped his arm along the mantle, also setting down his beer. "The person Kate's talking about is prepared to swear you knew Masters well enough to hang around her at her office an awful lot. And there are others, too, who'll say the same."

I looked at him, my heart filled with pride and

gratefulness. He was right on-line, all buttoned up with no emotion showing, just a cop doing the job he had to do.

Rhoads stood up and stalked across the room, hands thrust deep into his pockets. When he neared the door, he spun around and faced us, and his cheeks were dark, almost black, with anger. A scowl scored his forehead and his eyes were flashing madly.

"My best friend, my best friend and a cop I'd learned to trust! You turn on me like this? What kind of people are you?"

"Sit down, Charlie," I told him, and now my voice assumed a commanding tone he recognized immediately. He gave a start, staring at me hard.

"Okay"—he shrugged—"let's talk this out."

He lowered himself into a chair, holding his arms loosely, giving the appearance of being relaxed, but I saw his foot tapping rapidly on the floor.

"I'm going to ask you once again, Charlie, did you know the victim, Meryl Masters?"

"And I'm going to tell you once again," he said evenly, but through clenched teeth, "I didn't, those people have mixed me up with someone else. I maybe passed through that social services office looking for some information about Mitchell, but if she's the one I spoke with, I sure don't recall." He paused. "Wow, what a coincidence that would be!"

Smooth, I thought, very smooth. But yet giving us

a little more with every utterance. From absolutely not knowing her to maybe passing her to perhaps actually talking to her at her desk.

And as his answers progressed, his demeanor deepened, till I felt anew he was trying to contain something that wanted desperately to get out. Like a restless beast, he again rose and began pacing back and forth. I looked at Bobby and he nodded. The time had come.

"Charlie, can you deny *this*?" And I held up the smoothed-out photo for him to see.

He paused, one foot actually raised up in the air, and his eyes began to bulge as they fastened on the picture. He stared as if he could look at nothing else, and I saw a vein in his forehead start to throb.

"Gimme it!" he yelled, like a small child squabbling at a sandbox, and he lunged toward me, hand outstretched. I sidestepped his advance and handed off the snap to Bobby.

"Charles Rhoads, you have the right to remain silent . . ." He stood gaping at me like a wounded bull while I continued reading him his rights.

"You're so wrong," he whispered when I'd finished, "so very wrong. It isn't what you think."

"What, then?" Bobby asked. "Why don't you tell us all about it."

"She was a friend in passing, a long, long time ago. To tell you the truth, I didn't even recognize her or her name when we found the body. And when it dawned on me much later who she was . . . I know it was wrong but it just seemed so much easier to keep quiet."

"Won't work, friend," Harris told him, facing him with his back turned toward the fire. "We've got more than just the photo, we've got this." And he dangled the wad of silver tape.

"Found by me in your pocket," I told him, "I imagine you forgot to throw it away. And even though I touched it, I'm sure a lot of the surfaces stayed clean. I imagine the lab will find them covered with your prints."

Rhoads sank into a chair and began to shiver, cowering down and pushing his body into its back as if he ached to disappear.

"Oh, God," he moaned, "oh, God, that little baby. I never meant . . . I never planned to hurt either one of them. It happened—I just snapped—and then they both were dead."

He jerked his head up, staring at the two of us. Tears ran down his cheeks and his words came out in gulps.

"I loved her so very much, but she would only play with me. All the years we were together, she'd never commit. She'd not even tell her snotty family about us, scared they'd throw her out if they feared she might marry a lowly cop.

"Nothing but a doctor, lawyer, or rich dilettante would do for them. They wanted her to marry in her class and keep herself busy with the fuckin' Junior League. They'd have looked on me, a workingman in a rough profession, as near as bad as Sonny Mitchell. Drop down below that certain Masters level and you were lumped in with all the lowly masses. Character didn't count with them, position did."

"Tell us about it, Charlie," Bobby urged. "Tell us how it started and how it ended up."

Rhoads buried his head between his large strong hands and began sobbing once again, louder this time, as if a flood long dammed was finally breaking loose. So, I thought, this explains the oddness in his actions, explains why he was wired so tight. He'd already been nearing the breaking point before we confronted him, doing his best to keep control but letting it slip as every minute passed.

"I met her just by chance one day in Lodi. She was dating that bastard Mitchell then but I soon took her away from him, and not long after that, I busted him and sent him away. And she was mine for many months to come. *You* knew, *you* knew, Bobby." Rhoads wagged his finger at Harris. "You've known for several years there's been someone, but you didn't want to hear because of Jane."

Harris nodded calmly, then indicated to Charlie to go on.

"Meryl was a big teaser and she'd always torment me with the fact maybe she'd never gotten over Sonny. She knew how I hated him and she'd use that to jerk my chain. Man, a guy like him. With her. She was so fine. I despised his guts because of what he was, but mainly because he'd been with her.

"And then about nine months ago she threw me over. Said it was time she started getting serious and her family expected her to marry someone else. It killed me and I fought her over it but finally we split up, she moved south, and we didn't see each other after spring.

"But two months ago I couldn't stand it any longer and I phoned. We talked several times after that and she still said she didn't want to see me, but there she was again, the teasing showing in her tone."

Rhoads threw his head against the cushion and closed his eyes while tears continued running down his cheeks. I stayed with him while Bobby filled a glass with water and put it in his hand. He sat up and drank it thirstily, then set it down.

"I ached for her, I was no good without her, so I drove down unannounced that Friday night and rang her bell. She answered but she wasn't pleased to see me, and even though she let me in, she asked me not to stay. We began to argue and she said something about Sonny, and then she told me 'wait a minute' and went into another room.

"And when she came back, she was carrying this little baby in a plastic carrier and she set it on the floor, and I looked at it and it looked just like Sonny. She must've read my thoughts because she looked at

ne, teasing like, and said, 'Remind you of
omeone?' "

Again he sobbed, and his shoulders shook in
pasms.

"I . . . thought . . . it . . . was . . . her . . . baby,
ers and Sonny's, and I blew up. I had my hands
around her neck before I knew it and I was choking
er, and then the baby started crying and I gave it a
great big kick. I hated them, hated both of them and
ll they stood for, and I just went into a rage. She
uddenly slumped down in front of me but the baby
ept on crying, and I went to a kitchen drawer and
ot some tape and tore it off and taped the nose
nd mouth."

"But why remove the tape?" Harris asked. "Why
ake it off, then put it on again?"

"Carl got it right that day at the brunch," Charlie
old us. "I was hurrying and I put my prints all over
he first strip. I ripped it off, and the second time I
overed my fingers and only taped the mouth. Be-
ause by then the baby wasn't crying anymore."

"And you didn't know that Lucy wasn't
Masters's?"

"No," he wailed, "not till later. Not till I came
down to San Madera and learned for sure. I knew
ou'd told Bobby about the mother, but I didn't be-
ieve it. I thought there'd been some mistake. I was
ickened and stunned when I found out." He
cratched his head and then his ear and, in his agita-

tion, began to scratch his face as well. I vividly recalled the moment he referred to—how Rhoads had questioned if we were sure the child was Wanda's, coughed and mumbled when I'd told him yes.

"And then you disposed of the bodies?"

"Yes, but first I searched her album for any pictures, and I found that one and ripped it out. And then I put them in my van. I split them up. I wanted to leave the baby close to home—and I felt awful, so awful, about that little child—but I took Meryl up to Stockton because if she was ever found—and I thought she might never be because of hiding her in those woods—I could take control of the investigation and squash any links between her and me."

"But it didn't work that way, did it, Charlie?"

"It did," he cried, "it did. It was working just fine till you threw me off the case. And until you came up here."

He tried to light a cigarette but his hands shook too much. In desperation, he walked to the fireplace, bent down, and held it to the flame.

"What happened to their clothes?" I asked.

"I removed the baby's and wrapped it in an old shirt of Meryl's. No labels, unidentifiable. I took *her* things off when I reached the woods, then burned everything later in my fire. I was frantic, I didn't mean to do it. But once I did, I had to hide my tracks."

"And the purse? Why did you remove Meryl's purse?"

"To make you think she'd gone off on her own. No woman would leave her purse behind if she left home voluntarily. See, I didn't think the body would be found so quick—maybe never—so I wanted you to think she'd just walked away, maybe taken the baby with her. Or, if *it* was found, then killed the baby and disappeared."

So Meryl had been his lover, I thought as the three of us fell silent. Maybe I should've seen it sooner. I remembered the day Darrow had spoken about the "lack of randy studs" hanging around Masters and how Rhoads had quickly stiffened at the words. I'd thought it had been out of respect for the dead, but instead it'd been pure old-fashioned jealousy.

I sat down across from him, leaning forward.

"And even though you'd found another lover, Meryl still affected you enough that you killed her and a harmless baby out of rage?"

"Another lover?" Rhoads's head jerked up.

"Yes," I said, "the woman in Merced."

"You've got it all wrong!" he yelled, his eyes flashing. "Can't you see the way it is? There *is* no woman in Merced, I just made her up! I just kept pretending she existed so you'd think the girl I'd been seeing was one who was still alive!"

Bobby and I looked at each other and slowly shook our heads. Rhoads had played the big bluff and it'd worked so well. I'd fallen for the bit about the ultimatum, and given him sympathy and cut him slack he didn't deserve.

And I'd also bought the bit about going to see his lover the morning I'd learned of Farnham's death. The morning Karen had spotted Charlie out on the San Luis Road. He'd not been heading to hassle Brownfeld, as I'd thought, he'd simply been killing some time because he had nowhere else to go.

But without doubt the bluff had done its best work where he'd most intended. It'd served to make us believe the woman he loved was still alive. And if that were true, then of course we'd not think to ask if he'd been involved with Meryl.

"I'm sorry it ended like this, Charlie," I told him, reaching for the cuffs, "but you know we've got to go."

Without warning, Rhoads moved his hand to his hip pocket and started to draw his gun, screaming "I'm not going anywhere," and in that instant my own hand went to my revolver and I jerked it out and aimed.

But suddenly, as Charlie brought his weapon forward, an arm reached out and pushed me roughly back, and Harris stepped in front of me and fired. Rhoads staggered backward, bleeding from the mouth, then fell heavily down beside us and lay dead upon the floor.

I ran to him, disarmed the lifeless body, then put my fingers to his neck, just making sure. Bobby joined me and, sinking wearily down beside him, laid his head upon his back.

"My friend," he sobbed, "my dear, dear friend. How could it ever have come to this?"

"Why didn't you let me do it?" I cried. "Why didn't you let me help you out?"

Harris stumbled to his feet and wiped away the tears.

"Because I could never have lived with myself if I'd not handled it, Kate," he answered quietly. "It's just as simple as that. If I'd not been the one to take care of Charlie, I'd always have wondered if I'd shirked my duty because he was my friend. Surely you know what I feel, surely you understand."

I moved around the body, around the pool of blood forming on the floor, and took him in my arms.

"Of course I understand," I told him softly, "I understand and if it'd been me in your place, I hope I'd have acted just the same way."

CHAPTER TWENTY-FOUR

"It'd been simmering all along, Bobby—Charlie's propensity for violence—but because its escalation was so gradual, surfacing in isolated instances separated by months or even years, no one could really see it was ingrained in him."

It was two weeks later now, and we were sitting on a side porch off my den. The bitter cold had fled temporarily, along with the cloaking tule fog, and for the past few days a springlike warmth and brightness had filled the air.

"But the one he loved?" Bobby puzzled. "How could he kill the one he loved?"

"I think you know that," I told him, "we all know that, if we've ever been cops. Because we've seen enough examples of how love can turn to hate in just one blinding second when one cares very much.

"And the more you care, it seems, the more intense the black feeling, the more intense the white, each rushing to opposite extremes with no lukewarm ground between them. The volatility of love, I've heard it called."

Bobby rose from the wicker sofa and walked over to lean against the rail.

"But I thought I knew him," he protested, "I thought I knew that man inside out, even though we'd been apart."

"Do we ever really know anyone, Bobby?" I asked, looking up at him with saddened eyes. "We get used to them, tend to think of them as they were when we first met them, and blind ourselves to any change. Because usually it's slow and insidious and passes us by unawares."

He plucked a white jasmine from the vine winding around the porch post and stared at it thoughtfully, twirling the bloom in his hand.

"I feel he betrayed me," he told me, "I feel he twisted my trust."

"He betrayed all of us, Bobby," I answered. "You, me, his family, the badge. But he hated himself when he'd done it, that much I do feel for sure. In those crashing moments of violence, Rhoads crossed a line over which he could never go back, and I think he loathed himself later."

I squinted, looking up at the sun, as I tried recalling his words.

"I heard Charlie talking about the killer of Lucy," I said, "and calling him a 'misery of a man.' Bobby, I don't think he was posturing to throw us all off, I think he was hating and flailing himself."

Harris walked back and sat down beside me, laying the flower on my lap.

"It's over now anyway," he told me slowly, "over for them, over for him, the whole sad sorry waste."

"Yes," I said cheerlessly, "it's finally been all sorted out."

And while Meryl and Charlie passed through my mind, it was Lucy who floated up front, and suddenly I saw her the night that I'd found her—helpless, innocent, a soul who'd not had a voice. For unlike the others, who'd always been free to make their own choices, Lucy had lay at their mercy, a child who'd never done harm.

I ached for her, the forgotten victim, and my throat caught at her memory and I choked back a tear. And I knew I would never forget her, knew she would stay in my mind.

He reached out and hugged me against him and tipped my face up to his lips. His mouth moved to my eyes, to my cheeks, and he murmured and I strained for his words.

"But, Katharine, *we're* just beginning," he whispered, "our whole world is waiting to start."

And in the light of that moment my keen sadness fled and a powerful gladness replaced it, and surged and swept through my heart.

Her greatest fear . . . Her toughest case

A DESPERATE CALL

Kids are often late for dinner in the seductively long, hazy spring twilights of the California suburbs. Yet a seasoned homicide cop like Kate Harrod knows that sometimes a child is late because someone else has decided the child is never going home again. Kate will risk sacrificing her own family in her obsessive search for one unlucky young boy. She'll come to grips with her most deeply masked childhood terrors. And she'll willingly walk into the sights of a practiced killer . . . and dare to cross the line no woman—and no cop—must ever cross . . .

**MORE SHOCKING CRIME FROM
LAURA COBURN**

A shocking crime . . . A shattering truth

AN UNCERTAIN DEATH

At dawn, they found the body. The victim was Connie Hammond, star high school athlete, loyal friend, loving daughter. For homicide detective Kate Harrod, the question of who would kill this vital youth takes an unexpected twist. As Kate faces the possibility of losing her son in a bitter custody case, she finds an unlikely ally in the sister of her prime suspect. An intimate friend of Kate's long-deceased mother, she unleashes in Kate feelings she has struggled long to bury. But why, then, is she hiding what she knows about Connie Hammond's murder?

MORE THRILLING SUSPENSE FROM LAURA COBURN